A Murder In A Different Light

Brendan Gerad O'Brien

Copyright © 2023 Brendan Gerad O'Brien

All rights reserved.
***

This work is licensed under the Creative Commons Attribution-ShareAlike 3.0 Unported License.
To view a copy of this license, visit
http://creativecommons.org/licenses/by-nc/2.5/
Or send a letter to:
Creative Commons
171 Second Street, Suite 300
San Francisco, California 94105

Also by Brendan Gerad O'Brien

Dark September
Footsteps

Guard Foley Mysteries:

Gallows Field
A Pale Moon Was Rising
A Crack in the Ice

Short Stories:

Dreamin' Dreams

Chapter One

A wave of icy air followed Guard Eamon Foley through the door of the Tralee Garda Barracks, and even though he'd stamped the snow off his boots before he came in, he still created a trail of wet slush along the floor behind him.

'Ah, the very man.' Acting Sergeant John Guerin came out from behind the reception desk and pointed at Foley with his pen. 'I have a job for you.'

'Well good day to you too, John.' Foley gave a weary wave of his hand and kept on walking towards the canteen. 'I've come back for my break. I'm just on my way to get a cup of tea.'

'That's *Sergeant* to you, Guard Foley,' Guerin said in a deceptively soft voice as he stood in front of Foley and blocked his way.

Foley glanced at the shiny new stripes on Guerin's arm and he was about to retaliate with a sarcastic quip when he noticed Peter Cavendish behind the desk watching them closely. This was not the time for Foley to start sparring with his newly promoted best pal, so he took off his cap and gave his best contrite smile. 'Yes. Of course. Sorry, Sarge. So what's this important job you have for me?'

Guerin ignored Foley's mocking tone and handed him a note. 'A young fella has gone missing over there in Clash. According to the mother he was playing in the garden one minute and the next he was gone. She panicked and called the neighbours, and then she called us.'

'Oh, right.' Foley took the piece of paper and read the address on it. 'So how old is the little fella?'

'He's four. The mother says he's a bright boy, very inquisitive, and he loves exploring. Anyway, you'll have to postpone your break, I'm afraid.'

'I understand, shur. Tis a parent's worst nightmare, to be sure. I'll head over there right away. Who else is helping in the search?'

'Right now, just you and Guard Hurley …'

'Really? Hurley?' Foley groaned. 'Surely to God you're not serious, John.'

'*Sergeant!*' Guerin stressed the point again by raising his eyebrows.

Foley groaned even louder. 'Surely to God you're not serious, *Sergeant*.'

'I am serious, I'm afraid.' Guerin had a smirk on his face which he tried to hide by scratching his chin. 'Hurley is the only guard available right now. So find him and go and talk to the mother. Then ring me. I think she has a phone in her house you can use.'

'Oh, come on, Sarge.' Foley pleaded. 'Not Hurley. The fella's a sloth. If he moved any slower he'd be going backwards. Don't do this to me, please. I'll take anyone else. Just not Hurley.'

Guerin grinned even more as he glanced over Foley's shoulder. 'Ah, there you are, Guard Hurley,' he said. 'I want you to go with Foley. There's a missing child I want you to help search for.'

Foley spun around and sighed even louder as Hurley stood there hitching up his trousers over his huge stomach. Hurley looked at Guerin, then at Foley and back at Guerin again.

'Right,' he said, and his head wobbled as he scowled at Foley. And he hitched up his trousers even more. Then he raised his eyebrows and nodded at the front door.

'So lead on, McDuff,' he sniggered. 'Sorry, I mean McFoley.' This was followed by a loud splutter of a laugh.

Foley rolled his eyes and started to walk away when Guerin noticed that Hurley was wearing ordinary uniform boots. 'For God's sake,' he jabbed the pen at Hurley's feet. 'You didn't come to work in those?'

'What?' Hurley looked down at his boots.

'What do you mean *what*?' Guerin pointed to his own footwear. 'Anyone in their right mind should be wearing wellingtons in these conditions.'

Hurley bridled, and he did an angry little shuffle. 'Well, it's stopped snowing now,' he snapped. 'The wireless said it'll be dry for the next few days. Then it'll rain and wash all the snow away.'

Guerin shook his head in despair. 'What are you talking about, you mad eejit? There are snow drifts out there as high as telegraph poles. It's been snowing solid for the past two months and you think it'll all suddenly disappear because we have one day of rain?'

Hurley bristled even more. 'I'll be alright, Sarge. I'll stick to the road where the snow is flattened.' Then he scowled at Foley again. 'If it gets too deep I'll walk in his footsteps.'

He tapped the side of his nose. 'You'd love that, wouldn't you, Foley? Someone following in your footsteps?' Then he gave a dry chuckle, pulled up the collar of his overcoat and headed for the front door.

The snow was piled high on both sides of the road, narrowing the gap to the width of a single car. As the two guards walked over the Clash railway crossing, a dog was frantically digging in a shallow patch and growling like a swarm of angry bees. His tail was flapping in the air like a flag in a storm. Then something long and brown flew out of the snow in front of him, and the dog jumped so high he flipped onto his back with his legs kicking wildly in the air. By the time he recovered his prey had disappeared, but he still decided to chase after it.

A group of people had gathered outside one of the bungalows on the right-hand side of the road. Foley could see more people dotted along the road in the distance. They appeared to be poking in the snow with long sticks, obviously searching for the missing child. When one of the women by the bungalow saw the two guards she rushed towards them.

'Where's the rest?' she called in a raspy voice. She was a small woman with short black hair, and she spread her hands with the question. 'Surely they didn't just send two of you? Where are the others? We need more than two guards to find my boy. My boy is missing and they only send two of you? That's not enough.'

Foley took off his glove and stopped in front of her. 'Mrs O'Gara?'

'Yes, I'm Mrs O'Gara.' Her eyes were red from crying and her shoes had clumps of snow packed around them.

Foley held out his hand and she blinked several times before she reluctantly shook it. 'I'm Guard Foley,' he told her. 'And this is Guard Hurley. So before we go any further, can you tell me exactly what happened?'

'I told you that already.' She gave an exasperated moan. 'When I phoned the barracks I told you all that.'

'Yes, I know. But if you don't mind, we'd like you to tell us again.'

A taller woman put her arm around Mrs O'Gara's shoulder. 'C'mon Jane. They're only doing their job. Tell them what happened.'

Mrs O'Gara buried her face in her hands for a moment. Then she threw back her head and stuck her chin out in annoyance. 'My little boy Patrick was in the garden playing in the snow. He built a snowman and he was packing more snow around it. You know how it is with children. They love the snow. Anyway, I was washing the clothes in the sink and I could see him from the window. So I took the clothes over to the mangle and squeezed them before putting them on the clotheshorse in front of the fire. How long does that take? A few minutes? I don't know. When I looked out of the window again Patrick was gone.' She took a loud gulp of air and her friend held her tighter. When she managed to compose herself she said, 'Anyway, I ran outside and called his name but I got no answer. I could see the snow in the fields around us was untouched, so the only way he could have gone was down the path to the road. When I still couldn't see him I panicked and started screaming his name and that's when Breda came out.' She patted the tall lady's hand. 'Thanks be to God for decent neighbours because it wasn't long before everyone else came out too.'

'And did you look in his bedroom?' Hurley said in a tone that made Mrs O'Gara jerk up straight.

'Of course I looked in his feckin bedroom,' she spat. 'I'm not stupid. It was the first place I looked. I searched the whole house, the kitchen, the toilet, the living room. So don't take me for a fool. I'm not an eejit.'

'All right.' Foley put out his hand. 'No one thinks you're a fool, Mrs O'Gara. But you'd be surprised how many times that happens. We had a young girl only last week who frightened her parents half to death when she didn't come home from school, and after calling the guards they actually found her asleep in her own bed. She'd snuck in the back door because she'd fallen out with the mother. So it is an easy mistake to make.'

Mrs O'Gara flapped her arms and turned away. 'So what happens now?'

'Well,' Foley looked around at the figures farther up the road. 'It looks like you have people out searching already, and that's great.'

'But is it enough?' a tall man with a mop of white hair asked in a soft English accent. 'I'd say the more people we have looking, the faster we'll find the lad.'

'And you are?' Foley forced a smile.

'Sean McGrath.' The man held out his hand. 'I live across the road in that bungalow with the red door.'

'I'm Guard Foley,' Foley shook his hand. 'And this is Guard Hurley. Thank you for coming out to help. Can I ask how many people are out searching, do you know?'

'Well, there's four working the road up towards the crossroads.' He held up his fingers as he recalled their names. 'Percy and Teresa Metcalfe on the left, and Mossie Connor and Peter Lynch on the right. They're calling in all the houses too, but the priority is the deep snow on the side of the roads. It stopped snowing around six this morning so most of the snow will be untouched around the edges. Hopefully any disturbance will be spotted quickly.'

Foley was impressed with the man's calm confidence, but before he could comment on it McGrath waved towards the other end of the road. 'Oliver Cunningham went that way doing the same thing,' he added. 'But so far we haven't found any sign of the little fella.'

Mrs O'Gara and Brenda had moved back by the gate and were talking to two other women. When they all turned and glared at the guards Hurley stamped his feet causing a cloud of snow to fly up around them. 'Will I call Sergeant Guerin?' he said to Foley. 'What do you think? Will I ask for more guards to help us?'

Foley looked at McGrath. 'Have you got a phone we can use?'

'I'm afraid not,' McGrath pointed up the road. 'But there's one in Liam Brazil's shop on the corner of Racecourse Road.'

'I thought the Sarge said Mrs O'Gara had a phone,' Hurley argued.

'No,' McGrath told him. 'The only phones around here are the ones in Brazil's shop and the railway gatekeeper's cottage. But the snow brought that line down yesterday.'

'Right,' Foley undid the top button of his overcoat. 'We'll head over to the shop. We can keep a lookout for the lad on the way.'

'I'll come with you,' McGrath rubbed his hands together then stuck them back in his pockets.

As they walked along the middle of the road Hurley was muttering about the lack of discipline in children today. 'They should take the strap to that young fella when they find him for running away like that and frightening his poor mammy. A good belting is what he needs. They're too soft these days, those modern parents.'

'He's four years old.' Foley couldn't keep the irritation out of his voice. 'He's just a child.'

'Yeah,' Hurley continued. 'A child with no discipline. When I was that age I knew when to behave myself cos if I didn't I'd get the strap. My legs would be red raw for a week if I wandered off like that and worried everyone. I can tell you, my Dad wouldn't stand for it.'

Foley couldn't be bothered to answer and he turned to McGrath. 'You seem very well organised, Mr McGrath. What do you do for a living, can I ask?'

'Oh, I'm retired now.' McGrath gave a self-satisfied smile. 'I don't do much these days.'

Foley grinned too but didn't speak, letting McGrath fill the silence. 'I was a Detective Inspector with the Birmingham Constabulary,' McGrath continued. 'Thirty years.'

'Oh, right,' Foley stepped over a patch of packed snow. 'That explains the accent. So what brings you to Tralee?'

'I was born and raised here, in the bungalow I'm living in now. I didn't want to go to England, but like most of my generation at the time, I had no choice. We had to follow the crowd in search of work.'

'And you did very well for yourself,' Foley gave him an admiring glance.

'England was not the paradise we were led to believe, I'm afraid, Guard Foley.' McGrath rubbed his hands together again, blew on them and shoved them back in his pockets. 'I was very lucky, though. Blessed, as my mother used to say. It's a sad fact, but we were fooled by the stories of jobs that paid good money, and the great craic to be had. But it was all an illusion. The bottom line is, I struggled to find work and I got into serious trouble. I would have ended up in prison if it wasn't for a big ugly Irish bobby who slapped me around and gave me one last chance. He let me hide in his garden shed until the fuss died down, then he made me promise to go straight. But how could I go straight when I couldn't get a job? Anyway, he dragged me down to the police recruitment centre and as they say, the rest is my life story.'

'Wow. And what a great story it is too,' Foley admitted. 'I bet your family was impressed.'

McGrath gave a sour smile. 'Well, I couldn't come home after that. Given the situation here in Ireland at the time, you know? With the fight for independence and then the civil war, I would have been seen as the enemy. The only two times I did come home was when my parents died and I attended the funerals. I was assured by the lads that I had immunity out of respect for my parents.'

He saw the question in Foley's eyes and he nodded. 'I'm retired now. And things in Ireland have changed a lot too. I'm no threat now so I'm left in peace.'

Foley stopped in front of a large impressive iron gate with two big concrete pillars set in a high dry stone wall. He assumed there was a driveway under the blanket of snow leading up to the huge brownstone house on the crest of the hill. It looked magical with its enormous chimney-stack poking through a perfect layer of snow and complimented the baronial style turret attached to one corner. 'Who lives there?' he asked McGrath.

'That's the Appleyard's place.' McGrath pulled a face that was hard to read. 'The lads won't have called there though. The snow isn't disturbed, as you can see. No one has been on that drive today so they wouldn't waste their time.'

Foley studied the house for a moment, his attention focused on the turret. 'What are they like, the Appleyards?'

McGrath shrugged. 'I'm not sure these days. I remember the old man from when we were kids, and he was all right back then. But from what I understand now, he had some sort of a breakdown after his wife died and he took to his bed. So the farm has gone to the dogs. He has a married daughter up the country somewhere, and another daughter who's a nun. Apparently the nun came home to look after him. But the latest rumour is that he has dementia now, and the nun has to run the place singlehanded.'

'God, the poor woman.' Foley looked out at the surrounding countryside, all quiet and perfect under the snow. He tried to imagine what the place looked like under normal circumstances. 'How do they survive if the farm is in such a bad way?'

'I don't know.' McGrath answered. 'I've only been home a few months so all I know is what I hear from the neighbours. And I don't think I've seen the nun more than half a dozen times since I've been back. The only activity I've ever noticed around there is Liam Brazil's van going in and out delivering the groceries. Do you know Liam Brazil? He owns the shop we're heading to right now. He's a lovely fella. A saint, according to the locals.'

'Yeah, I know Liam. We were in school together.' Foley stepped closer to the gate and studied the house. 'So it's likely the daughter will be at home now, would you say?'

'I would,' McGrath made it sound like a question and followed it with a quizzical look.

'Right,' Foley said to Hurley. 'C'mon, we'll go and say hello to her.'

'What? Why?' Hurley dug his hands deep into his pockets. 'As your man just said, that snow hasn't been touched, so the young fella didn't go up there.'

'I know that.' Foley walked on. 'But if we ask the Appleyards nicely they might let us go up onto the roof of that turret and take a look at the surrounding area. We'll have a better chance of spotting someone in the snow from up there than we have from down here on the road.'

'That's a great idea,' McGrath said with an approving chuckle. 'It's definitely worth a try. So I'll carry on over to the shop and ring the guards, yeah?' he added, turning back to the road. 'Tell them I spoke to you.'

'Don't you want to check this out first?' Foley gave him a quizzical glance. 'We might spot the young fella, then we won't need to call for reinforcements.'

'I would love to,' McGrath gave a sheepish grin. 'But I'm afraid I can't stand cats. I react badly to them. I end up sneezing and gagging if I get too close to them.'

'Cats? What …'

'Miss Appleyard has a house full of them, according to Liam Brazil. Apparently they're everywhere. Dozens of them. Like a carpet of fur all over the floor. So if you don't mind …'

'Not at all,' Foley chuckled. 'But don't ring the barracks just yet. I'll come and find you when we're sorted here.'

Hurley flapped his arms as he struggled to keep his balance while following in Foley's footprints, and he mumbled and groaned all the way up to the front door. Foley ignored him as he pushed the large brass button on the wall by the heavy oak door. Chimes echoed deep inside the house, but there was no answer. Foley waited a minute before pushing the button again. When they still didn't get a response he stepped back and looked around at the windows. Then he crunched through the thick barrier of snow and tried to look in the nearest one. The dazzling glare of the sun on the snow turned the glass into a mirror and he struggled to see into the room.

'It's no use. I can't see anything through this,' he called to Hurley. 'Go around that way and see if you can see anything. I'll go around this side.'

Hurley was huddled in his coat and looked reluctant to do what Foley asked. Foley growled in frustration. 'Go on,' he snapped. 'Check around the back.'

Foley picked his way around the side of the house, making sure there weren't any sudden dips in the ground beneath the snow that could trip him up. This part of the building was in the shade. He approached the next window and held his hand against the glass. The room was large and bathed in a miserable grey haze that reeked of cold and neglect. There was a sadness about the place that made Foley shiver.

As he scanned the room he thought he could see what looked like a cat lying on the carpet over by the open door. He held his face closer to the glass, and when he noticed some more shapes by the fireplace he jumped back in surprise. They looked really odd. They were just lying there on the floor. He rubbed his eyes and looked again. What was he seeing? Bits of cat scattered around the room? A tail? A head? He rushed along to the next window to see if he could get a better look.

'Hey, this door is open,' he heard Hurley shout from the back of the house. 'Will I take a look inside?'

'Do,' Foley shouted back. 'Go on, I'm coming.'

Foley came rushing around the corner into the wide back yard just as Hurley was pushing the door open. And when some hissing and spitting cats flew out the gap at him, Hurley gave an almighty scream and threw himself back into the snow. His cap flew off as the cats raced past him, tore across the yard and disappeared down the field scattering snow in a cloud behind them.

'What the hell was that?' Hurley squealed as he rolled back onto his knees. 'Did you see that? I could have been killed. Those were wild animals. They could have ripped the throat out of me.'

Foley stepped around him, gingerly pushed the door wider and crept into the huge kitchen. Then he gagged.

'God Almighty. What *is* that smell?'

Chapter Two

Hurley looked disorientated as he struggled to his feet and grabbed his cap. It was a moment before he realised Foley had stepped back from the open door. Pulling his cap back on his head he shuffled across the yard, and when he reached the door and glanced inside he slammed his hand over his mouth.

'Holy shit! That is putrid. That is *not* cat piss. Cats piss is awful, but that is not the smell of cats.'

Foley took out his handkerchief and held it to his nose, and he moved cautiously into the kitchen. The place was bitterly cold. Ice glistened on the inside of the windows and freezing air seemed to radiate from the walls. Bits of cats were scattered on top of the big oak table and all over the worktops. They looked as if they'd been ripped apart, leaving just feet and tails and clumps of fur. The floor was a carpet of cat faeces and decomposing bits of dead animal. It was impossible to walk without something squelching under their feet.

'There's been some sort of massacre here,' Hurley mumbled through his gloved hand that was clamped to his face. 'What did this? Is there a mad dog in here?'

On the far side of the kitchen Foley could see a big range with a high backed armchair on either side of it. A sunbeam coming through the dusty window threw a sharp finger of light around the chair that had its back to Foley, distorting the outline into an odd shape. A sudden dread made Foley stop and take a deep breath, and he counted to ten before he forced himself to move around to the front of it. Then he jumped back with a shocked yelp. There was a body sprawled in the chair.

The flesh had been completely stripped away but the remaining tufts of blond hair and the shredded red dress told him it was obviously the remains of a woman. A large crucifix attached to a wooden rosary beads was hanging around her neck and dangling over the back of the chair, and a chewed pair of red high heeled shoes hung from her ragged feet. The carcases of several cats were scattered around her.

Foley sensed Hurley come up behind him and gasp. Then the vomit sprayed from between his fingers. Foley danced out of the way but he couldn't drag his eyes away from the body. It was only when the bile stung his throat and forced him to take another deep breath that he managed to turn away.

'Check the other rooms,' he shouted at Hurley. 'I'll check upstairs.'

Hurley was still leaning against the wall and gagging as Foley went through to the hall and trotted up the wide staircase. There were several bedrooms along either side of the corridors at the top of the stairs. They were all empty. Except for the largest one at the front of the house. And again Foley had to pause and take a deep breath before he went in.

The curtains were drawn. And a familiar smell made Foley press his handkerchief to his nose again. He crept across the room and pulled back the curtains. And he groaned when his worst fears were realised. The body of an elderly man was hanging out of the bed, his pyjama jacket ripped open and his hands grabbing at his throat. His face was contorted in agony. Foley didn't need to check for signs of life.

The room was so cold there were ice crystals all over the body. A tray with half a cup of frozen tea and some toast stood on a little table beside the bed, and a cereal bowl and spoon were lying on top of the blankets as if they were suddenly dropped there.

Then Foley noticed there wasn't any sign of the cats up here. Or on the stairs either, for that matter. It looked like most of them had been shut in the kitchen, apart from the few in the front room. So how long had they been locked in there? How long would they need to be trapped without food and water before they actually turned on each other?

He assumed the lady in the chair was the nun because of the rosary beads around her neck. So what happened to her? Did she do something to the old man, and then to herself? Then the cats were trapped when they couldn't open the doors and they had to fend for themselves? The thought of what happened next made the bile rise in Foley's throat again, and he coughed into his fist. He had to lean his head against the frozen glass of the window to help clear his mind.

Suddenly he remembered why he was here in the first place. He was supposed to be looking for a lost child. He went back out to the landing and found the stairs leading to the turret, and he climbed up onto the flat roof. The view was spectacular, a rolling white landscape shimmering beneath the rays of a sharp sun in a stunningly blue cloudless sky. The biting cold breeze helped clear the nauseous smell from Foley's nose, but he was struggling to concentrate on his reason for climbing up here. He rubbed his eyes and looked down at the road, and he was surprised to see that all the searchers were back outside Mrs O'Gara's house again.

He ran back down to the kitchen where Hurley was standing by the back door holding his head in his hands.

'C'mon. We need to get in touch with the barracks and tell them what we found here.' He manoeuvred Hurley around the corner of the yard. 'And something's going on with the search for the young fella too but we'll have to see what the sergeant wants us to do about that. So go over to Brazil's shop and phone Sergeant Guerin and ask him what we should do. Tell him I'm still here guarding the crime scene.'

Chapter Three

'Are you alright there, Danny Boy?' Acting Sergeant John Guerin held out a packet of cigarettes, waited for Foley to take one then picked one out for himself. He flicked his lighter and lit his own, then passed the lighter to Foley.

'I'm grand,' Foley lit his cigarette then blew out a cloud of smoke. 'I probably won't be able to eat my lunch today, but I'll be fine.'

Superintendent Brian Flynn had his swagger stick tucked under his arm as he came around the corner of the Appleyard's house, and when he spotted Guerin he came straight over to him. 'Two bodies, I understand, Sergeant.' He acknowledged Foley with a curt nod.

'Yes, Sir. We believe they're Mr Toby Appleyard and his daughter Bella.'

'So what does it look like? Fowl play, do you think?' The Super's deep voice was cultured but he couldn't disguise the odd hint of a Galway accent.

'Well, the doctor is still upstairs with the remains of Mr Appleyard. He seems to think the old fella was probably poisoned because of the colour of his lips and the way he was hanging half out of the bed. He appeared to be in agony at the time he expired. There are remains of a breakfast by the bed so the Doc is going to take them away with him to have them examined.'

'And the daughter? Where is she?'

Guerin pointed to the door with his thumb. 'Right there in the kitchen, Sir.'

For a moment Superintendent Flynn looked as if he was about to go in but instead he turned back to Guerin. 'And what does the doctor say about her?'

'He didn't comment on that, Sir. There's a cup on the floor near the body and he's taking that with him too. But the body is so badly damaged he can't establish the cause of death at the moment.'

'So what do you think, Sergeant?' The super's eyes were wide and anxious. 'In your opinion, what happened there?'

Guerin thought for a moment and blew cigarette smoke down his nose. 'Well, my guess is Miss Appleyard poisoned the old fella then took her own life.'

'So you don't think they were the victims of foul play by a third party? There's no sign of an intruder?'

'Hard to tell at the moment, Sir. The back door was unlocked so anyone could have walked in. And with dead cats all over the place, it's impossible to say if there was any sort of struggle. But the lady was sitting upright in the armchair, certainly not looking like she'd been in a confrontation. So, in my honest opinion, she took the same poison as the auld fella in the bed upstairs then sat back in the chair and waited for God.'

The Super turned away and stood with his hands behind his back as he studied the mountains in the distance. The stark sunlight on the snow made him squint and he pulled the peak of his cap down over his eyes. 'So this thing with the cats,' he asked after a few minutes. 'Is it feasible? Would cats do that, eat human flesh?'

Guerin wiped a bit of tobacco off his lip. 'It depends how long they were locked in there with nothing to eat, I suppose. There are bits of cat all over the place so they were desperate enough to turn on each other as well.'

The Super cringed and his shoulders twitched. 'How many cats did she have in there, for God's sake?'

'Not sure, Sir. But there are dozens of remains around the place.'

The Super nodded and glanced around at the house. 'Is there any indication how long the Appleyards have been dead?'

'No, Sir. The doc wouldn't even take a guess. The bodies were frozen solid, you see? Foley did a quick sweep of the house to see if there were any newspapers or post that might help us put a date to what happened, but there isn't anything that we could see.'

The Super stared out at the scenery again, and Foley and Guerin sucked on their cigarettes.

'So what brought us up here in the first place?' the Super glanced at the sergeant as if he suddenly thought of something. 'How did we find the bodies?'

'We were called out to a missing child, Sir,' Foley answered. 'A young fella who lives just along the road there.'

'So this was just a routine check?' The Super seemed impressed with the answer. 'Part of that search?'

'Yes, Sir. I noticed the turret on the side of this house and I thought if the owners let me go up to the roof I would have a good chance of seeing if the child had wandered into the fields.'

'That was good thinking, Foley.' The Super looked him up and down with an approving gaze. 'So what happened then?'

'Well, we didn't get an answer at the front door so we went around the back. This door wasn't locked so we opened it and called out. That was when we noticed the terrible smell.'

The Super cringed again then nodded for Foley to go on. 'Well, we could see dead cats all over the floor,' Foley continued. 'So we went in to see what was going on in there. That was when we found the lady in the armchair, or what was left of her.' Foley couldn't stop the shudder and he wiped his mouth with his sleeve. 'I told Guard Hurley to look in the other rooms downstairs and I went upstairs. That's when I found the old fella.'

'Had the cats been at him too?'

'No. It looks like most of them were locked in the kitchen where we found the lady. A few had been shut in the front room too but none got upstairs.'

There was a long pause as the Super stared out over the snow-covered fields again, then he gave a deep sigh and turned to Guerin. 'Right, Detective Dinane will be here soon. He's trying to dig himself out of his house. But in the meantime I want you to start talking to the neighbours. Foley, see what you can find out about this family. You know the drill. You've done it often enough.'

Foley threw his cigarette butt into the snow and straightened his cap. 'What about the missing child, Sir? Shouldn't I be helping to look for him?'

'Ah,' Guerin gave an apologetic grin. 'I meant to tell you earlier, Eamon. They found him. He was hiding in the pantry all the time. He went in to get a carrot for the snowman's nose and when he heard his mother shouting when she couldn't see him, he got frightened and hid behind the sack of potatoes.'

'Oh, so he's safe, thank God. That's great news. Is that where Hurley is now? I could meet up with him and tell him what's going on here.'

'No, he's not,' the Super held his swagger stick with both hands behind his back. 'He was in no state to carry on here so I sent him back to the barracks. He's manning the front desk until he sorts himself out. I told him to send Guard Casey over here to replace him.'

'Oh? Right.' Foley nodded to the Super and then to Guerin. 'I'll make a start so.'

The Super's car was parked across the gateway to the house leaving just enough room for one person at a time to squeeze between it and the gate post. His driver was standing in that gap. Guard Quilter was a bull of a man and he grunted at Foley as he stepped back to let him by. Most of the people who were gathered around Mrs O'Gara's house earlier had now gravitated up to the Appleyard's gate, and they watched Foley with curious eyes as he approached.

'What's going on?' one of them called out, and immediately all the others joined in. 'Is it true? Were they killed by the cats? Was it the cats that killed them? Where's the old man? Did the cats kill him too?'

'For God's sake!' Foley put up both hands as if he was going to push them away and he raised his voice in exasperation. 'The cats didn't kill anyone. Where did you get that rubbish from?'

Sean McGrath was standing at the back of the group and he gave Foley a sympathetic nod, and Foley rolled his eyes in recognition. 'Look, right now we don't know what happened. It's way too early to say. But as soon as we know anything we'll announce it, all right?'

He looked around at the faces who stared back at him. 'In the meantime, we're appealing for any information that might help us with our investigation.'

'What kind of information?' one man asked. 'How would we know anything?'

'Yeah,' a woman agreed. 'We rarely saw them. They kept themselves to themselves.'

'She was a bit odd, all right,' another woman added. 'As odd as two left shoes, I'd say. And she being a nun as well. I'm telling you, she was a bitter little wasp. Never cracked her face.'

'No, she didn't,' her friend agreed. 'I tried to speak to her once, a few years ago now, but she cut me dead with her sour look. I didn't dare try again. The look she gave me would have curdled milk.'

Foley pushed his way through them and stood in the middle of the road, getting them to turn around and face him. 'What we'd like to know is, when was the last time anyone saw the Appleyards? Did anyone notice anything unusual around the place these past few weeks? Anything at all, even if it seems trivial and unimportant. Any strangers hanging about, any unusual visitors, stuff like that.'

'So if the cats didn't kill them, are you saying someone murdered them? The two of them? Is that what happened? Someone broke in and murdered them in their beds?'

'No,' Foley's voice almost rose to a shout again but he checked it and held up his hand. 'I told you already, we don't know what happened there. But what we *do* need right now is your help to establish *when* it happened. So if you have any information that will help us with that, please tell me now.'

People mumbled and glanced at each other, shrugging their shoulders and shaking their heads. Sean McGrath pulled his collar up higher and blew on his hands as he shuffled over to Foley. 'Your best bet would be to speak to Liam Brazil. As I said earlier, he was a regular visitor to the house. He'd probably be able to tell you more about the Appleyards than anyone else.'

Chapter Four

A bell jingled above the door when Foley stepped through it and into Liam Brazil's grocery shop. The lights weren't on in the shop, but the sun coming in through the big front window was bright enough to highlight the empty shelves around the walls. A few packets of foreign lintels and a couple of tins of an unfamiliar brand of soup were all Foley could see. There were a few mops and a couple of tin buckets propped up in one corner at the back, and a rake and a shovel leaning forlornly in another. Apart from that, the place looked depressingly bare.

A middle-aged lady came out from the door behind the counter, wiping her hands in her apron. There were deep creases in her forehead as she looked Foley up and down. 'You're back again? What do you want this time?'

'Mrs Brazil, how are you?' Foley took off his cap and glanced around the shop. 'I wasn't sure if you were open.'

Recognition made the lady's face soften and she gave a tired smile. 'Eamon Foley? Hello.' She gave a resigned shrug and looked forlornly at the shelves. 'Ah, yes, we're open alright. Sure there's nothing else for us to do, Eamon. We're open for a visit and a bit of gossip and that's about the size of it.'

She brushed something off the counter and rubbed her hands together before she said, 'Tis hard to believe this is 1947 and everything is still being rationed. Not that there's much to ration anyway. But the war finished almost two years ago and there's less food now than there ever was. Tis nothing short of scandalous.'

'You're right there,' Foley agreed. 'And this weather didn't help. The coldest winter in living memory according to the experts. No one's seen snow like this before.'

'I heard them say that too, sure. But tis about to change now, they said today. So we might be able to get some deliveries again. Our customers are desperate, as you can imagine.'

'Who is it, Ma?' A man glanced out of the door and when he saw Foley he looked at the floor and pulled a sour face. 'Oh, tis you.'

'Liam,' Foley greeted him with a nod. 'How're you doing? I haven't seen you for ages.'

'I've seen you around the town a few times,' Liam replied dryly, still looking at the floor. 'But I didn't catch your eye in case you arrested me for something.'

Foley's laugh came out as a spurt. Then he realised Liam wasn't smiling. His eyes seemed unnaturally red in his pale unshaven face.

'So what's going on?' Liam turned his head towards his mother but still didn't look up. There was a distressed edge to his tone. 'That other guard who came in earlier to use the phone was in a terrible state. We couldn't get any sense out of him. He kept ranting about finding a woman's body over in the Appleyard's place that was eaten by the cats. He said they think the woman is Bella Appleyard. He was really upset. We tried to give him something to drink but he said he had to call his boss and then get back over there.'

'I'm afraid he's right,' Foley told him. 'That's why I'm here. I wanted to ask …'

'But he's wrong.' Liam slammed his hand on the counter so hard his mother jumped and stepped away from him. 'I tried to tell him but he wouldn't listen to me. I tried to tell him it can't be Bella Appleyard.'

'Liam,' Foley had stepped back too. 'I'm sorry, but he's *not* wrong.'

'He is, though.' Liam's eyes were wide and frantic now, and his long uncombed hair flicked as he shook his head. 'It can't be Bella. Whoever they think they saw, it wasn't Bella.'

Foley held his hand out. 'Why do you say that, Liam?'

Liam rubbed his mouth with the back of his hand and glanced at his mother. 'Because the Appleyards went away on New Year's Day. They went away for a couple of weeks on New Year's Day. And they haven't come back.'

Before Foley could ask another question Liam rushed back through the door into the kitchen. Mrs Brazil stepped to one side and waved Foley through after him. Then she followed behind. 'Will you be having a cup of tea, Eamon?' she asked as she moved the kettle onto the hotplate of the range.

Liam had dropped into an armchair and started rubbing his chin in sharp irritated movements. He glared at Foley as he waited for the obvious question, and when Foley asked how he knew the Appleyards had gone away he sat forward and clamped his hands together in his lap. 'Bella told me,' he said, studying the floor again. 'When I called over there on New Year's Day.'

'On New Year's Day?' Foley did the calculations. How many weeks ago was that?

'Yes.' Liam was defensive now. 'I called over to wish her a Happy New Year. And to make sure they were all right. You know, for groceries and stuff?'

Mrs Brazil smirked and wiped her hands in her apron again. 'And because he has a soft spot for her.' She rolled her eyes at Foley.

'No, I do not, Ma.' There was a sudden patch of red on Liam's cheeks and he sat back in the chair with a growl.

Mrs Brazil put tea in the pot as the kettle started to boil. 'He's always been soft on that one, Eamon. I can't figure it out. She's an odd little sausage. Much too serious. Never speaks to anyone if she can help it.'

'So did she tell you where they were going, Liam?' Foley asked.

Liam was still glaring at his mother and he took a moment to answer. 'No. She just said they were going away for a few weeks so they didn't need anything from us. She asked me to deliver some letters for her, and she said she'd give me a call when they got back.' He flicked his hand in the general direction of the farm. 'But we didn't hear from her so we assumed they were still away.'

Mrs Brazil put a cup and saucer in front of Foley then pushed the milk jug closer to him. 'She wanted you to deliver letters to whom?' Foley asked as he watched Mrs Brazil pour tea into the cup.

'To her tenants in the cottages, Percy Metcalfe, Oliver Cunningham and Tom O'Gara.'

'What was in them?'

'How the feck would I know?' Liam snapped. 'It was none of my business. I just delivered them.'

'Of course,' Foley nodded in agreement. 'Anyway, did she say *when* they were going away, do you remember?'

Liam rubbed his chin again. 'I got the impression it was sometime that day. It was a brief conversation, and then she was gone back into the house.'

'But you didn't actually see them leave?'

'No.' Liam gave an agitated tut. 'I just presumed, you know? And we didn't hear from them after that so ... look, if they hadn't gone away Bella would have contacted us. I know she would. And if she'd come back she would have contacted us too. So whoever that unfortunate woman you found in that house was, it wasn't Bella.'

Foley scooped sugar into his tea and took a sip, then added some more. 'Liam, did Guard Hurley tell you we found *two* bodies over there.'

Liam's head jerked back and his face creased. 'Two bodies?'

'Yes. An old man in his bed upstairs, and a woman in an armchair downstairs in the kitchen.

'No, no, no.' Liam squeezed his eyes shut and a sob stuck in his throat. 'That other guard only said they found a woman. He didn't say anything about any old fella. Oh my God. This can't be ... and the old fella is dead too? Or is it just ... What happened to them? Are you sure the woman is Bella?'

'They haven't been formally identified yet. All I can tell you is one of them is a woman and the other is an old man.'

Liam started to gag and his mother handed him a tea towel. He held it to his mouth for a moment then squeezed it in his lap, and his eyes sparkled with tears. 'And was she ... your pal said she was ... you know? The cats?'

'What was going on with all those cats, Liam?' Foley put the cup back on the table. 'What was she running over there? A cat sanctuary?'

Liam wiped his mouth again and handed the towel back to his mother. 'Bella loved her cats. She always had three or four of them hanging around the backyard.' He sniffed and wiped his nose with his sleeve. 'She had classy names for them. Her favourite, Miss Kitty, had a litter of about eight kittens just before Christmas. She blamed some ginger tom that appeared out of nowhere. Then a short time later she said if I ever saw that ginger tom on my rounds I was to run him over with my van because her second favourite cat, Lucy Lastic, also had a litter. So now there were cats and kittens all over the place. At least twenty of them. She asked me to offer them to anyone who wanted a kitten for Christmas.'

A tear escaped and trickled down his face but he didn't attempt to wipe it away. This was followed by an awkward silence. Foley picked up his tea again then sat back in his chair, and he waited a few moments before he asked, 'Liam, did you notice anything unusual that day? Anything out of the ordinary? Apart from Miss Appleyard saying they were going away, that is. Did you notice if there was anyone else in the house, for instance? Was there another vehicle, maybe? Did you notice anything at all that was different?'

Liam pursed his lips and this time he wiped the tear away with his finger. 'Well, I thought it was odd when she came out of the front door as I drove up. I usually go around the back and she meets me there, so she took me by surprise when she came out the front door and waved me down.'

'And what did she say exactly, do you remember?'

'Just that they were going away and she'd give me a call when they got back.'

Foley waited, then asked, 'Anything else?'

Liam sucked a long breath in through his nose. 'Well, she was ...I can't explain it, but there *was* something different about her all right. She seemed ... excited? She was smiling.' He gave Foley a sheepish grin then looked down at his hands. 'She rarely smiles. People think she's dour because she's always frowning. She can look a bit severe sometimes.'

'Sometimes?' his mother mocked.

'She's misunderstood, that's all, Ma. She had a rough childhood. You know that.'

'So, to get this straight, she told you on New Year's Day they were going away, yeah?' Foley queried. 'But that was almost three months ago. Didn't you think it was a bit strange they hadn't come back by now?'

Liam gave a defensive shrug. 'Well, no. Not with the weather we've been having. According to the wireless it snowed for thirty days out of the past fifty. So they probably thought it was wise to stay where they were.'

'And where do you think that was? At a guess.'

'Her sister's, I'd say.' Mrs Brazil said. 'They live somewhere near Dublin, as far as I know,'

'So who lives here in this big house?'

'Just old Toby and his daughter Bella.'

'Oh. Right,' Foley folded his arms. 'Someone said Bella was a nun. Is that right?'

'She's supposed to be,' Mrs Brazil sneered. 'And tis the best place for her too.'

'Ma,' Liam groaned. 'Don't be mean.'

'I'm not,' his mother insisted. 'All I'm saying is she was born to be a nun.'

'Don't you remember her?' Liam glanced at Foley. 'Her sister Lily was in our class in Moyderwell. Bella was a couple of years behind.'

'Moyderwell Infant school?' Foley rubbed his ear. 'God, that's going back a bit. I can't say I remember anyone from infant school.'

Liam sighed. 'I remember everyone from our class.'

Foley picked up his cup again, took a long drink and sat back in the chair. 'No, I don't remember her,' he repeated. 'I hated school so I probably blocked it out of my mind. I remember some of the nuns all right, but that's about it.'

'But you must know the Appleyards, surely,' Mrs Brazil pulled out a chair and sat at the table opposite Foley. 'You being from Tralee and all.'

Foley shrugged. 'I can't say I do, Mrs Brazil.'

'Really? They used to be the most powerful farmers around here. They've been farming here for generations. And they kept a lot of people in employment. They had a cook, a housekeeper, a couple of maids, and farmhands. All sorts of people worked there. Especially in the harvest season. Itinerant labourers came from all over the country to work there. Which was great for us because they came here for their bits and pieces. Do you remember, Liam? There'd be queues down the street.'

Liam gave a sour grunt. 'Yeah, I remember, Ma. They were the good auld days, as you keep saying.'

Mrs Brazil stared into the distance trying to recapture the memory, and she couldn't disguise the sadness in the sigh she gave. 'Then Toby's wife died suddenly about … what was it? Twelve years ago? And everything went to pot after that.'

'So Toby must be the old fella we found …?' Foley stopped when Mrs Brazil crossed herself.

'He was all right back in the day, God bless his poor soul.' She gave a respectful nod. 'You knew where you stood with him. He had no pretensions. He'd have a laugh and a joke at the local fair, and he'd come to all the flower shows too. He was a lovely man.' She shuddered and joined her hands in her lap. 'Which can't be said for the woman he married. She came from a well to do family and she brought the airs and graces with her, which didn't always sit well here in Kerry. I never trusted her. She'd pretend to be nice to you but you always knew it was because she wanted you to do something for her. Always a favour, of course. Didn't matter what it cost you, she never offered payment.'

She stood up, got a cup and took it to the table. 'And she was useless as a mother too.' She glanced at Foley to gauge his reaction but he didn't speak. 'She was horrible to Bella. She gave Lily all the attention and ignored poor Bella. No wonder she never smiled. Would you like a cup of tea, Liam?'

'I would. Thanks.'

'Yeah,' Mrs Brazil poured tea into the cup. 'Lily was the firstborn, you see? And her parents worshipped her. But they expected Bella to be a boy, the son they craved. She was as pretty as Lily, with her mother's green eyes and ash-blond hair. But she wasn't a boy, so she was a huge disappointment. And she didn't have Lily's sparkle either. Her parents thought the sun shone out of Lily's ear. Bella was a lesser light. A bit dour. A bit too serious for a child. So she was confined to her sister's shadow.'

'She didn't help herself by trying to live the life of a saint, either.' Liam took the cup of tea from his mother and held it in his lap. 'Ever since she was told she had a guardian angel she couldn't tell a lie. The thought of the guardian angel seeing her telling a lie horrified her. But everyone else thought she was just a bit simple. They didn't understand. They couldn't see how important it was to her. Especially the kids at school. When they got into trouble they expected her to cover for them, but she couldn't. She couldn't lie. That was when she felt the full force of their spite.'

'No wonder she joined the nuns the first chance she got.' Mrs Brazil decided she wanted tea too and she got another cup from the dresser. 'She joined the Bon Secures Sisters when she was sixteen,' she said as she filled the cup.

'So now she's back here looking after her father?' Foley was longing for a cigarette but he couldn't see any ashtrays so he was reluctant to ask.

'Yeah,' Liam continued the story. 'When her mother died her father took it very badly. As Ma said, he had some sort of breakdown and Bella was called home to look after him.'

Mrs Brazil gave a sarcastic snigger. 'Lily couldn't do it. She was married and had a business to run, bless her. Anyway, Bella was the holy one, they said. Surely it was her duty to look after her father. The Mother Superior thought so too, according to rumour, and Bella was dispatched home without ceremony.'

Mrs Brazil looked at Foley with a guilty grin. 'We hear all the gossip here in our little shop, Guard Foley. People love to drop in for a chat and a bit of banter. And they all have a story they need to get off their chest. That's how we knew Bella's father wasn't happy about her coming home to look after him. He wanted Lily. Of course he said he didn't need looking after anyway, even if it was obvious he had no idea how to cook a meal or wash his clothes. But if he ever did get to that stage, he insisted, he'd rather go and live with Lily. And he wouldn't let Bella wear her nun's clothes either. Nuns agitated him and he didn't want one creeping around his house.'

'So Lily doesn't help out at all?'

'God no.' Mrs Brazil snorted. 'She's too important for that. She's married to Sean Redigan. Sean doted on Lily since they were in school and he followed her around like a shadow. But she treated him like something that dropped off a dog's bottom.'

She looked at Liam and he agreed with a wave of his hand. 'She'd swat him away like an annoying fly. Then one day Sean's parents died suddenly and Sean became the sole heir to the biggest shoe factory in the west of Ireland. It was obscene the way Lily immediately hosed him down with her charm. The poor sod was overwhelmed by the sudden attention she was giving him. He couldn't believe his luck, and before he knew what was happening they were married. They'd both just turned eighteen.'

Mrs Brazil sat back and stared into the distance again. 'It wasn't long before Lily turned off the charm, though. Then the real Lily emerged from behind the rainbow mist. From what we hear, Sean might own the company, but everyone knows who the real boss is. She's harsh with the workforce, but charming with the customers. Fair dues, though, she built the business up and opened two more factories around the country. They live in a huge estate just outside Dublin. She visits her father a couple of times a year. People say poor auld Sean has shrunk to a shadow of his former self. He's become even quieter than usual. Very submissive too. And very sad.'

There was another long pause and Liam started rubbing his face again. Foley struggled to ignore it so he broke the silence with a question, 'How long has Bella been looking after the old man, Mrs Brazil?'

'God, it must be ten years,' she said. 'Maybe twelve.' She nodded at that. 'He has dementia now too, by all accounts. And he spends most of his days in his room. Sadly, the farm has gone to the dogs, but he refuses to sell it. The animals and equipment have all been sold. Heaven knows how they'd survive over there if Lily didn't pay the bills. When we deliver the groceries we give Bella the invoices, and we get a cheque from Lily at the end of every month.'

'Liam, you said Bella is about our age, yeah? So was she in good health? Was there any underlying problems that might have been worrying her, do you know?'

Liam frowned and rubbed his hands together. 'Well, she looked great when I saw her on New Year's Day. I've never seen her looking so well.'

'Why?' Mrs Brazil asked. 'Are you saying she might have died from some sort of illness?'

'We don't know at the moment.' Foley picked up his cap. 'But it's one of the things we're looking into. There's also the possibility Bella took her own life?'

'What?' Liam yelped and almost jumped out of the chair. 'Good God, no. She's a nun. She wouldn't even think that way.'

Foley stood up and buttoned up his coat. 'As I said, it's one of the things we have to look into. There are loads of questions we have no answer to yet, as you can imagine.' He nodded at each of them in turn. 'Well, thank you for your time. Lovely to see you again. We might have to call back another day. Would that be all right?'

'Yes. Of course, Eamon,' Mrs Brazil stood up too. 'Anytime you want.'

Liam was frantically rubbing his face again and he didn't look up.

Chapter Five

The crowd around the gate to the Appleyard's farm had grown to twice its size and now people were spread right across the road. Detective Brian Dinane was standing at the back speaking to a group of reporters, and when he saw Foley he waved at him with his famous pipe. The trousers of Dinane's usually immaculate suit and the bottom of his mohair coat were soaked, and Foley grinned.

'Det Dinane, you dug yourself out of your house all right then?'

Dinane glanced down and shook one foot, sending a spray of wet snow into the air. 'I have a great fondness for snow, Guard Foley,' he said without a hint of animosity. 'But only on a Christmas card. Or, at a push, on top of the Brandon Mountains where it can't cause any mischief.'

The reporters suddenly closed in around Foley and started pelting him with questions. 'Did you find the bodies? What state were they in? Were they really eaten by the cats? How many cats did you see in there? Was it the cats that killed them? Were they huge cats? As big as dogs, someone said?'

Dinane put his arm around Foley's shoulder and steered him towards the gate which was closed now and guarded by one young officer. When he saw them coming the officer opened the gate just wide enough for Foley and Dinane to squeeze through, then he shut it quickly behind them. But it didn't deaden the howl of questions that followed them all the way up to the house. The snow had mostly turned to slush up the middle of the drive where everyone had walked, and it squelched as it spattered up Foley's wellingtons. Dinane had his expensive shoes on and he chose to ignore the discomfort of the slush filling them.

'So your pal Guerin got his stripes.' This came with a cloud of pipe smoke from the corner of Dinane's mouth.

'Yes,' Foley grinned. 'They look good on him too. I'm proud of the man. He deserves them.'

Dinane gave him a sideways glance. 'And you don't?'

Foley paused. 'Me? Naw. I'm not made for stripes.'

'What does that mean, for feck sake?' Dinane gave an irritated puff on his pipe.

'Well, it means stripes wouldn't sit well on me. I'm happy doing what I'm doing.'

'So how old are you now?'

'What? Why?'

'Well, you're obviously in your thirties.' Dinane didn't break stride, walking straight up the middle of the road puffing on his pipe. 'Isn't it about time you thought about your future? And your pension?'

'I just told you. I'm not cut out for stripes.'

'I am surprised.' Another cloud of smoke popped out from behind the pipe. 'I thought you'd be eager to follow in your stepfather's shoes, live up to the reputation of the legendary Inspector Liam Edge.'

'God, no. I saw what the pressure of the job did to him. The job is hard enough as it is without taking on the responsibility for everyone else.'

'Then what about going for detective?' Dinane took the pipe out of his mouth and pointed it at Foley. 'And don't give me the bullshit about not having the skills.'

'Well, I ...'

'The Super mentioned you recently when the subject came up. He has a lot of time for you, Foley. He thinks you should be a lot higher up the ladder by now.'

They'd reached the house and Dinane nodded to the cluster of men waiting patiently to remove the bodies. They were shuffling from foot to foot and they kept their hands deep in the pockets of their long black coats. The cold made their eyes water.

'Sorry for the delay, lads,' Dinane gave them a sympathetic grin. 'I'll be as quick as I can.'

As they went in through the back door Foley braced himself against the smell and pressed the handkerchief to his nose again. Dinane puffed on his pipe and seemed to be unaffected by it. He walked slowly through the kitchen, ignoring the mess on the floor. His eyes scanned the worktops, the shelves, the remains of the cats. When he got to the body he stood in front of it and studied her in silence for a few minutes. Then he shook his head and blew out another puff of smoke from the corner of his mouth. 'So what do we know so far, Eamon?'

'Well, we believe the bodies are of Toby Appleyard and his daughter Bella. Toby had some sort of a breakdown when his wife died around twelve years ago, so Bella came home to look after him. He had dementia now too and rarely came out of his room anymore.'

'What a sad state of affairs.' Dinane bowed his head for a moment then glanced at Foley again. 'To think they used to be such important people back in the day. Huge farmers. Well respected.'

'You knew them?'

'I knew of them. Didn't you? I thought everyone in Tralee knew the Appleyards.'

Foley sighed. 'That's what Mrs Brazil said.'

'Mrs Brazil? Is that where you were, over in the corner shop?'

'You know them too, I suppose?' Foley couldn't hide the mockery.

Dinane rolled his eyes and hid a grin behind his pipe. 'They're in the best place to hear all the gossip, though. So what did you find out?'

'Well, Liam says Bella told him they were going away for a few weeks when he called to see her on New Year's Day.'

'On New Year's Day?'

'That's what he said. He said she was very excited about it and she'd call him when they got back. But Liam and his mother insist they didn't see her again after that. So they assumed they were still away.'

'New Year's Day,' Dinane repeated to himself. 'That would explain a lot.'

Foley realised he was shivering and he couldn't decide if it was from the dreadful cold of the room or from being this close to what was left of a human being. He tried to distract himself by stamping his feet but stopped when something crunched under his boot.

Dinane leant over the body again and examined the wooden rosary beads that hung around her neck like a necklace. The big wooden crucifix was dangling over the back of the chair. Dinane lifted it and examined its weight. 'So, what do you make of this,' he asked Foley.

Foley studied it but couldn't see anything unusual. 'It's a rosary beads. Nuns wear them all the time. It's part of their uniform. Bella was a nun. She's not wearing a habit now because her father wouldn't let her, but I suppose…'

'I mean the way it's hanging.' Dinane touched it again.

'It was probably shoved out of the way by the cats. If they were trying to … you know? They'd push it away, wouldn't they?'

Dinane gave it a sharp tug then let it go. 'The cord is thick and strong. It wouldn't break easily.' He ran his fingers along the beads to where they touched the bones of the neck. 'If she was taken by surprise, this would be a formidable weapon.'

Foley gasped behind the handkerchief. 'What are you saying? You think she was strangled by her rosary beads?'

'It's possible, don't you think?' Dinane stood up and looked around the room again.

'Damn.' Foley noticed the cup the doctor had been interested in earlier and he picked it up. 'The doc was supposed to take this with him. He thinks Bella probably took the same poison she gave her father, and he was going to examine the cup for traces of it.'

There was a long pause as Dinane puffed on his pipe and stared at the body again. Then he went to the range and opened the door on the front. 'If I remember rightly, New Year's Day was bitterly cold. I bet you a kitchen as big as this would not be warm enough to sit around in just a dress. Especially one with short sleeves.'

Foley was surprised at the observation and he had to agree. Dinane was right. The dress the victim was wearing was far too skimpy for a winter's day. She'd have to be wearing a jacket or a cardigan as well if she was going to sit here for any length of time. 'So what does that mean?' he asked.

Dinane chewed on the stem of his pipe. 'I have no idea.' Then he went over to the door that led to the hall.

Two long overcoats, obviously belonging to a tall man, and two shorter ones were hanging on a stand inside the front door. Dinane checked the pockets but he didn't find anything apart from a screwed up shopping list. In the large front room across the hall, the only thing out of place was the bodies of two cats. It was probably a very comfortable room at one time, but now it looked sad and neglected. It was tidy but obviously unlived in, and it reminded Foley of a doctor's waiting room.

On the other side of the hall, another large room was used as an office. A huge desk stood in front of the bay window so whoever was working at it had a fabulous view out over the fields to the town in the distance. The spire of St John's Church looked impressive in the shadow of the Slieve Mish Mountains beyond. Dinane shuffled the papers on the desk then looked in the drawers before studying the books on the shelves around the wall.

Finally he went back out to the hall and Foley followed him up the stairs where he looked into every room, just as Foley had done earlier. Most of the rooms seemed to be unused. The beds were dressed but there was nothing in the wardrobes or in the bedside drawers. They assumed the smallest room at the back was Bella's because it was as close to a nun's cell as anyone could get. A huge crucifix hung on the wall above the headboard, and a prayer book sat on the tiny stool beside the bed. There was a nightdress on the pillow and slippers under the chair. A nun's habit hung on the back of the door along with a black dress and two black cardigans. There was one pair of black shoes in the corner.

In the master bedroom Dinane stood looking at the body of the elderly man for another few minutes, his poker face blank and impossible to read. Foley studied the body too, trying to see what the detective was seeing. Eventually Dinane turned to the sideboard and examined the array of medicine bottles spread out on it with names that Foley couldn't even pronounce. There was also a clock, a prayer book, and a detective novel in large print.

'So what are your thoughts, Foley?' Dinane looked at him in the mirror. Foley glanced around the room as he considered his answer. 'Well, your man looks as if he was in agony when he died so my first instinct is to say he didn't die of natural causes.'

'Why?'

'What do you mean why?'

Dinane tapped the side of his head. 'What's to say the poor man didn't have a stroke and was struggling to get help, but he didn't make it out of the bed?'

Foley looked at the body again. He had no idea what a stroke did to a person. But he didn't know what a person who'd been poisoned looked like either. 'Well ... I see what you mean, but the doctor seemed to think ...'

'And we respect his opinion.' Dinane sucked on his pipe. 'But only up to a point. We can't hold up the investigation while we wait for the result of his examination. That could take days and we'd waste precious time. A killer could be putting some distance between himself and the crime, or building himself an alibi while we sit around twiddling our thumbs.'

'But surely the doc's findings are critical to what we do next. They'll point us in the right direction.'

'Yes. You're right. But in the meantime, we should gather as much information as we possibly can. So when the doc's findings land on our desk we can hold them up to what we've collected and see what fits where.'

Foley nodded and made the right noise, but he wasn't wholly convinced.

'Right, so what do you notice so far?' Dinane blew out another puff of smoke from the corner of his mouth.

'In here?'

Dinane waved the pipe like a conductor's baton. 'And downstairs.'

'Well, I ...'

'You've set your mind on this being a murder and a suicide, haven't you? And I don't blame you for that because there's a lot to justify that suggestion.'

'Is there?' Foley felt a strange surge of relief.

'Look around, Foley.' Dinane waved the pipe again. 'First of all, there's no evidence they were going anywhere, is there? Despite what the nun told your friend Liam Brazil, there's not a single suitcase anywhere. There are no folded clothes ready to be packed away. There are no toiletries gathered up to be shoved into a suitcase. So one possibility is that Miss Appleyard made up the story about going away because Liam Brazil surprised her by calling here unexpectedly on New Year's Day. Suppose she'd already poisoned her father. She'd want to get rid of Brazil as quickly as possible, and she wouldn't want anyone calling to the house too soon and discovering what happened. They would spoil her plans.'

'That makes sense,' Foley agreed.

'But then again, the opposite might be true.' Dinane folded his arms across his chest as he studied the body again.

'The opposite?'

'Yes.' Dinane paused again, and when Foley coughed into his handkerchief Dinane continued. 'Suppose the old chap hears Liam Brazil drive up and he goes to the window to see who it is. And he hears the daughter saying they're planning to go away. But he doesn't want to go away. He dreads going anywhere. So he goes down to the kitchen to challenge her and things get out of hand. He loses control and strangles her with her rosary beads.'

'Right,' Foley nodded. 'But if that's the case, how did he die?'

'Well, as we said earlier, he was so distressed by what he'd done that it brought on a stroke just as he got back into bed.'

Dinane looked at Foley as he waited for a reply. Foley studied the body again as he tried to imagine the scene. Then he noticed the man's bare feet. 'You said New Year's Day was bitterly cold, yeah? But his feet are bare. He wouldn't walk very far in bare feet if it was that cold.'

Dinane nodded. 'That would depend on how upset he was. Real anger deadens the senses. If he was in a rage he wouldn't have noticed the cold on his feet.'

Foley snapped his fingers. 'And then he locked the cats in the kitchen to destroy the evidence. But would he think like that? What kind of a mind would even come up with something like that?'

Dinane pointed at the man's feet. 'On the other hand, his feet are clean. If he'd walked downstairs and through the kitchen in bare feet, they wouldn't be this clean.'

Foley noticed a pair of tattered slippers behind the door. 'Perhaps he wore those then kicked them off when he got back in the room.'

'Then he got back in bed and continued eating his breakfast.' Dinane picked up the cereal bowl on the bed and put it by the mouldy toast on the tray on the sideboard.

'I thought the doc was going to take those with him.' Foley pointed to the tray. 'As well as the cup downstairs. They could be vital evidence.'

'No, he left them for us to see.' Dinane tapped his pipe out in the saucer. 'We need to see the scene as it was to check for any obvious clues. And since we're finished here we can gather them up and give it to the fella on the gate to take over to the doc.'

Chapter Six

Sean McGrath beamed when he saw Foley and Dinane coming in his front gate and he whipped the door open before they reached it. Foley introduced Det Dinane and McGrath put out his hand.

'Guard Foley tells me you're a detective too,' Dinane shook the hand warmly.

'Retired now, thank God,' McGrath grinned. There was an instant rapport between the two detectives and they were already comparing notes as McGrath guided them into the kitchen. The heat from the range was welcome and Foley unbuttoned his overcoat. McGrath invited them to sit down and they went to the opposite sides of the table. Foley put his cap on the corner of the chair while McGrath clattered pots around on the top of the range.

'Tea? That's all I've got, I'm afraid. Unless you'd like something stronger? Medicinal, of course. To keep out the cold.'

Dinane laughed and put up his hand. 'Tea will be grand, thank you.'

'So what's the story so far?' McGrath asked as he spooned tea into the pot.

Dinane let Foley tell it and McGrath didn't speak until he'd finished. Then he pulled a face that was full of questions.

'So you believe they've been dead since the beginning of the year?' He gave his head a sympathetic shake and clicked his tongue. 'God, that's dreadful. But do you think it's possible that no one called to the house in all that time? Three months almost? What about the postman? Were there any letters in the door, any signs of a newspaper being delivered?'

'That's the first thing we checked,' Dinane rolled his eyes in a way that said McGrath should have known that.

'But from what we can see they rarely got any letters anyway. The odd bill but nothing on a personal front. As for visitors, when you think what the weather was like you can understand why there wasn't any. The snow pinned everyone in their homes. They only went out if they were desperate, and that was only to the shops.'

'Yes. It's been a bizarre few months all right.' McGrath took cups from the dresser and put them on the table. 'The country has never been through weather like this before in all its history. So I suppose it *is* possible no one visited the house in all that time.'

'But even if someone did call, wouldn't they just assume no one was home and gone away again? Unless they looked in the window and saw the cats like I did.' Foley shivered as the picture came back to him. 'But then the cats might still have been alive at that time, of course.'

All three of them paused for a moment as they pictured the scene, then Dinane said, 'The thing is, for the cats to become so hungry they actually turned on each other, they must have been locked in that kitchen for a very long time.' He shook some tobacco into his pipe and packed it down with his finger. 'Which is something I haven't come across before, and I hope to God I don't ever again. What about you, Sean? Have you ever been called out to anything like that in your time as a detective?'

McGrath sat in an armchair on the other side of the range and rubbed his chin. 'Nothing like you described in the Appleyard's house. But I've had more cases where the family dog has attacked a child than I care to remember. I had one case where the parents left a three-year-old child in the house with the dog while they went to Blackpool for a holiday. They said they left enough food out on the table for them, but the neighbours heard the child crying and called the police.'

'But the child was all right?'

'Luckily, yes. I did have one where the dog killed the child and the parents hid the body under the bed.' He waited for the reaction and nodded when it came. 'Oh yes. They told the neighbours he'd gone to Scotland to visit the grandparents and he liked it there so much he wanted to stay there. But a teacher got suspicious when she noticed a distinct smell on his sister's clothes. The girl had become withdrawn and sad and the teacher managed to coax her into telling her what was wrong. It still took the council a week to send someone around to check.'

'And the parents were arrested?'

'They were, and the girl was put into care. But the parents were only charged with unlawfully hiding a body and got a fine. The council agreed the girl could go home on condition the dog was put down, but the father said the dog was like a child to him and he couldn't do it. So the girl stayed in care.'

'God,' Foley sighed. 'As the saying goes, there's nothing as queer as people.'

'So, getting back to the Appleyards, Sean.' Dinane waved his pipe at the detective. 'I get the feeling the neighbours weren't very fond of them. Am I right?'

'You're right, Brian.' McGrath clicked his tongue again. 'There's a lot of bad feeling about the way some people were treated by the Appleyards a few years back. It was before I came home, mind you, but I'm a good listener. Anyway, the three cottages you can see across the road from mine are owned by the Appleyards, and the tenants all used to work on the estate. Some of them had been employed there most of their working lives.'

There was another pause as he gathered his thoughts. 'But when Sinead Appleyard died suddenly about twelve years ago, everything changed. Her husband Toby had some sort of breakdown. The sad thing is, there were enough people with experience to keep the place running until he got better, but the daughter who came home to look after the old fella didn't have a clue how to treat her staff. She upset everyone. They were only trying to help her, but she couldn't see that. She was bitter and spiteful and gradually they were all shoved out until there was no one left to look after the animals or the crops. The older sister brought in an agent who sold off all the stock and the animals, but he was instructed not to sell the land. It was the family heritage. Toby wanted it to go to his first grandson, if there ever was a first grandson. The fact is, the daughter who was looking after him was a nun, and the other daughter had been married for years without producing an offspring.'

McGrath got a jug of milk and put it on the table then got a bag of sugar off the sideboard and put it there too. 'Anyway, it was agreed the tenants could carry on renting the cottages as long as they paid the going rate. Which was a huge problem, of course. They were all out of a job now. But the nun wouldn't allow them any grace. Luckily Percy Metcalfe and Oliver Cunningham got a job in the new bacon factory in town not long after they were laid off, which saved their homes.'

'What about Mrs O'Gara? Is she renting from the Appleyards too?'

'She is.' McGrath brushed something from the table into his hand then shook it into the bucket of coal beside the range. 'Luckily her father, the late Jimmy Lynch, bought small plots of land from Toby Appleyard over the years, and he built up a nice little business raising sheep and goats, and that kept them going when the shit hit the fan.'

'So he didn't work for the Appleyards?'

'Oh, he did. For many years. Then when Jimmy died his daughter Joan and her husband Tom took over the lease of the cottage. I think Tom is looking to build his own house nearby but there's some sort of legal wrangle holding him up.'

'So how well do you know your neighbours, Sean?' Dinane pulled a cup closer and poured some milk into it. 'I mean, in your opinion, is any one of them likely to have harmed the Appleyards?'

McGrath looked shocked for a second then chuckled. 'Naw. I can't imagine any of them being capable of doing what was done up in that house. Mind you, in the heat of the moment, who knows?' Then he clicked his fingers. 'So you're thinking, did one of them kill Bella and then decide to silence the old man too? But aren't the odds of that huge? Unless it was premeditated. No, if it was a sudden burst of rage the killer would have run away after he killed Bella and tried to cover their tracks.'

McGrath poured boiling water into the teapot. 'Anyway, from what you told me so far, I'm inclined to agree Bella poisoned her father then sat in the kitchen and drank the poison too.'

'But Bella was a Catholic nun,' Foley argued. 'She would consider suicide to be a mortal sin, and she'd be damned to the fires of hell. It would be against everything she believed in.'

McGrath shrugged. 'Well, if the stories *are* true, she's been putting up with her father's abuse for years. It would have been like a prison sentence, listening to him ranting at her day after day, jumping to his every whim. He wouldn't even let her wear her nun's habit, you know? She couldn't go out. He wouldn't even let her go to Mass on Sunday. She only ever left the house when her sister came to visit, and that was on a rare occasion. So maybe one day she just broke under the strain and couldn't take anymore? So she killed her father. Then out of remorse, she took her own life.'

Chapter Seven

Percy Metcliffe was shovelling snow off his front path and he didn't look up when Detective Dinane called his name as they crossed the road from Sean McGrath's house.

Despite the bitter cold, Metcliffe was dressed in just a shirt with his sleeves rolled up. His grey hair was long and uncombed and there was a sheen of sweat on his weather-beaten face. For a man his age, he was shifting a huge amount of snow on his shovel and throwing it away across the garden. Foley was impressed. Coming out from the warmth of McGrath's kitchen had him shrivelled up inside his heavy Garda overcoat with his collar pulled up as far as it would go around his face.

'Mr Metcalfe,' Dinane repeated. 'I'm Detective Dinane and this is …'

'I know who you are,' Metcalfe barked from behind a shovel full of flying snow. 'If you've come about what happened to the Appleyards you can feck off because it has nothing to do with me.'

Dinane stopped just out of reach of the shovel. 'That's interesting, Mr Metcalfe. Why would we think it did?'

'Because that's the way you people work,' Metcalfe spat. 'You look around for a suitable suspect then you make that person fit the crime. Anyone who had a beef with the victim is dragged in and accused of something.'

'That's very cynical, Mr Metcalfe.' Dinane had a chuckle in his voice. 'Are you saying you had a beef with the victim, as you put it so eloquently?'

'Everyone who knew that dreadful woman had a beef with her. Just knowing her made you hate her, even if she was a nun, God help us all.' Metcalfe gathered up another shovel full of snow. 'Still, whatever happened to her was unfortunate. But it had nothing to do with me. I haven't been up to that house since the day the miserable cow fired me, and that was years ago.'

'So you haven't been up to that house in over twelve years?' Foley sounded sceptical.

The snow scattered like a mini blizzard as Metcalfe threw it away. 'Well, yes. Apart from New Year's day, that is.'

Dinane glanced at Foley and he moved closer. 'You went over to the Appleyard's house on New Year's day? Why?'

'Because I was furious.' Metcalfe scooped up more snow and flung it away so hard most of it flew over the boundary wall.

'Right.' Dinane stepped back again. 'And why was that?'

'Do you know how long I worked for those people?' This time a spray of spittle came out with the words and Metcalfe wiped it away with the back of his hand. 'All my feckin life, that's how long. I was just a child when I started helping my father on the Appleyard's farm. Every chance I got. Weekends, school holidays, I'd be there. And I never got a penny for it.'

The shovel screeched as it hit the concrete and Metcalfe shuffled it into the next pile of snow. 'But I didn't mind because I loved every minute of it. So when I was fourteen I was taken on properly. And I never missed a day in all those years. Not one feckin day!' The shovel almost flew out of his hand with the angry throw of the snow. 'And this is the thanks I get. After everything we did for that family, this is how she treated us now. No respect. Not one feckin ounce of respect.'

Another shovel full of snow hit the wall. Dinane took his pipe out of his pocket and put it in his mouth. 'So what did she do that upset you so much you had to go and see her on New Year's Day, Mr Metcalfe?'

'She sent us that feckin notice.' Metcalfe rubbed his hands together then dug the shovel into the snow again.

'She didn't even have the guts to tell us herself. No, she got young Brazil to deliver it. I was fuming, I can tell you. Of all the days to give us the bad news, she chooses New Year's Day. Can you believe that? New Year's Day is supposed to be the beginning of a new chapter, the time for starting a new page. And she chooses to do this to us on that very day. I was mad enough to wring her scrawny neck with my bare hands, so I was. I couldn't believe she'd be so spiteful. We were already struggling. I'm working six days a week and just about getting by.' He started to cough and he had to lean on his shovel to steady himself. Dinane waved his pipe at him.

'So what was the notice about, Mr Metcalfe?'

'She was putting up the rent. Again!' The words brought on another cough. When he got his breath back he said, 'We were already struggling, as I just told you. So another rent increase would be the difference between us having food on our table or going without.'

He glared at Dinane and wiped his mouth again. 'I wanted my neighbours, Oliver and Tom, to come with me but they were too afraid to confront her. They said if we antagonised her she'd have us evicted. But I was livid. I had to do something. So I went across the top field. But when I came out through the trees by the back of the house I could see a car in the back yard and I stopped. That was when I heard the voices. Raised voices, like someone having a row.

'Did you recognise the voices?' Dinane took the pipe out of his mouth.

'No.' Metcalfe frowned as he thought about it. 'But one was a man. The other was a woman, or maybe two women. I'm not sure.'

'And it was a car you saw,' Foley asked. 'It wasn't a van?'

'I know the difference between a car and a feckin van,' Metcalfe grabbed the shovel and started digging at the snow again. 'I'm not a complete eejit.'

'All right,' Dinane said in his soothing tone. 'Mr Metcalfe, did you manage to get a look at whoever was in the house?'

Metcalfe grunted with the strain of lifting the snow and he turned to Dinane. 'I told you. I'm not a feckin eejit. I wasn't going down there now. I know when to pick a fight, and that wasn't it. So I came home.'

Foley sensed a movement behind him and he spun around in time to see a big man with a thick ginger beard bearing down on him.

Chapter Eight

'What's all the roaring about?' The man had the palest blue eyes Foley had ever seen. His hair was almost all gone leaving just the tuffs on either side of his head, but he made up for it with a thick beard.

'And who are you?' Foley stood in the middle of the path and the man sized him up before stopping in front of him.

'I'm ...'

'He's Oliver Cunningham, my next-door neighbour.' Metcalfe pulled a face. 'What do you want, Ollie?'

'I want to know why you're roaring like a bull with his bits caught in a door,' Cunningham chuckled.

'Feck off.' Metcalfe threw a lump of snow at him. 'The guards aren't interested in what you have to say so go back to your cosy fire and have your usual afternoon nap and stop bothering them while they're trying to do their job.'

Dinane held out his hand. 'I'm Detective Dinane.'

Cunningham took it. 'Nice to meet you, Detective Dinane.'

'And this is Guard Foley.'

'I know Guard Foley.' Cunningham nodded but didn't offer his hand. 'I've seen him around the town.'

'Can you spare us a few minutes of your time, Mr Cunningham?' Dinane gave him one of his unnerving smiles that let him know what the expected answer was.

'Yes, of course. But not out here in the freezing cold.' Cunningham waved his hand at the house next door. 'Come in the house and I'll make you a nice hot cup of tea like any civilised person would and not be keeping you standing out here in the snow like some inconsiderate people I won't mention.'

Metcalfe threw down his shovel and picked his jacket off a bush by the front door. Dinane gave him a nod. 'Thank you, Mr Metcalfe. We might be in touch again soon if we have any more questions.'

'You're grand,' Metcalfe said as he brushed past Dinane. 'C'mon, Ollie. Get that feckin kettle on. I'm frozen to the bone.'

Foley stepped out of his way and looked at Dinane, and Metcalfe waved them on. 'You'd better hurry up if you want that tea. He's known for changing his mind. Well, not changing his mind, exactly. More like forgetting what he's doing.' He rolled his eyes and went on down the path.

The woman washing clothes in the sink spun around when the four men piled into her kitchen.

'Sorry, love.' Cunningham pulled out a chair and offered it to Dinane then pointed Foley towards another one. 'These fellas are the guards. They're enquiring about what happened over in the Appleyard's place. Lads, this is the missus, Jessie.'

Jessie wiped her hands in her apron and she seemed lost for words so she went to the range and moved the kettle onto the hot plate. 'A cup of tea, so.'

'Please don't go to any trouble for us,' Dinane gave her a beaming smile.

'Not at all,' she smiled back but it was forced. 'Tis no trouble, sure.'

Then she wiped her hands in the apron again and her face creased in a worried frown. 'So you're asking about the Appleyards, are you? We heard what ... well, we got bits and pieces of the story. The poor woman. Do you know what happened to her? Well, of course you do, you being the guards and all. I mean, what *did* happen ...?'

Dinane held out his hand to her and she glanced at her husband before she shook it. 'I'm Detective Dinane, Mrs Cunningham. And this is Guard Foley.'

'Hello.' The handshake was quick and she nodded at Foley. 'How do you do?'

'I'm grand.' Foley sat down and the other men sat at each end of the table.

'I know Bella Appleyard was an odd little creature,' Mrs Cunningham addressed Dinane. 'But we wouldn't wish any harm on her. No one deserves that.'

Metcalfe snorted and scraped his chair as he moved nearer to the table. And Jessie glared at him. 'No, she didn't deserve that, Percy,' she argued. 'No matter what she did to us she didn't deserve to be eaten by her cats. That's a dreadful thing to happen to anyone.'

Metcalfe shrugged and turned to Dinane. 'So what's the real story? Only what we're hearing is bizarre. You know, they're saying the nun was savaged to death by her feral cats who had the run of the house. Is that possible?'

'And they said the old man starved to death because there was no one to feed him.' Cunningham looked from Foley to Dinane. 'But we didn't think he was so sick he couldn't get out of bed. Especially if he was starving.'

Cunningham produced a packet of cigarettes and passed them around, and Jessie put a saucer in the middle of the table.

'He broke the last ashtray.' She poked her husband on the arm and he grinned sheepishly as he cracked a match. He lit his own first then the other two. Dinane took the match and held it to his pipe and he disappeared behind a cloud of smoke as he sucked loudly on it. Then he shook out the match and dropped it in the saucer.

'Well, as things stand right now, we're waiting for the doctor's report,' Dinane told them. 'All we can say for sure is Mr Appleyard was in bed when he died, and Miss Appleyard was in the kitchen. It seems the cats were locked in the kitchen with her.'

'So did the cats kill her? Is that how she died?' Jessie's voice was almost a sob.

'No. We think that's unlikely. At this stage, we think she was already dead by the time they got hungry enough to … you know.'

'So how did she die then?' Cunningham demanded. 'Are you saying someone murdered her? Someone killed her in her own kitchen? Who?'

'As I just said, we don't know how she died.' Dinane used his headmaster's voice, slow and deep. And persuasive. 'We have to wait and see what the doctor says when he's had a good look at the bodies.'

Jessie Cunningham crossed herself and went back to the sink. 'The poor, poor woman. God rest her soul.'

'Well, I can't say I'm sorry.' Metcalfe held his fists under his chin.

'No, don't say that, Percy Metcalfe.' Jessie glared at him again. 'The poor woman is dead. Show some respect.'

'Show some respect?' Metcalfe snapped. 'How can you say that? When did that cow ever show us any respect?'

'That's not the point. You should still show respect for the dead.'

'I can't,' Metcalfe insisted. 'What she did to us is still too painful. And look at us now. We're worse off than ever. They're bound to sell the place now, along with our cottages. It's like bloody Déjà Vu. We're right back where we started.'

Oliver Cunningham saw the way Dinane was sitting quietly absorbing the conversation and he leant forward in his chair. 'Jessie was the housekeeper up at the big house, you know. Her mother was the housekeeper before that. They spent their whole working lives in that house. Then the Appleyards did ...'

'And I loved every minute of it,' Jessie butted in. 'I started working there when I left school, you know, back in the days when Tyrone and Anastasia Appleyard were alive. They had two chambermaids at the time. And a kitchen maid. Percy's wife Teresa ...,' she nodded at Metcalfe. '...was the cook. They were happy times. We felt like we were part of the family in those days. As long as we knew our place, we were treated very well.'

'I was the same age as Toby Appleyard when I started working there,' Metcalfe shook his head and sighed. 'The good old days, sure. Funny how we remember the good times and block out the bad stuff. But speaking for myself, I loved working there. Even during the troubles when things got a bit ...'

Cunningham groaned. 'The troubles? They were dreadful times all right, there's no denying it. But we were young and naïve and we didn't understand what was going on around us. Politics was beyond us so we tended to follow the direction of those we thought knew best.'

Jessie put four cups on the table. 'The troubles, yeah. They were the death of poor auld Tyrone Appleyard. He was an innocent man. He wasn't on anyone's side during the civil war, but that didn't count for anything when the moment came.'

'What happened to him,' Foley asked.

'Well, it was the time the Free State Troopers came down to Tralee because the IRA wouldn't behave themselves. There was fierce fighting all over the town. Then the troopers arrived at the Appleyard's, supposedly on a tip-off they were harbouring IRA fugitives. They made everyone leave the house while they searched it. It was raining and cold but they made us all stand out in the backyard for ages. In the confusion the two younger Appleyard boys, Toby's brothers Harry and Edward, ran away over the fields. The rest of us were threatened with prison if we didn't say where they went. The fact is we didn't know. No one knew. The family never discussed politics in front of us. We were just the hired help.'

There was a sudden silence as everyone turned in on themselves as they remembered the times. Then Jessie Cunningham said, 'They found the two bodies on the Castleisland road the next day. One story was that Harry and Edward tried to flag down a car in the dark and the driver didn't see them because it was raining so hard. Then someone said the IRA killed them because they were informers for the guards. Then we were told an army lorry hit them. It was all very upsetting. And poor Tyrone never recovered. He caught pneumonia, which was blamed on the way the army made him stand out in the rain for so long. But the grief played a big part too, and he died soon afterwards. Unfortunately, Anastasia gave up the ghost too and she died a few months later.'

When the kettle started bubbling, Oliver Cunningham jumped up and poured the boiling water into the teapot. 'Toby was the only surviving son, and he found himself in charge of the business quicker than he expected,' he said. 'And to be fair to the man, he did a great job. He had his father's charm and good humour. It was a pleasure to work for him.'

'It was. Even after he got married.' Jessie put a jug of milk and some teaspoons on the table. 'He met Sinead at some big farmer's event and it was love at first sight. You could see he was besotted with her.'

'Well, she was a beautiful woman,' Metcalfe added. 'I never saw a man fall in love so hard and so fast before.'

'Beautiful to look at anyway,' Cunningham said. 'Her manner was a bit brusque, though. They said it was because she came from a big shot family up the country somewhere. She had the bearing of a country duchess. But like we said, if you knew your place you were treated well.'

'Yeah, Toby worshipped that woman.' Jessie put a bag of sugar on the table. 'They had two daughters, Lily and Bella. Lily is married in Dublin and Bella went off to be a nun.'

There was another pause as the old days filled their minds again.

'Teresa and I were at a friend's wedding over in Killarney when we heard the news that Sinead had died.' Percy Metcalfe's voice was suddenly subdued. 'It was a dreadful shock. She was always so healthy and strong, full of energy. She was out riding and when she got back to the house she said she had a headache and was going to lie down for a while.'

Jessie took up the story. 'I brought her up a cup of tea around five o'clock so she'd have time to come around and get ready for dinner. But I couldn't wake her.' Jessie looked as if she was still in shock and her eyes filled up. 'I called Toby, and as God is my witness I have never seen a man crumble so completely in front of my eyes. It was pitiful. His face that day has haunted me ever since.'

'There was no consoling him,' Cunningham added. 'He was hanging onto her and pushing everyone away. It was heart-breaking. The doctor had to sedate him before he was able to look at Sinead to see what happened to her.'

'And that was the beginning of the end for us,' Percy Metcalfe glanced at Dinane and sat back in his chair. 'The daughter Lily and her husband came home and to be fair to the woman she didn't interfere with the running of the business. She could see we knew what to do and she trusted us to do it.'

'But when it became obvious Toby had some sort of breakdown and wasn't recovering, the younger sister Bella was brought home to look after him.' Cunningham tapped the ash from his cigarette in the saucer and then took a long drag on it. 'We could understand why she was so bitter and twisted, in all honesty, because from the moment she arrived home her father made her life a misery. He was dreadful to her, abusive and downright nasty. So she took it out on us. And one by one she pushed us out.'

Foley stubbed his cigarette butt out in the saucer. 'I can see why none of you was very fond of her.'

'I'd say we were more disappointed than anything,' Jessie said. 'We'd known those girls from the day they were born. They grew up around us. We washed them, we bathed them, and we dressed them for school. We bandaged their knees and combed their hair. Yet when Bella came home it was as if we were total strangers. We were just commodities, disposable assets.'

Foley smiled at the analogy.

'I always thought she got rid of us so her father would be forced to depend on her,' Oliver Cunningham said. 'He knew how to run a farm but he didn't know how to run a house. He couldn't even boil an egg. He'd been waited on his whole life, you see. There was a cook and a maid, and a housekeeper who catered for his every wish. So with us out of the way he'd be helpless. He'd need Bella if he was going to survive. So she began her campaign to force us out. Small things at first, snapping about the most trivial mistakes, like not attending the rosary at six o'clock every evening. Then she started ranting if the meals weren't ready at a specific time every day. Demanding the laundry be washed with a specific soap and hung out in a specific way.'

'And she wouldn't acknowledge you unless she had something to say to you,' Jessie added. 'And if you dared to speak to her she'd bite your head off. The whole atmosphere became uncomfortable and stressful in a very short time.'

'The maids were the first to go.' Oliver Cunningham gave his wife a sympathetic smile. 'So Jessie was expected to do their work as well as her own, and that was why she …'

'No,' Jessie contradicted him. 'That wasn't the reason I left. I could cope with the work, which irritated her, of course. No, I left because of her petty objection to me having my meals there. I was always at work by six in the morning, and after breakfast was served to the family and the daily routines were completed, I would sit down with the cook and the other staff and have my breakfast. One day she called me into her office and told me my meals were not her responsibility as I didn't live in the house. So from then on, I was to have my breakfast in my own house before I came to work. And I was to go home to have my lunch in my own house too.'

'Which was unfair,' Oliver growled. 'Our meals were part of the job. The wages on their own weren't enough to live on so without the meals it would be a struggle to survive. Even with both of our wages, it was a struggle.'

Oliver coughed and wiped his mouth with his sleeve. 'Then she did the same to me. Me and the rest of the farmhands. We were in at five every morning to milk the cows, feed the horses and do all the other chores that kept the farm going. And around eight we'd all traipse into the kitchen for our breakfast. It had always been like that. It was tradition. Then one day we turned up to find the cook Teresa really distressed. She'd been instructed to tell us that from then on we sorted out our own meals. We weren't even allowed to come in for a cup of tea. Teresa was so upset she took off her apron and walked out.'

'She was in a dreadful state,' Percy Metcalfe tapped the ash off his cigarette. 'And to make it worse, young Miss Appleyard told me I should leave too so as not to cause bad feelings amongst the other workers.'

'You can imagine how we felt,' Oliver Cunningham pulled a face. 'Suddenly we had no job, and we honestly believed we'd be thrown out of our house too. But she was too devious to do that. She saw a way to keep us in line and she allowed us to rent the cottages, but at the going rate.'

'Lucky Oliver and I knew someone who worked in Denny's factory and he managed to get us a job over here.' Metcalfe shuddered at the memory. 'We were grateful, of course. But it was a complete shock to our system. We'd worked outside all our lives, out in the open spaces, out in the changing seasons with whatever the weather threw at us. Now we were confined to one spot all day every day, locked inside a factory, no fresh air, no open spaces. It was a nightmare. But we had no choice and we said a grateful prayer of thanks every day that we weren't as badly off as other people.'

'Our two boys were out of short pants by then,' Oliver informed them. 'So Jessie was able to work in the kitchen of the Grand Hotel. She did the breakfasts and lunches so she was home when they came in from school.'

'My girls were a bit older and they went off to Dublin to become nurses.' Percy Metcalfe's chest puffed out with pride. 'They're doing well, thanks be to God.'

Jessie put the teapot in the middle of the table. There was another pause as they all sat back and watched Oliver Cunningham pour the tea into the cups. He glanced up at his wife. 'Will you be having some?'

'No,' she pointed to the sink with her thumb. 'I'll finish this first and hang it out while the sun is shining. Not that it'll dry properly in this cold. But the breeze will get some of the wet out of it before I put it on the clothes horse in front of the fire.'

'Right you are,' Oliver shoved the cups in front of Dinane and Foley. Dinane put his pipe on the table, took a sip of his tea and sat back in his chair.

'So can I ask you when you all last saw the Appleyards?' He nodded at Metcalfe. 'I know you said you went over there on New Year's Day, but has any one of you been over there since then?'

There was a collective shaking of heads and a mumble of denials, and Dinane took another sip of tea as he looked at each of them in turn. 'What about you, Mr Cunningham? When were you last over there?'

Cunningham looked up at the ceiling and dragged in his cigarette. 'God, it must be years since I set foot in that place.' He looked at his wife. 'It was around the time they were selling off the machinery, wasn't it, love? Remember? That agent was there. And Lily Appleyard. She was in charge of it. But I don't think we saw Bella. Which is just as well. She'd probably have got a belt around the head with a shovel if she dared to show her face, considering how many people she upset.'

'And you, Mrs Cunningham?'

'Me?' Jessie looked startled and rubbed at the items in the sink with a sudden urgency. 'I don't know. Tis years. It must be the time Ollie was talking about. Yes, it was. That was years ago.'

'Are you sure?'

Her eyes flashed and a glow appeared in her cheeks. 'Are you calling me a liar?'

Dinane turned around and gave her one of his silent stares, and Jessie shrivelled in front of it. 'Yes. Sorry. I'm sure.' She turned back to the sink. 'Why would I go up there anyway? There's no reason for me to go up there, sure. I have nothing to do with them now.'

Dinane glanced at Foley, and Foley asked, 'Did any of you know the Appleyards were supposed to be going away for a few weeks on New Year's Day?'

'Were they?' Cunningham looked at Metcalfe then at his wife. He looked genuinely surprised.

'Where were they going?' Metcalfe asked. 'I thought Toby was supposed to be too sick to come out of his room. That's according to the rumours. If he's that sick I can't see him wanting to go far from the house.'

'And I can't see him going anywhere with the nun.' Jessie said. 'He could barely tolerate her. He was brutal towards her so I can't imagine the two of them going on holiday together.'

'So Liam Brazil didn't mention it when he brought the letters to you on New Year's Day?' Foley put his cup down and dragged on his cigarette.

Metcalfe scratched his ear. 'He might have said something but to tell you the truth my mind went blank when I read the letter. I just saw red. It was like a physical punch to the belly. I think I came straight around here. I was furious. I think Liam Brazil was gone by then. But we were all in too much of a state to take any notice of what he said.'

'What about when you went over to his shop? You didn't hear him mention anything about it?'

Metcalfe gave a sheepish grin. 'Actually, we rarely go over to Brazil's shop these days. We get our groceries in town on the way home from work. We pass right by the shops so tis easier for us. It saves a lot of time.'

Dinane pushed his chair back and stood up. 'Well, thank you all for your time. And for the lovely cup of tea, Mrs Cunningham. It'll keep us going for a while.'

Foley stood up too and put on his cap. 'If you remember anything that might help us please get in touch. We appreciate all the help we can get.'

'We will, sure.' Cunningham and Metcalfe both jumped up and Cunningham opened the kitchen door. 'So if no one saw them since the New Year, does that mean they were dead all this time? Three months? I find it hard to believe no one called there in three months. What about the postman?'

Dinane turned and gave him a broad smile. 'Thank you, Mr Cunningham. We appreciate your help. Take care.'

Chapter Nine

Acting Sergeant John Guerin and Guard Casey were coming out the gate of the O'Gara's house as Dinane and Foley approached.

'How's it going, lads?' Dinane had his pipe in his mouth and he gripped it in his teeth.

'I think that's everyone,' Guerin checked his notebook. 'It's everyone along this road anyway. All we got was rumours and hearsay. No one admits to seeing the Appleyards in the last few months. They were more worried about the snow. They were concerned about how they'd survive if it went on for much longer.'

'I can understand that.' Foley looked back along the road. 'We were all starting to panic a little bit, wondering where the food was going to come from.'

'Well the latest forecast is looking much better, thank God.' Casey looked up at the clear sky and blinked when the sun caught his eyes.

'You could still freeze to death, you know.' Guerin stepped around a river of slush flowing along the gutter. 'So what's the plan now? Back to the ranch for a decent cup of coffee?'

Dinane glanced up and down the road. 'Are you sure we didn't miss anyone?'

Guerin pulled his collar up against the bitter breeze and pointed back at the house he'd just come out of. 'Well, the fella who lives here, Tom O'Gara, is out tending his sheep and won't be home till after six. We spoke to his wife. She's a lovely woman, but she does not have a nice word to say about the Appleyards.'

'Why's that?'

'Well, both she and her husband worked for the Appleyards for years, but they were sacked when the daughter Bella came home to look after her father. That was about twelve years ago but feelings are still a bit raw. Anyway, on New Year's Day the Appleyards sent them a letter saying their rent was going up. So there's no love lost between them. But Mrs O'Gara insists they haven't been anywhere near the house for years.'

'The Appleyards did the same to the other tenants too,' Foley told him. 'It's no wonder no one likes them.'

'That's for sure.' Dinane looked at his pipe as if he was deciding whether to light it or not. 'You can see why Percy Metcalfe lost his temper and charged over there. God knows what he'd have done if that car hadn't been there.'

'What car?' Guerin and Casey gathered around and pushed Foley out of the way.

'Well, you know Liam Brazil is saying Bella Appleyards told him they were going away for a few weeks, yeah?' Dinane moved into the middle of the road and started walking back towards town, stepping around the deeper pools of slush. He still gave off an air of not being concerned about his wet shoes. 'So Percy Metcalfe went over there on New Year's Day to confront Bella about the rent increase. But when he saw a car in the backyard he changed his mind and went back home. He said he heard raised voices but he couldn't see who was actually in the house.'

'So what does that mean?' Guerin asked. 'Liam Brazil is right? The Appleyards did go away for a few weeks with whoever was in that car? So whose car was it? Could it be a taxi? We should check that out, Guard Casey.'

Casey nodded and wrote it in his notebook.

'Or did whoever was in the car discover the bodies?' Foley suggested. 'Didn't your man say he heard raised voices?' When Dinane stared at him he shrugged. 'So they panicked and got out of there in case they were blamed for it.'

There was a pause as they strolled along the road and crossed the railway lines. 'What about the gatekeeper? Has anyone spoken to him?' Dinane pointed at the small railway house beside the tracks.

'I spoke to the son,' Guerin said. 'He didn't see anything of use to us. Lovely man, though. Very polite and respectful. His dad is away for a few days so maybe we'll talk to him another day.'

Guerin took his cap off and wiped his forehead. 'Suppose the Appleyards did go away for a few weeks in that car, isn't it possible they came back later and no one noticed them. Especially as the weather was so bad? And suppose the holiday had been a disaster and Bella had enough of her father's abuse and decided to put an end to it? Then the guilt became too much and she decided to end it for herself too?'

There was a ripple of agreement and they walked on in silence for a minute. 'I still find it strange that no one went to that house in all that time,' Foley dug his hands deeper into his pockets. 'I mean, is that likely? Or is it just that the people we spoke to didn't go there? But that doesn't mean no one at all called there. The house is isolated so would the neighbours even notice if someone went there?'

'Well, according to Mrs O'Gara, someone did.' Casey glanced at Guerin and hesitated. When Guerin nodded he continued. 'When we asked if they'd called to the house recently, she said she remembered her husband complaining about someone driving out of the Appleyards gate too fast and almost hitting him and the dog. He said the driver nearly lost control and skidded across the road before driving off towards the racecourse.'

'When was this?'

'Well, she wasn't sure exactly. All she knew was it was snowing at the time.'

'Did he recognise the car?'

'She thinks he said it was a van. She couldn't swear to it, but she got the impression it was Brazil's delivery van.'

Everyone looked at Dinane and he put his pipe back in his mouth. 'Well, well, well,' he mumbled out of the corner of his mouth. 'That *is* interesting. So when did the snow start? February sometime? That's a bit different from the story Liam Brazil gave us. Why is that? Eamon, can you go and see Mr O'Gara, ask if he remembers the exact date he saw the van. Then call over and talk to Liam Brazil again.'

Foley stopped and went to speak but Dinane waved him on. 'Not now, of course. O'Gara won't be home till after six. It can wait till tomorrow.'

'Speaking of the O'Garas,' Guerin grinned at Foley. 'Mrs O'Gara asked me to give her apologies to the good looking guard who came over to search for her missing boy this morning. She felt really bad about being so rude to him – the good looking one – who was only doing his job and she asked me to say sorry for wasting his time and to wish him all the best.'

Foley beamed, but before he could answer Guerin pulled a face. 'So I told her I'd pass the message on to Guard Hurley as soon as I see him again.'

This time the others laughed out loud and Foley kicked a lump of snow at them.

Back in the Detective's office, Casey passed the cigarettes around while Foley put the mugs of coffee on Dinane's desk. Dinane studied his notes as he stuffed tobacco into his pipe and took a long time lighting it, and the others sat back and waited for him to speak.

'Right,' he blew a cloud of smoke from the corner of his mouth. 'So what have we got so far? Two bodies in a house. Toby Appleyard is dead in his bed, and his daughter Bella is dead in the kitchen. We don't know how the old man died but we're guessing it was poison. We don't know how Bella died either, but we're guessing she took her own life after killing her father.'

They all nodded and glanced at their notes as they sipped their coffee and dragged on their cigarettes.

'However, it's possible Bella was strangled by the rosary beads she had around her neck. Unfortunately, any evidence is now destroyed by the cats.' Dinane took a sip of his drink and sucked on his pipe again. 'What did you make of the tenants, Eamon? Metcalfe and Cunningham?'

'Very bitter, I'd say.' Foley sat up straight in his chair. 'And with good reason, though. If what they said is true, they were treated very badly by the Appleyards. Well, by Bella anyway. But are they capable of killing her? And how did they do it? Where did they get the poison to give to the old man?' Foley wiped his mouth with his sleeve. 'Although I can see how someone might lose control with the nun if she was as horrible as everyone says she was. They might have grabbed at her out of frustration and in the struggle pulled on the rosary beads. She'd be dead in seconds. Then they panicked and decided they had to shut the old man up as well.'

'That's the bit I'm struggling with.' Dinane stretched and rubbed his neck. 'If it was an explosion of anger, the moment the attacker realised what they'd done their instinct would be to get out of there as fast as they possibly could. I can't imagine they'd hang around to poison the old man.'

'And why poison him,' Guerin asked. 'Did they think the old man could identify them? But if they felt they had to kill him, there are lots of quicker ways to do it.'

'And what's this thing with the cats?' Foley gave a long shiver. 'What was that all about? It almost looks as if it was planned, a clever way to get rid of the evidence. But what kind of mind would even think like that?'

'What kind of mind indeed. But if someone had called to the house wouldn't they have noticed all the cats, though? There must have been millions of them.'

'Millions of them?' Guerin chortled. 'I've told you a thousand times, Guard Casey. Do not exaggerate.'

'Well, maybe twenty,' Foley joined in. 'But if the callers knew Bella, they'd know she kept lots of cats. So they probably wouldn't think there was a problem.'

'True,' Dinane agreed. 'So all we know is that Liam Brazil went there on New Year's Day and was told the

Appleyards were going away for a few weeks. But did he make that up? Did he murder the nun, for whatever reason, and said they were going away to stop anyone calling there too soon. Did he deliberately shut the cats in with her, or was that just a fluke? And again, why would he waste time on the old man?'

'Unless he planned it all along,' Casey suggested. 'He delivered the groceries so he'd know the layout of the house, especially the kitchen. He might have fantasised about killing the nun for ages, playing it out in his head as he worked out the details, then timed it precisely.'

'What about the old man, though? How would he be able to poison him without having to fight him?'

'He probably went up to see the old man whenever he called to the house. So the old man wouldn't be suspicious if he brought him a cup of tea.'

'There was a tray with breakfast stuff on it.'

'So he brought up the old man's breakfast. And the poor auld fella didn't suspect a thing.'

The phone rang and Dinane answered it, and the next five minutes were a jumble of yes sir, no sir, right away sir. When he put the phone down again he sat back and rubbed his eyes.

'That was the Super. He won't authorise any overtime for tomorrow because he doesn't think we'll achieve anything by knocking on doors on a Sunday. He suggests we wait for the doctor's report, which should be ready by Monday, with a bit of luck.'

Guerin stood up and buttoned up his coat. 'So if it looks like a murder and suicide, then it'll be case closed, yeah?'

'Definitely,' Dinane waved them all out of his office. 'Now get lost. Have a good weekend and I'll see you when I see you.'

Chapter Ten

Eamon Foley was sitting in the pew at the back of the Dominican Church during the Sunday morning 12 o'clock Mass, and he was bored stiff by the dull monotonous drone of the elderly priest. He was giving a sermon in a voice that was much too soft for the ambient noise coming off the huge crowd of worshippers. They filled every seat, overflowed into the alcove, and latecomers crowded into the foyer. Some even stood outside on the steps by the entrance, straining to hear what was going on. And they were shuffling, coughing, blowing their noses and generally making random noises.

But Foley couldn't concentrate anyway. What he'd seen at the Appleyard's house yesterday was stuck in his head, going around and around like a film stuck in a loop. He couldn't cut away from what the cats had done to Bella. And the awful smell that lingered on his clothes and hair for the rest of the day. He wasn't even sure if the long soak in the bath last night had washed it all away because he could still catch a faint hint of it every now and again.

But apart from the fact two people were dead, there was something peculiar about what Foley saw in that kitchen, and it was niggling at the back of his mind. Something obvious, but elusive. And it was irritating him because trying to focus on it was like trying to grab a handful of fog. He glanced up at the Stations of the Cross dotted along the church wall as if they were going to give him the answer. But they didn't, and he looked down at his hands again.

He sat up again when the noise in the church suddenly increased and everyone crossed themselves and stood up. He'd lost track of time, and suddenly the Mass was over. He stepped out into the throng of moving bodies and let himself be pulled towards the front door. There was the usual buzz of excitement after this particular Mass every Sunday morning, because the pubs opened at 12.30. Now the men could engage with a completely different kind of spirit.

As he shuffled through the foyer, Foley became aware of someone standing by the big front door watching him closely. In the glare from the daylight behind him, Foley couldn't make out the man's features until he got closer, then he let out a groan. 'Detective Sheffield. What are you still doing here?'

'Please, call me Paul.' The detective had a weary look about him as if he hadn't slept for a while. When he held out his hand Foley got a whiff of stale alcohol on his breath.

'I thought you were finished here,' Foley gave the hand a reluctant shake.

'So did I.' Sheffield pulled a glum face. Then he nodded towards the town. 'Look, can I buy you a pint?'

'I don't ...' Foley checked his watch.

'Just the one,' Sheffield added. 'I'm staying at Sullivan's pub. That's on your way, isn't it?'

Foley buttoned up his coat. 'Just the one,' he agreed.

Sullivan's bar was already crowded by the time they got there and they had to squeeze into a gap at the far end of the counter. Sheffield called for two pints and two whiskey chasers.

'No!' Foley put his hand up to the bartender. 'No whiskey for me.'

But Sheffield repeated the order and the bartender nodded. While the pints were settling on the counter the whiskeys arrived, and Sheffield swallowed one straight down.

'Hair of the dog,' he mumbled as he picked up the second one and sipped it.

'Right,' Foley chuckled. 'I presume you had a good time last night. Were you celebrating something?'

'Drowning my sorrows, more like.' Sheffield studied the glass. 'Anyway, I just wanted a quick word with you about the incident with the late Inspector Liam Edge. There's a few things I'm trying to clear up and ...'

'For feck sake.' Foley picked up the empty glass and banged it down on the counter again. 'That was years ago. Why the hell are you dragging it all up again now, for God's sake?'

'I know, sure.' Sheffield waved his glass at him. 'But there's been a bit of a development and I've been sent back to have another look at it.'

Foley sighed, and when the pints arrived he picked his up and took a long swig. 'I don't understand. What do you hope to find now that you didn't find back then? You went through everything with a fine-tooth comb that time, and now you're raking it all up again?'

Sheffield put his whiskey down and studied his pint for a moment before sucking at it like a thirsty pilgrim. He swallowed almost half then wiped his mouth with the back of his hand. 'The thing is, Foley, the story should have ended right then. Alex and Seamus Cassidy were dead. And the two detectives who'd been following them for years also died. And your step-father too, of course, God rest his soul. In the real world that should have been the end of it. But instead it stirred up a whole new pile of questions.'

Another long swig of his pint and another wipe of his mouth. 'Now, I told you before, I have the knack of reading people, which makes me a bloody good detective. And when I read you back then, Guard Foley, I knew you weren't completely honest with us. I'd go as far as to say you were deliberately obstructive to our investigation. Why was that?'

'Why do you think?' Foley snorted. 'I was a serving garda officer, for God's sake. Yet I was treated like a common criminal.'

'No, you were not.' Sheffield swallowed the rest of his pint. 'Why are you saying that? No one treated you like a criminal?'

'*You* did. First, you raided my house, then …'

'We didn't raid your house. We searched it. And that was with your full permission.'

Foley groaned and turned to the man next to him who was puffing on a cigarette. 'Jackie, can you spare one of those?'

'Sure I can, Eamon,' Jackie Maher took a packet of Woodbines from his jacket pocket and passed it to Foley. 'And how're you this fine Sunday morning? We don't usually see you in here during the day.'

Foley took out a cigarette and handed the packet back. 'Tis business, I'm afraid, Jackie. They never leave you alone in this job.'

Jackie laughed as he looked Sheffield up and down, then he turned away without acknowledging him. Foley lit the cigarette from one in the ashtray.

'Look, you know the story, Foley,' Sheffield glanced around him and moved closer in a colluding huddle. 'The Cassidys had stolen something from a very important Government Minister. An envelope of some sort, yeah? So every law enforcement officer in the country was on the lookout for them. There was a huge reward out for them too but that was beside the point. So when we heard the Cassidys were in Tralee we came straight here expecting to recover the envelope. But to our horror, it was nowhere to be found. Imagine the frustration. People were fit to be tied.' He nodded gravely and sipped his pint. 'Then your nephew told us Alex Cassidy had been to *your* house looking for an envelope. She told your nephew she'd left it there when she was living there years ago. It was very important, she told him, and she swore him to secrecy.'

He stared at his pint for a moment before taking another gulp. 'Of course he told his mother, who told you. But you told us the woman who died in the shoot-out was not the Alex Cassidy you knew. And your sister said the same thing. So who was the woman you knew? An imposter of some sort?' He poked Foley on the shoulder. 'And there it was – the big million dollar question. Why did *our* Alex

Cassidy believe *your* Alex Cassidy left the envelope in *your* house? So you can understand why we had to search your house. For all the good it did us.'

'What's so feckin important about this stupid envelope anyway?' Foley muttered from behind a cloud of smoke. 'You've been busting your arse trying to find it. Anyone would think it was the secrets of Fatima. Or maybe evidence of some corrupt politician's sneaky deals. Is that what it is? Or is it some state secrets that could bring down the government?'

Sheffield frowned as he stared at Foley for a moment then he threw his head back and gave a laugh that had people jerking around to see what was happening.

'My God, Foley.' His whole body rippled as he beat his chest and swallowed a breath. 'You make me laugh.' He put his face in his hands as he tried to control his spluttering and he wiped his eyes with his sleeve. Then he picked up the whiskey glass and swallowed what was left.

'Another round here,' he roared at the bartender.

'No,' Foley protested. 'I'm only having the one. I told you. One's enough for me.'

Sheffield patted him on the arm. 'Tis my round. Don't be worrying about having to pay.'

'I'm not worried,' Foley insisted. 'Tis just that I don't usually drink during the day.'

But Sheffield was still chuckling. 'My God, but you're right, Foley. What you said just now is spot on.'

'What are you talking about?'

'That envelope. What you just said. Is it a state secret that could bring down the government? Or the secrets of Fatima?' That bit came out as another laugh. Then he swallowed the dregs of his pint and wiped his mouth again. 'But the sad fact is it's nothing like that at all. It's actually really pathetic. I don't know why I didn't see it before. How can I have been so stupid? Am I that naïve? All that cloak and dagger nonsense? My God, this is so pathetic. Such a load of hypocritical bullshit. I can't believe I'm part of it.'

Foley took a drag on his cigarette as he tried to keep up with the slurred ramblings of his colleague.

'But,' Sheffield clicked his fingers, 'I suppose he who pays the piper calls the tune. Isn't that how it goes? If you take the King's shilling you must do his bidding.'

When the next round of whiskeys arrived he grabbed one and swallowed it straight down again. Then he picked up the second one and raised it to Foley. 'Your good health.'

Then he drank it straight down too. And it was followed immediately by a grumbling burp.

As the pints were put in front of them Sheffield handed the bartender a ten-shilling note. 'Set them up again, young man. And have one for yourself.'

'No. I told you already. I'm not drinking anymore.' Foley stubbed his cigarette out in the ashtray. 'And judging by the cut of you, you shouldn't either.'

'Don't feckin tell me what to do?' Sheffield swung around so sharply he staggered against the counter. 'And tis Sergeant to you, *Guard* Foley.'

Foley felt his face start to burn and he stepped back. 'No it feckin isn't.' He pulled his coat tighter around him. 'I'm not on duty now. And neither are you. So I'm going home. And I suggest you don't ever come near me again unless tis on official business.'

Sheffield tried to stand in Foley's way but mistimed it and fell back against the counter again. 'Don't walk away from me, you feckin culchie prick,' he called, but Foley had already pushed through the door and was out in the street.

As Foley slowed down to button up his coat against the biting wind, the door behind him crashed open and Sheffield staggered across the pavement and into the road, almost slipping into the wall of snow piled up in the gutter. Then he swung around and focused on Foley.

'All right.' He put his hands up. 'I'm sorry. I was a complete pig's arse back there. I didn't mean any of it. Look, come back inside. I need to ask you a few things. There's a couple of things confusing me and they're driving me mad. So can you just come back inside and talk to me? I promise I'll behave myself. What do you say, Foley?'

'No. I don't think that's a good idea right now.' Foley started walking away. 'You've had too much to drink and you're not thinking straight. So why don't you go up to your room and sleep it off? Get them to bring you a pot of strong coffee, get into bed and just sleep it off.'

Sheffield scrubbed his face with his hands. 'Look, I just want to clear a few things up with you. That's not too much to ask, is it? One cop to another? Colleague to colleague?'

'Colleague to colleague?' Foley spluttered. 'More like the big city detective and the stupid country cop. Anyway, you've had too much to drink. Whatever we discussed now would be lost in a boozy haze and you wouldn't remember a word of it in the morning. So just go to bed and sleep it off.'

'I'm not that drunk.' Sheffield spread his arms as if he was going to fly and he walked along the middle of the road. 'See, I'm as sober as a judge. Honestly. So I had a few drinks. But that was just to … well, as I told you, I was drowning my sorrows. And I was on my own last night. Tis hard to know when to stop when you're on your own, when there's no one to bounce off. No one to tell you when to stop.'

Foley sighed. He didn't want to get caught up in this. He didn't know Sheffield well enough to get involved in his personal life.

'All right, I'm bitter and twisted right now.' Sheffield was still trying to walk in a straight line, ignoring the pools of slush that splashed up his legs. 'That's because I'm a good detective, Foley.' He patted his chest with both hands. 'I've been involved in some serious cases and I've proven my worth over and over again. I have put my life on the line several times to bring criminals to justice. I've faced some really bad people and didn't flinch from my duty. And that's a fact. I'm not boasting, but I'm a bloody good detective. And do you know how those lousy gobshites treated me? Do you?'

It came out as a wounded yelp. 'They passed me over for Inspector. Again! Three times. That's three times I've been passed over for promotion now. So you can understand why I'm pissed off with the whole lot of them'

He stepped off the road and onto the pavement where the snow had been cleared. 'I joined the guards when I was eighteen, you know. Tis all I ever wanted to be. Ever since I was a small boy I dreamed of being a guard. And I loved every minute of it. I made detective at twenty, and I was a sergeant by the time I was twenty-five. Then I was fast-tracked into the Special Branch. It was supposed to be an automatic step up to Inspector. But around the time I joined the squad, someone upset a Government Minister called D'Lacey. Have you heard of him? Rich, powerful, arrogant, obnoxious. A man with a dreadful temper. Not the kind of person you'd want to be on the wrong side of. Anyway, someone stole something precious from him and the shit hit the fan.'

Sheffield patted himself on the chest again. 'And my promotion was put on hold until this mess was sorted out. The culprits had gone to ground and we didn't have a clue where to even start looking for them. But D'Lacey was screaming for an answer and the pressure was fierce. Heads rolled. Senior Gardaí were demoted and involuntary resignations followed quickly. People were falling like dominos. Careers hit a brick wall.'

Sheffield looked up and spotted another pub and he dashed across the road to it. 'C'mon, Foley. We can't talk properly out in the street like this. Come in here and I'll stand you another round.'

'No.' Foley carried on walking up Rock Street. 'But if you want to talk, my house is just over there. Come in and have a cup of coffee. You can say what you have to say then you can feck off and leave me in peace. One cup of coffee and that's it. All right?'

Sheffield thought about it for a moment then gave a reluctant nod.

Chapter Eleven

Vicky almost dropped the saucepan she was holding when she saw the two men come into the kitchen.

'Vicky,' Foley was already taking off his coat, 'you remember Detective …'

'I know who you are.' Vicky had to rest the saucepan on the edge of the sink. 'You got a feckin cheek coming here. What do you want now?'

Sheffield rubbed his face again. 'Look, I'm sorry, Vicky. May I call you Vicky?'

Vicky carried the saucepan to the range and banged it down. 'Call me what you like. Just tell me what you're doing in my kitchen. I thought you'd finished your inquisition.'

Foley pulled out a chair and Sheffield dropped onto it, and he put his elbows on the table. His eyes were red and for a moment they seemed to be unfocused.

'I'll make him some coffee,' Foley took a mug from the dresser and got the coffee off the mantelpiece. 'Strong and sweet, then he'll be on his way.'

'So what does he want?'

'Six years,' Sheffield was muttering. 'Six whole feckin years. Oh, sorry. I didn't mean to swear in front of a lady. Please forgive me. I'm feeling a little bit sorry for myself at the moment so I'm being a bit of a pain in the arse.'

'As I said, what do you want?'

Sheffield rubbed his eyes again as he thought about his answer. 'Well, what I really want is that famous elusive envelope, the one the late Alex Cassidy was so determined to find.'

'But that envelope is not here.' Foley poured the boiling water into the mug, added coffee and stirred it with a spoon. 'You established that the last time you were here. You and your heavy mob looked under every stone in the place and you decided there is no envelope here. So whatever you're hoping to find now, it won't be that stupid envelope. You're wasting your time. You're wasting everyone's time.'

Sheffield took the coffer and spooned three sugars into it before adding milk. 'It's here somewhere.'

Foley let out an agitated snort. 'No, it bloody isn't. So just drink your coffee and feck off.'

Vicky was stirring something in a small pot. 'All this grief over some ridiculous envelope. For God's sake. You're all obsessed with the bloody thing but none of you knows what's in it. Every time we asked you what's in it, you looked blank as if you hadn't got a clue yourself. So if no one knows what's in the stupid thing, why are you so frantic about finding it? Why can't you just accept tis lost and get on with whatever it is you're supposed to be doing?'

Sheffield sat back in the chair and unbuttoned his overcoat. 'You are right, Vicky. And I wish it was that simple. But we're guards and we have to follow orders. And we were sent to find something even the bosses weren't privy to. The orders cascaded down the line and we all rushed off to obey them. Dutifully. Slavishly. Blind obedience, that's what it is. Ours is not to reason why and all that shit.'

He cupped the coffee mug in both hands. 'The thing is, our initial brief was simple. A couple called Seamus and Alex Cassidy stole something from a Government Minister called D'Lacey. But they fell out with Seamus Cassidy's brother Tommy and killed him. So we were supposed to be looking for a couple of dangerous killers, but behind the scenes there was fierce pressure to find whatever they'd stolen from D'Lacey. And when a huge reward was put up for the capture of the Cassidys and the return of the stolen item, the rumours went wild. But the reward was on the strict understanding that the stolen item remained confidential. If even a whisper of what it was became public knowledge the reward would not be paid.'

Sheffield's voice was getting more slurred and he cleared his throat to steady it. 'But all I was concerned about was my promotion. It was all that mattered to me at the time. But it depended on us finding that stolen item. I'm just a foot soldier, after all, so I was prepared to do what was necessary to find it. I'd have liked the rewards too, of course. But I wanted my promotion more.'

'Well, at least you're honest about it.' Vicky stopped stirring the pot and wiped her hands in her apron. 'And that's why you're back again? Looking for your promotion?'

Sheffield took a sip of the coffee and pulled a face. Then he spooned more sugar into it. 'To be honest, it was. Right up to the moment your brother opened my eyes to how pathetic the whole thing is.'

Foley and Vicky stared at him and he gave a splutter of a laugh. 'I mean it. Honest to God, right up to that very moment I didn't even think about the hypocrisy of it all. The sheer arse-licking and the arse crawling that was going on, all the way up to the very top of the Gardaí.'

Now his smile disappeared. 'When I think about all the decent hard-working detectives who were thrown on the scrap heap because no one had the guts to stand up to some lousy rich fella. He's got the whole country dancing to his tune like puppets on a piece of string. Tis not right. Tis not feckin' right.'

He put his mug down and his head drooped. Foley pulled out a chair and sat down beside him. 'So what are you planning to do now, Detective?'

Sheffield's head snapped up. 'Well, right now I just want to tell them to take their job, stick it in their ear and blow it out their arse.'

He laughed at that and took another swig of coffee. 'For six long frustrating years I have been dancing to that eejit's jig and I'm feckin tired of it now. I should just walk away this very minute. But I have to ask myself, what am I going to do if I quit my job? Being a guard is all I know. Tis in my blood. I spent my whole working life doing what I love, so what right have those lousy pricks got to force me out because some high flying politician lost the deeds to his feckin house?'

Vicky gave an audible gasp. 'He lost what?'

Sheffield looked up quickly, his eyes darting between them in a confused blur. 'Oh, my good God.' He put his coffee down with a thump. 'I didn't mean to say that. Oh my God. You have to forget I ever said that. That is confidential. You must forget I ever said that.'

Vicky's voice was as shrill as a train whistle. 'Are you telling me that bloody envelope contained the deeds to a house? You can *not* be serious. My good God and his Holy Mother. Are you telling me we had to go through all that torment because some dopey politician lost the deeds to his house? Are you telling me my step-father, a hero Garda Inspector, died because some feckin important piece of shite lost the deeds to his house? How in God's Name did that happen? How is it even possible?'

'No, no, no.' Sheffield put his hands up. 'Inspector Edge didn't die because of the envelope. He died trying to arrest two murderers. He died doing what any guard would do, trying to apprehend a couple of killers. It had nothing to do with that envelope. Well, not directly, anyway.'

'But it must be linked,' Foley insisted. 'Why else would you have come down mob-handed from Dublin the minute the Cassidy's were dead? You were like a mob of mad monkeys swarming all over the place. And all because of the deeds to a house?'

'Well, tis not just any old house. Tis an enormous estate in Dublin. The grounds touch on three counties, tis that big. It's been in D'Lacey's family for centuries, ever since some English king gave it to D'Lacey's ancestors for services to the Crown. So you can understand why he wants the deeds back.'

'And all this time you knew what was in that envelope and you didn't let on? You acted as if it was …'

'No. I didn't know what was in that envelope. I promise you. I only found out a few days ago.'

'So what did you think was in it all along?'

'I don't know. There was so much secrecy surrounding it we all assumed it was something valuable, like a piece of jewellery. You know, a million-pound diamond or something like that? There was such a big reward put up for its recovery we just assumed it was something precious. Then someone suggested it might be something incriminating. You know? Something D'Lacey was trying to cover up to prevent a scandal.'

He gave another burp and rubbed his stomach. 'But there were loads of different theories. And as time went by we thought it would all die down. But it didn't. I'd get involved in some big case and I'd spend long weary hours on it. Then just as I'm about to close the case I'd be called away because some chancer swore he'd seen the Cassidys and was demanding the reward. So I'd be sent to some God-forsaken hole where I'd waste precious days only to find out it was a pile of crap. And of course I'd get back to find the case I'd been working so hard on was already closed and my colleagues were wallowing in the glory. And all I got was a bollockin for not bringing D'Lacey's missing item back with me.'

Foley decided to get himself a strong mug of coffee too and when he brought it back to the table Sheffield had his head on his arms and appeared to be sleeping. Vicky stuck a knife into the potatoes boiling in the saucepan. 'What'll we do with him now, Eamon? Stefan will be back from Mass any minute.'

But before she could decide, Sheffield sat up straight and picked up his coffee. 'When we heard the Cassidys had been killed down here in Tralee we naturally thought it was all over. But to our horror, there was no sign of the mysterious stolen item on their persons. And in all honesty, we still didn't know what we were looking for at the time. Then your nephew informed us Alex Cassidy had been to your house looking for an envelope. Which we didn't find, as you pointed out. And we were back to square one.'

He took a long swig of coffee. 'Anyway, last month my review for Inspector was coming up again, so I thought I'd better show some initiative. As every good detective knows, when a case goes cold you go right back to the beginning. And that's what I tried to do. But I quickly discovered I was not allowed to interview any of D'Lacey's family or friends. Only the top Garda brass was allowed to approach the big man, and that was only on bended knee.'

He burped and wiped his mouth with his sleeve. 'Anyway, while I was sitting out in the corridor waiting to be called for my Inspector's review, I could overhear the Super and another Garda officer having a heated discussion about that very situation. They didn't realise I could hear every word even though the door was shut. The Super wanted to interview the staff of a casino where D'Lacey's son Rupert had gambled away a pile of money on the night of the alleged theft, and he was furious because he was warned off by D'Lacey's legal team.'

Sheffield tapped the side of his nose. 'And that made my blood boil. What were they so afraid of? I needed to know why we were treated like mushrooms, kept in the dark and fed a load of shit. And as I might have said once or twice before, I'm a bloody good detective. So I did a bit of digging and I found one young lady who worked in the Casino who was not as innocent as her bosses believed her to be. I discovered there was a married fella who knew exactly how *un*-innocent she was. So I mentioned this fella when I managed to have a quiet word with her. And to her credit she was more than happy to discuss the events of the night in question.'

He tapped his nose again and gave a self-satisfied grin. 'And would you believe it, everyone in the Casino knew exactly what had happened that night? Even the auld fella who cleans the feckin toilets. They all knew about it. But as

I said, we – the feckin Gardaí, the guardians of the people – were treated like simpletons.'

Vicky almost ran at him with her fist held out like a weapon. 'So tell us. What did you find out?'

Sheffield flinched and backed away from her, and Vicky dropped her hand.

'Well,' Sheffield continued, 'it turned out Rupert lost the deeds to the family estate to Seamus Cassidy in a card game. No one stole anything from D'Lacey. The only crime was Rupert acting like an eejit in a card game.'

He laughed and sipped his coffee again. 'But the truth was poison to D'Lacey. His reputation was sacrosanct. The very thought of the plebs laughing at him behind his back was more than he could stomach. His son was an embarrassment, and that was common knowledge in the circles they moved in. But to us mere mortals it was something to be denied at all cost.'

Another snigger and another sip of coffee. 'Anyway, this week it was announced in the Times that D'Lacey's American wife was suing for divorce. And because they were married in New York it was going to be very quick. And very messy. Mrs D'Lacey was looking to get half of everything. And as you can imagine, it was as if someone stuck an electric probe in the pants of the Gardaí top brass. They were hopping up and down in panic, and the hysterical wail cascaded down to all serving personnel. Find that feckin stolen item. Now! And I was dragged out of bed on a Saturday morning and dispatched to Tralee and more or less told not to come back without it.'

He waited for a reaction, and both Foley and his sister looked furious and gave him a dark stare. He continued. 'Anyway, now that I knew exactly what I'm looking for, I thought I could have another go at it. Quietly and calmly go over all the paperwork, re-visit all the interviews. No fuss, just a careful, methodical look back over everything. What was Inspector Edge doing in Tralee that day? What were Detectives Lane and Grey doing here that day? How long had the Cassidys been in town? You know the kind of stuff, Guard Foley. You're an intelligent man. You've got your head screwed on the right way.'

He sucked a breath through his nose and wiped his eyes. 'Then yesterday, just as I arrived in Tralee, I got a phone call. I hadn't even unpacked my feckin suitcase yet. *I'm sorry to tell you, Sheffield, but you've been unsuccessful in your application for Inspector. Never mind. You can re-apply again in another year or two. Good luck.*' Anger flashed in his eyes. 'My God, you can imagine how disappointed I was. I was furious. I was fit to be caged. My first reaction was to jack it all in, go straight over to the Kerryman and tell them all about D'Lacey's lost deeds. Spill the beans and watch them make a huge mess all over D'Lacey's nice clean carpet.'

He reached out and absently picked a cigarette butt from the ashtray, looked at it then put it back. 'Of course, I knew in my heart they wouldn't touch the story with a mile-long barge pole. If the big boys in Dublin were too scared to say anything detrimental about the famous D'Lacey, you can bet your mother's last penny a small rural paper won't provoke him. So I decided to pour my soul out to a bottle of Ireland's best whiskey. And do you know what the whiskey told me? It said stop feeling sorry for yourself. Get off your fat arse and prove to those useless whores in Dublin what a fantastic detective you are. Find that stupid envelope and take it back to them with your head held high and wave it under their stupid noses. Then they'll have to reconsider their judgement of you. They'll have to promote you immediately. And who knows, the next step could be Superintendent.'

He clicked his fingers and pointed at Foley. 'But the whiskey also told me I can't do it on my own. Look around you, it said. Who do you know in Tralee you can trust? Who would be discreet enough to ask for help? And that is why I was waiting for you this morning outside the church.'

Foley stifled a laugh. 'I don't believe that for one moment. After the way you treated us the last time? You must need your head examined if you think you can trust me now.'

Sheffield swallowed the last of his coffee, and when he tried to stand up he slipped and crashed down again. 'All I ask, Foley, is that you think about it. You're a good policeman. You have a cop's instinct. I know we can crack this case between us. I feel it in my bones.'

This time he did manage to stand up and he pulled his coat tighter before buttoning it up. 'So I'll trot off back to my hotel room and let you good folk get on with your Sunday. Thank you for the coffee, Vicky. And I'm sorry for disturbing you. Good day to you both.'

Chapter Twelve

'What the hell is wrong with you today?' Acting Sergeant John Guerin swallowed the last of his tea and slammed his mug back on the table. 'You've got a face on you like a robber's dog.'

Foley flicked the ash off his cigarette into the ashtray and took another long drag on it as he stood up and pushed his chair back. Guerin stood up too and pulled on his overcoat.

'Well?' Guerin growled, determined not to let it go. The atmosphere in the Garda canteen was almost carnival. The weather forecast had told them the unprecedented period of relentless snow was over, and everyone was feeling as if they'd been released from some sort of straight jacket. No one relished the rain, of course. Until now. With a bit of luck it would wash away the snow in a few days, and the country could return to some sort of normality.

But the chatter from their excited colleagues, and the scrape of chairs being pushed and pulled on the wooden floor, made a quiet conversation almost impossible. And Foley took advantage of it to brush the question aside.

Guerin knocked on the table with his knuckles. 'C'mon, spit it out.'

'There's nothing wrong with me.' Foley took his coat from the back of his chair and started walking towards the door. 'I didn't get much sleep last night, that's all. You know how it is. A head full of rubbish tormenting the life out of me.'

'Oh, right.' Guerin nodded to a group at the table by the door and they nodded back. 'Is this about what happened to the Appleyards? That's understandable, I suppose. It was gruesome enough to give anyone nightmares.'

'Yeah. Something like that.' Foley pushed past him into the corridor, and he was still buttoning his greatcoat when they reached the front door. Guerin pulled it open and held it for a stocky man who grinned a thank you as he slid past into the reception area. And Foley spun around and pretended to be looking for something in his inside pocket. Guerin looked from Foley to the man and back at Foley again, but Foley pretended to be too distracted to notice. The stocky man was already climbing the stairs to the Inspector's office.

Out in the street Foley pulled his collar up against the sharp breeze that whipped straight down from the mountains. The weather forecast had promised no more snow today but the thick low clouds seemed to be about to contradict that assumption.

'So what was that all about?' Guerin asked as he straightened his cap, and his breath came out in a cloud.

'What?'

'Don't give me *what*.' he growled. 'It was bloody obvious. You were trying to duck that fella I opened the door for.'

Foley turned left and headed for Bridge Street without answering, and Guerin stepped over a pile of snow stacked up on the pavement to keep up with him. Lots of people were out shovelling the snow from the front of their shops. Now it was piled up in the gutter, and it turned the rest of the road into a narrow strip of snow that had been flattened into a dangerous sheet of ice by the workers traipsing back to their jobs after the big freeze.

A group of schoolboys on the opposite side of the street shouted something at the two guards before throwing a snowball at them. Guerin moved with the speed of a feral cat and snatched the snowball out of the air, and the boys roared with glee when it exploded in his hand and showered him in a spray of snow dust. Guerin laughed too and scooped up enough snow to throw back at them, but the boys had already run out of range. Guerin threw the snowball anyway then clapped his hands together to clean his gloves.

'He's Special Branch, isn't he?' Guerin moved into the middle of the road. 'I remember him now. He came down from Dublin back when Inspector Edge and the two detectives were killed. Yeah, I remember him. He was one of the investigating officers.' Then he snapped his fingers and his voice rose a couple of octaves. 'Is that why you were trying to avoid him? Because of why he was here before? In case he sees you and brings up all those bad memories again?'

Foley gave him a sideways glance and shifted deeper into his overcoat.

'Look, Eamon, I can understand what you're feeling.' Guerin gave a sympathetic shake of his head. 'That was a rough year for you and your family. Seeing him again can't have been easy for you.'

'Paul Sheffield.' Foley pushed the words out through clenched teeth. 'His name is Detective Paul Sheffield.'

'Detective Paul Sheffield,' Guerin repeated, and he grinned to himself. 'Yeah, he was all right, that fella. For a detective, that is.'

He caught the look in Foley's eyes and pulled a face. 'Well, he was all right when he spoke to me, that's all I can say.'

'When did he speak to you?'

Guerin shrugged. 'I don't know. When he was here about the shooting over in the Green. We were all interviewed at the time.'

They walked on in silence for a moment then Guerin said, 'I remember he was concerned about you at the time, you know. You were in the hospital because you nearly got yourself killed trying to rescue that young fella in the Blennerville windmill.'

Foley rubbed the faint scar on the side of his face. 'He was only concerned about me because he wanted answers. He wanted to know why Liam Edge was here in Tralee. But all I could tell him was what Liam had told me. He was here as a witness in a court case.'

A wedge of snow slid off a roof and hit the ground in front of them making them jump back from the spray it caused. Guerin laughed and wiped the front of his coat which looked as if he'd been showered by a hailstorm. Foley stepped around him and carried on walking. When Guerin caught up with him he clicked his tongue. 'So what's Detective Sheffield doing here now? There's nothing going on that would concern the Special Branch. Is there? So what's he doing back here?'

'He's opening up old wounds and upsetting everyone, that's what he's doing back here.' Foley spat the words out.

'What do you mean?'

'He's been sent back to take another look at the case.'

'What case?'

'The Liam Edge case?'

'Why?' Guerin looked shocked. 'I thought that was all settled years ago. Liam Edge and two detectives went to arrest some murder suspects. The suspects shot the detectives and Liam Edge shot the suspects. Unfortunately Liam Edge had a heart attack and died at the scene. An open and shut case, surely to God.'

'That's what we were led to believe,' Foley sighed.

'So why are they poking around it again? Have they discovered something they missed the first time?' Guerin stepped over an abandoned shovel and kicked a lump of snow out of the way. Then he paused when he realised something else. 'And he's been in contact with you already, hasn't he? That's why you're in such a foul mood. Because dragging it all up again has upset you. That's it, isn't it? I can tell.'

Foley nodded. 'I saw him at Mass yesterday.'

'Really?'

Foley didn't answer and Guerin grunted as he kept in step with him. 'So what did he have to say?'

When Foley still didn't answer Guerin cursed out loud. 'For feck sake, Eamon, I'm only asking because I want to help. You know that. But if you're going to be a prick and refuse my help, that's grand. But we have a lot of people to see today and I don't want you frightening the life out of them with your sour face. I mean it. You're no use to me if you're going around looking like Frankenstein's monster all day. So what's it to be?'

'It's complicated, John.' Foley tried not to look at the sergeant.

'I don't mind complicated,' Guerin told him. 'So go on. What's he looking for this time?'

'I can't say.'

'For God's sake, Eamon. Just tell me.' Guerin grabbed Foley's arm and spun him around. Foley pulled away and started to cross the street.

'All right. They're looking for an envelope,' he called over his shoulder.

'A what?'

'An envelope.' Foley moved back into the middle of the road. 'It seems all this shite started with the theft of an envelope.'

Guerin's mouth opened and closed several times before he repeated, 'An envelope?'

'Yeah. The story began when Seamus Cassidys was accused of stealing something from a very important Government minister called D'Lacey, and the shit hit the fan.'

Guerin's eyebrows almost hit his hairline. 'D'Lacey? You don't mean D'Lacey who's a big shot in the government? Oh my good God. That's not good. He's not someone to be messing with. When did this happen?'

'Around the time I came back home to Tralee. Early 1941,' Foley said. 'Anyway, Seamus Cassidy was also accused of killing his brother, and he and his wife Alex went on the run. They were never heard of again until they were spotted in Tralee a few years later. That's when Liam Edge and the detectives tried to arrest them. You know the rest.'

Guerin squinted as he tried to process the story. 'So whatever they stole from D'Lacey fitted into an envelope? I wonder what that was. And I take it they didn't find it on the Cassidys at the time. Otherwise they wouldn't be back now. So what happened to it, do you think?'

'I wish I knew,' Foley sighed. 'As you said, it wasn't with the Cassidys when they were killed. And that's where it got even stranger. Because not long after Liam Edge died, Special Branch turned up at our house and tore it apart looking for that same envelope. Of course they didn't find it there either.'

'Why did they think it was in your house?' Guerin's voice was high with surprise.

Foley took his time to gather the memory, then he said, 'Do you remember Alex Cassidy?'

'The woman who was killed? No. How would I?'

'No,' Foley tutted. 'Not *that* Alex Cassidy. I'm talking about Alex Cassidy who was in the Local Security Force with us back during the Emergency?'

Guerin shook his head and looked as if he was going to ask another question. But instead he said, 'No, I don't think so.'

'Yes, you do.' Foley flapped an impatient hand at him. 'She was the one who used to follow Liam Edge around like a love sick pup. She was like his shadow. It was obvious to everyone there was some sort of relationship going on between them at the time. Everyone was talking about it. It was the talk of the barracks.'

Guerin sucked at his teeth. 'No. Not off hand, I'm afraid. I was more interested in my own life back then. I was just after getting married, you know. There was a war on and we were worried about being invaded by the Germans. So I had my own stuff to be concerned about. I didn't pay much attention to the gossip in the guard's barracks.'

'Oh, you knew her all right,' Foley insisted. 'The night Joe McCarthy was shot in Delaney's pub, you were called out. I remember all of you making comments about why

Liam Edge was there when he was already off duty. You were implying it was because he was on patrol with the pretty young Alex Cassidy.'

Guerin looked up at the sky and a grin played on his lips. 'Oh yes, I remember now. Wasn't she a small woman? She barely came up to his elbow. That's right. I remember now. But I don't remember the name.'

A car turned into Bridge Street and the two guards had to scramble over the bank of snow to get out of the way. The driver grinned and waved at them. Guerin decided it was safer to go across the Square and Foley shuffled along beside him.

'So what about her, Eamon? Are you saying she had some connection to the woman who stole the envelope from D'Lacey?'

'I honestly don't know, John.'

'So why are you talking about her?'

'Because that's where the complication comes in.' Foley rubbed his nose with his glove. 'Look, I was working in a hotel in Dublin before the war and I got into a bit of trouble, and this young woman came to my rescue. She told me her name was Alex Cassidy. Well, I had no reason to question it. I had no reason to think she was lying about something as simple as a name. I mean, why would she?' He looked at Guerin to see his reaction but the sergeant was staring straight ahead with his mouth in a tight line.

'She said she was an orphan,' Foley continued. 'She had no family and nowhere to go, so I brought her back to Tralee with me and my boy Mickey. And Liam Edge took an instant shine to her. He let her have a room in his house in Rock Street, the house me and Vicky are living in now. And he got the both of us into the LSF, and Alex stuck closer to him than a tinker's vest. Which is how the rumours started.'

Guerin waved to a group of men working on a coal lorry and they all called out a greeting. 'So where are you going with this story, Eamon?'

'It's ...' Foley rubbed his eyes. 'The thing is, Alex was with us here in Tralee for less than a year. She disappeared around the time Joe McCarthy was shot in Delaney's pub. Liam Edge said she went home, but as far as I knew she didn't have a home to go to.'

They stepped out of the way of a man pushing a wheelbarrow with an assortment of shovels in it. Guerin stayed on the road and Foley stepped back onto the pavement.

'Right, so she went home. What about it?'

'Well, I believe to this day that she was dead. I can't explain why, and I had no evidence, but I just know she never went home.'

Guerin stopped in the middle of the road. 'What are you saying? Are you saying she was ... how is that related to the missing envelope?'

'It's related because a couple of days before Liam Edge and the detectives died, my sister caught Joe, her oldest boy, in my room.' There was a sudden sadness in Foley's voice. 'Vicky was mortified because she thought he was stealing from me. He denied it, of course. But then Vicky saw a woman sneaking out of the house. She was moving too fast and Vicky only got a quick look at the back of her. Anyway, Joe told his mother he'd been approached by a woman who said she was Alex Cassidy, and that Joe should remember her because she used to live in his house. She desperately needed his help, she told him, and she swore him to secrecy. She said she'd left an envelope behind when she moved out of her room all those years ago, and it was imperative she got it back. Her life depended on it.'

Guerin was even more interested now and nodded for him to continue.

'So Joe let the woman into the house when his mother went to the shops,' Foley said. 'She searched my room because that was where Alex Cassidy used to live, but of course she found nothing. So the woman went up to Vicky's room. But Vicky came home too early and disturbed them.

The thing is, Vicky insists the woman couldn't have been the Alex Cassidy we knew because she was too tall, and a lot chunkier.'

'So who was she?'

'Well, Special Branch identified her as the Alex Cassidy they had a warrant out for. So either there were two Alex Cassidys, or the woman who came back to Tralee with me was not who she said she was.'

'That is a strange one all right,' Guerin agreed. 'So is there a connection between the woman you knew and the woman who was killed?'

'I really don't know, John.' Foley stepped into what looked like a soft heap of snow and cursed when it turned out to be a pile of rubble. He flapped his hands to regain his balance and he walked out onto the road. 'And I don't expect we'll ever know now. Liam Edge came to Tralee the same week as the Cassidys, and the next thing we knew they were all dead.'

Guerin crossed himself and shuddered. 'That was an awful thing all right. Five people dead, and for what? I never knew about any envelope, though. Or if I did I forgot about it. I'd swear I didn't hear anyone else mention it either. We were all interviewed, you know. We were asked what we knew about Inspector Liam Edge, and if we knew why he was in Tralee. But what could we say? We knew nothing.'

'Vicky and her children were grilled too, and myself as well,' Foley told him. 'We were treated like criminals, the way they questioned us. Why was Liam Edge here in Tralee, they asked? Did we know the Cassidys, they asked? Did we know why they were in Tralee, they asked? What did Liam Edge say about them? Did he tell us he was going to try and arrest them?' He gave a sarcastic chuckle. 'Then young Joe told them about Alex Cassidy calling at our house looking for an envelope and they went crazy. A mob of them turned up and spent days going over every inch of our house. But there was no sign of any envelope.'

'And that's why your man is back again. But why does he think it'll be different this time?'

'I don't think it was his idea to come back,' Foley said. 'Apparently D'Lacey is getting divorced, and he needs what's in that envelope to settle his wife's demands.'

'What?' Guerin looked amazed. 'So what *is* in that envelope, for God's sake?'

Foley hesitated. There was so much secrecy around the envelope he wasn't sure if he'd be putting his best friend in danger by telling him. However, now Sheffield knew, it wouldn't be long before everyone connected with the case found out too.

'According to Detective Sheffield, it's the deeds to the D'Lacey estate.'

This time Guerin laughed out loud. 'Are you serious? How … Why in God's name would anyone steal the deeds to an estate? What did they hope to do with it? They couldn't just move in and claim ownership. I never heard anything so stupid in my whole life.'

'Actually, Detective Sheffield said the deeds were never stolen in the first place,' Foley told him. 'Seamus Cassidy won them in a game of cards. For some strange reason D'Lacey's son Rupert put them up instead of cash. Everyone expected Cassidy to fold, considering D'Lacey's reputation. But Cassidy wasn't intimidated by D'Lacey and he called his bluff, took the envelope and left. However, D'Lacey wasn't going to let a lowlife like Cassidy make a fool of him, so he reported the deeds as stolen. D'Lacey, the government minister, has huge influence with the Gardaí, and they were only too willing to do his bidding. Then Seamus Cassidy killed his brother, and now they had the perfect excuse to put up a generous reward for the arrest of the Cassidys and the return of the stolen deeds. But the Cassidys went to ground.'

Guerin gave his nose an angry rub. 'You're damn right, Eamon. It is complicated. So the reward was more for the return of the deeds than the capture of the Cassidys. God, it makes me sick of the way we're played by the rich and famous. They have no shame. If they were open about what happened from the start the Cassidys might have behaved differently and Liam Edge and the others might not be dead now.' He spat out the words, 'May God blast their rotten souls?'

'It's all become too much for Vicky,' Foley said. 'She was in a right state last night. It was well past midnight before Stefan got her to bed. Then I heard them talking long after that. It all seems like a bad act in a dreadful play.'

'So what happens now?' Guerin asked.

'I have no idea.' Foley dug his hands deeper into his pockets. 'It depends what Detective Sheffield comes up with.'

Chapter Thirteen

Tom O'Gara's face stretched in surprise when he opened his front door and saw two uniformed guards standing there, one of them with sergeant's stripes. He turned around as if he was going to call someone, changed his mind and put his hand on the doorpost. 'Lads, what can I be doing for you?'

'Mr O'Gara? I wonder if we could have a word.' Guerin gave him his best business smile.

'Is it about what happened to the Appleyards?' O'Gara's eyebrows knitted into a serious frown. 'Only the missus said you called on Saturday and she told you everything we know.'

'That's right, sure.' Guerin held the smile. 'But tis you we'd like to talk to.'

O'Gara only came up to Foley's shoulder but he had the build of a fit young wrestler. He was wearing a thick pullover and faded dungarees, and he was struggling to stand still. His whole body seemed braced for action, and he stepped from foot to foot as he thought about his answer. Then he stepped back and invited them into the house with a flick of his hand.

'Come in, come in.' He went ahead into the kitchen. 'There's tea in the pot. I expect you could do with a cup to warm you up. Jane love, a cup of tea for the guards.'

Jane O'Gara jumped up and went to the dresser, and when she caught Foley's eye she gave him a look that had a hint of embarrassment in it. She put two cups on the table then pointed to the chairs. 'Why don't you sit down? Help yourself to milk and sugar.'

Tom went to the range and picked up a pot. 'How about some porridge? We have loads here.'

'They don't want your porridge,' Jane laughed as she grimaced at Foley. 'He likes it so thick you could build a wall with it. It's always a case of one slice or two.'

Foley was surprised how different Jane looked now compared to how she appeared on Saturday. Her hair was as black and shiny as a raven's wing and her eyes were bright and playful. He found himself laughing too as he picked out a chair and sat on the inside of the table. Jane sat back down opposite him and she poured tea into the two cups. Guerin sat at the other end opposite Tom.

'I'm so sorry about Saturday,' Jane glanced at Foley again and gave him a contrite smile. 'You came all the way out here to help look for my boy and he was hiding in the scullery all the time. I feel so stupid after all the trouble I caused.'

'Not at all,' Foley insisted. 'Sure I'm delighted he was found safe and well. So how's he doing? I hope he wasn't too upset by all the fuss. It can be frightening to see all those grown-ups gathered around and looking down on you. It must have seemed like an attack of the giants.'

Jane chuckled at that, then she said, 'Sorry, I shouldn't be laughing at a time like this. You're here about the Appleyards, aren't you?' She crossed herself and touched her lips with her thumb. 'A desperate tragedy, so it is. Dreadful altogether.'

Guerin put his notebook on the table and turned to Tom. 'Your wife told us neither of you has been up to the Appleyard's house in years.'

'Not to the house, no. Definitely not.' Tom picked up a piece of toast and started buttering it. Foley and Guerin watched him in silence and he suddenly realised they were waiting for him to elaborate. 'My fields are around the edge of their land.' He drew a circle in the air with his finger. 'So I've been up that way every day. I can see the house from the top field but I haven't been over to it since …I don't know when. It must have been when Sinead … Toby's wife… died. That was …what? Twelve years ago?'

'And you haven't been to the house recently?'

Tom took a bite of the toast and washed it down with a slug of tea. 'God, no. I never had any reason to. From what

I heard I probably wouldn't have been welcome anyway. Not while the mad nun was looking after the place. She's a right …'

'Tom!' Jane reached out and grabbed the hand with the toast. Tom looked startled and gave a long sigh.

'Sorry. Of course. I shouldn't speak ill of the dead. God rest her soul, the poor woman. I can't pretend I liked her but no one deserves to die like that.' He looked up at Guerin. 'So how did she die, Sergeant? Only we're hearing some very strange stories.'

Guerin sipped his tea then said, 'We're still waiting for the doctor's report.'

'Since Saturday? I thought you could tell how someone died in a few hours, science being what it is these days.'

Guerin sat back in his chair. 'This case is a bit different, I'm afraid. Because of the freezing weather we can't even be sure *when* they died. Which is why we're trying to find out when they were last seen alive.'

Tom nodded and took another bite of his toast. Guerin tapped his notebook with his pencil. 'I understand you saw Liam Brazil's van coming out of the Appleyard's gate on the day the snow started.'

Tom looked surprised at the question and he turned to his wife. 'You told them about that, did you?'

Jane put her cup down. 'I did. I thought it might be important.'

Tom looked back at Guerin. 'Is it?'

'It could be,' Guerin informed him. 'Right now every bit of information is important. It might not seem like it at the time, but all of the pieces tell a story. The question is, where do all the pieces fit in the big puzzle.'

'Oh, right.' Tom nodded as if he understood but by the way he was munching his toast Foley wasn't convinced he did.

'So what exactly do you remember, Mr O'Gara?'

'Well, I remember the date alright.' A flake of toast flew out with the words and Tom brushed it off the table.

'January 22nd. My birthday. I had planned to finish early because Jane wanted to cook me a special lunch.' He smiled at his wife and she beamed back. 'But it started to snow and I got bogged down trying to sort out the sheep. Anyway, by early afternoon the snow was so bad I couldn't do anymore, and I was heading home along the main road. It was the safest way to go, or so I thought. But when I reached the Appleyard's place this van came flying out of the gate and missed me and the auld dog by the width of a cigarette paper. It shot across the road and nearly fell into the ditch on the other side. Luckily it managed to straighten up and it roared off up the road.'

'Did you see who was driving it?'

'No. I got such an almighty fright I danced back out of the way. By the time I gathered myself it had disappeared into the snow.'

'But you recognised the van?'

Tom munched on his toast again and shook his head. 'At the time I would have sworn it was Liam Brazil's van. You know, because it's in and out there all the time. But in the present situation, I'm not so sure.'

'Why?'

'Well,' he glanced at his wife and she nodded for him to go on. 'Because of what happened to the Appleyards. I don't want to point a finger at anyone, especially if he's innocent. I'd feel terrible if I said something that got an innocent person arrested.'

'That's very commendable, Mr O'Gara.' Guerin looked up from his notebook. 'But as I said, every bit of information is important. Two people are dead and you seeing that van might be a critical piece of the puzzle. It might give us an indication of when the Appleyards were last seen alive.'

'I understand that. Of course, I do.' O'Gara ran his fingers through his hair. 'But I still don't want to make any definite identification.'

Jane picked up the plate of toast and held it out to Foley. 'Would you like a piece? Go on, there's loads here.'

Foley waved it away and so did Guerin. 'So, just to be clear, you were coming home along the road when a van came out of the Appleyard's place.'

'That's correct. It missed me by inches. I'd say my Guardian Angel was looking out for me that day.'

'Thank God.' Jane crossed herself again.

'So why were you coming home that way, did you say?' Foley asked. 'Where is your farm again?'

'Actually, we have four smallholdings.' Tom glanced at his wife for confirmation and she nodded. 'They're scattered around the perimeter of the Appleyard's farm.'

'Yeah, that's right,' Guerin said to Foley. 'Mrs O'Gara's father bought them off the Appleyards.'

'No, no. He didn't buy them,' Jane corrected. 'Toby Appleyard gave them to my father.'

'He did.' Tom nodded and waved a piece of toast at Foley.

Jane gave a smile that showed a deep pride in her father. 'The thing is, my Da and Toby Appleyard had a wonderful working relationship. My Da had a sort of affinity, I suppose you'd call it, for the land. He could read the land like you'd read a book. He had a gift of knowing what crops to plant in which fields, which meadows were the best for cattle grazing. Toby respected his advice and they would often spend the whole day walking the fields together. Toby wanted my Da to be the farm manager, and he asked him many, many times. But my Da wasn't that kind of person. He was a decent, honest hard-working man, and he wasn't comfortable telling others what to do. So he always turned the job down.'

She looked at her hands and then rubbed them together. 'My Da hated seeing land going to waste. He always said every bit of land had a use. So it annoyed him that there were several pockets of land the Appleyards had written off as useless. My Da thought they were ideal for sheep and goats. But Toby had a thing about sheep. He said the way sheep looked at you was creepy, and the way they followed each other with no regard for their own safety irritated the life out of him.'

Both of them chuckled at that. 'He would not allow a single sheep on his farm. It was like the Wild West with the cattlemen and the sheep farmers. They hated each other. Anyway, it became a bit of a running joke between my Da and Toby Appleyard.'

Tom looked up at the ceiling and smiled. 'They were great together all right. Toby always looked happy when Jimmy... Jane's Da ...was around. They always had a great banter going on, and it cheered up everyone who was in earshot.' He looked at Jane and pulled a face. 'I don't think he got on too well with Toby's wife though. He never said anything bad about Sinead, mind you. All he'd say was Toby loved her and that was all that mattered.'

'So did you work for the Appleyards too, Mr O'Gara?' Guerin asked.

'Straight from school,' Tom beamed. 'My first job. I was the gopher.'

'The what?' Foley sucked back a laugh.

'The gopher. You know, go for this, go for that. I was at the bottom of the pecking order so no job was too lowly. If something went wrong and they needed someone to kick, they kicked the gopher.'

Foley laughed out loud at that. 'It sounds like a great job, all right.'

Tom sighed. 'It didn't last long, though. Sinead died and everything collapsed like the walls of a sandcastle. They were very dark days indeed. I was the first to go. No notice. I turned up for work and the nun said *what do you want, you don't work here anymore.*'

Jane sniffed. 'So my Da took him on to help out with the land Toby had given him.'

She saw the bemused look on the faces of the two guards, and she took a sip of tea before explaining. 'Toby called my Da into the office one day and my Da thought it was to discuss the manager's job again. But instead, Toby put four sheets of paper on the desk in front of him. There was another man in the office who turned out to be the Appleyard's solicitor, and he explained to my Da that Toby was handing over four of the pockets of land to him. There was a separate contract for each piece. And there was a string of conditions attached to them. If my Da intended to use the land for sheep, the land had to be properly fenced off so they didn't stray onto Appleyard land. No sheep were allowed to set foot on Appleyard land, so if my Da wanted to move them it had to be done on the back of a truck. Or a donkey and cart. Toby had a dread that the sheep would leave droppings that would poison his cows, or destroy his crop.'

'How did your father feel about that?'

'He was delighted. He knew he could make a good go of it.'

'But there was a twist.' Tom tapped the table with his finger. 'Toby was using it as a bribe to get Jimmy accept the farm manager job. If he did accept the job he could use the Appleyard farm hands to help him every Monday and Wednesday afternoons. If he did not, he was on his own. If he hired anyone he would have to pay them himself.'

There was a pause and everyone sipped their tea and reflected on what they would have done in those circumstances. Eventually Foley asked, 'So what did he do?'

'He brooded over it for a couple of days. He asked Jane about it but she was just a teenager at the time and she had great faith in her father.' Tom glanced at Jane who was staring into the middle distance as she picked at the memories. 'She told him she would support him in whatever he decided.'

'What about your mother, Mrs O'Gara?'

A sad shadow crossed her face. 'She died years ago when I was six. She had a seizure while walking into town and by the time they got her to the hospital it was too late.'

'God, I'm so sorry for your loss,' Guerin said, and Foley mumbled in agreement.

Jane smiled as she accepted the condolences. 'So I was looking after the house and my Da. But I helped out with his new project whenever I could. And it was fierce hard work. My Da put every spare minute God gave him into making it a success, sometimes not getting home until well after dark.'

Tom raised his cup of tea in salute. 'God bless the man. He was a miracle worker. In less than a year he had all four places up and running, and Toby Appleyard was as pleased about it as Jimmy and Jane were.'

'The only time my Da got worried was when he was trying to build up his flock of sheep,' Jane added. 'He was the Appleyard's manager now so he was expected to be at work early every day to make sure things were running smoothly at the farm. By the time he got to the monthly fair in town, all the best sheep would have already been sold. But he would rather wait another month for the next fair than bring back animals that weren't up to his standard.'

Tom took up the story. 'The thing is, Jimmy was such a lovely man everyone wanted him to succeed, so a lot of the men worked with him for nothing on their days off. Maybe just a few hours here and there, but each one made a difference. And a couple of them who knew about sheep went to the fair and brought back the kind of sheep Mossy wanted. Yes, it was hard work but in the end Jimmy was pleased with how it turned out.'

There was another pause and the only sound in the kitchen was a log in the range crackling. Tom glanced at it. Then he said, 'It sounds like you already know the gory details about what happened to the workers when Toby Appleyard's wife died?'

'We do indeed,' Foley said, and the two guards nodded. 'A terrible business.'

'It certainly was.' Jane closed her eyes for a moment then took a deep breath. 'It was the finish of my father, that's for sure.'

Tom reached out and took her hand. 'Toby's daughters Lily and Bella came home for the funeral. Lily was the one making decisions, and to give her her due, she let us do our job. For a while, anyway. Eventually Lily went home and left the nun in charge. But the nun didn't have the foggiest idea about running a farm and in a very short time she'd fallen out with everyone. Within weeks most of the staff had left or were fired. Needless to say the farm went to pot. It was suddenly running at a loss and haemorrhaging money, so Lily had no choice but to call in an agent to sell off the livestock and the machinery. We think she realised Toby wasn't going to get any better and she was trying to put him into a home. But he was having none of it. So she sold everything of value to make sure there was enough money to keep a roof over his head.'

'Including my Da's sheep.' Jane spat out the words. 'The stupid cow let the agent do whatever he wanted.'

'Oh, really,' Guerin looked at Tom and then back at Jane. 'Surely she had no right to do that.'

'She didn't. The first my Da knew of it was when he saw two men driving the sheep across a field towards a lorry. There was a dreadful row. The men had bought the sheep in good faith and they weren't going to give them up without a fight. But my Da stood his ground and eventually the guards were called. My Da had the papers to prove he owned the sheep, and the men were told to put them back until it could be sorted out properly.'

'Toby's solicitor was nowhere to be found,' Tom continued the story. 'His office said he got a new job with a law firm in Tipperary and he took all his files with him, so they couldn't comment on the contracts. But they would get in touch with him and sort it out. It took two weeks, during which time Jimmy was distressed with the worry of having to feed the sheep and generally look after them. Anyway, the solicitor took it to the magistrate who decided the farmers bought the sheep lawfully, and the Appleyards had to pay Jimmy the money the farmers had given them for the sheep. Jimmy was raging because the agent had sold them for a fraction of what Jimmy had paid for them in the first place, and now he had to start all over again.'

'I can understand why he'd be raging,' Foley gave Jane a sincere smile.

Jane's mouth tightened and she rubbed her eyes. 'The nun was raging too. She said my Da had cheated Toby out of the land, and he was stealing from them too by using the farmhands and equipment without permission. Then she dropped the bombshell. Because most of the farmhands had been dismissed by that time, there was no need for a manager anymore. Needless to say my Da was heartbroken. But what hurt him most was that Toby refused to see him. Toby was like a wounded animal, lashing out at everyone around him, but my Da thought their friendship would count for something. It didn't.'

A tear sparkled in Jane's eye and slowly dropped onto her cheek. She wiped it away with her finger. 'Luckily my Da and the neighbours had a lease agreement that allowed them to rent the cottages for ninety-nine years. The nun was furious about that too, and she tried to force them out by putting the rent up by obscene amounts. But the solicitor pointed out a clause in the small print that limited the amount of yearly increase the Appleyards could enforce.'

Toby poured himself another cup of tea and offered to refill the other cups but Foley shook his head. Guerin held out his cup and nodded.

'A lot of the lads who were laid off, me included, went to help Jimmy and he was really grateful.' Tom filled Guerin's cup and put the pot back on the coaster. 'But he couldn't pay them, so when they found another job they had no choice but to take it.'

Jane beamed and took Tom's hand again. 'But you stayed.'

Tom blushed and glanced at the guards. 'It was love, you see? The moment I set eyes on this stroppy young mare I was mesmerised. I would have worked for Jimmy for nothing just to catch a glimpse of her in the kitchen every morning.'

'He was so shy he couldn't even speak to me.' Jane squeezes his hand. 'Just a grunt when I asked him if he wanted an egg with his toast.'

'That's cos you terrified me. One of your sideways looks would curdle the milk in the jug.'

'You cheeky monkey.' Jane pretended to throw a spoon at him. Tom laughed and sat back in his chair, and another pause had them all drinking their tea again.

'So what happened to Jimmy, your Da?' Guerin asked.

Jane studied the cup in her hand for a moment then put it down on the table. 'You've heard the expression, he worked himself into the ground? Well, he did. Even the day Tom and I got married he was up and out by five o'clock. He turned up in time to walk me down the aisle then he was off again halfway through the reception.'

Tom leant over and took Jane's hand again. 'It started out as just an ordinary cold, but Jimmy wouldn't take time off to rest. It took five long hard years to get the four patches back up to the standard Jimmy wanted. He was terrified that if he took his eyes off it for a day it would all fall to bits again.'

Jane wiped her eyes again. 'He did his best to hide how sick he was from us. And then it was way too late. Pneumonia, well advanced, they said at the hospital. He was worn out and he didn't have the fight left in him anymore.'

'I'm so sorry for your loss,' Foley bowed his head in respect.

Jane and Tom nodded in unison. 'Thank you.'

'So do you run it all by yourself now, Mr O'Gara?'

'I do, sure.' Tom pointed over his shoulder with his thumb. 'Jimmy laid the foundations and all I have to do now is keep it maintained. It's still fierce hard work, of course. I have an agreement with a couple of the adjoining farmers. They let me move the sheep across their land when I need to spread them between the sites. I'm actually in talks with them about buying a strip of land that would let me join three of the sites and also allow me to build a bungalow there too. It would mean we'd be in the middle of it all. And we wouldn't be beholden to the Appleyards anymore.'

Jane curled her lips as if she just tasted something unpleasant. But she didn't comment and Guerin pushed back his chair. 'Well, thank you for your time. And for the tea. It was very welcome.'

He stood up and Foley followed him. 'Hopefully we won't have to disturb you anymore. But if you remember anything at all about the Appleyards that might be relevant, please give us a call.'

'Definitely,' Tom jumped up and walked with them to the door. 'I'm sorry I couldn't be of any more help.'

'I hope you find out what happened to the Appleyards, Guard Foley,' Jane called after them. 'I didn't like them, but I wouldn't like to think they were the victims of something horrible. They should be allowed to rest in peace now.'

Chapter Fourteen

Mrs Brazil was standing on a box wiping down the shelves when the two guards walked into her shop, and her face clouded.

'What do you want *now*?' Her voice was shrill. She threw down the cloth and stepped off the box, and Foley was surprised by the darkness of her features.

'Good morning, Mrs Brazil. Is Liam in?'

'What do you want him for?' She practically ran at them with her hand raised, and her eyes were full of rage. Foley stepped back away from her in surprise but Guerin didn't move.

'Is he here, Mrs Brazil?' Guerin's sharp tone made her hesitate but her lips were still pulled back over her teeth in a vicious snarl.

'Why?'

'Because we'd like to have a word with him. If that's all right with you?'

'He's not here.'

'Mrs Brazil, where is Liam?' Foley took off his cap and kept his voice as calm as he could.

'I just told you, didn't I? He's not here. Are the two of you feckin deaf? Liam is not here, all right?'

'No, it is not all right.' Guerin pushed past her and went around the counter and through the door into the kitchen. Mrs Brazil screeched as she followed him and she tried to grab his arm.

'How dare you come into my home, you feckin maggot. You have no right to just walk into someone's home without permission. I'll have you fired for this. I'm going straight down to the barracks and making an official complaint about the brutal way you treated me.'

'Mrs Brazil,' Foley got between her and Guerin. 'Just tell us. Where is Liam?'

Mrs Brazil flapped her arms and almost turned around in a full circle. Then she sighed and said in a softer tone, 'He's in Killarney, all right?'

'Killarney?'

'Yes, Killarney.' The shrill was back in her voice again. 'That's what I said, you deaf feckin ... What do you want him for? Why are you raiding my house like those Gestapo thugs? You have no right to ... '

'Sit down, Mrs Brazil, for God's sake.' Foley took her arm and guided her to one of the armchairs by the range, and she was still spitting abuse as she sat in it.

'Look, we just want to ask him a few questions, all right?' Guerin leant on the back of the other armchair.

'What about? He doesn't know anything. He didn't do anything.'

'It's about the Appleyards.' Foley flicked through his notebook until he found a page he was looking for. 'He told us the last time he went to the house was on New Year's Day.'

Mrs Brazil spluttered. 'That's right. It was. It was on New Year's Day. What about it?'

'Are you sure about that?' Guerin stood up straight but still kept his hands on the back of the armchair. 'Are you sure he didn't go back there a few weeks later?'

Mrs Brazil's eyes were even pinker now as she glared at Guerin, and her nostrils flared. 'He did not! He never went near that place again. What are you saying?'

'We're saying we have a witness who saw Liam's van coming out of the Appleyard's gate several weeks after the time he told us he was last there.'

'No.' Her voice was a screech again. 'That's a lie. They're mistaken. I'm not listening to this bullshit. Who is this witness? They need their eyes tested if they saw anything like that.'

'It doesn't matter who the witness is, Mrs Brazil. We're here to get Liam's version. So when are you expecting him home?'

Mrs Brazil buried her face in her hands and bent forward with her elbows on her knees, and her body shook for a moment before she snapped back up straight again. 'I don't believe you.' Her voice had lost its fury now and the words came out subdued. 'When is this witness supposed to have seen him?'

'In late January, they said.' Foley tapped the page of his notebook. 'January 22nd to be precise. The day the snow started.'

A whimper escaped from Mrs Brazil's tight lips and she blinked several times. 'Then it couldn't have been him.'

Guerin wagged his finger at her. 'Why can't it have been him? It was his van.'

'Because he was in Killarney then too.'

'Mrs Brazil,' Foley could feel his patience starting to wane. 'How long does it take to drive to Killarney and back? He could have called in to see the Appleyards on his way home. He'd have to pass that way, wouldn't he?'

'No. It wasn't him, I'm telling you.' Mrs Brazil pushed it away.

'But if he was driving past on his way home ...'

'That's just it,' Mrs Brazil almost shouted again. 'He didn't come home.'

Guerin swore under his breath and shook his head. 'What does that mean? He didn't come home?'

'He didn't come home because he was locked up in the bloody looney bin.' Mrs Brazil pushed herself out of the armchair and her face was back under the furious scowl again. 'So go on. Mock me all you want. Laugh at me, why don't you? Mock me because my boy was locked up in the looney bin. My boy was carted off to the nuthouse and it's a huge joke. So go on, say what you're dying to say.'

Guerin did step back this time. 'Mrs Brazil, I'm so sorry to hear that.'

Mrs Brazil sneered and wiped her hands in her apron so hard she almost pulled it off. 'Yeah? Well...'

'I promise you we don't think it's anything to laugh about.' Foley closed his notebook and put it back in his pocket. 'And we would never mock you because of it. Please, sit back down. And please accept my sympathy.'

Mrs Brazil dropped down into the armchair and clamped her hands in her lap. Foley sat down too. 'So what happened, Mrs Brazil? Why was he taken to Killarney?'

'He always suffered from his nerves. You know that.' She glanced at Foley. 'You went to school with him.'

Foley looked at Guerin and pulled a face that said no, he didn't know that.

'It got worse after his father died.' Mrs Brazil's eyes filled up and the tears dripped down her cheeks. 'Liam found him in the backyard. He was moving the dustbins out for collection and he just dropped dead. Liam was fifteen. He never got over the shock.' She wiped her eyes with the apron. 'Then about six years ago he had some sort of breakdown. No one knows what started it off, but I think it was because the business was starting to struggle and it was bothering him more than he was letting on. Anyway, they took him to Killarney for a few weeks. Then they sent him home with a bag of medicine that was supposed to help him cope.'

She brushed more tears away with the back of her hand. 'The trouble is, the medicine makes him feel good, and after a while he thinks he doesn't need it anymore. So he stops taking it. Then something upsets him and off he goes again.'

'Is that what happened back in January?' Foley asked.

'No. Not exactly.' Mrs Brazil took a handkerchief from her sleeve and wiped her eyes. 'It was a lot of things. The medicine was very expensive, and because of the rationing and the lack of stock, the business was struggling more than ever. Our credit was no good anymore, and some of our suppliers were no longer delivering to us. Then the pharmacies in town stopped our credit. Our biggest customer was the Appleyards, you see, and that wasn't very big anymore. But it was regular. So when they decided to go away for a few weeks it was awkward. Liam put on a good show of being all right, but he couldn't keep it up. After a few weeks without his medication, the demons were back and I had no choice but to call the doctor again.'

A pause had Guerin standing awkwardly in the middle of the room while Foley sat by the table with his hands joined in front of him.

'So how long did they keep him in Killarney for?' Guerin asked.

'Four weeks.' She shivered and rubbed her eyes again. 'They sent him home with enough medicine to last a month. He seemed to be coping well, then you turned up last Saturday with the dreadful news about the Appleyards and that set him off again. Not long after you left on Saturday I had to call the men in white coats again, and they came and took him away.'

Guerin looked around him then sat in the other armchair by the range.

'With hindsight, we made a huge mistake with the Appleyards,' Mrs Brazil said in a soft sad voice. 'We'd put all our eggs in the one basket. When my husband Ben was alive the Appleyards were the biggest farming family in the country, and he always put them first. Which is understandable, of course. We were the nearest shop, so all the workers came here too. But we neglected the loyal locals. If we got something new we took it straight over to the Appleyards first. The regulars would gripe about it but Ben would say it was first come first serve. No one believed that. The Appleyards never actually came here, we always took it to them. Then calamity struck. Sinead died and Toby took to his bed, and our business quickly bled away. The staff up at the house were being sacked almost every day, and in the end we were living on the dregs the nun bought from us. But it was a steady income. Now that's gone too.'

Then the tears came freely and her shoulders rocked with the sobs.

Chapter Fifteen

Eamon Foley was sitting at one end of the kitchen table idly picking at his supper of boiled bacon, cabbage and fluffy potatoes bursting out of their skins. Vicky's husband Stefan was sitting at the other end writing in a huge ledger with his nice new fountain pen. The nib was making scratching noises as it hopped across the page.

Vicky had the ironing board in front of the range and she was pressing the laundry in time to the music coming out of the radio on the sideboard. She sang along, totally out of tune and with the wrong words too.

Foley was finding it hard to shift the heaviness in his heart that had stayed with him all day. It was hard to believe that one person dying could have such a devastating effect on so many others. It wasn't just the family of Sinead Appleyard who felt the repercussions, but the dozens of workers who depended on the Appleyards for their employment too. Even the local store keeper was touched by the cold hand of fate that changed their lives forever.

When they'd left Mrs Brazil's shop she was sitting in the armchair hugging herself and staring into her own corner of space. The fight had gone out of her. She was a deflated version of herself, and she didn't have the strength to go on anymore. Foley couldn't imagine what it was like for a mother to have her son hospitalised with a condition that couldn't be treated with a sticking plaster.

But despite the compassion Foley had for Mrs Brazil, Liam being committed to Killarney only added another question to the pile that was already stacking up in Foley's head. Was Liam's breakdown triggered by something he'd done? According to his mother he had feelings for the nun, Bella Appleyard. Did he make awkward advances towards her on New Year's Day, only to be rejected? Was it possible that, without his medication, he'd lost control and attacked the Appleyards? Then the enormity of what he'd done overwhelmed him and he collapsed under the weight of it?

But that leaves the question of the van Tom O'Gara saw coming out of the Appleyard's gate. The first thing Foley did when he got back to the barracks was ring Killarney to determine the exact dates Liam Brazil was confined there. The hospital confirmed the dates Mrs Brazil had given them. So whoever was driving that van, it wasn't Liam Brazil.

It was only when Vicky slammed the iron back on the cradle on top of the range and said *'I'll get it,'* that he realised someone was knocking on the front door. She gave both men an evil look as she squeezed around the ironing board and went into the hall. Stefan looked at Foley with worried eyes, and Foley picked up another sliver of bacon and chewed on it as he answered with a contrite smile.

They heard the front door open and Vicky's voice giving a warm greeting to someone. The voice that answered was too soft to make out what was being said, but they heard Vicky say 'come in, come in.'

The other voice sounded reluctant but eventually followed Vicky into the kitchen.

'Eamon, look who's here.' Vicky's face was glowing with a wide smile. Both Foley and Stefan stood up to greet the visitor, and Foley felt his mouth go dry when he saw who it was. Her hair was shorter and her face was a bit fuller, but even wrapped in a big warm coat she didn't appear to have changed at all.

'Miss Kite.' Foley put out his hand and she took off her glove before giving it a quick delicate shake.

'Guard Foley.' She gave a smile that Foley couldn't interpret. The last time he'd seen her she was glaring at him with a furious face because he was arresting her father for murder. 'I told you before, call me Florence.'

'Yes,' Foley nodded. 'Of course. Florence.'

Vicky caught Stefan by the arm. 'Florence, have you met my husband?'

'I almost did,' Florence looked the big seaman up and down. 'But unfortunately I didn't make it to the wedding, for which I'm really sorry.'

'Not at all,' Vicky brushed it away. 'It wasn't your fault. Anyway, this is Stefan. Stefan, meet Florence. She's a friend from school.'

Stefan put out the hand with the pen in it and quickly withdrew it again with a chuckle. He changed the pen to the other hand and tried again. Florence beamed at him. 'Nice to meet you at last, Stefan.'

Stefan beamed back. 'Nice to meet you too.'

Vicky steered her visitor towards the armchair by the range. 'Take your coat off and have a cup of tea.'

'No,' Florence gripped the front of her coat. 'I'm interrupting your meal. I'm sorry.'

'Not at all,' Foley told her. 'I'm almost finished.'

'Anyway, I only called to give you this.' Miss Kite took a small lady's purse from her pocket and held it out to Foley. 'I was clearing out the house and I found it at the back of a drawer. I must have shoved it there when I originally found it and forgot all about it. Then today I remembered your mother used to live in our house, and I wondered if it might be hers.'

Foley took the purse and turned it over in his hand. 'You found it while you were clearing out your house?'

'Yeah. I've put the house up for sale. The removal men came today and took away the last of the furniture.'

'You're selling your house?' Vicky had taken a cup and saucer from the sideboard and was handing it to Miss Kite who didn't seem able to refuse it. 'So where are you going to live?'

'I have a small bungalow in Waterford close to my brother. And I have a job now too. I'm working for a timber wholesaler, in the office.'

'So you're leaving Tralee for good?' Vicky was still trying to get Miss Kite to sit down.

'I am.' Miss Kite held the cup while Vicky poured tea into it, but she still didn't sit down.

'I thought you had already left Tralee.' Foley studied the purse again. 'The house always looked empty whenever I passed by it. And I didn't see you around town for a while.'

Miss Kite stared at Foley over the rim of her teacup as she took a sip of her tea. 'No, I haven't been in town much since my father was …'

She turned to Vicky. 'I only came back once in a while to light the fire and give the place an airing. You know how it is? I didn't want it getting damp and musty over the winter.'

Foley sat back down at the table and Stefan did the same. Vicky moved the ironing board and dropped into the armchair, and eventually Miss Kite sat down in the other armchair, but she perched on the edge of it.

Every time Foley looked over at her she was staring back at him. He'd forgotten how bright and intelligent her eyes were, and the way she held her mouth in a Mona Lisa pout. He was never sure if she was smiling or not. She was unnerving him now, so to distract himself he opened the purse and looked inside. There was a key on a ring with a St Andrew medal attached to it, and a small brown envelope. He picked out the envelope and turned it over, and when he read the name on the front of it he almost dropped it like a red hot egg.

Mrs Alex Cassidy
Doon House
Doon
Dublin

He felt the blood drain from his face, and he must have made a noise because everyone looked over at him.

'Are you alright there, Eamon?' Vicky put her cup on the range and went to stand up.

'Yes,' Foley answered quickly, and he waved the envelope at Miss Kite. 'Where did you say you found this?'

'Remember that big dresser behind the door? Well, when we first moved in we thought it would look better by the other wall. Anyway, we found the purse behind it. We assumed someone had put it on top of the dresser and it slipped down the back. I did intend to find out who it belonged to but ... well, as you know, life got in the way and I forgot all about it. I'm sorry.'

'Don't be.' Foley studied the envelope again. 'It's very kind of you to bring it over.'

'Not at all.' Miss Kite started to unbutton her coat as the heat from the range became uncomfortable. 'As I said, I assumed it belonged to your mother. Is it hers?'

'Let me see it.' Vicky got up with her hand out. Foley passed it to her and she turned it over a few times before she put it back on the table. 'I don't recognise it.' She looked at the key and shrugged at that too. 'I don't recognise that either.'

She went back and sat down, and she shook her head at Miss Kite. 'I don't remember my mother having a purse like that, but it doesn't mean it wasn't hers. Do you know what I mean? She might have bought it after I left home when I got married. Isn't that right, Eamon?'

Foley was staring at the envelope trying to understand what he was looking at.

'Eamon?' Vicky's voice was full of concern.

'What?'

'Are you alright?'

'No,' he wanted to scream at her. 'How can I be all right?' He felt as if he was holding a stick of dynamite with a very short fuse.

Was it possible this was the envelope everyone was looking for after Liam Edge was killed? So what was it doing in their old house? Did it have anything to do with the Alex Cassidy who came home with him when he left Dublin? He tried to think back to the day he brought her to Creamery Lane. Did she have a purse with her? He couldn't remember. It was years ago. He couldn't even remember what she was wearing. Could she have hidden it in a coat pocket? He knew it was raining that day, but everything else was a blur.

He took the sheet of handwritten paper from the envelope and smoothed it out on the table before reading it. *'Alex, you won't know what this means and it's best that way because if anything happens to me I don't want them coming after you. Just give this picture to Billy McStay. He will know what it means. Seamus.'*

Also in the envelope was a battered photograph of a woman and two young men. They were posing for the camera in front of a big range in the kitchen of an old house. The woman had her arms around the young men, and her beaming face told Foley this was a proud mother with her sons.

But he didn't recognise any of them. And he didn't recognise the room either. On the back, someone had written: *'Safe in the Sacred Heart.'*

Foley turned it over and studied it again. There was nothing unusual about the scene. Two half burnt candles in silver holders stood on either side of the mantelpiece above the range along with the usual assortment of everyday things. Pride of place in the middle of the mantelpiece was a statue of The Sacred Heart. A couple of nightlights were placed in front of it, and several Mass Cards were propped against the wall behind it. It was the kind of scene you'd find in any Irish kitchen.

He folded the paper and tried to put it back in the envelope but his hands were shaking so much it took several attempts.

'So,' Miss Kite asked. 'Is it your mother's, do you think?'

'I honestly don't know.' Foley slipped the envelope into his jacket pocket and put the purse on the table, touching it as if it was sacred.

Vicky clicked her tongue at him and sat back down. There was a moment of silence when the only noise was the sipping of tea and the scratching of Stefan's pen. Eventually Miss Kite said, 'I saw you in the paper, Guard Foley. You looked fed up standing in the snow outside the Appleyard's house.'

'Isn't it awful?' Vicky squeezed her eyes shut and shook her head in disbelief. 'The two of them murdered in their own house. Holy Mother of God, who would do such a thing to someone in their own house?'

'No,' Foley turned around in his chair. 'We don't know if they were murdered, Vicky. That's just speculation. You should know better than spreading stories like that. You've seen the damage it can do to an investigation.'

Vicky frowned at him then turned to Miss Kite. 'Well, that's what I'm after reading in the papers. The Kerryman is saying it looks like they were murdered.'

Miss Kite didn't agree. 'I read it was murder and suicide.' She leant forward and pointed at Vicky with her cup. 'I wouldn't put it past Bella Appleyard. You remember her, don't you? She was a miserable little thing, even back then. She had a face on her, always frowning. No one ever saw her smile.'

Vicky sat forward too and looked at Foley. 'Don't you remember her, Eamon? She was in my class.'

'Her sister Lily was in your class,' Miss Kite reminded him.

Foley was struggling to listen to the conversation. His mind was full of the letter in his pocket. What was he supposed to do with it now? He'd have to take it to Detective Sheffield and see what he made of it.

'Eamon?' Vicky called again.

'What?'

'Florence was saying Lily Appleyard was in your class.'

'I know. Liam Brazil was saying the same thing. But I can't remember her. It was too long ago.'

Vicky picked up her cup off the range and took a sip of tea. 'I remember Lily was a terrible show-off. But because she came from a rich family all the nuns sucked up to her.

She could get away with anything. And she was the biggest mischief-maker of them all, you know?'

'I remember she always wore bright cheerful clothes which made her look beautiful and attractive.' Miss Kita added. 'But she was so spiteful, wasn't she? Remember how she would egg the others on, then she'd give the nuns her big innocent smile as she melted into the background while everyone else was dragged to the Mother Superior's office.'

'Me included,' Vicky laughed.

'Do you remember how terrible she was to her sister?'

'I do, sure. Whenever she was causing trouble she would try to get Bella involved. But Bella wouldn't play ball and Lily would be absolutely vicious towards her. She would get all her friends to torment Bella every chance they got.'

They sat in silence again for another few moments. Then Miss Kite said, 'Isn't it strange how two sisters could look so alike and yet be so different? How can one be such a huge show-off always craving attention, and the other one be like a sour little mouse?'

'What was that horrible name Lily called Bella?' Vicky clicked her fingers. 'Yeah. She had a funny name for her. What was it? Something to do with her limp. Limping Lulu, or something like that.'

'Wasn't it Lolloping Lulu?'

'God, yeah. Lolloping Lulu. Yes, she was really mean to her sister all right.'

Vicky looked at Foley to see if he was paying attention, but his focus was still on the letter. He glanced up and frowned, but Vicky had already turned to Stefan and was explaining the story to him.

'Bella got tangled up in the rope of a hay cart. It was during the harvest time on the farm. Her leg was crushed,' she told him. 'She was just a child but the bones didn't heal properly, so one leg was shorter than the other and it gave her an awkward gait. Her sister Lily thought it was hysterical, and she called her some horrible names.

Lolloping Lulu and stuff like that. And she thought it was great fun when her so-called friends joined in the mocking of Bella.'

'Even her mother thought it was funny. Remember how she used to turn up at the school gates posing like the queen in her big posh car?' Miss Kite gave a mock regal wave. 'She was one of the few people in town with a car, and she would park it right in the middle of the road to make sure everyone saw it.'

Vicky gave a mocking sneer and Miss Kite said, 'Anyway, I was coming out the gate after school one day and poor Bella was sobbing her little heart out. She started telling her mother what the other kids were calling her, and would you believe it, her mother actually laughed out loud. W*ell, it is funny,* she said. *And you do walk funny. But it's nothing to be upset about, is it? It's only a bit of harmless teasing.* Yeah, the mother was as heartless as her sister Lily was.'

Vicky gave a huge sympathetic sigh that said she understood the pain of being mocked and not getting much support from the people she most expected it from.

'Anyway,' Miss Kite drained her cup and put it on the range, stood up and began buttoning up her coat. 'I'm sorry I have to dash off like this. Thank you for the tea, Vicky.'

Stefan and Foley both stood up and took her hand as she held it out to them. 'It's lovely to see you all again. Maybe we'll meet up again the next time I'm back in town. You never know.'

Vicky saw her to the front door. Then she was gone.

Now the music was back on and Vicky was ironing in time to it. She made some observations about Miss Kite that Foley answered with a vague comment, but his mind was too busy fluttering around the meaning of the letter to be listening to what his sister was saying.

Was it possible this could be the actual envelope the real Alex Cassidy was so desperate to find? The thought of it was squeezing the knot in his stomach and making it impossible for him to sit still, so he went for a wash and shave. Then he sat in the armchair and tried to read the newspaper while ignoring his sister's tone deaf version of whatever was blaring from the wireless.

A hint of perfume reminded him that Miss Kite had been sitting in this chair, and the news she was selling her house in Creamery Lane sent a sad ripple through him. Not only was he likely to never see her again, but he actually liked that house. The memories of his time there were mixed, but it was a comfortable place all the same.

Then an idea popped into his head, and he felt a sharp twang of embarrassment for even thinking of it. But it did make sense.

He knew he couldn't wait for the morning to find out, though. The anxiety would keep him awake all night, fretting about how Sheffield would react to his suggestion. So he put his tie back on, grabbed his coat and checked what money he had in his wallet.

'I won't be late,' he told Vicky, and he nodded to Stefan as he went out. 'I have my key, so don't wait up.'

Chapter Sixteen

Sullivan's bar was quiet, which was to be expected considering it was a Monday night. Three men were hunched at the counter nursing their pints of stout, and a couple sat at the table in the glow of the fire.

As Foley looked around, the bartender caught his eye and asked what he wanted with just the flick of his head. Foley indicated a pint of the black stuff, and the bartender nodded, took a glass off the shelf behind him and started filling it.

Foley unbuttoned his overcoat and turned back to the room, and he stopped dead when he realised who was sitting at the table by the fire. The woman had her back to him but he recognised her immediately. What in God's name was she doing in Sullivan's pub? And more to the point, what was she doing with *him*?

Detective Sheffield looked up and saw him, and a wide smile creased his face. 'Foley? What are you doing here? I thought you were banned.'

Miss Kite spun around and it took a moment for her to realise who was there. Her eyebrows raised slightly with a hint of amusement but her smile was still hard to decipher. 'Guard Foley,' she chuckled. 'Are you looking for me?'

The question made Foley pause and his reply seemed to stick in his throat because his mouth was suddenly dry. When the words did come out they were, 'No. I was looking for Detective Sheffield.'

Miss Kite turned back to Sheffield. 'Detective? You're a detective? You didn't tell me that.'

Sheffield shrugged. 'Well, it's not something you advertise. Not everyone feels comfortable in your company when they know what you do for a living.' He gave her a knowing smile. 'And I didn't want to make you feel uncomfortable.'

She studied him for a moment before looking up at Foley again. 'That's a shame. I was hoping you came here to ask me about buying my house.'

'You thought I was going to buy your house?' Foley flinched.

'Well, yes.' The look was serious, not a hint of a smile. 'I think it would be ideal for you. You used to live there once, so it would hold no surprises for you. And you wouldn't need to arrange a visit to view it.'

'I ... well, it would be ideal for me,' Foley agreed. 'But right now it's beyond my means, I'm afraid.'

'Really?' Again the serious look. 'But you're a guard. You have a good job. Any bank manager would willingly give you a mortgage. You'd be a good investment.'

The log in the fireplace crackled and threw up a bright finger of light, and Foley caught the tiniest hint of amusement in her eyes again. And it confused him because he couldn't decide if she was playing with him or not. But before he could answer her, Sheffield joined in.

'Come on, Foley. Look at you. You're still living with your sister after all these years. You need a place of your own, a place where your boy can call his home. You ...'

'I already have a place, thank you,' Foley cut in. 'And my boy is very happy there, I can assure you. So ...'

Sheffield pulled out a chair with his foot and motioned for Foley to sit down, but Foley waved it away. 'No,' he said. 'I won't, thank you. I don't want to interrupt your evening.'

'Not at all,' Miss Kite insisted. 'Please, join us.'

Foley took a moment to decide, then he sat down and shuffled the chair closer to the table. And he frowned when he realised they were both waiting for him to say something. But the bartender appeared, put his pint of porter in front of him and nodded to Sheffield. 'Can I get you another? And the lady?'

'Yes. A pint and ...' Sheffield looked at Miss Kite but she shook her head.

'Not for me, thank you.' She put her hand over her glass. 'I'm not staying long. I need a bath and an early night.'

'So soon?' Sheffield asked, and she gave him a tired smile. Sheffield shrugged and picked up his glass, and he waved it at Foley.

'So you were looking for me, were you?'

Foley took a sip of his porter. 'I was. But I didn't think you'd be having company this evening.'

'I'm staying here,' Miss Kite glanced around the bar with an approving look. 'For a few days anyway. My house is empty now, so while I'm waiting for a buyer I'm staying here.'

'That's how we met,' Sheffield beamed. 'We got talking over dinner. You know what it's like, two ships passing in the sea of time. Two lonely people and all that stuff you only ever see in the cinema.' He took another sip from his glass. 'And I have to say, it's not often you meet such a delightful fellow traveller in a place like this. So you have to take advantage of the opportunity.'

Miss Kite grinned and studied her glass before draining it. 'That's a very nice thing to say, Paul. Thank you. And on that note, I bid you both goodnight.'

Both men stood up, and Sheffield took her coat from the back of her chair and passed it to her. 'I'll see you at breakfast, so,' he added. 'Goodnight, Florence.'

'Good night, Guard Foley,' she answered, then she gave a jokey smile. 'And goodnight, Detective Sheffield,' she said, stressing the word *detective*.

Sheffield flinched, and his expression said he was looking for a suitable answer to that. But before he could find one she was already walking towards the stairs behind the bar.

Sheffield was still staring after her when he sat down again, and he took a long drink from his pint before putting the glass down. 'So, how long have you known Florence?' he asked Foley.

Foley thought about it for a moment. 'Well, it's a long story.'

'I'm not going anywhere,' Sheffield sat back and picked up his glass again.

'She bought our house - well, my mother's house in Creamery Lane - after Liam Edge was promoted and sent to Limerick.'

'So why is she selling it?' Sheffield sounded genuinely interested.

Foley grinned. 'Didn't she tell you?'

'Tell me what?'

'Why she was selling her house,' Foley mocked. 'Listen, anyone who saw the two of you cosied up by the fire would have assumed you were close enough to know what the other one was up to.'

It came out sharper that Foley intended, and it made Sheffield throw back his head and laugh out loud. 'My good God,' he spluttered. 'You're ... well, well, well, I would never have guessed it, Foley. It's not the house you have your eye on, is it? It's who's living in the house you're interested in.' He threw his hands up in mock surrender. 'And I can't blame you. She is a very attractive woman, I have to say.'

'Stop it,' Foley snapped. 'It's nothing like that.'

'Oh, don't give me that rubbish,' Sheffield countered. 'I'm a detective, Foley. I read people. I can read you like an open book with huge letters. Your face was all twisted out of shape when you saw me here because you were hoping to meet her on her own.'

'I was not. I didn't even know she was staying here.'

'Rubbish. Admit it, Foley, you ...'

'I'm telling you.' Foley took the envelope from his inside pocket and put it on the table. 'I came here to show you this.'

'What is it?' Sheffield frowned at the envelope but didn't attempt to touch it.

Foley pushed it towards him. 'I want to know what you make of it.'

Sheffield looked at it for a long moment before gingerly picking it up, and his mouth was tight in a suspicious line as he studied the address on the front. Then he took out the photo and turned it over in his hand several times before sitting back in his chair again.

'So where did you get this?'

Foley nodded at the stairs. 'Florence found it when she was clearing out her house. It was in a lady's purse and she thought it must belong to my mother.'

'I'm confused,' Sheffield waved the photo at him. 'Why would it be in her house?'

'Well, all I can think is the woman I thought was Alex Cassidy had it with her when she came to Tralee with me back in '41. Florence said she found it down behind a large dresser in the kitchen. Maybe Alex - that woman - put it on top of the dresser for safe keeping but it fell down the back and she couldn't recover it.'

Sheffield rubbed his eyes. 'So what are you thinking? Are you saying this could be the mysterious envelope everyone is chasing?'

'Well ...'

'But how can it be?' Sheffield flipped the photo over and dropped it back on the table, then he studied the envelope again. 'The envelope we're looking for is supposed to be big enough to hold the deeds of an estate. And this is not.'

Foley reached out and took the envelope. 'But it has to mean something. It has to be significant, doesn't it? The real Alex Cassidy came to our house in Rock Street because she thought the fake Alex Cassidy had been living there, yeah? She had no idea the fake Alex Cassidy actually lived in Creamery Lane first, before Liam Edge gave her a room in Rock Street. So the real Alex Cassidys assumed the fake Alex Cassidy had the envelope in her room in Rock Street. When she told Joe Junior about it, everyone - especially your mob - thought it was the envelope with the deeds in.

But suppose the envelope they were looking for was this one, a photo that held the clue to where the deeds are actually hidden.'

Sheffield put back his head and rubbed the back of his neck. Then he reached out for the envelope again, but Foley held it to his chest. Sheffield frowned then leant closer with his hand stretched out even farther. 'Let me see it,' he growled. 'What's the matter with you?'

Foley moved back from the table. 'The reward for finding the deeds, what is it?'

'What?' Sheffield looked as if he was going to shout but he lifted his glass and drained it instead. Then he said, 'What are you talking about? What's the reward got to do with anything?'

'A lot,' Foley answered. 'Because if this turns out to be the clue that solves the riddle, I want half of the reward.'

This time Sheffield slammed down his glass and gave a bellow of a laugh. 'For feck sake, Foley. You can *not* be serious. What makes you think you deserve half of … what kind of wild notion has filled your head and made you think you deserve half of the reward? I've put years into finding that envelope, years of pain and sweat and many tears. If I do recover those deeds I will not be sharing the reward with anyone, especially someone who tried to block my investigation from the very start.'

Sweat glistened on his top lip and he swiped it away with the back of his hand. Foley waved his glass at the detective. 'So how close are you to finding the deeds right now, Sheffield?'

'I'm this close.' Sheffield held up his thumb and finger an inch apart.

'No you're not,' Foley mocked. 'You're on the wrong side of the river, and you'll stay there forever if you carry on being the prick you are.'

'Oh, for God's sake, Foley. You've got nothing. A battered old photograph of … what?'

'But that battered old photograph might be the life raft you're looking for to take you across that river, right over to the side where x marks the spot of the buried treasure.'

Sheffield's face had taken on a darker shade of puce and he squeezed his eyes shut again. 'You've got nothing, Foley. You're so full of bullshit it makes me want to vomit.'

'*I'm* full of bullshit? You need to take a good look in the mirror, you feckin moron.'

'Don't you …'

'What happened to all that crap about the reward not being important to you, that all you were interested in was getting your promotion?'

'Well, my promotion is important. But it doesn't mean I'm stupid enough to give the reward money away to the first dope that thinks he's entitled to it. Who do you think you are, Foley?'

Foley gave a sharp laugh and pointed to his chest. 'I think I'm the one you came looking for to help you look for D'Lacey's missing deeds. Remember? Someone that you could trust? Someone who had some common sense and who would cover your back?'

Sheffield smarted and turned his face to the fireplace, and the flames glistened on the sheen of his angry face.

'Anyway,' Foley put the envelope back in his pocket and pushed back his chair, and Sheffield spun around and glared at him.

'What are you doing?'

'I'm going home,' Foley told him.

Sheffield's mouth opened and closed a few times and he gave a long angry sigh. 'All right,' he snapped. 'Go. But don't think this is the last you'll hear about this, Foley. This could be a very important piece of evidence, and you could be in serious trouble for concealing it.'

Foley snorted, picked up his glass and swallowed the last of his porter. Then he waved the empty glass at Sheffield. 'I thought you said it was just an old battered photograph that meant nothing.'

'It probably is. But you can't withhold it from the investigation.'

The bartender appeared and plonked another pint in front of Sheffield, and he gave the two men a look that said he was discreetly not paying attention to what they were arguing about.

'I'm not withholding anything,' Foley argued as the bartender walked out of earshot. 'But I am asking for a share of the reward money if this proves to be a vital clue.'

'A vital clue?' Sheffield scoffed.

'Yes,' Foley insisted. 'Look, you said you'd already gone back to square one with the investigation, yeah? And you quickly discovered the Cassidy's didn't rob D'Lacey at all. They actually won the deeds in a card game. So what's your next move, Detective Sheffield?'

Sheffield shifted in his chair. 'Well …'

'Well, you should find out what Cassidy did next, shouldn't you? Where did he go when he left the casino? Did he go straight home?'

The glare he got from Sheffield told him the detective had already thought of all that. 'Look, Sherlock, I'm not a complete fool. I've been down that road already,' he hissed.

'But you didn't have the photo back then. So if it was me, I would go back to Cassidy's house again and take another look around, see if the photo has any relevance to it.'

Sheffield sat up straight and held out his hand. 'Show me that address again.'

'No,' Foley gave his pocket a defensive pat. 'You already know it. You've been chasing the Cassidys for years so you should know it by heart.'

'I do not,' Sheffield still held out his hand. 'I never saw that address before.'

'Don't give me that …'

'That is not Cassidy's address.' He clicked his fingers impatiently. 'Cassidy lived on the other side of the city.

Henry Street, just off O'Connell Street. That envelope you got there said Doon. I have never been to Doon.'

Foley studied him closely, trying to decide if he was actually telling the truth. Then he shook his head again.

'For feck sake, Foley. Show me the bloody envelope.'

This time Foley clicked his fingers. 'Talk to me about the reward.'

Sheffield looked as if he was going to explode. 'Talk to you about the bloody reward?' he mocked. 'I cannot believe you're so concerned about the stupid reward, Guard Foley. I had you down as someone who was only interested in justice. Especially justice for fallen colleagues. But you're just as prone to self-interest as the rest of us. You've got your price too and …'

Suddenly his face lit up and he slapped the table. 'For feck sake,' he chuckled. 'I just realised what this is all about. This is about the delectable Florence Kite. Oh dear God, Foley. You're doing this so you can buy her house. That's it, isn't it? You're doing this to impress the lady of your dreams.'

This time he threw back his head and gave a whoop of a laugh that had the three heads at the bar swivelling to look at him.

'I'll tell you what I'll do, Foley, you soft eejit. Give me the photo and the address, and if it turns out to be useful in finding the deeds, I will buy Florence Kite's house for you. How does that sound?'

'It sounds like a plan,' Foley agreed. 'But the photo and envelope stay with me.'

'Oh, for God's sake. What is the matter with you?'

'Next Saturday,' Foley continued. 'It's my weekend off. So you and I will go on a day out to Dublin, and we'll visit the address on the envelope and see what information we can get from it. Then we'll take it from there, right?'

Sheffield buried his face in his hands to stop the angry howl from escaping, then he threw back his head and growled.

'Seriously? You and I … what? … The two of us …?'
'Yep. Just a couple of pals visiting the big city. What do you say, Detective? Is it a plan?'

Chapter Seventeen

'Good grief, will you look at that?' Eamon Foley pushed his cap back on his head as he walked in through the huge metal gate and stared up at the house at the end of the wide drive.

'What?' Sheffield glanced up as he held out his hand to the taxi driver for his change which he put straight in his pocket.

'This house,' Foley said. 'It's almost identical to the Appleyard's house in Tralee.'

'Is it?' Sheffield had a look on his face that said he wasn't actually interested. He just wanted to get the formalities out of the way and get on with the real reason they'd spent four hours on an overcrowded train with no buffet car. And that was to track down the missing D'Lacey deeds.

Sheffield had spent a miserable, sleepless night in his room in the pub staring up at the ceiling as his mind danced from one uncertain scenario to another, and hit every kind of roadblock in between. He'd get a burst of excitement at the thought that Foley's photo was the final piece of the puzzle. But in a heartbeat the excitement would evaporate and be replaced by the chill of crippling doubt. What exactly had Foley got? A photo of a woman and two men in an ordinary Irish kitchen. But what did it mean? And the message on the back? Safe in The Sacred Heart? There was a statue of The Sacred Heart in Sheffield's kitchen when he was growing up. Every Catholic house had one. Either that, or a statue of The Virgin Mary. The images were the glue that kept the faith fixed to Irish Catholic lives. They were a beacon of hope and strength. People took great comfort from their presence.

The big question had to be, where did the fake Alex Cassidy get the envelope in the first place? If the story

Foley told him was true, the real Alex Cassidy had come to his house looking for it, and at a very real risk of being exposed to the pursuing Garda detectives. So it had to be important, as Foley pointed out. And Foley seemed to have a strong instinct about the photo, which meant Sheffield had no choice but to take it seriously too. So it made sense to take Foley along, go back to square one with him and see where it leads them. It's possible Foley could spot something that Sheffield might not even be aware of.

But he couldn't wait until Saturday to get started. It would kill him to just sit around doing nothing. So he was waiting in the office when the Superintendent arrived this morning. The Super had already been briefed about why Sheffield was in Tralee, and he'd offered every assistance at the time. Now it was time to provide that assistance.

Superintendent Flynn was delighted to release Guard Foley for a few days to help in the investigation. Especially if there would be reflected glory for him and his department if one of his officers was involved in closing this very high profile case.

To justify Foley's absence, it was agreed they would call on Lily Appleyard first to offer their condolences. And also gather what information they could regarding the death of Bella and her father.

Unfortunately by the time they'd contacted Foley and gave him the good news, the next train to Dublin wasn't until noon. And having to take a taxi out to Lily Appleyard's house meant the daylight was fading fast. The thick clouds and misty rain didn't help Sheffield's mood either, and he strutted up to the front door and rapped on it with overzealous force.

The maid who whipped the door open glared at the two men like a hawk about to attack. Her white cap was nesting in a mop of wild red hair that wrapped around a long thin face, and her sharp grey eyes were like two shiny pebbles.

'What?' Her voice was sharp too, like cracking ice.

'Oh,' Sheffield was taken by surprise by her tone and it took a moment for him to react. 'We'd like to speak to Lily Appleyard, if you …'

'There's no one here called that,' the woman spat, and she slammed the door shut.

Sheffield jumped back with an angry yelp. 'You ignorant …' he gasped. 'How the feck can you …'

'She's Lily Redigan now,' Foley told him as he stepped forward and rapped on the door again.

'What?'

'Her name isn't Appleyard anymore,' Foley added. 'It's Redigan. She's married to Sean Redigan of the Redigan Shoe Company.'

When the door opened again Sheffield ran forward waving his warrant card. 'Gardaí. We want to speak to Mrs Redigan *now*.'

This time the maid looked them up and down before reluctantly pulling the door wider. 'Why didn't you say that?' she screeched. Her bottom lip wobbled and she turned and stomped down the hall in front of them. 'How am I supposed to know who you want if you don't know their name? It isn't my fault. I'm only after starting here this week. How am I supposed to know everyone's name when I'm only working here for a few days?'

She pushed open a big white door at the end of the hall and called out, 'Sir, Madam, the guards are here to see you.'

As Sheffield and Foley walked into the enormous drawing room, the two people sitting by the fire drinking tea looked frozen in shock. Then the man put down his cup and stood up with an angry jerk. The blood seemed to have drained from his thin face as he glanced from his wife to Sheffield, then at Foley before looking at his wife again. 'What's this about?'

The woman was dressed all in black, and Foley was stunned when she looked up at him. She had the most perfect face he'd ever seen. Her ash blonde hair was cut in a modern bob and the high collar of her black blouse made her face appear the colour of milk. A delicate nose above an equally delicate mouth, and bright green eyes that were almost luminous.

A shadow flashed across those eyes and for the briefest moment Foley thought he saw the look of a startled animal. But in less than a heartbeat her features reset and she held Foley's stare.

Sheffield prodded Foley with his elbow, and Foley took off his cap. 'Am I speaking to Mr and Mrs Redigan?'

'Yes,' the man said with a defensive tone.

'We're so sorry for your loss.' Foley gave his most contrite smile, and he flinched when the man rushed towards them with his fists bunched.

'Who the hell are you?'

'I'm Detective Sheffield and this is Guard Foley from Tralee.' Sheffield stepped in front of the man. 'We were asked by Superintendent Flynn to call in and …'

'You came all the way from Tralee?' Redigan puffed out his chest. 'So you've discovered what happened to … you've come to tell us you know what happened to our family?'

'Well, no.' Sheffield glanced at Foley for support. 'I'm afraid we don't know exactly what happened to them. It's just that …'

'What? So why did you come here?'

'Because Superintendent Flynn asked us to call in and offer you our sincerest condolences for your loss.'

Redigan rolled his eyes and snorted. 'You came all the way up here from Tralee to offer your condolences?' Then he paused. 'Right. Yes. That's very kind of him. Tell him thanks. But I still don't see why it was necessary to come all this way if you didn't have anything more to tell us.'

'Actually, we were coming to Dublin anyway on another matter. The Superintendent asked us to call in as we were passing to say how sorry we are for your loss.'

Redigan nodded but didn't respond.

'And to ask if you'd mind answering a few questions, to help us with our investigation.'

This time Redigan's head jerked up and his lips became a thin angry line. 'What kind of questions? For God's sake, can't you see we're grieving? My wife is already distressed enough about what happened to her family, and you want to ask us questions?'

'We're so sorry,' Foley said. 'But you can understand we're doing all we can to find out what happened to them.'

'But we already told the detectives who called here yesterday everything we know.' Redigan looked Foley up and down with a condescending sneer. 'They were a Superintendent and an Inspector, you know. So we have nothing else to say to their junior colleagues. We just want to be left alone to grieve in peace.'

Foley forced a smile. 'We understand, of course. It must be very difficult for you. But right now we have no idea about what happened in Tralee. Or when it happened, for that matter. So anything you can tell us will be very helpful.'

Redigan looked at his wife again. She gave a sharp nod of her head, then she pointed at the sofa opposite. 'For God's sake, gentlemen, sit down. Sean, call Agnes. You'll have tea, Guards?'

'Thank you.' Sheffield unbuttoned his coat and sat on the side nearest the fire. The side Foley sat on was directly in front of Lily Appleyard, and he had to force himself to stop staring at her. He could understand why every man with a pulse would think she was beautiful. And every woman would worry if her man was anywhere near her.

When the maid appeared Mrs Redigan said, 'Bring two cups, please. And maybe a sandwich for the guards. They're probably hungry after their long trip up from Kerry.'

'Right you are, missus,' the maid answered as she disappeared back out the door.

'So what do you want to know?' Sean Redigan dropped back into his armchair.

Foley put his cap on the seat beside him and opened his notebook on his lap. 'Well, when was the last time you saw Bella and her father?'

Redigan looked at his wife again as if he needed prompting, and she answered for him. 'It was in the beginning of December.'

Foley waited for more and when it didn't come he said, 'You haven't seen them since before Christmas?'

'Yes.' Redigan's tone was shaky and uncertain, and he glanced at his wife again.

'We were just after buying this house.' Lily looked around the room and nodded with a hint of pride. 'There were complications.'

She studied the two guards for a moment before deciding to explain. 'We thought the property came with staff. We were wrong. Our own cook and maid didn't want to come with us because of family commitments. And our gardener and handyman were useless and we had to let them go anyway. So with a busy Christmas workload, and trying to sort this mess out, we spent Christmas in the village hotel. And we didn't get the chance to visit Tralee to see my father. Or my sister.'

'So you didn't call to see them on New Year's Day?'

'No.' Redigan's voice was sharp. Then he blinked several times before repeating, 'No.'

Foley let the silence hang between them and Redigan was first to fill it. 'Why?'

Foley pretended to consult his notebook. 'According to the young man who delivers the groceries, Miss Appleyard told him she and her father were going away for a few weeks.'

Sean Redigan swallowed loudly and his Adam's apple bobbed up and down. 'That's rubbish. Bella and I certainly …'

His wife threw him a look that stopped him in mid-sentence, and he did another bout of nervous blinking. His mouth moved but nothing came out.

Agnes the maid appeared, put two cups and saucers on the coffee table and headed back to the door.

'Agnes.' Lily gave a sharp bark. 'What are you doing? Pour the tea for the guards.'

The maid spun around and did a confused shuffle before picking up the teapot. When she finished and left, Sean Redigan gave a disapproving grunt. 'Stupid girl. It's impossible to get good staff anymore.'

Foley and Sheffield picked up their cups and took a sip of tea, and Sheffield added two spoons of sugar as he said, 'Getting back to New Year's day.'

Lily stared at him for a moment. Then she turned to Foley. 'What did the delivery man tell you?'

She was obviously aware she was making him uncomfortable by holding him with her unblinking gaze. But he couldn't afford to become intimidated by her so he stared back. 'He said Bella told him they were going away for a few weeks and she'd let him know when she got back.'

'Why would she let the delivery boy know when she got back?'

Foley shrugged. 'Maybe to bring groceries. You know, have stuff in the house ready for when they get home? Especially as she would have her father with her who would need looking after.'

Lily gave a slight shake of her head and turned to Sheffield, and Foley felt as if he'd been released from a hypnotic spell. But he still couldn't stop staring at her. Her whole demeanour fascinated him.

Then he remembered what someone had told him about Sean Redigan, how Lily used to treat him before his parents died and left him one of the most successful businesses in the country. Foley glanced at the man slumped in the armchair with a haunted look on his thin face. He was only about Foley's age but he was already round shouldered and losing his hair.

But there was something else. The eyes were wary, flicking from his wife to the guards and back to his wife again as if he was petrified of saying the wrong thing.

The maid rushed in and put a plate of sandwiches on the table and turned to go again, caught Lily's eye and picked up the plate again. She held it out to Sheffield who took two, and then to Foley. They were thick cheese in soda bread and he took two of them as well. When he realised Lily was watching him his face reddened as he struggled to bite into the sandwich with some dignity.

'You look familiar,' she said suddenly, and Foley felt the bread stick to the back of his mouth. He had to take a drink of tea before he could answer.

'Do I?'

'You remind me of a girl I was in school with.' She tapped her face under her eye. 'She had an accident with a bike. Left her with a nasty scar.'

'My sister Vicky.' Foley was surprised. The impression he got was that Lily was so self-absorbed she saw nobody outside her own field of vision, unless they could be of use to her. She nodded and sat back in her chair, and the hem of her dress rode up slightly to show she was wearing long lace-up shoes with a thick sole. The way she was sitting in the large padded armchair made it hard to judge how tall she was. But Sean wasn't as tall as Foley. Foley knew some petit women felt uncomfortable about their lack of height, often feeling slighted and dismissed because they didn't command a presence. Did Lily feel that way? Did she feel the need to grow a few inches to add to her sense of authority?

Foley didn't think so. Her face held all the authority she needed. There wasn't a man alive who could resist her demands, especially when she captured them in her unblinking stare.

She brushed down the front of her skirt and sat up straight in the armchair and said, 'I'm afraid your delivery man was mistaken,'

'He was very insistent,' Foley told her.

'Even so,' Lily dismissed it with a flick of her hand. 'There is no way my father would agree to go anywhere in his condition. Where would he go, for God's sake? Who would have him?'

'A relative?' Sheffield suggested. 'Family, maybe?'

Lily Appleyard pulled the kind of face she'd have pulled if she tasted something bitter. 'My father was the most obnoxious man on this earth,' she spat. 'He sat in his bed all day long howling his demands like a big spoiled child. Nothing was good enough for him. Everyone was stupid. Nobody could do anything right by him. But he would not come out of his room and do anything for himself. He drove us to despair with his bitterness and his spite. So no, Guard Foley, he would not have been invited to visit family. And certainly not relatives.'

She picked up her cup and raised it to her mouth, and she held it there for a long time without actually drinking from it. And Foley thought she was hiding a sadness behind the anger.

Sheffield reached out and took another sandwich, and as he sat back he said, 'But your father was not a well man, I understand.'

'That was not an excuse for his dreadful behaviour.' Sean crossed his legs and sat back in his chair. 'I know his wife was after dying on him, and I have the greatest sympathy for the man. But for God's sake, how long ago was that? How many people lose their loved ones every day of the year and they don't take to their beds like that.'

'We all felt the loss of my mother.' Lily took the cup away from her mouth. 'We cried and grieved as much as he did, but we didn't crumble like that. It wasn't our fault she died. But he turned on us as if it was, blaming us for his pain and taking his pain out on us.'

The pause that followed exaggerated the sound of Sheffield munching on his sandwich. Sean Redigan sighed behind his fingers that he held to his lips. Lily sighed too, and this time took a sip from her teacup. Foley wasn't sure if he should be feeling sympathy for her because, if what everyone had told him was true, she had abandoned her sister to the mercy of her very angry father. But there was something about the sparkle in her eyes that touched him.

'Am I right in thinking your sister was the only one looking after your father in that big house?' Sheffield asked through a mouthful of sandwich.

Sean Redigan gave his mouth another nervous swipe. 'That's because she was the only one left,' he snapped. 'Everyone else had gone. Rats abandoning the sinking ship.'

Foley looked at Lily and she gave a condescending nod, and Foley couldn't stop himself saying, 'Some of the ex-employees told us that Bella drove them out. Several of them ...'

'That's a bloody lie.' Lily's face clouded and she almost dropped her cup. 'Who the hell told you that? That's a horrible thing to say.' She had to take a deep breath before she could continue. 'People left of their own accord. No one drove them out. The farm was falling to pieces and my father wouldn't get out of bed to take charge of things. So there was no money to pay them anyway. But you can't blame me ... us ...for any of that. Staff left because they weren't paid. We did our best to keep the place going, but how could we do it on our own? He controlled what little money there was, and he controlled me ... us ... making our lives a misery. He was not a nice man.'

A tear escaped and she wiped it away, and she stared at Foley again. 'He was not a nice man. What more can I say?'

Foley looked away and took another bite of his sandwich, and he washed it down with a drink of his tea. Then he asked, 'When was the last time you heard from Bella?'

'Why?'

'Well, right now we don't know when they actually died, so we're trying to establish the time they were last seen alive.'

'Surely to God you could tell that by the cut of the … remains?' Sean Redigan gave a sarcastic sneer.

'No, we could not,' Foley told him. 'They were frozen solid when we found them because of the fierce weather we had recently. But I thought you would have been told that, considering that you were briefed by a Superintendent and an Inspector.'

Sean muttered and sat back in his chair again. 'We haven't heard from Bella since she sent us the bill for the groceries. Sometime in January. We sent her a cheque.'

'Oh, so she would have been alive in January? What date was that, do you know?'

Sean sat up and looked at his wife, and he had the panicked look on his face again. 'I don't remember. Sometime in January.'

'Can you find out for me?'

'No,' Sean almost shouted. 'This has gone far enough. I don't know what you're trying to achieve by this line of questions but I'm …'

'It was December,' Lilly snapped and silenced both men. 'Before Christmas. I added a few pounds to help her buy a few extras for the festivities.'

'And she didn't get back to you to say thanks? Or to wish you a happy Christmas?' Foley asked.

'For God's sake,' Sean rocked back in his chair.

'No, she did not,' Lily gave Sean a look that said stop talking. The look in her eyes was hard to read, but the tightness of her mouth showed a hint of anger.

'So you didn't contact her either?' Foley put the cup back on the coffee table. 'And she was looking after her father alone? That must have been hard.'

'Of course it was bloody hard.' The look in her eyes was obvious this time. She was furious. 'It was dreadfully hard. Day after day, no let up. No respite. Of course it was bloody hard.'

'But wasn't there anyone who could give her a break? Let her take a few days off?'

'Like who?' It came out almost as a cry, and Lily had to check herself by taking another deep breath. 'It took a saint to put up with the torment that man put us through. When my mother died and he first got sick, people said if you need anything just ask. But that didn't last long. It never does. It's human nature. People make the right noises and mean it at the time because they're caught up in the emotion. But actually subjecting themselves to my father's abuse quickly eroded any goodwill they might have had. Family and friends disappeared like fog when the sun came out.' She brushed her eyes and the sigh she gave was bitter. 'Even Lily abandoned us. Too bloody busy running her business to be ...'

Her eyes widened and Foley saw the startled animal again, and he caught the way she looked at Sean as if she'd suddenly revealed a dreadful secret. Her mouth tightened and she swallowed hard before she looked at Foley again. 'That's what Bella told everyone, that Lily had abandoned her.'

Sean nodded and gave his nervous blink again. 'Yes. That's what Bella told everyone. Lily was too busy. Too bloody busy. But it wasn't like that. We had to work to keep the business going so we could afford to support them, and that big house they were living in. It wasn't cheap, you know.'

'Anyway,' Lily took a handkerchief from up her sleeve and wiped her eyes. 'I'm sorry we can't be more helpful. But I can assure you that my father and my sister were not going anywhere on New Year's day. Where were they supposed to be going? And how were they supposed to get there? Neither of them drove, and they didn't have a car anyway. And I can't see my father walking all the way to town to catch a train dragging a suitcase after him.'

Sean gave a growl and then cleared his throat before saying, 'I can't believe Bella and her father could spend time in each other's company without killing ...'

Lily's glare shut him up again and he looked down at his hands.

'Call Agnes,' she told him, and he got up and pulled the cord by the fireplace. 'Agnes will ring her father to come and collect you in his van.' She didn't look at Foley this time, just stared past him into the fire. 'He will take you as far as the village. There isn't a bus until the morning so you will have to spend the night in the village pub.'

Chapter Eighteen

The rain was so heavy Foley had his face right up against the windscreen so he could see where they were going, because the wiper on the car they'd borrowed was as useless as a chocolate teapot. It was the only car left in the Garda vehicle pool, and when Sheffield booked it out it was obvious why. It was old and rusting, and they were frightened to slam the door in case something fell off. The seats were frayed and covered in cigarette burns, and the steering wheel and gearstick were sticky with grime. Tea stains and the residue from dropped food had discoloured the fabric in the footwell, and the door to the glovebox was dangling on one hinge.

The noise from the engine and the rattling of the bodywork made it impossible to hold a conversation, so they sat in silence for the hour it took them to reach the address on the envelope. Now they were approaching a huge brownstone house at the end of a potholed lane.

'Are you sure this is it?' Sheffield rubbed the glass and strained to look at the building.

Foley checked the map he had spread out on the dashboard. The route from the city to Doon was marked in red ink, and Doon House was circled in red too.

'This is it,' he said.

Sheffield parked as close to the front steps as he could and Foley dashed up to the big battered door. And a strange sense of foreboding made him hesitate before hammering on it. The unlocked door creaked open letting Foley see into the large hall. The winding staircase was overlooked by portraits of severe looking men in military uniform trying to look important, and again the sense of unease had Foley pausing before he stepped inside. He jumped when a young woman appeared from behind the door and said, 'Hello.'

'Oh, hello,' Foley took off his cap and shook the wet from it. 'I'm Guard …'

The young woman was already walking away, and she pointed to a door on the left of the stairs as she went past it.

'He's in there,' she called, then she was gone around the corner.

Sheffield rushed in behind Foley rubbing the rain from his face, and Foley beckoned for him to follow. Foley's stomach was already tight with an anxious pull, and when they reached the open door the young woman had pointed to his heart nearly stopped. Because he realised why this house had held such dread for him.

The big man with the mop of white hair sitting behind the old oak desk looked up at them with his blank shark-black eyes.

'Gentleman,' the man's mouth smiled but his eyes did not. He looked Foley up and down and his eyes narrowed, then he studied Sheffield. 'How can I be of assistance?'

Sheffield took a quick glance around the room. 'Who are you, Sir?'

The man uncurled his huge frame from his office chair and stretched before answering in a deep rumble of a voice. 'Maranus. Leo Maranus. And who are you?'

Sheffield took out his warrant card and held it out. 'Detective Sergeant Sheffield, attached to the Special Branch.'

Maranus snatched the card and studied it, then he shoved it back at Sheffield. 'I have one of those,' he smirked. 'Only mine says Detective Inspector.'

Sheffield's hand froze in mid-air before he could take back his warrant card, and when he did he held it to his chest.

'I don't understand.' He glanced around the office again then turned back to Maranus. 'What is this place?'

Maranus squinted at him again. 'What do you mean *what is this place*? If you don't know where you are, what the feck are you doing here?'

Sheffield smarted and straightened his tie, and he looked at Foley as he struggled with his answer. 'We're following a lead in an ongoing investigation,' was how it came out.

'What investigation?'

'Well, we're trying to trace the movements of a Mrs Alex Cassidy, and we're led to believe she once lived here.'

'Holy Mother of God,' Maranus threw his hands up in an angry sweep and dropped back into his chair. 'How many more of you feckin eejits are going to come here asking about Mrs Alex Cassidy? How is it the moment that gobshite D'Lacey snaps his fat fingers, the whole of the feckin Garda Siochana jump to their feet and start running around like a band of headless chickens? And they all end up here desperately hoping to find some sort of magic revelation. It's so feckin ridiculous.'

Sheffield waited for the right moment to ask, 'So you know about the D'Lacey incident?'

'Of course I know about the D'Lacey incident,' Maranus snapped. 'I'm feckin Special Branch too, the same as you. And I'm sick of the whole wretched thing. It's because of the D'Lacey incident that I'm stuck behind this desk in this shithole doing a job that would bore the pants off the world's most workshy pig's arse of a lazy bastard.'

He threw back his head and put his hands over his face for a moment, then he sat forward again and slammed his fist on the desk. 'So you can both feck off because there's nothing here for you.'

Sheffield did a nervous shuffle as he put his warrant card back in his jacket pocket. 'But ... look, we're sorry if we upset you, Inspector. But right now we're under fierce pressure, as you can imagine. So we thought if we went back to the very beginning ...'

'... just like all the other poor eejits before you.' The cold grey eyes seemed to almost pop out of the dark angry face. 'I told you already. A million detectives have traipsed through here hoping to find the Holy Grail. It is not here.'

When Maranus glared at Foley the furious eyes burnt a hole in his brain, and Foley flinched.

'Have you got something to say, Guard?' Maranus leaned forward even more.

'I ...'

'You look like you're going to fall off a cliff. Spit it out.'

Foley clasped his hands in front of him. 'I don't suppose you remember me.'

A blank stare was the answer he got, and he continued. 'I was working in the Black Bird Hotel back in '41 when my boss Raymond Price was shot and killed.'

A hint of a smile curled the side of the Inspector's mouth, and he put his hand on his chest with a dramatic pout. 'The Black Bird Hotel? My God, that brings back some memories. Well, well, well. We closed down a huge illegal operation that night. It had taken a huge amount of time and effort, but it was worth it all right.' He pointed to Sheffield and chuckled. 'I got my Inspector's warrant card because of that, God bless them all.'

He took a moment to wallow in the memory, then he looked Foley up and down again. 'So how were you involved in that?'

'As I said, I worked there, and I was wounded in the crossfire. And for some strange reason you got me mixed up with Raymond Price.'

A twitch of his shoulders said Maranus didn't remember that at all.

'Well, that was why you brought me here, to this house.' Foley pointed at the door as if that was going to help.

'Me?'

'Yes. It was you who interrogated me.'

'Interrogated you?' Maranus mocked. 'What the feck are you talking about?'

'You interrogated me. You wanted to know about a ledger that had gone missing. You kept me in a locked room and ...'

Maranus gave a throaty grumble and waved his hand as if he was swatting away a bluebottle. 'I do not remember that. And I don't see where you're going with it anyway. So unless you have something useful to say, please feel free to feck off out of my sight.'

The dark stare held Foley in its grip and he had to force himself to keep his nerve and continue with his story. 'The point I'm trying to make, Inspector, is that the young lady who helped me and my son to escape ...'

'Escape?' Maranus barked. 'Escape from what, for God's sake?'

'You locked us in our rooms. She let us out, and she helped us to get out of the house. In the dark.'

'This is absolute rubbish.' The Inspector's voice had dropped to a sinister purr now. 'I don't know anything about this. A member of my staff helped you to escape from a locked room? What an utter load of ... why *are* you telling me this?'

'Because she told me her name was Alex Cassidy.'

Maranus was about to spout another dismissive comment when the name caught him with his mouth open. It took a moment before he closed it again, and his stare was even more intimidating. 'She told you her name was Alex Cassidy?' he repeated.

Foley nodded, and Maranus leant across the desk and bushed a button on a black box. A female voice answered.

'Come in here, will you?'

'Right you are.'

A door opened nearby and shoes pattered across the wooden floor, and when the nun glided into the office she glanced at Sheffield. Then she looked at Foley and she gave a thoughtful frown.

'Sister Michael has a memory like a steel trap.' Maranus beamed up at her. 'Once you're in there, you are never forgotten.'

The nun's eyes were fixed on Foley and tight with curiosity, and she nodded when Maranus said, 'This fella says he was mistaken for Raymond Piece and we brought him here after the Black Bird Hotel incident back in ... when was it again?'

'I remember,' Sister Michael said. 'You weren't a guard then, obviously.'

Before Foley could answer she continued. 'You had your young fella with you, yeah? How is he, sure?'

Foley was thrown by the question and he took a moment to answer. 'He's grand, thank you.'

'Tell her about the woman who helped you to escape.' Maranus gave an impatient snort.

'Escape? Escape from where?'

'I'm after telling *him* that already,' Foley pointed to Maranus. 'We were locked in a room, and she let us out, and we got away.'

Maranus and the nun exchanged looks, and Maranus shrugged.

'Ah,' Sister Michael said suddenly. 'So that's what happened to you. We were wondering about that at the time, sure.'

'What do you mean *that's what happened to you*?' Foley gasped. 'Didn't you know what happened to us? Didn't you even bother to find out?'

'Why would we?' Sister Michael leant back against the desk. 'It didn't take us long to find out you were not Raymond Price, so you were no longer of interest to us. So when you and your boy weren't in your room the next morning we assumed you'd checked yourselves out and gone home.'

'I don't believe this,' Foley wiped sweat from his top lip. 'You just ...'

'For feck sake,' Maranus snapped. 'Just tell her what that woman told you.'

Sister Michael raised her eyebrows and looked severe as if to say get on with it. Foley did.

'She told me her name was Alex Cassidy.'

This time the nun gasped, and she looked at Maranus. 'Not *the* Alex Cassidy?'

Maranus put his hand up as if to say it was news to him too.

'No, it couldn't have been her.' Sister Michael rubbed her hands together in disbelief. 'Sure she was still working here when we got the call about her husband Seamus, and what happened to D'Lacey. So it couldn't have been the woman who ... you know, who let you out of your room, as you say.'

She turned around and stared into the fire as she rubbed her hands again in agitated bursts.

'Well, that's what she told me,' Foley insisted. 'She was desperate to leave this place because of the way you mistreated her. She was terrified of you and couldn't get away fast enough.'

Sister Michael glared at him 'What are you talking about? When did I ever ... she told you I mistreated her? When?'

'I saw you with my own eyes. You hit her in the face because she let me out of my room to see my boy.' He turned to Maranus. 'You were there. You saw it.'

'Oh, for Heaven's sake,' Sister Michael rolled her eyes. 'That was not Alex Cassidy. That was Mary what's-her-name, that useless mare who was upsetting everyone with her lies and her stories. She was a waste of human skin. We were going to dismiss her anyway.' She gave a sour chuckle. 'So that's what happened to her. She ran away with you. Well, well, well. That's another little mystery cleared up after all these years.'

Maranus gave another impatient grumble and sat back in his chair. 'And now your mind is put at rest, Guard. The woman you left here with was not Alex Cassidy. So if that's all, gentlemen, please excuse us. And feck off.'

Sister Michael chuckled at that and joined her hands in front of her as if she was going to pray. 'Will I be showing you out, so? Unless there's anything else, of course.'

'Yes.' Foley pulled the envelope from his pocket, picked out the photo and handed it to Maranus. 'Can I ask you something before we go? Do you know who these people are?'

Maranus leant forward and took the photo, and after studying it closely for a moment he handed it back with a shake of his head. 'No idea,' he mumbled.

As Foley leant over the desk to take back the photo, Maranus jumped up and snatched the envelope out of his hand. 'And what's this?'

Foley cursed and tried to grab it back, but Maranus had pushed his chair too far back from the desk. The Inspector squinted when he read the name and address on the envelope, and he turned it over before picking out the note. As he read the note he passed the photo and the envelope to Sister Michael, and she muttered under her breath as she studied them. She turned to Maranus with her eyes wide in amazement. 'Surely this can't be the … you know, what everyone is looking for?'

'Where did you get these?' Maranus made another deep grumble of a noise and he glared at Foley.

Foley glanced at Sheffield, and he took a moment before he answered. 'We found them in my mother's house in Tralee.'

The eyes that looked back at Foley were hostile, and he thought it was best to elaborate. 'When Alex … whatever her name was … helped us to escape, we went straight to Tralee and she stayed with us in my mother's house. But she left after about a year and we never heard from her again.'

Maranus drummed his fingers on the desk again. Foley flinched and rubbed his mouth. 'We found a purse that had fallen down behind a dresser in the kitchen. The note and the photo were in it. Det Sheffield was in Tralee at the time so I took it to him. And that's why we came here today, hoping to find out more about Alex Cassidy. And to see if we can identify the people in the photo.'

'Why take it to Detective Sheffield?'

Sheffield nodded at Foley. 'Guard Foley knows all about the D'Lacey affair. His step father was Inspector Liam Edge, who died trying to capture the Cassidys. So Guard Foley was briefed about the missing envelope, and anything else that was relevant to the case.'

Maranus wasn't impressed, but he didn't comment.

'Can it be true that Alex Cassidy was telling the truth all the time?' Sister Michael said to Maranus. 'She swore someone stole her purse from her room. Mary what's-her-name was sharing the room with her at the time. The thieving cow must have taken that purse when she disappeared. Yes, it all makes sense now.'

'For God's sake,' Maranus groaned. 'And you didn't think they were connected at the time?'

Sister Michael flushed and threw the photo and envelope back at him. 'I did not. How many times have those girls from the orphanage come here to work and then run away at the first opportunity? Anyway, I wasn't sorry to see the back of that one, I can tell you.'

'After you slapped her,' Foley added, and the nun gave a sharp gasp.

'You don't know anything, so shut your fat face.' Her eyes blazed and she looked like she was going to slap Foley too, so he stepped back away from her. 'A whole tribe of Gardaí top brass descended on us like a swarm of mad wasps, and they tore the place apart looking for something Seamus Cassidy was supposed to have stolen from a government minister.' She patted her chest as she drew breath. 'We were treated like something that was squeezed out of a cow's arse, like it was all our fault. One minute Leo … Inspector Maranus is a hero, and the next he's just a gobshite who couldn't be trusted to help in the investigation. So we were effectively put under house arrest. So don't you even …'

'Sister Michael,' Maranus put his hand out to her. 'Easy now. They don't need to know the details.'

He sat back and studied the note again, and it was hard to know what he was thinking behind the blank mask. Then he handed it to Sister Michael. 'So who is this Billy McStay? Is he someone who worked here?'

'I never heard of him,' the nun said. 'Maybe he's one of the young fellas in the photo.'

Maranus sucked at his lips. 'I don't think so. I'm sure the woman is Seamus Cassidy's mammy, and I'd put a bet on that the fella on the left is Seamus himself when he was probably still in school.'

He pointed at the photo to show Sister Michael and she squinted at it, but then she stepped back. 'How do you know that? When did you ever see Seamus Cassidy?'

'His wife had a picture of him in her room. Don't you remember? When the heavy mob arrived they kept asking us if we ever saw him here. They wouldn't believe he lived in town and never came near the place, even though his wife worked here, and lived here too. It was one of those strange relationships you read about in American magazines. She lives in one place, and he lives somewhere else.'

Sister Michael gave a lopsided grin. 'There's many a woman here in Ireland who would love to be in a relationship like that, only seeing the old fella once in a while when it suited her.'

Maranus threw the note at Foley. 'So do you know this Billy McStay?'

'I do not.' Foley folded the note and then picked up the envelope. 'We were hoping someone here might know who he was.'

Maranus sat back in his chair and put his hands over his face again, and he made a noise by sucking air through his fingers. 'I have to say, Detective Sheffield, you don't know very much at all.'

'Well, I can say the same about you, Inspector.'

Maranus dropped his hands from his face and the nun stepped away from the desk, and the air suddenly became a lot more charged than it already was.

'So what exactly are you two thinking?' Maranus gave a twist of his mouth. 'Do you think this note and this photo are some sort of clue to where the missing D'Lacey envelope might be hidden?'

'Well,' Sheffield was thrown by the change in tone, and he looked at Foley. 'That's what Guard Foley thought the moment he found the note. And I have to admit, when he showed it to me I felt the same.'

'And that's why we came up to Dublin,' Foley added, looking at Sister Michael to avoid having to face the dark glare Maranus was giving him. 'As we said, if we start at the very beginning, maybe we can retrace the steps Seamus Cassidy took after he … acquired? … the D'Lacey envelope.'

Maranus looked at Sister Michael too, and she gave the slightest of nods. Then Maranus growled as he sat back in his chair with a weary thud. 'Best you go now, Detective. And you too, Guard. I will see if I can find out who Billy McStay is. In the meantime, go and see Seamus Cassidy's mother and ask her if the photo means anything to her.'

Before any of them could answer, Maranus started writing on the back of the photo. 'She lives on this street. The second house on the left hand side by the streetlight. Don't ask me for the number.'

He shoved the photo at Sheffield. 'Come back in the morning and report to me here.' Then he stood up and pushed out his chest. 'But don't be wasting my time. If you don't have anything to report, do not come back.'

Chapter Nineteen

'You're not from around here, with your culchie accent.' The elderly woman sitting on a chair outside her front door sucked on a clay pipe, blew out a cloud of smoke and pointed the pipe at Foley. 'Cork, I'd say.'

Foley flushed at the mocking tone and his jaw tightened. 'Kerry, actually.'

'Thought so. You look like a culchie too. You can't hide that by putting on a garda uniform, I can tell you.'

Foley felt the colour rise in his face. 'That's not very nice …'

'You're a guard,' the woman answered, her eyes still mocking him. 'Who is ever nice to a guard? If you want nice you should become a priest or something. I ask you …'

'And I ask *you*, missus,' Foley couldn't hide the annoyance in his voice. 'For the second time, do you know where Mrs Cassidy is? We knocked on her door but we didn't get an answer.'

'And why would you?' Another cloud of smoke gushed from the corner of her mouth.

'What?'

'I said, why would you get an answer? The fella who lives there works on the buses, and his wife cleans in the council offices. They're out all day, so they are. They won't be home till the evening.'

'Right,' Foley said. 'So what about Mrs Cassidy? When will she be home?'

'Not today, I'm afraid.' Again the mocking tone. 'Mrs Cassidy hasn't lived in that house for years. Not since the day she fell down the steps and broke her back.'

Foley cringed, embarrassed by the fact they were the guards and they didn't know this. 'Oh, right. And when was that exactly?'

The lady spat on the pavement and wiped her mouth with her sleeve. This time the mocking tone was replaced with a contemptuous sneer, and she sucked on her pipe again before adding, 'I'll never forget it as long as I live, the poor creature. It was one of the worst days of my life seeing her lying on the street like that and everyone running to help her and calling for the guards, for what good it did her with her broken back and her son dead on the kitchen floor.'

'So you were there?' Sheffield was studying the three steps that led from the pavement to Mrs Cassidy's front door.

'I was, sure.' Another spit and a wipe of her mouth. 'Didn't I hear it all through the wall of my kitchen and me cooking the dinner for my lads for when they come home after a hard day working down in the docks. It was terrible all together. Really terrible.'

She sat back and soaked up the attention she wasn't expecting when she dragged her chair out to her usual spot on the pavement to smoke her daily dose of pipe tobacco. She had a gleeful glint in her eyes and she dragged out her moment until Foley eventually said, 'So what happened? What did you hear?'

She braced her mouth and took another moment to say, 'Well, first it was raised voices that went on for ages, then a sudden burst of screaming. It was Mrs Cassidy herself howling at the top of her voice, so I ran outside to see what in God's name was happening. And just as I got there didn't she come flying out of the door as if the devil himself was trying to grab her. Her face had the look of sheer terror on it, I swear to God. Anyway, she missed the step and she hit the pavement like a sack of spuds. There was a terrible crack, then total silence. But only for a second, mind you, because the pain hit her then and the howl of agony she let out made my stomach turn.'

She nodded gravely as she took another drag of her pipe.

'So what happened then?' Sheffield was paying more attention to her now and she blew a cloud of smoke at him.

'Didn't all the neighbours come running because that's the kind of people we are when one of us gets hurt? Betty Lynch was a nurse and Liam Fitzgerald was studying to be a vet, and they were on their knees trying to comfort her while the rest of us stood around looking to see if we could help at all. As I said, it was a terrible thing to witness, so it was.'

'And what about the son Tommy? Did you see what happened there?'

'No, I did not. There was a lot of commotion, what with poor Mrs Cassidy screaming in agony on the ground and all the neighbours buzzing around trying to help her. So no, I did not see what happened to Tommy.'

'So you didn't see his brother Seamus at the time?'

The lady snorted and blew another cloud of smoke at Sheffield. 'Seamus was never there. What the guards have been telling everyone is a pack of lies.'

Sheffield glanced at Foley who shook his head. 'But the Garda report said Seamus killed Tommy. That's the ...'

'Bullshit. Even someone with only half a brain wouldn't swallow that pile of crap. It's just a pack of downright lies.'

'How can you be so sure?'

'Because I was there.' This time it was closer to a scream. 'Seamus was not ever there, no matter what those ...' she indicated Foley with a nod of her head. '...ignorant bastards insist on telling you.'

Foley stepped back from the wagging pipe. 'Look, missus ...'

'Look yourself.' She swiped at him again. 'The only people who came out of that house were the two fellas with the long coats and trilby hats. No one else was in that house so don't be listening to those lying bastards anymore.'

She gave another smug grin when Foley and Sheffield stared at her with blank looks on their faces.

'I was the first to arrive at the Cassidy's front door after I heard all the roaring and screaming,' the woman nodded in emphasis and gave another dramatic sweep of the pipe.

'And I was the one who saw Mrs Cassidy miss her footing and fall down the steps right there. So I was right there when all our neighbours came running. I was right in front of the door and looking that way when I saw the two men sneaking out. They looked really shifty, I can tell you. Eyes everywhere like cornered rats. And as the crowd got bigger they slipped out and went off down the street never to be seen again.'

Sheffield gave her a cynical grin. 'And did you tell that to the guards?'

'The feckin guards?' she yelled. 'The feckin guards saw them too.' She almost took the end off her pipe with the angry bite she gave it, and she glared at Foley again. 'The guard who was there saw them too. And what's more, he knew them.'

'What guard?' was all Foley could get out.

'It was the usual fella who'd been around here for ages. We saw him nearly every day doing his rounds. So when Mrs Cassidy fell he came running too. And when I saw the two men appear at the door I looked over at the guard and he was staring up at them. And from the look on his face it was obvious he knew them. He actually nodded at them. They nodded back and one of them touched his nose as if to say you never saw us. The guard winked and turned away pretending to be distracted by what was happening to Mrs Cassidy.'

Sheffield thought about that for a moment then sucked at his teeth. 'So how did you find out Tommy Cassidy was dead? Did you go into the house?'

'I did not,' the woman snapped. 'I stayed with Mrs Cassidy until the doc arrived and they took her to the hospital.'

'So …'

'But I do remember her front door was shut because someone was asking where Tommy was because he needed to be told about his mammy. And when they knocked on the door they didn't get any answer. So they tried opening it, only it was locked. And I swear it was the fellas with the hats that pulled it shut behind them because they were trying to hide what they'd done.'

'What?' Foley stayed out of reach of the pipe as the question spurted out. 'Are you trying to say Tommy was killed by those men? How did you come to that conclusion, for God's sake?'

The lady's eyebrows leapt up to her hairline with the sharp laugh she gave. 'Because not long after they took Mrs Cassidy away, a wagon full of guards arrived and beat the door down. Then were shouting about a body being found in the kitchen with his head caved in.' She wiped dribble from her chin and rubbed her hand on her shirt. 'So how did they even know there was a body in there, in the kitchen? Who told them that? It wasn't Mrs Cassidy herself because she was knocked out by the medication they gave her for the pain. And why did they immediately start blaming Seamus when no one saw Seamus anywhere near the house? No, it had to be the two gobshites I saw coming out of the house while the poor Mrs Cassidy was roaring in agony on the pavement outside her own front door. So tell me that's not as odd as two left shoes.'

'So why didn't you tell them all that,' Foley insisted.

'Told who?'

'The guards. When they were knocking on the doors looking for witnesses. Surely you told them what you saw.'

This time the lady almost choked on the laugh that spurted out with a cloud of smoke. 'No one came knocking on the doors, you feckin dope. They were in the house for less than half an hour banging and clattering before they took the body out wrapped in a blanket. And then they were gone. They didn't speak to any of us, or any of the people who were outside in the street gawping at them as they went about their charade.'

'What about the guard you said came running when Mrs Cassidy fell? Didn't you speak to him?'

'Well, surprise, surprise, we never set eyes on him again. An older fella turned up the next day but he was a crusty old maggot who looked like he'd give you a belt of his stick if you didn't keep out of his way.'

She studied her pipe as if she was debating lighting it again. Sheffield stepped back into the road and looked up and down the street. 'So where is Mrs Cassidy now?'

'If she's still alive.' The woman decided her time with her pipe was over and she shuffled to her feet. 'I'm told she went to live with her late husband's sister out in the country when she came out of hospital. A place called Patch. It's about thirty miles out on the Cavan road.'

She tapped the side of her head and gave a sad frown. 'But from what I heard she was never right up there after what happened to her. But how can you blame her for that? One of her young fellas was dead and the other was hunted like a fox for something he couldn't have done in the first place because he wasn't even there.'

She picked up her chair and paused as she put one foot on the bottom step. 'Anyway, that all happened years ago. So what is a Kerry guard doing here now asking about it and digging it all up again?'

Foley took out the photo and showed it to her. 'Before you go, can I ask you, is this Mrs Cassidy?'

The woman put the chair down on the step and held the photo up to the light as she squinted at it, and her face creased. 'Oh, you poor wee lamb. What did they do to you? Doesn't she look so happy there? She was so proud of her boys, you know? And they were such lovely young men. It's not fair, is it?'

She handed the photo back to Foley. 'Seamus was a gambler, you know. But he was a kind and gentle soul. He always looked after his mammy. If he had a big win he'd take her out and treat her like a queen.'

Then her face fell and she shook her head as she picked up the chair again. 'We did wonder if what happened here was because of his gambling. Do you know what I mean?

Did Seamus get on the wrong side of some bad people and they came looking for him? Only Tommy got in the way. You never know, do you?'

She gave Foley another contemptuous glare and carried on up the steps, pushed the door open and went into the hall. 'And the guards were feckin useless. We often wondered if they were part of it too. The whole thing had a rotten stink about it.'

She didn't look back as she slammed the door.

Chapter Twenty

Patch was at the end of the longest straight road Foley had ever seen. At least five miles long, it followed the contour of the land, often sweeping down sever dips into deep valleys. Several times Foley had to hold on tight to the dashboard while Sheffield's fingers were white from gripping the steering wheel as the car rattled and rocked over the rough surface that had patches of packed snow and potholes that could have swallowed a small dog. Then the road would traipse back up even steeper slopes on the other side of the dip, and it was sheer will power that got the old jalopy all the way to the top.

From the crest of the last hill they could see several cottages dotted around the patchwork of fields that swept away into the haze hovering around the base of the distant mountains. Foley checked the handwritten note they'd been given by the duty guard back at the barracks. 'Drive on until you reach a sharp bend. You can't miss it. Patch will be right in front of you, through the gate and over the cattle grid.'

The bend was a lot sharper than Sheffield expected, almost at right angles. Which didn't matter if you were approaching it while driving a pony and trap. But if you were travelling any faster than that and you weren't warned about it, it could have been lethal. Sheffield was through the gate to Patch, over the cattle grid and skidding to a halt in the middle of a cobbled courtyard before he had time to adjust his bearings.

The young woman with the yard broom gave them a casual look as if to say bemused travellers appearing out of nowhere was not unusual, and she kept on sweeping the sludge into the gutter as the two men got out of the car and strolled over to her.

'Good day to you,' Foley said. 'I wonder if you can help us.'

The young woman had soft warm features and an easy smile, and she raised her eyebrows in question. Foley said, 'We understand Mrs Rose Cassidy lives here.'

He gave a quick glance around the cobbled yard. There were stables on one side and a huge barn on the other. Straight in front of them was the main house. It was surrounded by a small wall that separated it from the courtyard, and the neat patch of garden had borders of winter flowers and neatly trimmed bushes.

'Yes, Aunty Rose lives here.' The young woman nodded towards a narrow path that skirted the far side of the house and she gave Foley a suspicious glare. 'Why?'

'Well, we were wondering if we could have a quick word with her,' Foley answered, and when he looked at the young woman properly he realised that, behind the gentle features, there was a sharp intelligence in her bright blue eyes. And for some strange reason he suddenly felt as if he was about to be caught lying to the teacher. He quickly checked himself and said, 'I'm Guard Foley, by the way. And this is Detective Sheffield.'

'I'm Peg.' She nodded at each of them. 'I'm the youngest. My sisters are all out in the fields. My dad is out there too, and my Mom will be in the house somewhere.'

'Right,' Foley turned towards the house but Peg put out her hand.

'Aunty Rose won't talk to you,' she told him. 'She would never talk to the guards.'

'Oh?' Sheffield pulled the collar of his coat up against the icy breeze that was rippling around the corner of the barn. 'Why would that be, so?'

Peg blinked as if the question was incredibly stupid, and she shook her head in disbelief. 'Because she blames you for killing her son.'

The frown on Sheffield's face deepened and he looked at Foley. Foley shrugged and Peg gave a sigh that was loaded with annoyance.

'So why do you want to talk to her now?' she asked. 'You didn't want to talk to her all those years ago, so you didn't. All the times she tried to tell you what happened to her son Tommy, and you treated her like an imbecile. She was in a wheelchair after breaking her back and she was frightened and hysterical after seeing her son beaten to death by two detectives. But all you did was try to have her committed to a lunatic asylum because you were desperate to cover up what your colleagues had done. So you can understand why she looks on the guards in the same way she'd look at a field full of cow shit.'

Her face had darkened with the flash of anger and she brushed back a strand of hair that had escaped from under her woollen hat.

'I'm ... we are so sorry to hear that.' Foley tried to hold eye contact with her but the intensity of her stare forced him to look away. 'We don't want to ...' he started to say, but he was suddenly conscious that he sounded as if he was just making a load of insincere noises. So he looked at Sheffield for guidance. Sheffield rubbed the inside of his collar with his finger and made some grumbling sounds, then he put his hand on Foley's shoulder.

'Sure that's the reason we're here now,' he said, and his head was nodding as the sudden thoughts came pouring into his mind. 'We're part of a unit that follows up on cases that are still unresolved. We look for any new information that might help us with the case.' He put on the most sincere face he could muster. 'Fresh eyes and a bit of old fashioned detective work, our Inspector always says. So we were asked to look into Mrs Cassidy's case, which is why we're here today.'

Peg stared at him in silence, and her mouth was a tight line that said she didn't believe a word of it. Sheffield was like Foley, the intensity of Peg's stare made him look away and he tried to distract her by walking towards the house.

'Is it alright if we go in?'

'She'll be in the sunroom at the back of the house.' Peg reluctantly fell into step with him. 'But let me go in first and warn her the guards are coming so she won't be taken by surprise and start throwing things at you.'

There was a strange glee in Peg's voice at the thought of that. She pushed ahead and looked through the window before gently pulling the door open. The lady in the wheelchair had a shawl around her shoulders and a cup of tea in her hand, and she was staring into the distance with a contented smile on her face.

Peg pointed to a tray of medication on the sideboard on the far side of the room. 'You should know, Aunty Rose takes some very strong medicine because of the pain in her back,' she said to the guards in a stage whisper. 'And because of that she'd often ... well, confused would be the word I'd use.'

'Oh, right,' Foley said, and he waited until Peg walked over to her aunt and put her arm around her shoulder before he followed her into the sunroom. Sheffield came in behind him and stood back by the wall.

'Aunty Rose?'

Mrs Cassidy looked up at her niece and gave a beaming smile. 'Hello darling, is dinner ready?' She put her cup on a small table beside her and started taking the shawl off. 'What are we having today?'

'No, Aunty Rose.' Peg took her hand and gave it a gentle squeeze. 'You have some visitors.'

'Oh,' Mrs Cassidy's smile was even brighter when she turned to Foley, and when she spotted Sheffield she gave a joyful gasp.

'Mossie Hobbert,' she beamed. 'How nice to see you again. What brings you all the way out here? It must be months since we last saw you.'

Peg looked at Sheffield and shook her head. 'No, Aunty Rose. That isn't Mossie.'

'What?' Mrs Cassidy tried to turn her wheelchair around to get a better look at the man by the wall.

'Aunty Rose, these gentlemen are here about your accident.'

Rose Cassidy looked at her niece, then at Foley, and finally at Sheffield who came closer and gave her a quick wave. Her smile had already frozen and now it faded into a serious pout.

'Mrs Cassidy,' Sheffield put on his most concerned voice. 'If it's alright with you, can we ask you about the day you fell and injured yourself?'

Mrs Cassidy's eyes flickered from Sheffield to Peg and back to Sheffield again. Then she gave a cautious nod and Sheffield asked, 'Can I ask you about Seamus?'

The frown on Mrs Cassidy's face deepened into a sadness that made her turn away and stare out of the window, and her hand went to her mouth to smother a sob. Peg rushed over and put her arm around her shoulders again and she glared at Sheffield.

'Maybe this is not a good idea,' she said to him, but then Mrs Cassidy took Peg's hand and held it to her chest.

'Seamus,' she sighed. 'My poor wee lamb.' And she gave an even deeper sigh. 'I see him every day, you know. And he still looks as handsome as the first time I ever set eyes on him.'

The pause that followed was awkward, and Peg was about to speak again when Mrs Cassidy sat back up in her wheelchair. She let go of Peg's hand before clasping both of hers to her chest. 'It was such a beautiful summer evening. We were gathered as usual by the crossroads waiting for Sean McCarthy to arrive with his fiddle so the dancing could begin. Sean was never late, but this Sunday he was, and we were starting to get worried. Anyway, when he did turn up he brought the most handsome young fella I'd ever seen in my whole life with him. He had one of those small banjo things ... you know, a yuke something.'

'Ukulele?'

'Yes, he had one of them. And Holy Mother of God and the wee baby, didn't he make the most beautiful music come out of it. We hopped and we bopped all night until we could hardly stand on our poor weary feet anymore. And I was totally smitten by that young fella. I'm ashamed to say I practically threw myself at him and he had no choice but to walk me home.'

Her eyes sparkled and a tear escaped and slipped quietly down her cheek. 'They were such happy, sweet times. Me and my beautiful Seamus. Such sweet times. Then one day he was gone, taken from us in the blink of an eye, leaving me a widow with two young boys to bring up on my own.' She brushed the tear away. 'And not a day goes by when I don't say good morning to him. I still miss every bone of his beautiful body.'

Her gaze drifted off into the distance again as she savoured the memories, and a respectful silence filled the sunroom. Peg got a glass of water from the side table and Mrs Cassidy took it but she didn't drink from it.

After a while Peg took Mrs Cassidy's hand again. 'Aunty Rose, is it alright if the gentlemen talk to you again? They want to know what happened on the day you fell down the steps.'

Mrs Cassidy looked around at Sheffield. 'Why? Sure didn't I tell you all that already, Mossie? What more can I tell you? I told you everything I know.'

Peg tucked the shawl around her aunt's shoulders as she gave Sheffield a wide eyed look, and she went across to the sideboard pretending to fetch something as she beckoned him to come closer. Just out of Mrs Cassidy's hearing she said, 'She thinks you're the family solicitor, Mossie Hobbert. He's a great friend and a lovely man. Mossie supported her from the very beginning. It was Mossie who stopped them having her committed to the lunatic asylum when she was hysterical and showing off. But apart from that, he got nowhere when he went up against the guards. They threw a wall of obstacles around everything he tried to do, blocking and dodging every question he asked about what went on in her house that day.'

Sheffield nodded and his face was set in an understanding frown. He straightened his tie and moved closer to Mrs Cassidy. She glanced up at him and gave an inpatient wave at the chair by the window.

'For God's sake, Mossie. Will you please sit down and not be hovering around me like a nervous butterfly.'

Sheffield was reluctant to get too close in case Mrs Cassidy realised her mistake, but she had an adamant look on her face and didn't really scrutinise him.

'So,' Sheffield sat down and tugged the collar of his coat a little bit higher. 'Can I ask you about Seamus, your boy? Did you see him on the day you had your accident?'

At that moment Mrs Cassidy noticed Foley and she jerked up straight with an angry gasp. 'What are … you brought a guard here? You brought a guard to my house? Why in God's name would you bring a guard to my house, Mossie?'

Peg moved between her aunt and Foley and put her hand Mrs Cassidy's shoulder. 'No, Aunty Rose. It isn't what you're thinking. I promise you. These gentlemen are here because they're looking into what really happened the morning you had your accident.'

'But I told them all that already. I told them a million times and they didn't believe a word I said then. They made out I was mad and they tried to lock me away. They made out it was all in my mind and I was suffering from some sort of hallucinations and I needed to be strapped into a straightjacket and locked in a padded cell. They didn't believe a word I said then. So why would they pretend to believe me now?'

'Mrs Cassidy,' Foley put out his hand to her but she sat back away from him. 'We just want to know the truth.'

'The truth?' she yelped. ''Tis the same truth that was there from day one but you ignored it completely. Why are you going to accept it now?'

'Because it's what we do.' Foley started to repeat what Sheffield had said to Peg, but he caught the smirk in her eyes and he couldn't bring himself to lie so brazenly. So he said, 'We just want to know exactly what happened that day.'

Mrs Cassidy took a long drink of water from the glass she was still holding, and she straightened up in her wheelchair. Peg rubbed her aunt's shoulder and adjusted the shawl around her, tucking it in at the sides. ''Tis all right, Aunty Rose,' she purred. 'You can talk to them, all right?'

Mrs Cassidy closed her eyes and bent her head forward as if she was in the Confessional box at church. 'All right,' she whispered.

'Thank you,' Sheffield said. 'So can you tell us if you saw Seamus at all on that morning when you were hurt?'

'I did.' She smothered the sob with her hand. Then she took a deep breath and added, 'Tommy was still in bed and I went out to the lavatory in the backyard. When I came back in Seamus was standing by the fire looking up at the statue of The Sacred Heart on the mantelpiece. I nearly jumped out of my skin because he looked so much like his late father. But he had an odd look on his face as if he was saying his prayers. When he saw me he pretended to be fine, but I could tell there was something troubling him. At first I thought it might be his wife, Alex. She had been getting broody lately, saying she wanted more from their marriage. Like a proper home where they could live together. And children. You know, all that kind of stuff. But he said there was nothing wrong with Alex. Everything was fine between them. So I immediately thought it was something to do with his gambling, and he might be going to ask me for money to get himself out of a bit of trouble. And I felt sick to my stomach because I was in no position to help him. I didn't have two brass pennies to rub together myself, so I had no money to help my son out of a bit of bother. And I have regretted it every day of my life since.'

She rubbed her eyes with her fingers then joined her hands together in her lap again. 'But he didn't ask me for anything. I said the kettle was on and would I be getting him a bit of toast or something, but he said he couldn't stop because he had to meet Billy McStay in town. Then he kissed me on the cheek and that was the last time I ever saw my baby boy.'

She took a handkerchief from her sleeve and wiped her nose, and she clasped it in her hand on her lap. Peg rubbed her shoulder again.

'So who is Billy McStay?' Sheffield asked after a pause.

'He was a cousin,' Peg answered. 'He and Seamus were best pals. They grew up together. You'd think they were joined at the hip, the way they hung around together. No two greater friends could be found in Dublin, I can tell you.'

Mrs Cassidy sighed and sat back in her wheelchair, and Peg looked over at Sheffield and raised her eyebrows as if to say *is that it?* Foley took the envelope out of his pocket but before he could take the note out too Mrs Cassidy continued with her story.

'But there was obviously something wrong,' she said in a voice that was more strained and angry now. 'Because he'd hardly been out of the house for ten minutes when there was a loud banging on the front door. And would you believe it, before I could open the door and see who it was, didn't these two big fellas come barging in and pushed me all the way back into the kitchen. And all the time they were roaring and screaming wanting to know where Seamus was. I told them I didn't know and that I only saw him once in a while but they kept saying he robbed someone and if I didn't tell them where he was I'd be charged with aiding and abetting a criminal and I'd be dragged off to jail and locked up for years.'

She seemed to choke suddenly and covered her mouth with her hand. Then she looked up at Peg before she continued. 'That's when Tommy came flying down the stairs, and when he saw the way they were pushing me around he tried to protect me. But the two of them started belting him with their truncheons. They hit him such a ferocious belt around the back of the head he dropped straight down and cracked his face on the floor. I couldn't believe what I was seeing, my little boy lying on my kitchen floor with his head cracked open like a busted egg. There was a dreadful silence. The two fellas were stunned. They just stood there staring down at what they'd done.'

Mrs Cassidy gave a huge ripple of a shiver and clasped her hands tighter in her lap. 'The next thing I remember is the screams tearing from my throat and me running down the hallway, then I'm lying on the pavement with a pain that was impossible to describe. After that everything was a blur. I'm in the hospital dosed up to the eyeballs with all sorts of medication. I'm screaming in agony not just from the pain in my back but from knowing my boy was lying dead in my kitchen, and some guards turn up to tell me they're looking for Seamus for the murder of his brother.'

She gave another huge disbelieving shiver. 'I'm afraid I lost all control of myself. I tried to tell them about the two detectives who came to my house looking for Seamus, and that it was them that killed Tommy. But I was pinned to the bed and stabbed with needles. Whatever they injected me with made me even more agitated, and they threatened to put me in a straight jacked and lock me up in a looney bin. But I wasn't going to let those maggots get away with it. I was going to make such a fuss it would be heard across the whole country. They were not going to shut me up, I can tell you.'

Another pause and another angry shiver. 'But of course they *did* shut me up. They could shout louder than me. They had the ears of all the newspaper editors in the country. They painted me as a hysterical mother who couldn't accept that one of her sons robbed someone then killed his brother who was probably involved in the robbery as well. They implied it was because I was such a rotten mother that the boys turned out the way they did. So no matter how many times I tried to tell my story, no one would listen. Their reaction varied from pity for the disillusioned auld mad woman, to rage that I was allowed to bring such horrible monsters into the world in the first place. So gradually they wore me down. Pick your fights carefully, my auld da used to say. Stick with the ones you believe you can win, and walk away from the rest.'

She looked up at Foley with wet eyes. 'I haven't got the strength to run with this anymore, Guard. Will you take the baton and run with it for me?'

Foley jerked up straight and glanced at Sheffield, and the detective gave a lopsided grin as Foley struggled to answer. Instead he held out the photo he was holding.

'Mrs Cassidy, do you recognise this photo?'

Mrs Cassidy rummaged down the side of her wheelchair and pulled out a pair of reading glasses, and she screwed up her nose as she put them on before she took the photo. She held it up to the light to study it. Peg leant in to get a look, and she gave a joyous squeal. 'Oh look, tis the lads. Don't they look grand? When was this taken, Aunty Rose?'

But immediately a shadow clouded Peg's face and she stepped back, and instinctively her arm went around her aunt's shoulder. Mrs Cassidy's hand went to her mouth and the sound that filtered through her fingers was a mix of grief and rage.

'Oh my beautiful boys. Look how happy they were, standing there with their whole future before them.' She touched each face with her finger and then held the photo to her lips. 'My beautiful, beautiful boys. What did they do to you?'

When she looked up at Sheffield again her eyes seemed enormous behind the thick reading glasses. 'How did you get hold of this, Mossie? The last time I saw this it was on the mantelpiece in my kitchen.'

'Well, from what I understand, Seamus sent it to his wife Alex.'

'What? Why?'

Foley took the note out of the envelope and handed it to Mrs Cassidy. 'He wanted her to give it to Billy McStay.'

Peg took the note from her aunt and read it out loud. Then she read it again and waved it at Sheffield. 'Why would he do that?'

'Well,' Foley said, 'we're hoping your aunt might know the answer to that. What would it mean to Billy McStay?'

Peg looked at her aunt who just shook her head. 'Well, don't ask me. Billy and Seamus were close all right, but what this picture would mean to him I have no idea. I remember it was taken by the fella who did the school photos, and it cost a few bob for him to come around and take one in your house. But Billy wasn't there. Well, as far as I remember anyway.'

She looked at the photo again and then held it to her chest. Foley took the note from Peg but Mrs Cassidy was clutching the photo too tightly, so he put the note back in the envelope as he waited for the opportunity to recover the photo.

'So where does Billy McStay live?' he asked Peg. 'Perhaps he can tell us what it means to him.'

'In St Patrick's cemetery.' Mrs Cassidy looked up at Foley and nodded at the look on his face, and she waited for the obvious question before she elaborated. 'He died years ago too. And there was a big question about that as well, but again the guards covered it up.'

'Careful, Aunty Rose,' her niece wagged her finger at her. 'That's a guard you're talking to. You don't want to get yourself into trouble for saying things like that, now do you?'

Mrs Cassidy gave an angry groan and tapped the arm of her wheelchair with her finger. 'But isn't it strange that he should die so soon after they came looking for Seamus? And I blame myself. I must have mentioned Billy to the men who were attacking me, so they went after him too. The bastards were determined to get my boy. And I still have no idea why. No one would tell me who he was supposed to have robbed. Or what he was supposed to have stolen. But it must have been important enough to kill Tommy and Billy over it. But no one would tell me anything. Even after they shot Seamus and Alex down in Kerry, they still wouldn't tell me what it was all about.'

She swallowed and wiped her mouth, then she pressed the photo against her chest again. 'In fact no one told me anything at all. I only found out about the shooting from a reporter who was following the story, but he went away and never came back.'

Foley felt an angry bubble swell up in his stomach and he got a mad impulse to let it all spill out. Tell Aunty Rose about the whole bag of lies and deceit. That a whole country was dancing to the tune of one man who was fortunate enough to be born into a rich and powerful family. How can it be that brave people who risk their lives every day to uphold the law can be cowed down by someone like that? Why are they so afraid to challenge him, expose the hypocrisy of the whole system? Too many people had died already to cover up one man's embarrassment. Enough was enough.

'So what happened to Billy?' Sheffield asked, and Foley's moment was lost. 'How did he die?'

'He drowned while fishing, according to the guards.' Peg closed her eyes as if to say she didn't believe that was what really happened, and she leant against the arm of her aunt's wheelchair.

'According to the guards?' Sheffield queried.

Peg gave an angry pout. 'The thing is, Billy fished in the same stretch of the river since he was big enough to fit into a pair of waders, so he knew every inch of it. But they found his body farther upstream in a place where Billy would never fish because he said it was useless. So why was he even there? The guards said he must have slipped and hit his head on a rock, knocked himself out and landed in a deep pool by the bank where he drowned. His broken rod was found some distance away.'

'God, that's awful.' Foley made a sympathetic gesture with his head.

'But there were questions which the guards refused to answer.' Peg's face had turned an angry shade of pink again. 'Like, why was his tin box of handmade flies still on the rock by his usual spot? Billy spent hours making those flies and there's no way he would leave them there if he was fishing somewhere else. Also, if the rod broke when he fell and hit his head, why was it so far away from the body?'

'I suppose it's possible he …'

'And then, why were there so many bruises on the body? Obviously if he fell onto the rocks there would be some defensive wounds, like to his hands when he tried to break his fall, and maybe to his knees as well. But along with the bruise on his head that was caused when he hit it on the rocks, his jaw was dislocated and his nose was broken. Several teeth had been knocked out and three ribs were cracked. According to Billy's family, the doctor who attended to the body thought Billy had been in a car crash, there were so many cuts and bruises on him. Yet on the death certificate it just said death by drowning. So that was the end of it. No inquest. No guards report. No witnesses. Maybe tis another case for your special unit to look into, isn't it, Guard Foley?' She gave Foley a curious look as if challenging him to respond.

But all he did was nod and look away.

'So,' Sheffield injected. 'That still leaves the big question. Why did Seamus want his wife to give the photo to Billy McStay? It must have meant something. But now Billy and Seamus are … no longer with us, we will probably never know. Which is a shame.'

'A shame indeed,' Peg said and she raised her eyebrows at Foley. 'So what happens now? Where do you go from here?'

Her mocking tone made Foley cringe, and he grunted as he struggled for a response that wouldn't sound like an obvious lie. 'Well,' he heard himself saying, trying to inject some sincerity into his voice. 'We will have to go back to the beginning and look at all the reports about Seamus and Tommy ...'

Peg snorted and turned away, and she folded her arms tightly across her chest.

'When we go back to ...' Foley continued, but Peg put her hand up.

'Don't,' she snapped.

'What?' Foley was startled by the sharpness of her voice, and her eyes were tight in a furious squint as she turned back to him.

'Do not continue with this ridiculous charade.'

'Look, I'm very sorry if we upset you,' Foley put his hand on his heart. 'But I really think we ...'

'... should be going now.' Peg went across to the door and pulled it open. ''Tis obvious you haven't found what you were hoping to find, so there's no point standing there like a couple of eejits anymore. I'm sorry you came all this way out here for nothing, but I wish you the best of luck anyway.'

Foley had the mad urge again to tell her the real reason they'd come here today. Tell her about D'Lacey's deeds and the enormous cover up of Tommy's murder. Tell her about the reward money, the poisonous thirty pieces of silver that justified it all. But Sheffield pushing past him to the door stopped him, and instead he put on his cap and gave Peg a regretful nod.

'I am really sorry for your loss,' he told her.

Peg shrugged and pulled the door open wider, but she didn't answer.

'So where's my statue now?' Mrs Cassidy called out, looking around at the parting figures. 'Mossie? Do you know? Where is my statue now?'

Sheffield pulled his coat tighter around him as he looked at Peg for an answer, but she held the door open and nodded for him to leave.

'Peg,' Mrs Cassidy called out again, and this time her voice had a rasping irritation to it. 'What's going on? Where's Mossie? Mossie, where are you?'

She leant forward and reached for the brake so she could turn her wheelchair around but she knocked her glass of water off the table. And in her desperation to stop it hitting the floor she almost toppled out of her wheelchair. The roar of frustration drowned out the crash of the breaking glass, and Peg ran to grab her. Sheffield moved fast too, and he managed to catch her arm and help her to sit back in the wheelchair. She cursed with embarrassment and shifted herself back into a comfortable position, and Peg straightened the shawl around her shoulders.

She gave an angry hiss as she glanced up at Sheffield, and for a second a shadow of confusion crossed her face. She turned to Peg and then back to Sheffield, but he'd moved away from her and in that brief second she seemed to have forgotten what was bothering her.

She held out the photo to him and asked again, 'So what happened to my statue? The one in the picture. The statue of The Sacred Heart.'

Sheffield turned to Peg but she shook her head because she had no idea what happened to it.

'Will I go and ask Mammy?' she said to Mrs Cassidy. 'She'll know what happened to your stuff when they cleared out your house.'

'Well, it isn't in my room.' Mrs Cassidy was clearly agitated now and she gripped the arm of her wheelchair.

'But you have a lovely statue of The Virgin Mary, don't you Aunty Rose? Tis a beautiful statue. You said so yourself. You say your prayers to her every night.'

'I know that, Peg my darling. It is a beautiful statue and thank you for putting it in my room. But my statue of The Sacred Heart was special, you see? And I can't believe I'd forgotten about it. How could I forget about our special statue? Our secret place? It was so precious to us, and yet I forgot all about it. How could that happen? I must be doting or something.' Her eyes filled up suddenly and a tear escaped and trickled down her cheek.

'Ah now, Aunty Rose, please don't be crying.' Peg had a sob in her own voice as she put her arm around her aunt's shoulder. 'I'm sure tis around here somewhere. I'll go and find Mammy and I'll ask her. She will remember where it went, I'm sure.'

'Tis not just the statue, though,' Mrs Cassidy took Peg's hand and squeezed it. 'I don't remember how much money was in it at the time, but whatever it was I'd rather you had it, Peg. It might only be a few pounds but it should be yours because you deserve it for the kindness you show me every day.'

'Aw, that's really kind of you, Aunty Rose.' Peg smiled and kissed the top of her aunt's head. 'But I'm not sure I know what you mean. What money are you talking about?'

Mrs Cassidy squinted and her eyes became distant again as she looked out the window. She licked her lips and rubbed her mouth, and for a moment she seemed to be confused. But just as quick she sat back and her eyes lit up again.

'Any spare change we had left at the end of the week we used to put in the statue,' she told them. 'It was like a safe to us. If any gobshite broke in to rob the place, they would never think of looking in a statue of The Sacred Heart. They'd be too frightened to touch it anyway in case they were struck down dead by the good Lord himself.'

There was a chuckle in her voice as she smiled up at Peg, and Peg gave her a sympathetic smile. But her eyes said she still had no idea what her aunt was talking about.

'I'll go and ask Mammy,' she repeated, and Mrs Cassidy stared out the window again as she remembered the good old days.

'I kept stuff in there if I needed to hide it from Seamus,' she said in such a soft voice Foley thought she was speaking to herself. He moved closer and watched her reflection in the window, hoping to lip read the bits he couldn't hear.

'If I got a bill I didn't want him to see I'd shove it in the statue so he would never know I got it.' She gave a deep sad sigh. 'He never even knew about the statue. The boys did, of course, and they would put the odd couple of bob in it every now and then. Especially in the run up to Christmas so I would be able to buy something extra for the big day.'

'How did you do that?' Sheffield couldn't contain his curiosity any longer. 'I mean, how do you put stuff into a statue?'

'Ah sure, wasn't there a big hole in the back of it? Back in my mother's day, the statue got knocked over and a thick sliver broke off the back. It came away in one tidy piece and it fitted on again by gently pushing it back into place. Me and the boys could do it blindfolded, and if anyone looked at it they wouldn't even know it was there at all.'

Foley didn't need to look at Sheffield to know the detective was intrigued by this bit of information. He knew exactly what the detective was thinking. How big was that statue? Mrs Cassidy was holding the photo out in front of her and Foley leant closer to get a better look at it. On the mantelpiece above the range the statue looked quite big, but in relation to Mrs Cassidy and the boys, it was hard to tell. Foley calculated it as being no more than eighteen inches tall. He glanced at Sheffield to gauge if he was thinking the same thing. Would it be big enough to hide an envelope with the deeds of a house in it? Both of them remembered Mrs Cassidy saying Seamus was standing in front of the statue when she saw him on the morning of the accident. It was as if he was saying his prayers, she said.

Foley wondered about the note to Billy McStay. Would Billy have known about the statue? He probably would, because it's one of those strange family secrets close pals would have joked about. And that is why Seamus wanted him to have the photo. He would instantly know what was meant by *Safe in The Sacred Heart.*

All they needed now was for Mrs Cassidy to remember what happened to the statue. And it wasn't long before they found out.

The woman who came rushing in the door was an older version of Peg, with the same kind open face and the same bright intelligent eyes. But she wasn't pleased to see a uniformed guard and a detective questioning her vulnerable sister-in-law, and she threw a protective shield around her with her arms.

'Rose, what's going on here?' She glared at Foley as she shouted the question.

Mrs Cassidy held out the photo to her. 'Eileen love, I was just asking young Peg about my auld statue of The Sacred Heart I used to keep on my mantelpiece. Do you know what became of it? I'm afraid I forgot all about it until Mossie showed me this photo.'

'Mossie?' Eileen gasped and glared even harder at Sheffield. 'That's not Mossie. What the feck are you trying to pull here, you maggot? Why are you pretending to be Mossie?'

'Eileen, do you know where my statue is or not? I want to know if there's any money in it. And if there is, I want young Peg to have it because she deserves every penny. I don't want it going to anyone else.'

Eileen looked from Sheffield to Foley, then at Mrs Cassidy and back at Sheffield again.

'What are you talking about, Rose dear? What money are you … I don't understand what you're saying, I'm afraid.'

'My statue of The Sacred Heart,' Mrs Cassidy pointed to it in the photo. 'Do you know what happened to it?'

Eileen studied the photo. 'Oh yeah. I remember now. You gave it to Sister Gabriel, remember?'

'Who?'

'Sister Gabriel. The nun who looked after you when you were in St Kevin's. You were very fond of her.'

Mrs Cassidy's brow became a jumble of confused lines and she stared at the photo as if it would remind her of what happened during her time in hospital. But it was still a long moment before her eyes suddenly lit up again.

'Oh right. Sister Gabriel. I remember her now. She was a lovely lady.' Mrs Cassidy stared at the photo again and the lines on her forehead came back. 'But why would I be giving her a statue of The Sacred Heart, for heaven's sake? It was just an auld statue. It was old and battered. Why would a nun be wanting an old thing like that?'

'Don't you remember?' Eileen told her. 'It was when we had that terrible storm and it blew the branch off a tree right through the chapel window. It broke the beautiful stained glass window and shattered the statue of The Virgin Mary, along with the picture of Our Lord on the Cross. The nuns were really upset about it all, so you told them they could have your statue of The Sacred Heart so they would have something to pray to while the repairs were carried out.'

Mrs Cassidy took another moment to recapture the memories and when she did she beamed. 'Oh shur, I remember now. They put it up on that high shelf behind the small altar. They had to use a ladder to get it up there. And they were so grateful for it, didn't the priest say a special mass of thanksgiving?'

'So what's this all about?' Eileen asked again. 'Why are the guards here asking about a holy statue?'

Sheffield gave her his best unthreatening smile. 'We're sorry to have imposed on you out of the blue like this, but we're following up on an old case.'

'What old case?' Eileen's eyes flashed with the same angry look Peg had given him earlier. 'Are you talking about what happened to Rose? After all these years you're following up on what happened to Rose? Why? You won't get anywhere with that now, even if you were serious. Too much water has passed under that bridge. Those guards who killed Tommy deny they were ever there, so there won't be any written reports about it. No records for anyone to look at. No witness statements. What happened to Tommy and Rose has been buried so deep even the worms can't get that far down.'

She rubbed her nose and glared at Sheffield again. 'But I suspect this is just a meaningless exercise anyway. Because you didn't want to listen to Rose the first time around. You dismissed her version of what happened and even called her a hysterical lunatic. You laughed when she told you it was two of your detectives that killed Tommy and caused Rose to fall and break her back and put her in a wheelchair for the rest of her life. What I don't understand is why you're digging it all up now. Has something happened? Has someone stirred up the gravy and discovered some unexplained lumps floating in it?'

She spread her arms as if she was a bird about to take flight. 'So go on, Detective. Please explain to us why you're really here now. What are you really looking for? Tommy is dead. Seamus is dead. His wife Alex is dead. And all of them were killed by Garda detectives. So what exactly are you doing here now, today?'

Sheffield kept his noncommittal expression, looking every inch the experienced detective who was unfazed by confrontation. Foley handed Eileen the note and she held it out in front of her before cautiously reading it.

'All I can tell you is we were asked to look into a photo and a note that was brought to the attention of the Gardaí.' Foley pointed to the photo in Mrs Cassidy's hand. 'We're trying to establish if there's a link to what happened on the day Tommy Cassidy died and his mother was injured. Is it connected to Seamus? Is it a clue as to why he killed his brother?'

'That's a feckin lie,' Mrs Cassidy yelled and she spun around so fast the wheelchair almost toppled over again.

Foley put up both of his hands. 'I know, I know. And I'm sorry about that. But why did the guards believe Seamus did kill Tommy?'

'Because they were covering up the fact it was detectives that killed my Tommy,' Mrs Cassidy shouted. 'There were witnesses who saw the detectives coming out of the house, but no one bothered to interview them. And those same witnesses swore on oath that Seamus was nowhere near that house at the time Tommy was killed.'

Mrs Cassidy was waving the photo at Foley, and Eileen snatched it out of her hand and took it to the window to study it. 'Why do you think this is going to throw any light on what happened to Rose and Tommy that day? Tis just a photo of Rose and her boys.' She turned it over and read the inscription out loud. 'Safe in The Sacred Heart.'

She flipped it around again and studied it more closely, and she gave a long loud groan. 'Oh my good God. I get it now. This is all about what Seamus is supposed to have stolen, isn't it? You didn't find it when you searched the house that day when Tommy was killed. And you didn't find it when Seamus and Alex were shot and killed by the detectives in Tralee. Now the photo has got you thinking maybe he did hide it in the house and left this as a clue for Billy McStay. But I don't get it. The note was addressed to Alex, so how has it turned up now, years later? If she had it on her when she was killed, why are you only investigating it now?'

Foley took the note and the photo back off her and he put them in the envelope. 'As I said already, Detective Sheffield and I were asked to look into this. Where it came from I don't know. We're just following orders.'

Mrs Cassidy reached out and grabbed Sheffield's arm. 'Mossie, you're not taking that photo, are you? Tis mine. Tell him to give it back to me. Tis the only picture I have of my boys.'

'Rose, stop calling him Mossie,' Eileen snapped. 'That's not Mossie. That's a detective and he's here trying to get you to answer questions that should have been asked years ago.'

Mrs Cassidy's hand went to her throat and she gave a shocked cry. 'What are you saying? Mossie is a detective? When did Mossie become a detective? Mossie, how could you? Get out of my house, you feckin turncoat. And don't ever darken my door again. Go on. Get the feck out of my sight.'

Chapter Twenty-One

Sheffield was leaning as far forward in the driver's seat as he possibly could, his whole body willing the old car to go faster. He was gripping the steering wheel so hard his fingers were white.

The wave of impatience came off him like a toxic cloud. He was like a long distance runner at the front of the pack who was almost in reach of the tape. But there was still the final lap to go before he could safely claim the prize. And anything could happen in those few precious moments. Another runner could muster an unexpected burst of speed and go racing past him in a blur of motion. And the fear of this happening was etched on Sheffield's face. His jaw was clamped tight and his eyes were two slits under a heavy wrinkled brow.

Foley was pressed back in the passenger seat holding on tightly to the door handle. He could understand Sheffield's unease. After all those years following the trail of the missing deeds, he was closer to finding them now than anyone had ever been before. He imagined himself being regaled by the whole of An Garda Síochána for finally putting an end to the whole embarrassing episode. D'Lacey would have what he wanted. Sheffield would get the recognition he craved. Then there would be the question of the reward. Yes, it was all so close now. They had found St Kevin's Hospital on the map, and in less than an hour they'd have the statue. More importantly, they'd have what was inside it.

Foley knew he should be feeling the same excitement as Sheffield, but for some strange reason he couldn't. His heart felt heavy, as if he was carrying a huge sack of guilt on his back. The whole sorry charade with Mrs Cassidy made him cringe with embarrassment. And his face turned red when he remembered Peg's eyes burning into him. Because she knew there was a hidden agenda to the whole pretence of looking into an old case. Did they think she was too stupid to know they were on a fishing exhibition, hoping to find some elusive nugget of gold amongst the dross? Foley felt bad because he didn't have the courage to say why they were really there, mainly because he dreaded the consequences if he did. It would be like lighting a match while standing in a lake of petrol. What chaos would that tiny spark cause? The ripple of destruction would spread wide and wild, and destroy a lot of innocent people as well as those responsible for the debacle in the first place.

So what was he going to do now? Was he just going to go along with Sheffield, find the deeds, take his share of the reward money, and bury the story Mrs Cassidy had told him in some dark corner of his mind?

He took a sideways glance at Sheffield, an experienced cop who had learnt long ago to control his feelings and mask his thoughts behind a blank expression. The only evidence of any emotion at all was the obvious impatience that radiated from his tense body.

'So what do you make of it all?' Foley had to almost shout to be heard above the rattle and roar of the car.

Sheffield gave him a sour look. 'All what?'

'All that stuff about Tommy Cassidy being killed by Garda detectives. Do you think there's anything in it?'

Sheffield stared straight ahead without offering a reply.

'Doesn't it bother you?' Foley continued, annoyed at Sheffield's unresponsive attitude. 'Surely, as a detective, you should feel some sort of regret. Shame even, if any of that is true. Any decent cop would want to know if there was any truth in it. And they would want to do something about it. Wouldn't they?'

Again Sheffield didn't offer a response. He kept staring straight ahead and kept a fierce grip on the steering wheel. Foley had to look away to stop himself from swearing at him.

Then a sudden thought made Foley jerk up straight in his seat. 'Oh my Good God.'

Sheffield snapped up too. 'What?'

'You knew about this already, didn't you?' It came out in a higher voice that Foley intended and Sheffield bent his head towards him but didn't make eye contact.

'You knew, didn't you?' Foley deepened his voice. 'You already knew Mrs Cassidy accused Garda detectives of killing Tommy. So why were you pretending you didn't? Why were you so frightened to admit it?'

'For feck sake, Foley. What are you talking about?'

'I thought it was odd when the neighbour was telling us about the two men she saw coming out of Cassidy's house after she fell down the steps. It was the way you reacted. Or didn't react, to be precise. Any decent guard would have been disturbed by an accusation like that. They would be anxious to know more about what happened afterwards, if the accusation had been followed up. Any decent cop would be mortified to know the witnesses weren't even questioned. But you didn't blink an eye, did you? Because you already knew about it.'

'Oh piss off, Foley. You're talking out of the wrong hole.' Sheffield's body shifted position and he hunched his shoulder even more, and now his face was almost touching the windscreen.

'So what did you know about it?' Foley asked. 'What did you hear? Did you know the detectives who were involved?'

Sheffield grunted but pretended to be too engrossed on the road to answer.

'Did you know who they were, Sheffield? Were you involved?'

'Of course I wasn't involved,' Sheffield spat out the words. 'I had nothing to do with any of that.'

'But you knew about it?'

'For feck sake, everyone knew about it.' Now it was more of a resigned groan. 'But it was just speculation. You know what it's like, Foley. You hear it every day. It was the detectives' word against an injured woman who was heavily sedated and very confused. There was no evidence to back up what she was saying. The detectives admitted they were there looking for Seamus. The mother became abusive and erratic and she started screaming for her neighbours to come and help her. She ran out into the street, missed the step and … well, you know the rest.'

'And that was it?' Foley sneered. 'The detectives' word was taken and the witnesses weren't even approached?'

Sheffield shrugged. 'I can't answer that, can I? I wasn't there. As I said, there were all sorts of rumours going around. I just heard bits and pieces. You know how it is, Foley? Stories like that grow legs and take off in all directions. I heard so many different versions, but I never heard anything official.'

'But surely you wondered about them saying Seamus killed his brother?'

'No, I did not.' Sheffield slapped the steering wheel. 'The detective swore they did not see Tommy in the house that morning. If he was there, they insist they didn't see him.'

'So why did a bus load of uniform garda descend on the house shortly after they took Mrs Cassidy away? How did they know there was a body in the kitchen?'

'They got a phone call,' Sheffield told him. 'Someone who wouldn't give their name said they saw Seamus coming out of the house covered in blood. That's the version I heard, anyway.'

'So what happened to those two detectives? Were they even investigated? Or did they just carry on as if nothing happened?'

Sheffield gave a funny grin that bared his teeth. 'Well, if you're hoping for some sort of retribution, Foley, you're out of luck. Those two detectives caught up with Seamus and Alex Cassidy down in Tralee a few years back. And died for their troubles. You'll remember the incident? Your step father Inspector Liam Edge was caught up in it too.'

It took a moment for Foley to absorb the information, and when he did he couldn't decide whether he felt cheated or avenged. He wondered how Peg would react, although he was sure Mrs Cassidy wouldn't feel that justice had been done. All she really wanted was the opportunity to tell her version of events, and to have her story properly investigated.

As they struggled up a long steep hill the old car began to shudder with the effort, and Sheffield cursed under his breath. He shook the steering wheel, willing the old jalopy to keep going. There was less than twenty yards to go and they would be over the crest of the hill, then it was plain sailing down the other side.

So when a lorry poked its nose out from a side road in front of them, Sheffield yelled and sounded the horn. He had no choice. He knew if he stopped now they would never make it to the top of the hill, so he cut in front of the lorry, throwing up clumps of turf from the grass verge. Then the car rocked and wobbled before straightening up again and finally crept up the last few yards to a huge sigh of relief.

Sheffield was actually smiling when the ferocious crash threw him back in his seat. Foley's head slammed against the door frame and turned everything into a wave of noise.

Sheffield instinctively slammed on the brakes and his face became a mask of fury that said he was going to rip the head off the stupid lorry driver who had crumpled the car boot and shattered the rear window.

He instantly regretted doing that because now the car was being shunted forward with smoke belching from the burning tyres. He grabbed the gearstick, changed down gears and pressed the pedal to the floor. The car detached itself from the distinctive bull-nose grill of the Bedford lorry and spurted forward, but the space between them never grew more than two feet. The lorry was keeping pace with them. Foley struggled to focus through the blinding pain in his head, the screaming of the car engine, the roar of the lorry and the howl of the breeze coming in through the broken window. It felt as if his skull was cracked.

'What the hell did you do to that eejit?' Foley croaked.

Sheffield's face was pasty grey and glistening with the sheen of sweat. 'This is no feckin accident,' he yelled. He reached inside his jacket and tried to extract his Smith & Wesson .38 service weapon from his shoulder holster, but the effort of trying to control the car prevented him from grabbing it properly. He shouted at Foley, 'Get my gun. C'mon. Get my gun and shoot the bastard.'

'What?' Foley shouted back. 'Are you mad? You can't just shoot someone for colliding with your car.'

'This is not an accident, Foley. This lunatic is trying to shove us off the road. He's trying to kill us. Can't you see that? So get the feckin gun and shoot the fool. Come on. Do it now before he kills us.'

For a moment it looked as if the car was actually pulling away from the lorry but when a huge pot hole appeared in the middle of the road Sheffield had to skim around it. The wheels sank deep into the soft grass verge and caused enough drag to close the gap again.

The next wallop almost spun the car around in a circle. Sheffield roared as he fought the steering wheel, just righting the vehicle in time for the next impact. Metal screamed and the back door windows exploded, but the car was hit hard enough to push it farther away from the lorry. Sheffield rocked the steering wheel and bellowed at the car to go faster, keep the pace going, widen the gap.

All Foley could see when he looked back was a cloud of steam belching from the bonnet of the enormous lorry. It looked obscenely menacing and dangerously close. But he could not see who was in the cab.

'Come on, Foley,' Sheffield was shouting at him above the din. 'The gun. Get the gun. Do it, you moron. Stop him. Stop him now.'

'We're half way down the hill already,' Foley shouted back. 'Once we start up the other side he won't be able to keep up. So just go for it.'

Sheffield roared like a wounded bear and slapped the steering wheel. 'What are you talking about? I have never heard so much shit in my life. We'll be dead by the time we … look, just get the feckin gun.'

Sheffield tried to reach the weapon again and this time he managed to release it. But he couldn't hold it and it shot out of his hand and into the foot well. And he roared even louder.

Then up ahead he spotted a gap in the hedge where the road appeared to widen. If he timed it right he could swing into the gap unexpectedly, catching the lorry off guard and unable to react in time. The lorry would be forced to drive on past. He didn't think the driver would risk stopping once the odds had changed. He would try and make a run for it, and Sheffield would relish the chase. The hunted would be the hunter, and he'd have a gun to enforce his revenge.

He sniggered as he braced himself. He only had to keep his nerve until the last second then swing off the road and slam on the brakes. He counted down the yards in his head.

Unfortunately the reality was different from what he imagined. The gap was an illusion. The recent rain had melted most of the snow but there were still stubborn patches. And this was one of them. What looked like a strip of road was actually a ditch full of packed snow, flat and shiny and shimmering in the weak sunlight. The thin hedge behind it was hiding a deep drop down into a field that sloped away to a bank of rocks and trees.

But Sheffield had committed himself and he had no choice. He slammed on the brakes. The car didn't respond. There was no grip on the snow and the car slid back out onto the road just as the lorry raced past. It slammed into the back corner of the car and catapulted it through the hedge and down into the field.

The thud knocked the wind out of Foley but he was still conscious enough to feel the car rolling over several times before finally slamming against the rocks. Then came a deafening silence. Nothing stirred. Nothing. Just an unsettling silence. Foley sensed something trickling down his face and he rubbed it, and he gagged at the thickness of the blood that smeared his fingers.

His instinct was to sit up and try to stop the bleeding, but every move was agony. The car had landed the right way up and Foley was squashed into the foot well. And from where he was sitting it looked like Sheffield was in an even worse position. He was bent over the back of his seat with his head at an unnatural angle. And he was perfectly still. There didn't seem to be any sign of breathing, nothing to show signs of life.

Foley forced himself to turn onto his knees and crawl back into his seat so he could do an assessment of his injuries. Every movement created a more vicious pain than the last. Finally he was sitting back up, and he leant his head against the window to gather his senses. The car was facing back up the field, and through the cobweb of the battered windscreen he could see a movement. A wave of relief pushed up a gush of air that became a cheer. Someone was coming down the field towards them. Help was here. Help was on the way.

He bent forward to shout encouragement, but before the words left his throat they turned into a fractured gulp. Above the line of the hedge up on the road he could see the top of the lorry. Why had it stopped? Was it possible the driver realised the enormity of what he had done and decided he had a duty to help? Was that him coming down the field? Foley squinted to focus, and immediately every nerve in his body was telling him this was not good news. Because the figure was not moving in the manner of a saviour. He was furtive, hesitant, hunched in a sinister stoop as if he was stalking his prey. And he was carrying something in the cradle of his arm. A shotgun? Surely to

God Foley was mistaken. No one in their right mind would become that demented just because someone cut him up in traffic? Was this because Sheffield honked his horn at him?

Or was it because the driver thought he was in so much trouble for causing such a horrendous accident his only option was to silence the witnesses?

Foley grabbed the door handle and threw his weight against it, but nothing happened. The door was bent out of shape and jammed solid. He tried to wind down the window but that was stuck too. There was no way out. He pushed his legs against the dash to try and heave himself into the back seat. Maybe he could squeeze out through the broken rear window. But the avalanche of pain that rolled through him pinned him to the seat. It was no use. He was trapped. He scanned the inside of the car with frantic eyes, conscious that the strange whining noise was coming from him. Is this how it was going to end? Blown to bits by a lunatic pissed off about being cut up in his lorry?

Foley made one last frantic effort to extract himself from the situation, and he reached across to the driver's side and pulled the door handle. But that was jammed too. At the same time he saw Sheffield's gun lodged under the brake pedal. Despite the howl of pain from every bone in his body, he reached down and grabbed it, raised it in one continuous sweep and fired it in the direction of the approaching figure.

The explosion from the shot and the pop of the windscreen disorientated Foley for a moment. But he recovered quickly enough to see the figure scarpering back up the field and vanishing through the hedge. Seconds later the lorry jerked, then rolled forward and raced away down the road.

Foley's stomach heaved and bile burnt the back of his throat, but he managed to stop his breakfast from coming up. Another wave of pain made him rest his head back in the seat and he squeezed his eyes shut. He really needed to sort himself out, and fast. Establish to what degree he was injured. Sitting here feeling sorry for himself was not an option. He had to go for help. But first he had to find out how badly he was injured.

He started with his feet, his leg bones, his knees. They all moved without too much agony. Bit by bit it became obvious that most of the pain was from pulled muscles and torn ligaments. There was no evidence of broken bones, though his ribs and back felt close enough.

He knew he couldn't waste any more time. Sheffield looked seriously injured. Foley searched for a hand and tried to find a pulse. There was one but it was very weak. Sheffield needed help now. Foley needed to get himself out of the car and back up onto the road. And the only way he could see that happening was to kick out the remains of the windscreen and crawl out that way.

It took just one solid blow from his heavy garda boots to dislodge most of the remaining glass, but squeezing his battered body through the gap was not as easy as it looked. Even with his thick garda greatcoat and uniform jacket to protect the top of his body, the stubborn shards of windscreen that were still poking out of the frame sliced his legs and drew blood.

He rolled over the bonnet and dropped onto the mud that was churned up around the wheels, and slowly and carefully he rose up onto his knees.

'Guard?'

The sound was as violent as a gunshot in Foley's fragile mind, and he swung around with Sheffield's gun in his hand, pointing it wildly in the direction of the voice.

The two elderly farmers threw their hands up and dropped to their knees.

'Don't shoot,' screeched the nearest one, and Foley dropped back on his heels and lowered the gun with a gasp of relief.

'Sorry,' he called out. 'I'm very sorry.'

The farmers stood up and rushed over to Foley, and one of them took a tattered rag from around his neck and pressed it to Foley's head. 'Hold it there,' the man said. 'It'll check the bleeding.'

'Jasus, Gabby, this poor fella looks bad.' The second man was leaning in through the window poking at Sheffield. 'He should be in hospital.'

The first man joined him and together they pulled at the door, rocking and jerking it until eventually they got it open. Then very carefully they lifted Sheffield out onto the grass.

'Hang on here.' The first man pointed at Foley. 'I will go and fetch the auld tractor from the lower field and take it to the house where I'll collect the trailer. I'll be back quicker than you can shake a stick at a herd of cows. Paddy will stay here and look after you. Won't you, Paddy?'

Paddy muttered something that Foley couldn't hear and he gave the guard a wide assuring smile. 'Go on, sure,' he said to Gabby. 'But hurry on back, won't you? Don't be getting distracted and go wandering off to do something that's got no bearing on this disaster and end up forgetting all about us here and us in desperate need of assistance.'

Gabby was already scurrying off across the field towards the gap in the fence and the curse he shouted back at his pal was blown away in the breeze.

Foley shuffled over to Sheffield and cringed at the state of his face. It had bloated to twice the normal size and was a brutal shade of puce. He did not look good at all.

Paddy had his hand inside Sheffield's coat and pressed against his chest. 'We'll get him to St Kevin's in no time. His heart is sound at the moment so things are not looking too bad. But what about yourself? You look like you're after being in a car crash.'

He gave a wicked chuckle then rapped the door with his knuckles. 'Seriously though, how did you end up like this?'

Foley glanced down at his mud covered coat and ripped trousers. 'Did you hear the crash?' He cringed as the words annoyed his bruised lips.

'No, no.' Paddy pointed over his shoulder. 'We heard a gunshot so we switched off the tractor and came up from the bottom field to see what feckin poacher was hunting on our land. And we were shocked to see a car stuck in the rocks with a guard crawling out of the front window looking like someone out of one of those horror films you'd see in the Theatre Royal cinema. Jasus, we said, someone looks like they might need a bit of help.'

Foley inspected the cloth he was still holding to his head, squeezed some of the blood out and pressed it to his wound again. 'Yeah, we had a bit of a misunderstanding with a lorry,' he said. 'We came off worse.'

Paddy studied Foley for a moment, unsure if he was serious or not, then he nodded at Sheffield. 'Is he your prisoner? Only if he is a prisoner why isn't he wearing handcuffs? Aren't all prisoners supposed to be wearing handcuffs?'

Foley couldn't help the splutter that escaped his bruised lips. 'That fella is Special Branch Detective Sheffield. We were on our way back to the city.'

A frown wrinkled Paddy's weathered brow even more and his eyes tightened. 'So why did you shoot him?'

'What?' Foley looked down at Sheffield then back at Paddy, and the ache in his back seemed to sweep around and tighten his chest making him gasp like a badly blown tuba. 'No, I didn't shoot him. He wasn't shot. No one was shot. He was hurt in the crash.'

Foley swept his hand around at the trail of torn grass and mud leading down the field from the road. 'Look how far we tumbled, all the way down here, rolling over and over. Tis a wonder we weren't killed stone dead. I'm lucky to be able to stand up at all. I'm battered and bruised from head to toe, but thank you God, I can still stand up.'

Foley realised his voice was getting more and more whiney and was about to break into a hysterical sing-song, so he sagged back on his heels and took a deep breath. 'No. No one was shot,' he mumbled.

But Paddy didn't look convinced and he leant over Sheffield, discreetly looking for any sign of a puncture hole while pretending to make the detective comfortable.

'It was a loud bang all right,' Paddy added in a tone that was full of suspicion. 'We heard it above the tractor. That's why we came up to see who was sneaking around our land shooting our stock.'

'It's his gun.' Foley had an irrational need to explain his actions to the man who had rushed to his assistance, but he realised he couldn't just admit to wildly taking a pot shot at a random shadow because he thought it was about to do him a mischief. How would that sound if it was said out loud? Frantic guard goes mad with a gun?

'We were trapped in the wreckage.' Foley joined his hands as if in prayer. 'Sheffield looked in a really bad way and I couldn't do anything to help him. So I fired a shot to try and get someone's attention. And thanks be to God, you heard it and came over to help us. So thank you, Sir.'

Paddy turned when he heard the tractor coming across the field scattering slush and mud at the two women who were racing along beside it. When they reached the car one of the women dropped to her knees beside Sheffield, and the other one began fussing around Foley, taking the rag from his head and inspecting the cut on his scalp. But Foley guided her to the prone figure of the detective. 'See to him first, please. He's in a bad way.'

With amazing accuracy Gabby turned the tractor around and backed the trailer right up to the injured detective. Then all four of them manoeuvred him onto a blanket, grabbed a fistful each and lifted him in one smooth movement onto the bed of straw they'd put there to soften the harshness of the wooden floor.

Then they hauled Foley onto his feet, shuffled him onto the trailer and laid him down beside Sheffield. The two women squashed in beside them and Paddy stood on the back of the tractor beside Gabby.

Gabby glanced back at his passengers, shouted a warning and put the tractor into gear before slowly taking them back up to the road and over to St Kevin's Hospital.

Chapter Twenty-Two

Foley wiped his face with the towel and studied himself in the mirror. The nurses had shaved the top of his head so they could stitch the cut, and they rubbed ointment on the swollen lumps that had marked his face. The ill-fitting pyjama jacket he was wearing hung open to display the patchwork of bruises all over his chest, but none of them hurt like the deep cuts in the back of his legs. Every time he moved, the stitches pulled and stung like an attack of angry ants.

The assortment of drugs they made him swallow dulled the pain a little bit, but they did nothing to soothe the panic that was dancing around inside his chest. All because of what Sheffield had said.

They had been less than a mile from the hospital when the detective suddenly jerked awake, his face distorted with confusion when he saw the two women holding onto his shoulders trying to keep him still. When his wild eyes spotted Foley he grabbed a fistful of Foley's sleeve.

'Where's your man?' A spray of blood came out with the words. 'Did you see him? Did you see the feckin eejit?'

'What man?' Foley rose up onto his elbow and groaned at the rip of pain.

'Your man.' Sheffield pulled angrily at Foley's sleeve. 'You must … the fella driving the lorry.' Red dribble splashed down his chin. 'Surely to God you saw him. He was there. He was right there.'

'Easy now.' One of the women put her hand on his forehead. 'Stop talking and lay down. You have to lay down. C'mon.'

But Sheffield rose up on his elbow too and pulled harder on Foley's sleeve. 'You know who it was, don't you? It was that fella … we were talking to him. That fella … you know … you must have seen him, for feck sake.'

The detective's eyes rolled and his jaw sagged, and he was barely audible as the women eased him back onto the hay. But he kept trying to tell Foley who he'd seen driving the lorry and the louder he shouted the less coherent he became until his words were just a jumble of noise.

But above the rattle of the tractor and the thumping of the trailer on the country road, Foley could hear the urgency in Sheffield's voice. The injured detective was trying to warn Foley of imminent danger. Foley leant closer but was blocked by one of the women wiping Sheffield's face with a wet cloth and making soothing noises. Sheffield was still agitated and spitting out words.

'What's he saying?' Foley shook the woman's arm. 'What's he trying to tell me?'

'Ah sure, he's delirious. Isn't he talking rubbish? He had a bad crash and he isn't himself so don't be taking any notice of him.'

'No. I need to hear what he's trying to tell me.'

The woman manoeuvred her ample backside between them and ignored Foley, but the other woman started to call out what she thought the detective was saying.

'You know the fella, is what he's saying,' she told Foley. 'There was ... what's that? Something about a ... what?' She looked at Foley and pulled a face. 'A nun? Did you say a nun?'

Sheffield gave a cough and spattered the woman with a red mist. His voice had become a weak purr. He gave a deep sigh and lay as still as the rocking trailer would let him. And despite the pain that raged through every part of Foley's body, the words still stabbed him into a nervous wreck. Surely to God he didn't mean Maranus? Why would Maranus try to kill them? It didn't make sense. Unless he thought they were too close to finding D'Lacey's deeds. But surely it wasn't so important to Maranus that he would actually try to kill fellow officers of the law.

By the time the tractor rattled to a stop outside the hospital Foley was seeing danger everywhere. Was that a real doctor, or Maranus in a white coat? Anyone could put a stethoscope around their neck and spout long medical sounding words. That nurse is tall. How tall is Sister Michael?

The rush from the tractor to the beds in the ward was a blur of crashing doors and flashing lights, then hands stripping off their clothes and poking at their wounds. Sharp pinching where the cuts were stitched and foul tasting medicine forced down their throats. Followed by strong sweet tea.

Sheffield was prepped for surgery and wheeled away leaving Foley in the ward with two other occupied beds, and all the time his eyes were like a cornered rat's scanning everyone and hosing them down with suspicion.

In the sudden calm of the ward Foley tried to organise his thoughts. Maybe Maranus wasn't actually trying to kill them, or even injure them. What if he'd found out where the deeds were actually hidden. Did someone at Patch give him the heads up when they realised the importance of what Mrs Cassidy was telling them, and he was trying to get there first? Had he tried to even the odds by putting Foley and Sheffield out of the race? Was it a plan that tragically backfired?

But why a lorry? Wouldn't he have had a better chance in a car? Unless Maranus was already at Patch listening to the conversation, and he got someone there to lend him the lorry. Were there two people in the lorry? Foley tried to remember the figure coming down the field after the crash. On reflection, he didn't look like Maranus. Well, not exactly. But then Foley was under extreme pressure and concentrating solely on surviving, so he couldn't swear to what he saw.

As he lay on the bed with his eyes squeezed shut, he tried to spread the questions out on the table of his mind like a deck of cards. But every time he tried to focus on them the cards flew at him, so all he could see was a shower of black and red dots scattering across his brain.

Of course the obvious answer was to go to the chapel and see if the statue was still there. If it was Maranus who ran them off the road, he would have had loads of time to get to the statue before Foley and Sheffield were even found in the wreckage. And that would be game over. D'Lacey would have his deeds back and this madness would stop once and for all. Or would it? Was Maranus one to leave loose ends? Would he feel the need to erase all traces of his involvement?

Foley shook his head. Surely not. Once Maranus took the deeds out of the statue and put the statue back in its place, no one would even know he'd been there. Foley was fretting over nothing. But he still needed to know. So he got out of bed to take a look.

He got as far as the toilet when his shaky legs started to wobble even more, so he went in and hung onto the sink. And he splashed cold water in his face.

The sight of himself in the mirror wasn't pretty. He buttoned up the pyjama jacket and pulled it tighter around his shoulders, but it still looked like a badly fitting sack.

It was a few minutes before he felt composed enough to carry on looking for the chapel. He swallowed his discomfort, pulled open the door and limped out into the corridor where two Gardaí were waiting for him.

'Ah, there you are.' The sergeant scanned Foley with cold grey eyes set in a weather beaten face. Clumps of grey hair poked out of his cap and his long arms waved around like loose sails on a windmill. 'I want to talk to you, fella.'

Foley sagged back against the wall. 'I feel dreadful,' he mumbled. 'I need to lie down.'

The sergeant stepped back and waved him towards the ward. Foley exaggerated his incapacity and held his hand against the wall as he staggered down the corridor. But it didn't impress his escort. They followed behind, walking slowly with their hands clasped behind their backs.

When Foley dropped onto the bed, the sergeant pulled his pillow up in such a way that Foley was forced to sit up, and he couldn't avoid eye contact with the guards. He licked his swollen lips and tried to smile. 'So what can I do for you, Sergeant?'

'You can tell me what a Kerry guard is doing in our neck of the woods.'

'I was visiting a friend.'

'Were you now? And do you always wear your uniform when you visit a friend?'

Foley glanced at the small bedside locker where the nurses had stuffed his uniform. 'It was an unexpected visit. I came straight from work.'

The click of his tongue said the sergeant wasn't amused. 'And does this friend have a name?'

Foley shrugged. 'I don't think that's any of your business.'

The sergeant slapped his hand on the locker making the water glass jump and splash water all over the floor.

'Do not play games with me, Guard.' The voice was as clipped and deeply sinister as the one Maranus used. 'We play with the big boys up here in the dirty city, so a culchie on a day out should think twice about being a smart arse.'

He flicked some of the splashed water off his sleeve. 'So do not make me ask you again.'

The other guard was older than the sergeant and he had the bearing of an officer who had experienced many years on the city beat, and his impassive features warned Foley to behave himself.

'All right,' Foley sighed. 'My Super sent me up here to offer condolences to the sister of a murder victim.'

The sergeant shuffled his feet. 'Why?'

'Well, the murder victim was found in Tralee.'

'So what? Condolences could have been done over the telephone. I suspect there is more to this than just passing on condolences. Yeah?'

Foley relented and gave a submissive nod. 'Well, yeah. The victim had been dead for a few months. We have no witnesses and no evidence of how she was killed. The Super thought by sending me to speak to the sister she might be able to throw some light on what happened to our victim.'

Both men smirked at that. 'That doesn't explain what you were doing way out there on an isolated country road. Or why you took your car for a spin down a farmer's field. Were you driving? Did you think you were still on Kerry roads? Your friend is in a very bad way because of …'

Foley glanced at the empty bed beside him. 'My friend is actually a Special Branch detective …'

'We know who he is,' the sergeant snapped. 'What we want to know is what a Dublin detective was doing with a Kerry guard - in uniform – in a Garda pool car on a road in the back of beyond. Where were you going? Or, more to the point, where were you coming from?'

Again the two officers stared at Foley. Foley closed his eyes as if he was suffering a sudden relapse of pain, and when he opened them again the men hadn't changed their expressions one bit. Their silence was more painful than Foley's injuries and he licked his lips again.

'Detective Sheffield had some people to see. I don't know who they were. He didn't discuss it with me.'

The sergeant gave a tiny shake of his head and his eyes squinted. 'Why were you even with him in the first place? You said you came up here to see the sister of a person who was murdered in Tralee. So why were you and a Special Branch Detective driving around the Dublin countryside?'

Foley's head thumped from the barrage of questions that he struggled to find rational answers to. It was a weakness he hated, being unable to think fast enough. A fog usually descended and blurred everything in his head and he'd be unable to assemble a coherent answer even if his life depended on it. The only thing that ever made sense to him was to just tell the truth.

But right now telling the truth could be the death of him. These two men were not Foley's idea of friendly beat cops. They reeked of menace. What would they do with the truth if Foley told them his version of it? No, his best bet was to play dumb.

'Det Sheffield was in Tralee when the Super asked me to go and see the murder victim's sister. Sheffield said he knew the area well and, as he was going back to Dublin anyway, he'd be happy to take me to the sister's house. We came up by train, Sheffield booked out a car, took me to see the sister, and on the way back he called to see some people.'

The sergeant sniffed the air and pulled a face. 'What is that smell, Guard Kavanagh?'

Kavanagh gave a lazy blink. 'Bullshit, Sarge,'

'Bullshit,' the sergeant repeated.

Foley rested his head back on the pillow. 'Then ask Detective Sheffield.'

'We will, sure.' The sergeant pointed at the empty bed. 'That is if he makes it, God help us.'

Foley looked at the empty bed too and felt a stab of regret that he knew absolutely nothing about the detective. He didn't know where he lived, or if he had a family. What if he didn't make it? A horrible vision filled Foley's imagination. He would have to face the investigation into how Sheffield died all by himself. It would be a nightmare trying to negotiate the questions that would rain down on him. Suspicion would wrap around him like a cheap overcoat and his vague answers would condemn him to a future under a cloud. That is if he was allowed to continue as a guard.

'Where's the gun?'

Foley snapped back in the bed. 'What?'

The sergeant leant closer to Foley and just stared at him with unblinking eyes.

'I don't know,' Foley was forced to answer.

The sergeant groaned again and moved even closer, and he continued to stare at Foley without speaking.

'I haven't got it.' Foley's voice crackled with the strain.

'We have a witness who saw you waving it around.'

'I ... yeah, well I haven't got it now. I used it all right because we were trapped in the wreckage and Sheffield was badly injured. I fired the gun to get help. But I don't know where it is now.'

'You were waving it around when you were out of the car.'

Foley's voice crackled even more. 'I know. But we were all trying to help Sheffield. I don't know what I did with the gun. I must have dropped it in the mud. But I certainly haven't got it now. I swear.'

The sergeant bent down and pulled open the door of the locker. Then he pulled everything out onto the floor. Slowly and deliberately he lifted Foley's greatcoat and checked the pockets. He did the same to Foley's jacket. Finally he patted down the rest of the clothes before leaving them in a heap on the floor. And the look of surprise on the sergeant's face matched that on Foley's, and Foley had to disguise it by feigning annoyance at the sergeant's actions.

'Are you going to put that back?' he growled.

'Guard Kavanagh will be outside your room tonight if you need him.' The sergeant pulled his shoulders back and turned towards the door without looking at Foley.

'Why?' Foley called after him.

The sergeant gave a dismissive wave. 'Just in case the gun turns up. We don't want any more accidents tonight, now do we, Guard Kavanagh?'

Kavanagh sniggered and straightened his cap before giving Foley a dark sideways look. 'We certainly do not, Sarge. Tis bad enough being shunted off the road and miraculously living to tell the tale. But an accident with a gun, well ... that could be fatal all right.'

The blood that flowed in Foley's veins suddenly turned to ice, and every hair on his neck stood to attention. How did they know the car was shunted off the road? Were Foley's instincts right after all? These two men were sent here by Maranus?

A nurse appeared in the doorway pushing a trolley with a large urn of tea and a stack of cups, and she almost collided with the sergeant.

'Get out of the way,' he bellowed and waved an angry fist at her.

The nurse jumped back in surprise and the trolley clipped the end of the bed by the door causing several cups and saucers to fly off and smash on the floor.

A tiny woman in a matron's uniform came out of nowhere and her face blazed with fury. 'How dare you speak to my nurse like that?' The voice was surprisingly deep and crackled like breaking ice, and the sergeant's face stretched out of shape with a mix of surprise and annoyance. He puffed out his chest but Matron was in front of him and staring up like an angry elf before he could react.

'What are you doing here anyway, annoying my patients? Who gave you the right to come in here in the first place?'

'We're here on garda business, I'll have you know, madam.'

'Don't *madam* me.' Even up on her toes she barely reached his top button. 'You might have no respect for my nurses, but by God you will show respect to me.'

The sergeant's mouth made a selection of shapes with no sound coming out of it. Then he managed to compose himself. 'As I said, Matron, we're here on garda business.'

'Which can wait until the morning.' Matron dismissed him with a sharp nod and went over to Foley's bed.

Foley studied her, trying to remember if she was one of the people who attended to him when he was brought in. He knew Sheffield's gun was in the pocket of his greatcoat when he arrived, and he assumed it was still there when the coat was taken off him and shoved in the locker along with the rest of his clothes. He was stripped and poked with professional efficiency, stitched and smothered in ointment and wrapped back up in extra-large pyjamas.

So what happened to the gun?

Matron wasn't pleased to see the contents of his locker littering her shiny floor. Her stern face turned into an angry grimace and she glared at Foley with a look that said she would pick it up but he wasn't getting any tea tonight.

'That isn't my fault.' Foley tried a smile but it was frozen by her icy glare.

'Honest.' He tried again but she was already bent down and gathering the clothes up in angry fistfuls and shoving them back in the locker.

Guard Kavanagh and the sergeant had melted away, but Foley could still sense them out in the corridor. 'It was that sergeant,' Foley said in a stage whisper, reaching out to take Matron's arm, but she slapped it away.

'I'm telling you.' He swung his legs out of the bed. 'They were looking for a gun.'

Matron stood up and shut the locker door with her foot, and her face softened. 'A gun, you say.'

'Yes,' Foley answered. 'It was in my coat pocket when I came in.'

'Why were you carrying a gun? Sure only detectives carry guns in Ireland, don't they?'

'The fella I came in with is a detective. The gun belongs to him. I had to use it to attract help when we were trapped in the wreckage. But for some reason it isn't in my coat anymore.'

Matron studied him with severe brown eyes that had a web of tiny lines in the corners, then she beckoned for the nurse to bring the trolley over. As the nurse poured the tea Matron felt Foley's wrist and timed it with her watch. After a minute she dropped the hand and turned away.

'You're well enough to go home tomorrow. I'll arrange some medication for you to take with you. Come and see me after breakfast.'

Chapter Twenty-Three

Foley was conscious of the state of his uniform. His overcoat was stiff with mud and his trousers were ripped in several places, and his shoes were caked in all types of detritus. He stood close to the reception desk in the hope that Matron wouldn't be forced to make a comment. The nurse behind the desk smiled at him and told him Matron wouldn't be long.

It had been a long uncomfortable night. When they brought Sheffield back from surgery they'd made positive noises about his condition. They had relieved the pressure on his brain and repaired the damage to his skull, so he had a good chance of a full recovery. But he was heavily sedated and would be unresponsive for a while. He would probably be in hospital for several weeks. And Foley lay in the next bed, suddenly feeling all alone in the big city. What was he supposed to do now?

He knew he should take a look in the chapel, just to check that the statue was actually there. And if it was, he would try to open it and remove the deeds. Then put it back as if it hadn't been touched.

However, it was something he didn't get to do. Because Guard Kavanagh was perched on a chair right outside the ward door. The nurses had supplied him with cups of tea, and he'd acquired several newspapers which kept him amused, and awake, all night. And unnaturally alert.

Sometime, in the early hours of the morning, Foley heard Kavanagh stand up and stretch, then patter off down the corridor. Foley had noticed the nicotine stained fingers, so he assumed the call of tobacco was too strong and he was sneaking outside for a smoke.

So Foley slipped out of bed and pretended to head for the toilets while keeping a lookout for any sign of the chapel. He went down the length of the main corridor and along two of the other passageways, but there was no sign of a chapel anywhere.

There was a wide staircase at the end of the second corridor, but there was no mention of a chapel amongst the list of departments up on the first floor.

Foley retraced his steps and when he came back out into the main corridor he groaned. Kavanagh was back in his seat munching on a baguette and reading a magazine. Foley had no choice but to brazen it out, and he walked casually back to the toilet and went in. And annoyingly, Kavanagh didn't even glance in his direction.

After a reasonable delay Foley emerged from the toilet and headed back to the ward. And as he passed by him, Kavanagh pointed with the baguette and said, 'You should put some shoes on, you know. You could catch your death of cold walking on these bare tiles.'

The nurse who brought breakfast at six o'clock also brought Foley a cup of medication, and a little pot of ointment to rub on his stitches. Sheffield was still asleep as Foley got dressed, and Kavanagh sprang to his feet when he saw Foley coming out of the ward.

'Where do you think you're going?' he growled.

Foley ignored him and went over to the reception desk. Kavanagh muttered something obscene and followed him, and he leant his elbow on the desk. 'I said where do you think you're going?'

Foley smiled at the nurse behind the desk. 'Matron wants to see me,' he said, aiming it at Kavanagh.

'What for?' Kavanagh took his elbow off the desk and glared at the nurse as if she was going to tell him.

Foley gave him a sideways glance but didn't answer. Kavanagh puffed and stood up straight. 'Well, you're not going anywhere until the sergeant gets here. He'll be wanting a full statement from you and that's a fact.'

'That's not a problem.' Foley still didn't look at Kavanagh.

Kavanagh puffed even louder and stool closer to Foley so their toes almost touched. 'So go back to your bed and wait for him there.'

'I can't, I'm afraid,' Foley told him with a smirk.

'Why not?'

'Matron has decided I'm fit enough to be discharged, so my bed is no longer my bed. In fact there's probably some other poor eejit in it already.'

Kavanagh glared at the nurse again but she unnerved him by glaring back at him, so he stepped away from the desk. 'Then you'll just have to wait here in the corridor until the sergeant …'

'Guard Foley.' Matron stood up on her toes to look over the desk. 'Come into my office.'

Kavanagh stepped between Foley and the office. 'What's going on?'

Foley stepped around him again, and when he walked into the office Matron closed the door behind him. Then she went behind the big oak desk and pushed a paper bag at him.

Foley hesitated before gingerly picking it up and taking a look inside. Wrapped in a tea towel was Sheffield's gun, and when he looked up at her, Matron raised her eyebrows.

'Well I didn't want that ignorant sergeant to have it. God knows what he might do with it.'

Foley nodded and put the gun back in the bag. 'Thank you, Matron.'

'Don't thank me. This isn't about you.' Matron bared her teeth. 'This is about that bully out there throwing his weight around. He's hoping to make a case out of your car accident and have you arrested for something trivial. He will blow it out of all proportion and then bask in the five minutes of fame he'll squeeze out of it.'

Foley put the bag in his pocket. 'And I thought he was here because we're garda officers. You know, a show of support for fellow cops. Especially since one of them is seriously hurt.'

The shape of Matron's mouth could have been a smirk. 'God, no. That nasty man hasn't got a compassionate bone in his skinny body. I bet he didn't even report your accident to the bosses. He'll hold onto that until he sees what he can get out of it.' She slapped her hands together in fury. 'He comes here nearly every day to harass some poor eejit who got themselves in enough trouble to need medical attention. As I said, he pounces on the weak when they're at their most vulnerable. I suppose tis easier than chasing the real criminals. He won't chase the real bad guys because if he caught one he wouldn't know what to do with him.'

This time the matron's smirk was real because she was pleased with herself, and she scooped up a pile of files from the desk and waved Foley towards the door.

Foley pushed the paper bag deeper into his pocket. 'How do I explain this?'

'They're your sandwiches. For your journey home.'

Kavanagh jumped back from the door when Matron whipped it open and his face folded in embarrassment at being caught listening at keyholes. Matron flicked him away with the paperwork in her hand and she flounced off towards the wards.

'Did I hear her say she made you sandwiches?' Kavanagh's voice was full of amazement. 'Why would Matron make you sandwiches?'

'For my journey home.'

'Oh, no.' Kavanagh threw his shoulders back. 'You're staying here until the sergeant gets here. I told you that already.'

'Oh, stop it,' Foley snapped. 'I'm not going anywhere until I know Detective Sheffield is on the mend. But I need to go back to the pub we were staying in to collect our things. I'll bring them back here.'

'I'm not supposed to leave you out of my sight. I have my orders.'

'Then don't. Come with me. Have you got a car? If you have a car it wouldn't take us an hour to get there and back.'

As Kavanagh thought about it, he did a little shuffle around the desk. Then he checked the clock on the wall behind him. 'You can do that later, after the sergeant has spoken to you.'

'Then I'll be charged for another day, which I will have to explain to my Super. He examines every penny we spend, you know.'

'Well that's tough luck, but I'm not ...'

'Look, just point me to the bus stop. The sooner I go, the sooner I will be back.'

Kavanagh looked at Foley's battered clothes and clicked his tongue. 'Have you another uniform in your luggage? Cos you look like a right hobo dressed like that. It'll serve you right if you get arrested as a vagrant.'

'The bus stop?'

Kavanagh rolled his eyes and pointed to the main door. 'Out the gate and turn left. You can't miss it.' Then he poked Foley in the chest. 'And don't even think about jumping on a train back to the bog cos we'll come after you with a list of misdemeanours as long as your arm.'

The sharpness of the breeze after the warmth of the hospital made Foley's eyes water and he stood in the shade to wipe them with his handkerchief. The medication had deadened the concoction of pain, and he was still wary of sudden movements. So he walked on with considered steps towards the main gate.

He glanced back to see if Kavanagh was watching him, and to his surprise he noticed the small annex at the back of the hospital. It had a large oak door and a beautiful coloured window. No wonder he couldn't find the chapel last night. It was in a separate building.

There was no sign of Kavanagh so Foley did a detour across the grass, and as he approached the door it swung open and two nuns came out. They held the door open for him and gave him a sympathetic smile as they scanned his battered uniform. The younger one looked as if she was going to make a comment, but thought against it and just nodded at him instead.

Foley gave them a courteous nod back and let the door swing shut behind him. Then he studied the inside of the chapel. It was larger than he expected, almost as big as the chapel by St Catherine's Hospital in Tralee. And as beautifully decorated.

The hum of the silence gave him that wonderful sense of peace that he always felt when he went to Mass in the Dominican's Church on Sunday. He would wallow in it, and for just a short time it would cancel out the real world.

Instinctively he genuflected in front of the altar and crossed himself with holy water. Then he knelt on the pew at the back. From there he could see everything, and he focused first on the wall behind the altar. Peg's mother back in Patch said they'd put the statue up on a high shelf behind the altar. But from where Foley was kneeling he couldn't see any shelves on that wall. There were two big paintings of the Crucifixion, one on each side of the window. But no shelves.

He stood up and walked down the middle aisle, studying both walls as he pretended to be following the Stations of the Cross. There was no one else in the chapel but it didn't mean he wasn't being watched from a hidden door somewhere. So he stopped every few yards to pay attention to a picture or a plaque on the wall.

When he reached the altar a sense of disappointment started to creep in, because the few shelves he could see on the walls held only candles.

He knelt in front of the altar and closed his eyes. Was this the right time to say a prayer or two? He felt so deceitful even thinking of praying. He was more like a criminal creeping around looking for an opportunity to steal something that wasn't his.

His knees groaned when he stood up and he had to lean on the altar rail as he gave one last look around the chapel. Sheffield was going to be disappointed too when Foley gave him the bad news. The detective was so sure the statue was here in St Kevin's Hospital.

But now it seems that information might have been misinterpreted. They did say St Kevin's, but time and memory can play cruel tricks on people.

Also, the chapel would have had a major uplift after the storm caused so much damage. It was an opportunity to update the decor and rearrange the layout. The only positive outcome of this was that Maranus wouldn't have found the statue either.

Foley spun around when a small door behind the altar opened and a young priest carrying a bundle of prayer books swept into the chapel. He paused when he saw Foley and watched him with suspicious eyes, taking in the dirty overcoat and battered face.

Foley nodded and the priest nodded back. He looked like a boy, fresh faced and tight curly hair.

'Good morning, Father.' Foley tried to sound as unthreatening as possible, and the priest smiled before putting the books on the front bench.

'Good morning, Guard.' He nodded at Foley's uniform. 'It is Guard, I take it.'

'It is,' Foley chuckled. 'Guard Eamon Foley.'

'Father Donnie Callaghan.' The priest held out his hand. Up close Foley could see the lines on the priest's face and the flecks of grey in his hair. There was also a hardness in his eyes that comes from dealing with the underbelly of society. 'Am I right in assuming you're one of the guards from the car crash?'

'You know about that?'

'Nothing much happens here that I don't know about.' Fr Callaghan glanced around him and smiled. 'And also it was mentioned on the news.'

Foley couldn't disguise the sharp intake of breath. 'It was on the news?'

'It was, sure.' The priest frowned at Foley's reaction. 'The guards were asking for witnesses to come forward. So far all they know is your car skidded on a patch of snow and went off the road into a field. Two officers were injured, one of them seriously.'

Foley felt an even deeper sense of foreboding. He was not pleased by this level of publicity. Being recognised was not helpful when you're trying to be discreet.

'Are you all right, Guard?' Fr Callaghan put his hand on Foley's shoulder. 'Should you be sitting down? You look like you should be sitting down.'

'No. I'm grand,' Foley insisted. 'I was surprised it was on the news, that's all. No guard likes being the focus of attention. It brings a lot of adverse reactions, some people pouring out sympathy and some people pouring out animosity.'

Fr Callaghan pointed at the door behind him with his thumb. 'Would you have time for a cup of tea?'

Foley thought about it for a moment then shook his head. 'I would love a cup of tea, Father. But I have to catch a bus. I have to go and collect our cases from the pub we were staying in. Otherwise we'll have no change of clothes. And we'll be charged for another night.'

'Oh, right.' Fr Callaghan said. 'So where is this pub? How far will you have to carry your cases?'

Foley took out the card the landlady had given him and handed it to the priest. 'The bus stops outside the hospital gate every twenty minutes, according to my source.'

'Your source?' the priest chuckled. 'Anyway, never mind all that. I know the place well. Come and have that cup of tea and I will drive you over there.'

'Ah, no,' Foley protested. 'I couldn't put you out like that.'

'Actually you'd be doing me a favour.' The priest gave a conspiratorial wink. 'I had one Mass today, and the rest of the day is taken up with studying. I have a big exam coming up and already my poor brain is at bursting point. So going to fetch your cases will be a wonderful distraction.'

As they waited for the kettle to boil on the tiny primus stove, Fr Callaghan disappeared into another room, and when he came back he was holding a long black overcoat.

'Try this on, Guard.' He held it out in front of Foley. 'We're about the same height, although you're a bit more solid around the middle.'

Foley shook off his coat and put it over the back of a chair. And he suppressed a groan as he slipped his arms through the sleeves of the coat being held by Fr Callaghan. It was a tight fit and it was clean, and Foley transferred his bits from his old coat to the inside pockets of the new one. But the outside pockets were a lot shallower, and Foley couldn't fit the paper bag with the gun into either of them. He didn't want to draw attention to the gun so he put it back where it was and folded his coat around it.

When the kettle started to bubble and spit, Fr Callaghan got distracted making the tea, so Foley quickly retrieved the gun and stuck it into the belt of his trousers.

'So why have you come here?' Fr Callaghan asked as he handed Foley the mug of tea.

'What?' Foley scooped a spoonful of sugar into the mug and stirred it.

'The chapel. What were you praying for?' Fr Callaghan gave a soft smile and sipped his tea.

'Well, to tell you the truth, Father, I was looking for a statue of The Sacred Heart.'

The priest looked around the walls. 'A statue of The Sacred Heart?'

'Yes. A lady we were talking to yesterday had an accident about seven years ago. She ended up here in St Kevin's where she was treated very well. Afterwards she went to live with relatives and she donated the statue to the chapel here. It was to replace the one that was damaged when the window was broken in a storm.'

'Oh, right.' Fr Callaghan looked around the room again. 'I wasn't here then, I'm afraid. So I don't know anything about that. But I don't think there's a statue of The Sacred Heart here in this chapel.'

Foley gave a resigned shrug. 'Well, it was a few years ago. Anything could have happened to it since.'

'And the place has been decorated not so long ago too.' Fr Callaghan pointed at the brightly painted walls. 'If the statues were taken down it might have been given to one of the parishioners.'

He pulled a packet of cigarettes from his inside pocket and held it out to Foley. Foley shook his head and Fr Callaghan pulled one out with his teeth, shoved the packet back in his pocket and cracked a match.

'Or maybe the nuns took it back to the convent,' he said through a cloud of smoke. 'They love their statues, don't they? Will I ask them for you? Tell me what it looks like and I'll ask them when I see them in the morning.'

Foley cursed inside. It was all slipping away again. It was like the elusive Pimpernel. You see him here, you see him there ...

Fr Callaghan's car was a lot more comfortable than the one Sheffield had borrowed. Nothing rattled or looked like it was going to fall off.

They'd gone about three blocks when Fr Callaghan slowed at a junction and Foley noticed a small shop on the corner of the street. The weak sun highlighted the gold writing across the middle of the window: Maurice Hobbert, Solicitor.

The whole row of shops along the street looked neglected, and Hobbert's was no exception. The paint on the window had flaked in patches and the door had chunks taken out of the paint.

Fr Callaghan noticed Foley's interest in the shop and he took his time pulling out of the junction.

'Do you know Mossie Hobbert, Eamon?' he asked as he joined the traffic on the main road.

'No,' Foley sat back in his seat. 'The lady I told you about who gave the statue to the hospital, she mentioned that Mossie was her solicitor. She spoke highly of him.'

'Ah sure, everyone who has dealings with Mossie Hobbert speaks highly of him. He's one of the good guys, as the Yanks would say. He's an honest man, very humble and very brave. He's faced down many a tough character when he's defending a client, so he has.'

'I'm surprised at the cut of his place, though.'

Fr Callaghan glanced in his rear view mirror and nodded. 'Ah sure, doesn't he do a lot of work for people who might be a little short of funds. I hear he's owed thousands. Most people do try to pay him back, but that would be just a few bob a week.'

'So you've had dealings with him, father?'

'Note directly, no. But sometimes people who have dealt with him confide in me. And they all say the same thing. He has saved their lives.'

The journey to the pub didn't take as long as Foley expected, which was probably because Fr Callaghan never stopped talking. He seemed to know so much about everything, the places they passed, the buildings in the distance, who was related to whom, and who got married to their best friend's daughter. He knew who owned what farm, and who ran the village pub. And every story was told through a prism of kindness and understanding. Fr Callaghan didn't have a bad word to say about anyone.

There were still pockets of partially melted snow around the outbuildings at the side of the pub. Fr Callaghan parked as close to the front door as he could get, and they dashed inside to avoid the sharp breeze that swept around the gable.

'Will I get you something to drink while you're getting your cases?' Fr Callaghan had already selected the table by the fire in the cosy bar, and he dropped his trilby on it as he pulled out a chair.

'No. I'm grand.' Foley smiled as he approached the young woman behind the bar, and her own smile vanished as he got closer and she noticed the bruises on his face.

'Hello, Mrs Counihan, can I have the keys for room four and five.' He nodded at the board on the wall behind her, and the young woman frowned as she looked him up and down, taking note of his long black coat. Then her face lit up when she realised who he was.

'Ah, Guard Foley,' she beamed. 'I didn't recognise you for a minute there because of the ...' She made a circle around her face with her finger. 'What in the name of God happened to you?'

Foley grimaced. 'Do not get into an argument with a lorry, that's all I can say about that.'

Mrs Counihan shook her head in sympathy as she handed him the keys. 'We were wondering if you would be staying another night. Where's your pal? Don't tell me ...'

'Yep. He's in hospital. So I've come to collect our things and settle the bill.'

As Foley headed for the stairs he sensed someone watching him, and when he looked back the man leaning on the bar holding a pint of stout turned away sharply. He had his collar pulled right up and a cap down over his eyes, but for some strange reason Foley felt he knew him.

When the man looked up again Foley made eye contact and nodded, but the man straightened up and put his glass down with a thump. Then he pulled his collar even higher and practically ran out of the bar.

Foley gave a loud snigger and spun around to speak to Mrs Counihan, but she had her back turned and was busy making out his bill. Foley shrugged and went up the stairs.

Chapter Twenty-Four

As Foley came back down stairs with the suitcases, Fr Callaghan was at the bar getting two large brandies from Mrs Counihan.

'No, no,' Foley called out. 'Not for me. I'll just have a glass of stout.'

Fr Callaghan seemed to freeze, and from where Foley was standing it looked as if his face twisted into a snarl. He clicked his tongue. 'In that case I'll have the two brandies and Guard Foley will have the ladies drink.'

He picked up the two glasses and gave Mrs Counihan a huge smile. 'Guard Foley will be adding these to the bill,' he called over his shoulder as he walked back to the table by the fire.

Foley watched the priest with an unsettling swell of disquiet. Foley didn't really know the priest, of course. He'd only met him this morning. But in that short time he'd created an impression about him. He appeared to be thoughtful, considerate, at ease with the world. Then suddenly there is this awkward blip in that image, and Foley didn't like it.

As the glass of stout was being poured Foley took the cases over to the table, and he noticed the two other empty glasses on the table. Fr Callaghan was staring into the fire while holding one of the brandies, and Foley could see his eyes were already becoming disconnected with his surroundings as his head rocked gently to whatever music he was playing in his head.

When he realised Foley was standing there he raised the glass in salute. 'You're a good man, Guard Foley.' Then he drained the glass in one gulp.

'Thank you, Father,' Foley replied. 'That's …'

'To all the guards in Ireland,' Fr Callaghan continued. 'God bless them and those who sail in them.' He gave a cackle of a laugh and banged his fist on the table.

Foley looked around and was relieved to see that the only other person in the bar was Mrs Counihan, and she was busy doing something with a cloth in her hand.

'So how many brandies have you had there, Father? Wasn't I only gone for less than fifteen minutes, sure?'

Fr Callaghan picked up the other glass of brandy and waved it at Foley. 'Not enough, I'd say.'

Foley wondered how many times he'd seen this over the years. A quiet and inoffensive person, seemingly contented in his own world, but secretly engaging with a demon that's impossible to control.

Foley went back to the bar and took a long swig from the glass of stout as he paid his bill.

'Right,' he said to Fr Callaghan as he came back and picked up the suitcases. 'Time to go.'

'What?' Fr Callaghan's eyes were read and teary, and his mouth was fixed in an angry sneer. 'I thought you were getting another round in.'

'No,' Foley struggled to control his annoyance. 'I have to get back. I have a lot to do back in the hospital.'

'Then good for you,' Fr Callaghan slurred. 'But I'm staying for another drink.'

Foley shook his head and went back to the bar where Mrs Counihan was watching them now with curious eyes. 'Will you order me a taxi, Mrs Counihan?'

'I will of course.' Mrs Counihan went into the small office behind the bar, but before she could make the call Fr Callaghan came rushing over and put his hands up.

'All right, all right,' he called to her. 'I'll take him. For feck sake, I was only joking. I should have realised that guards have no sense of humour.'

'Too late, Father.' Foley couldn't look at the priest. 'You made your point. Thank you for bringing me here. I do appreciate it. But you can go back and sit by the fire. I will be grand with a taxi.'

Fr Callaghan went to pick up one of the cases but misjudged it and staggered against the bar. 'Oh come on,' he spat. 'I'll take you back to the hospital. There's no need for all this feckin drama.'

'As I said,' Foley grabbed the priest's arm to steady him. 'You go back and sit by the fire. Relax. Take it easy till you're sober enough to drive again.'

Fr Callaghan stepped back away from Foley and looked him up and down with disdain. 'What are you saying? Are you saying I'm not fit to drive? Is this the officious guard talking now? The guardian of the law telling a priest he's not fit to drive? Well, feck you so. I'm not bothered ...'

Foley picked up the suitcases and called over his shoulder, 'Taxi please, Mrs Counihan.'

Fr Callaghan followed him to the door making all sorts of noises, then he grabbed Foley's arm. 'All right, I'm sorry. I'm sorry. I'll take you ... look, I'm very sorry. C'mon. Please. Just let me ...'

'All right.' Foley held out his hand. 'Give me the key.'
'What?'
'Give me the car key. I'm driving.'

Fr Callaghan sighed and seemed to shrink into himself as he reluctantly handed Foley the key.

As Foley opened the car boot and put in the cases he got the strangest feeling he was being watched again. So he took his time as he closed the boot and got in the driver's seat, casually scanning the surrounding area for signs of life. But he couldn't see anyone. Fr Callaghan was sitting stiffly in the passenger seat watching every move Foley made to his nice motor car.

They drove in silence for the first few miles. Fr Callaghan had gradually slipped lower in the seat and stared out of the window. When he made a sudden peculiar noise in his throat Foley glanced at him.

'Are you alright there, Father?'

Fr Callaghan put his hand over his eyes. 'No, I'm not alright. I have not been all right for years, if you want the truth.'

Foley studied him for a moment then looked back at the road, but he didn't reply. He waited for the priest to continue, which he did.

'I don't know what I'm doing here.' He sounded weary. 'I'm in the wrong place. This isn't where I want to be.'

Foley still didn't comment, and the silence continued for another couple of miles. Then Fr Callaghan sat up straight in his seat.

'I have these severe panic attacks,' he said, looking out of the window as if he was telling the whole world. 'I look at my life and all I can see is a long dark tunnel stretching ahead of me, dark and hopeless. Never ending. On and on, day after day, dark and meaningless and depressing. There is no light at the end of my God forsaken tunnel. It goes on and on into empty blackness.'

This time the sob closed his throat and he leant his head back on the seat.

'So where do you want to be?' Foley was trying to stop the sob developing into anything more.

'I want to be where you are.'

'Me?' Foley chuckled in surprise, but the look the priest gave him was serious.

'Yes. I want to be a guard. All my life I wanted to be a guard. My Uncle Mike was a guard, and I dreamt of following in his footsteps. I saw how everyone looked up to him, spoke of him with pride, and respected his wisdom and his status.'

Before Foley could contradict that illusion, Fr Callaghan continued. 'But when I applied to join the force I was rejected without even an interview. My response to some of the questions raised concerns about my suitability to be a serving police officer.'

Foley couldn't stop himself saying, 'Oh?'

'Yeah. Not even an interview. But do you know what hurt the most? My family weren't the least bit surprised. Not one of them. It was a foregone conclusion that I was never going to be a guard.'

Fr Callaghan rubbed his eyes with the flat of his hand and lay his head against the window.

'So how did you end up being a priest?' Foley asked.

Fr Callaghan thought about this, and he sat back up again. 'There was a young fella I was in school with. We weren't friends or anything, but I knew he was studying in Rockwell College. Anyway, he was home for the summer holidays and I met him in town one day, and it turned out he was in Rockwell studying to be a priest.' Fr Callaghan nodded gravely at this. 'He was so full of enthusiasm, so excited about his future in missionary work. When I told my mother about him she said she already knew, and her face lit up at the thought of having a priest in the family. How proud his mother must be feeling, she said. How the whole family must be thrilled about it.'

He stared out of the window again. 'I know it sounds pathetic, but I craved that kind of response for myself. I desperately wanted my family to feel the same kind of pride for me too. So I went back to Rockwell with him, and I was accepted immediately.'

'And your family was proud of you after all?'

Fr Callaghan thought about that. 'They were, yes. Very proud,' he answered.

Then he added, 'But I wasn't ready for all the attention that was suddenly heaped on me. I craved their attention, as I said, but I didn't realise how intrusive it was going to be. You hear talk about famous people being in a goldfish bowl, where their every move is watched and commented on. You have to smile when you're introduced to every Ton, Dick and Harry your family wants to impress. And God help you if you don't react properly. You can feel the animosity drip from someone who feels slighted by something you said. Or didn't say.'

'You surprise me,' Foley said. 'Most priests I've met seem to be comfortable with all that.'

Fr Callaghan was annoyed by that and he rolled his eyes. 'Most of them are, to be sure. But I am not. I find it a struggle every day.'

He rubbed his hands together. 'Tis not just that. There's the other side of it too. I have seen some really horrible things, things that, once seen, can never be unseen. I've had desperate people on their knees in front of me pleading for a miracle, begging me to help them in their grief and pain. But I'm just a conduit. Because my Master walked on water, they think I can too. They think that just by laying my hands on them I will make them well again. And because I can't cure the sick, I feel like a fraud. I'm racked with guilt and I feel their pain sticking to me. And the only way I can deaden it is by having a conversation with my pal Vodka. He's the only one who will not betray me. No smell, you see. Colourless, odourless, silent. Non-critical.'

He chuckled at this and patted his chest.

'So you're telling me you made a mistake by becoming a priest?' Foley said after a pause.

Fr Callaghan nodded and rubbed his eyes again. 'If I'm honest, I suspected I was making a mistake before I was even ordained. But I was in denial. I believed I could brazen it out, and in time everything would be grand.'

'But it wasn't?'

'No,' Fr Callaghan said. 'The big revelation came suddenly and bitterly. I was booked to marry a young couple, and when the bride to be came to see me I was immediately captivated. I had never seen such a pretty young woman in my whole life. She haunted me.'

He shuddered. 'Anyway, at the wedding reception that evening she got me up to dance with her, and just being so close to her made me dizzy. Holding her hand and with my arm around her waist, I lost control for a moment. She had the most beautiful mouth, and I leaned in to kiss it. But she turned her head away at the last second. So my kiss landed on her neck.'

He shuddered again. 'I can still feel the way her whole body stiffened with the shock. Her eyes almost popped out of her head, and she pulled away from me. The rest is an embarrassing blur. She didn't tell her husband, luckily enough, because he didn't react. But she avoided me like the plague after that.'

'Celibacy,' Foley chuckled. 'That's the part I can't understand. To me tis the most natural thing in the world to admire the female form. And there's nothing wrong with that. There's nothing wrong in admiring a field of beautiful flowers, but being denied the chance of picking a special one and taking it home to lovingly care for it is just cruel.'

Fr Callaghan gave a resigned smile and stared out of the window again. They had reached the outskirts of the city and as Foley drove down a wide street Fr Callaghan suddenly shouted, 'Turn left. Turn left.'

Foley braked and shouted back, 'What left?'

'There.' Fr Callaghan pointed to a big arch between two large warehouse type buildings.

Foley hesitated and Fr Callaghan waved him on. 'I just remembered,' he cried. 'I think I know where your statue is. Go in there. Go in through the arch.'

The arch took them into a courtyard that was overlooked on three sides by big red brick buildings. Right in front of them was a large black door with three steps and two pillars giving it an air of importance. There was a row of tall windows on each of the four floors of that building. On the other two sides of the courtyard the windows were smaller and the doors were the size of an average house.

The yard was littered with rubbish. Piles of broken slates and bricks filled every corner. Rotten mattresses and the remains of tables and chairs took up whatever space was left.

Foley drove right up to the big door and parked facing the steps. As he stepped out of the car he could feel the despondency of the place. The air was bitterly cold and reeked of decay and neglect. Every window was either broken or cracked, and the big front door was pockmarked with rot.

'What is this place?' Foley stepped over some rubbish and walked up the steps.

'It started out as a workhouse.' Fr Callaghan skipped past Foley and pushed the door open with his foot. 'Then it was a lunatic asylum, which no one speaks about because of the brutal regime that was in place at the time. During the civil war it was taken over by the anti-treaty side, and later re-captured by the Free State Army. Finally the nuns took over the running of it. They turned it into an orphanage.'

The once impressive hall was now desperately sad. Parts of the ceiling had collapsed and massive lumps of plaster had dropped off the walls.

'The nuns still own it, of course,' Fr Callaghan continued. 'But they can't afford to run it anymore. They were forced to abandon it during the Emergency when everything was scarce and there was no money coming in.'

'So what are we doing here?' Foley pulled his coat tighter around him and blew on his frozen hands.

'Looking for your status.' Fr Callaghan pointed down one of the corridors.

'Why do you think the statue is here?'

'Because I think I saw it. Or one that looked like it anyway. I only remembered when we were passing by just now. I had completely forgotten about it, I have to say.'

Fr Callaghan hurried down one of the corridors and pulled open a door that led to a big room with tall windows and a high ceiling. Two rows of tables were lined up along the centre of the room, and a long table on an elevated platform had a huge painting of a severe looking lady staring down at it.

And surprisingly, everything in the room was stacked tidily. Boxes and books were lined up in neat piles along the table, clothes were folded, and crockery was laid out safely.

'So how do you know about this place, Father?'

'Well, when I took over St Kevin's the sacristy was a right mess. Everything was scattered in heaps, there was nowhere to put things. I mentioned to Sister Agnes that I was looking for a table, or some sort of filing cabinet to store the prayer books, and she brought me here.'

He went across to the far side of the room and pointed to a row of assorted statues standing like a small army against the wall. 'I remember seeing these because I was thinking of taking one of the small ones to put by my bed.'

The nuns had separated the statues into groups, The Virgin Marys first, then Jesus, and at the far end all The Sacred Hearts.

'Shit.' Foley didn't mean to say it out loud and Fr Callaghan looked at him with a question in his eyes.

'Well, all the Sacred Hearts look the same. How will I know which is which?'

Fr Callaghan dropped into an armchair and created a cloud of dust and a ping of annoyed springs. 'What does it matter? If the poor woman just wants to know if it's still in existence, surely she'll be happy you found it for her. Are you saying she wants it back?'

'She would like it back, yes.'

'Then pick the best looking one. How will she be able to tell?'

'Well, it was in her house since before her children were born, so they grew up praying to it every night. I imagine they know every chip and crack in it.'

Fr Callaghan had closed his eyes, and his elbow was on the arm of the chair with his head resting in his hand. Foley chuckled and started looking through the row of Sacred Hearts. And it wasn't long before he realised there was only three that fitted the description of Mrs Cassidy's statue. Tall enough and wide enough to hide a big envelope inside. He picked up the most battered one and gave it a shake. Something rattled inside and he turned it over, and he could just make out the impression where the sliver of plaster had been stuck in place on the back of it. He ran his thumb nail along it, but it didn't shift.

His first thought was to take it away with him and break it open later when he was alone. He looked over at Fr Callaghan, and he was surprised to see the priest sitting up and watching him closely.

'All right there, Father?' Foley put the statue on the table as Fr Callaghan extracted himself from the armchair with a long weary groan.

'I have to go to ... you know? The little boy's room?' He patted his stomach. 'It's right down the hall. I won't be long.' He wobbled and held onto the back of the chair to get his balance, then he shuffled across to the door.

This was his opportunity. Foley looked around for something sharp to prise the back off the statue. There was a damaged picture against the wall. The frame was split and the glass was broken. Foley used his handkerchief to pick up a long sliver of glass, and he began scratching at the join with it. But it didn't even dent it. He tried tapping it, then pressing it, but whatever Mrs Cassidy had used to stick it together with all those years ago, it had solidified. The piece was solidly embedded and was not going to yield.

Perhaps he should just drop it on the floor and apologise later to Fr Callaghan. But his instinct was to avoid drawing attention to what was inside the statue. Fr Callaghan would understand if Foley took the statue with him on the pretence of returning it to Mrs Cassidy, so that was the safest thing to do.

Out of curiosity Foley checked the other two Sacred Heart statues. Neither one rattled, so he picked up the chipped one and headed back to the car.

Sheffield's case was the bigger of the two and large enough to take the statue, so Foley opened both cases on the back seat. He took a heap of clothes out of Sheffield's case and stuffed them into his own, then he wrapped the statue in a shirt and put it in Sheffield's case.

Foley was about to close the door when he heard footsteps coming out of the building behind him, and he turned around. Fr Callaghan was buttoning up his coat as he came out into the cold yard, and he was taking cautious steps, desperately trying not to stagger.

'All right there, Father,' Foley greeted him. 'Did you find the little boy's room?'

'I did.' Fr Callaghan patted his stomach again and grinned. Then he looked past Foley and his face stretched in horror.

Foley instinctively ducked behind the car door as the blast from a shotgun peppered the car window above his head and showered him with broken glass.

The second shot went wild. Then Foley heard the sound of a shotgun being broken and two spent cartridges hitting the ground. It was his chance to run for cover. He forgot the agony of his battered body and sprinted for the open door of the building.

Fr Callaghan had vanished. But he hadn't gone far. Foley found him lying on the stairs holding the stump of his hand, trying to stop the blood that was pulsing through the fingers of his good hand that he'd pressed against it.

Foley ran over and knelt beside him. The priest's face was already drained of colour and his eyes were red and staring in horror at his wound. Foley pulled up the leg of his trousers and whipped off the bandage the nuns had wrapped around his stitches. He folded it into a thick pad and pressed it to what was left of Fr Callaghan's hand.

'Hold this,' he shouted, then he ran back and threw himself at the door, slamming it shut. The bolts were rusting and loose but he shut them anyway. Then he ran back to the priest.

'Is there another way out of here?' It came out harsher than Foley wanted, but Fr Callaghan's eyes were already unfocused and his head wobbled. He didn't answer.

'We have to move. We have to hide,' Foley shouted again, hoping to shake the priest into action. He grabbed Fr

Callaghan's good arm and put it around his neck, then he lifted him to his feet and dragged him as far as he could away from the door.

He found a solid oak table and propped Fr Callaghan against the wall behind it. Then he turned the table onto its side and pulled it between them and the front door. He drew his revolver and pointed it in the direction the gunman would have to come. He had five bullets left. The odds seemed useless. A .38 against a shotgun? Even worse, Foley had rarely fired any kind of gun before.

His heart was pumping and his hand shook so hard the gun was making tapping noises on the table. He took a deep breath and sat back on his heels. And he suddenly became aware that the moaning sound was coming from him, because his stitches were pulling and stinging every part of his legs.

Fr Callaghan's head was slumped on his chest and his good hand was hanging limply in his lap. And the blood was still pulsing from his wound. Foley ripped the bandage from his other leg and this time he pulled the sleeve of Fr Callaghan's coat as far up his arm as he could. The first bandage was soaked so he squeezed the blood out of it and put it back over the stump. Then he used the second bandage to secure it as tight as possible. Next he took the lace from the priest's shoe and tied it around the arm in a tourniquet.

Finally he pulled the priest's coat sleeve right down and tied it in a bunch with the lace from his second shoe to keep everything in place. And all the time his nerves were on edge waiting for the gunman to kick the front door open.

Fr Callaghan's head suddenly jerked up and he gave a howl of agony. Foley jumped.

'Easy there, Father,' he said. 'Take it easy there.'

'Holy Mother of God, what have they done to me?' Fr Callaghan was staring in disbelief at his damaged arm. He howled again and beat his good hand against his chest.

'The pain,' he wailed. 'I can't stand the pain. Help me. For feck sake, help me. Stop this pain.'

His legs started to jerk as if he was having a fit, and he banged his head against the wall behind him. Foley grabbed him and pulled him away from the wall, and he lay him down with his head in Foley's lap.

'I'm sorry, Father.' Foley looked around at the massive hallway. 'We're trapped in here. You need to get to a hospital, but we cannot risk going out that door. So do you know if there's another way out of here?'

'My pocket.' Fr Callaghan raised his head and grabbed at his coat with his good hand. 'The flask. Get the flask. C'mon, man. Help me.'

It took a moment for Foley to understand what the priest meant. He patted him down until he felt the bulge in his inside pocket. He reached in and recovered the whisky flask. It was monogrammed and expensive. And filled with vodka.

Foley unscrewed the top and held it to Fr Callaghan's lips, and he sucked at it loudly like a drowning man grabbing at a float. He only stopped when he had to draw breath. He smacked his lips, then very slowly raised his damaged arm. And he looked at Foley with a strange, almost resigned smile. 'My hand?'

'I'm afraid it's …'

Fr Callaghan closed his eyes and made a funny sound. 'So I won't be able to play the piano now?'

Foley didn't know what to say to that. 'You play the piano?' was what came out.

'No,' Fr Callaghan gave a mocking snort. 'But suppose I want to learn?'

A weak smile danced around the priest's lips and he gave a big sigh. Foley waited a moment before asking him again, 'Is there another way out of here? I have to get you to the hospital. But we cannot go out the way we came in, just in case they're waiting for us.'

The vodka seemed to have pacified Fr Callaghan and he looked around before answering. 'There's two doors that I know of, but they both open onto the courtyard.'

'That's no good,' Foley groaned. 'They're probably waiting for us in the courtyard.'

'Who are they?' Fr Callaghan queried. 'Why are they trying to kill you? What did you do to them?'

'I have no idea,' Foley lied. Then a thought hit him. If they saw him putting the statue into the suitcase on the back seat of the car, they would probably have taken it already. Maybe that was why they didn't chase him into the building. If they found the statue there was no reason for them to hang around. Unless they were instructed to clean up any mess.

Something banged deep inside the building, a sharp slap like a door slamming shut, and both men turned towards it with their ears straining. Foley lay the priest's head down carefully and dashed over to the stairs. From the fourth step up he could see the whole of the courtyard through the tall window near the door. He swore out loud when he saw the door on the left wing swinging open in the breeze.

'Shit, shit, shit.' He spun around in a circle, desperately trying to decide what to do now. The gunman was coming in behind them. How far away was he? The noise they heard was hollow and could have been just an echo, so it was impossible to judge the distance.

He jumped back down off the stairs and unbolted the front door, and he opened it just a couple of inches. The car was less than ten feet away. If the gunman was creeping around the other side of the building trying to catch them unawares, then the car was considerably closer to them. The key was in the ignition. He hoped.

He stuffed the gun in his pocket and ran back to Fr Callaghan. 'C'mon.' he put his hands under the priest's arms and tried to lift him. 'We have to go.'

Fr Callaghan yelped and his eyes screwed up in pain. 'I can't. I can't.' He tried to push Foley away with his good hand. 'Tis no use. You go. Go and get help. They're not after me so just leave me here.'

'I can't leave you, you big eejit. You need to be in the hospital. So come on. Help me get you on your feet and I can haul you to the car.'

Both men staggered with the effort, and once Fr Callaghan was on his feet they shuffled across the great hall to the door.

Fr Callaghan was whimpering every step of the way. 'Sweet Jesus, Sweet Jesus,' he sobbed. 'My Lord, I know what you went through was far, far worse than this, but I was never a strong person. Please, please, please make the pain go away. Make the pain stop.'

When they reached the door Foley propped the priest against the wall and peered through the gap into the courtyard. It seemed clear, but there were a dozen places a gunman could be hiding. If he had time, Foley could stand there and watch for movement when the gunman became impatient. But they didn't have time because another crash deep in the building rippled down the hall behind them.

'Go,' Fr Callaghan shouted at Foley. 'Leave me here, for feck sake. They won't hurt a priest. Save yourself. Get away and bring back some help for me. Go on, you big clown. Just go.'

Adrenalin took over and Foley grabbed Fr Callaghan, and he ran the both of them out of the door and down the steps to the car. He shoved the cases onto the floor and threw Fr Callaghan across the back seat, then he dived into the driver's seat and turned the key. Nothing. Just a click. A stream of curses poured out of Foley's mouth as he turned the key again. Another click.

'Come on, you stupid heap of shit.' He slapped the steering wheel in frustration.

'Use the choke.' Fr Callaghan was trying to sit up but the pain was pinning him down. 'Pull out the choke.'

'What choke?'

'By the key. There's a knob. Pull it out and turn the key.'

Foley pulled the knob as far out as it would go, and this time there was a welcome growl when he turned the key. Another stream of curses poured out of his mouth and this time they were from relief. He threw the gears into reverse and pressed the pedal to the floor, and caused a roar from the engine and a screech of protest from the tyres.

His nerves were still tingling, waiting for someone to appear at one of the doors, or even at one of the windows, as he spun the car in a circle around the yard. Then at the last minute he slammed the car into second gear and raced through the arch, causing a woman with a pram to leap back and scream at him. The driver of a bread van waved a fist at him and shouted abuse as Foley cut in front of him.

They raced down two streets before Foley realised he was lost, so he pulled into the kerb and asked a newspaper seller for directions. He caused another session of abuse when he pulled back into the traffic at full speed.

He got the car as close to the front door of the hospital as he could then ran into reception shouting for help. The nurse at the desk called to some others and when Foley opened the car door there was a cry of horror. 'That's Fr Callaghan. What did you do to him?'

'He was shot. He lost his hand.'

Foley and the nurse eased Fr Callaghan out of the back seat, then several people lifted him onto a trolley and raced him away. Foley followed, and he got as far as the reception desk when he saw who was standing by Det Sheffield's ward door. The commotion had drawn everyone out to see what was going on. Leo Maranus was one of them, and he was staring at Foley with his cold dead eyes.

Foley ran back out to the car and drove away down the street. His mind was in turmoil. He had the statue. He had D'Lacey's deeds. But now he didn't know what to do with them. He had no idea who he could trust anymore. He assumed Sheffield had a plan, and he never questioned it. He assumed the plan involved taking the deeds straight to D'Lacey and collecting the reward. Simple. But now he was on his own and he felt too vulnerable. Here in the big city he was out of his depth. He didn't know a soul. He didn't even know what part of the city he was in. He had no idea where D'Lacey lived, and he dreaded drawing attention to himself by asking.

In the ideal world he would go straight to the nearest garda barracks and report to the duty inspector, but that felt like walking into the enemy camp and surrendering.

An idea popped into his head. He checked the fuel gauge. Just over half a tank. Was that enough to get him to Tralee? At least he would be amongst friends there. The Super was a good man and he would support Foley. He had been briefed about D'Lacey's deeds so he would decide on a strategy to get them back to their owner.

When Foley slowed down at a junction and looked across the street at a shabby little shop, he suddenly had an even better idea.

He caused another round of honking and swearing when he swung across the road and pulled up in front of the shop that had *Maurice Hobbert, Solicitor* on the window.

Chapter Twenty-Five

The young nurse behind the reception desk did a double take when she saw Foley walk through the front door of St Kevin's Hospital. Her brow creased in a frown because she knew she should have recognised him, but she couldn't remember why. He was familiar, of course, but different. Wasn't he a guard? So why did he look like a priest now?

She flashed him a smile but he didn't respond. Anxiety had frozen his face. His stomach was tight and uncomfortable as if he'd swallowed a cannon ball. And for the umpteenth time he questioned why he was doing this.

Common sense told him he should take Fr Callaghan's car and go back to Tralee. But something else was pulling him in a different direction. As some clever person once said, it ain't over until it's over. And Foley's problem would never be over until all the players knew it was. Running away home to Tralee would just delay that happening. It would prevent the final curtain from coming down, even when the performance was already over.

No, Foley had to confront his demons and face up to the people who tried to do him and Sheffield a serious injury. So he took a deep breath and walked into Sheffield's ward.

Sheffield was propped up on a stack of pillows. The bit of his face Foley could see under the bandages was swollen and pasty white. And it was obvious from his vacant eyes that he was still heavily sedated. He looked at Foley but didn't seem to respond.

Guard Kavanagh and the sergeant were sitting on hard chairs.

'Holy Mother of God.' The sergeant's eyes squinted with curiosity when he saw Foley, and he flicked Kavanagh on the arm. 'I thought you said he'd be on the train back to the bog already?'

A nurse who was spooning medicine into the mouth of the patient in the next bed looked up at the visitor, and she screwed the cap back on the medicine bottle as she said, 'If you're looking for your friend, Father, I'm afraid he isn't in this ward.' She pointed down the corridor with her thumb. 'Try down there.'

'He isn't a *Father*,' Kavanagh sniggered, and he shifted nervously in his chair when the nurse glared at him. He indicated Sheffield with a flick of his head. 'Sure isn't he the guard who was brought in at the same time as your man in the bed there.'

The nurse studied Sheffield for a moment then looked back at Foley. 'So why are you dressed like a priest?'

Foley looked down at his long black coat. 'Fr Callaghan lent this to me. Mine was torn.'

The nurse gave a shake of her head, gathered up her tray of medicines and went out, staring at Foley under her eyes. Foley waited until she was gone before asking, 'Where is Inspector Maranus?'

Kavanagh's eyes flicked from Foley to the sergeant then back at Foley again. 'So why didn't you?'

'What?'

Kavanagh gave a mocking pout. 'Why didn't you feck off home?'

'That is none of your business.' It came out as a dry croak and Foley coughed into his hand.

'Of course it's our business.' The sergeant unfolded himself from the chair. 'We came all the way back here so we could get a statement from you, you inconsiderate maggot. So don't play the clever dick with us.'

'Well, that's your tough luck,' Foley answered. 'I came to speak to Inspector Maranus.'

The sergeant looked around the ward with a sarcastic smirk on his face. 'Who the hell is Inspector Maranus?'

'Oh, don't give me that shit,' Foley growled. 'He was here. I saw him.'

'Who are you talking about?' Kavanagh joined in. 'There was no one here when we got back.' He looked at his watch. 'And we've been here for over ten minutes already.'

Detective Sheffield gave a sharp moan and lifted his head a fraction, then he let it drop again. Foley rushed over and put his hand on the detective's arm. 'What's the matter? Can I do anything?'

Sheffield's pink eyes blinked and he gave a feeble wave of his hand. His battered lips parted in a smile that immediately turned into a grimace, and he tried to raise his head again. 'The statue,' he whispered

Foley learnt closer. 'The statue?'

'He knows.' Sheffield licked his lips.

'Who?'

'Inspector ...'

Foley looked around at Kavanagh and the sergeant who were hovering like a couple of vultures. '*Maranus?*' he asked in the softest voice he could muster.

Sheffield nodded and groaned again, the pain obvious in his features. 'I didn't mean to. It just came out when he was asking about the crash.' He swallowed again and licked his lips which were starting to bleed with the effort of talking. 'I wanted to explain what we were doing on that road and it sort of slipped out. I told him ... you know ... the statue ...' He gave a weary sigh and closed his eyes, and Foley patted him on the arm.

'It doesn't matter now,' Foley told him. 'I already found it.'

Sheffield's eyes snapped open and he tried to speak but his bruised lips wouldn't respond. And Foley wasn't sure if the look on Sheffield's face was of relief or worry. He gave the detective's arm another squeeze.

'Look, don't be worrying about this now. Maranus is too late. The merchandise is back where it belongs. So you get as much rest as you can. Make sure you're well enough when the time comes to collect your promotion.'

Sheffield blinked again and Foley smiled at him. 'Well there's nothing to stop you getting your promotion now, is there? You've done your job. It's all over.' Foley pulled his coat tighter around him. 'Look, there's a few loose ends I have to tie up first, then I'll be back to bring you up to date.'

As Foley turned around the sergeant stepped between him and the door. 'Where do you think you're going?'

'I told you. I have to see Inspector Maranus. So if you'll excuse …'

But the sergeant wasn't in the mood to be fobbed off again. 'No. You are not going anywhere until I have your statement. So sit down …'

Foley tried to side step around him but the sergeant moved with him.

'Get out of my way,' Foley growled and the sergeant's face curled into an angry mask. He went to grab the front of Foley's coat but Foley slapped the hand away.

'You hit … how you dare strike a superior officer?' the sergeant gasped, and Kavanagh jumped up and let his chair drop to the floor with a loud crash. 'I could have you arrested for that.'

Foley put his hands up. 'Look, just tell me where Maranus is. I have to speak to him, then I'll come back and you can have whatever you want. All right?'

'We don't know who the feck Maranus is.' Kavanagh had his chest puffed up and his fists in a ball.

'But he was here.' Foley's voice rose in tune with his impatience. 'I saw him.'

'But *we* didn't.' The sergeant had dribble on his chin and he swiped it away with his hand.

Foley made another attempt to get to the door but the sergeant grabbed his arm this time. 'Stop. You are staying here until I get a full statement from you. So sit down and …'

Foley slapped the hand away a second time and the sergeant's face turned purple with the flash of fury that took hold of him.

'Right,' he shouted. 'Guard Kavanagh, put your handcuffs on him. Foley, I'm arresting you for resisting arrest so get those hands behind your back.'

'Holy Mother of God and the wee baby in the crib. What is all this noise?' Matron shot into the ward waving a pencil like a baton in an orchestra, and she shoved herself between Foley and the sergeant. 'And what are the two of you still doing here?' She stood up on her toes as she addressed the sergeant.

'We were waiting for this fella to come back.'

'I told you to leave my hospital ages ago. There are very sick people in here and they don't want a bunch of grown men howling at each other like a gaggle of fishwives.'

When she looked at Kavanagh he physically shrank away from her. 'Sorry, Matron. I was only doing what the sergeant ordered me to do. I'm only a guard. I have to do what I'm told.'

The sergeant opened and closed his mouth like a goldfish in a bowl but no words came out as he glared at Kavanagh.

Matron looked Foley up and down, frowning at his long black coat. 'And you, what are you doing back here? You were discharged. You have no business back here now, so get out of my hospital.'

'But that's my pal in the bed there.' Foley gave a pitying whimper. 'I have to know how he's doing.'

Matron glanced at Sheffield who forced a smile. 'Well if you're going to behave like a mob of school boys, I don't think he would want you anywhere near him,' she growled.

She waved her hands as if she was rounding up a flock of sheep, and in the blink of an eye all three men found themselves out in the corridor and being herded towards the door.

'Matron,' Foley turned to face her and had to sidestep the swipe of her pencil.

'C'mon,' she snapped. 'Get out of my sight.'

'Listen,' Foley persisted. 'There was a fella here earlier when I brought Fr Callaghan in. Do you know where he went?'

Matron rolled her eyes. 'Do you know how many fellas …?'

'This fella is big. Well over six feet. And he has a mop of grey hair. His name is Leo Maranus.'

'Ah, yes. He's a garda officer.' A smile played on the corner of her mouth and in the artificial light of the corridor it looked like she actually blushed. 'What about him?'

'I need to speak to him.'

Matron stared into space for a moment, lost in her imagination. 'Yes,' she said. 'He's a real gentleman, that fella. A real gentleman.'

'Is he still here?'

Matron pointed down the corridor. 'He was asking about Fr Callaghan. He might still be with him.'

Kavanagh and the sergeant were paying close attention to the conversation, and when Foley started heading back into the hospital they both rushed towards him. 'Now hold on …'

But Matron got between them again and stabbed at them with her pencil. 'The door is that way. Go!'

'Now look, Matron. We need to get a …'

'Do not '*now look, Matron'* me, mister. I need you gone. And I mean right now.'

'But this is garda business. We have …'

'Go!'

Rage made the sergeant's eyes almost pop out of his head. He turned sharply and shoved Kavanagh in front of him towards the door. 'You won't get away with this, Foley,' floated in the air behind them.

Fr Callaghan was sitting up in his bed with a prayer book on his lap. His eyes were closed and his lips moved in prayer. When he sensed someone standing by his bed he half turned his head but continued praying while he considered his reaction. After a moment he made the sigh of the cross and opened his eyes, casually observing his visitor.

'Oh, it's you. I would shake your hand only ...' He forced a smile and waved his bandaged arm at Foley. 'I suppose I should say tis nice to see you, but I'm conflicted. Is it nice to see you? Or am I going to lose another limb?'

His eyes twinkled and he indicated for Foley to sit on the chair beside the bed.

'No, I won't sit, Father.' Foley wasn't sure if he should let out the chuckle that was tickling his throat so he wiped his mouth with his fingers instead. 'This is a flying visit, but I promise to come back tomorrow, if that's all right.'

'No, no.' Fr Callaghan dismissed it with a shake of his head. 'A flying visit is good. I don't think my nerves could cope with anything longer.'

This time Foley did laugh and Fr Callaghan's eyes twinkled even more. 'So why am I honoured with this precious moment of your valuable time, Guard Foley?'

'Matron told me you had a visit from Inspector Maranus earlier.'

Fr Callaghan shifted up in the bed and closed the prayer book in his lap. 'I did,' he said. 'Isn't he a lovely man? He was *so* concerned about what happened to me. I think he said he was in the Special Branch. Is that right? Special Branch?'

'It is, Father. So what did he have to say?'

'Well, he was wondering how a priest got his hand blown off by a lunatic with a shotgun.'

'And what did you tell him?'

Fr Callaghan frowned. 'Why?'

'Why what?'

'Why are you so worried about what I said to him?'

'I'm not,' Foley stuttered. 'But like you said, he's Special Branch. You know what they're like. They put their own slant on everything you say. They could hang you if you're not careful.'

Fr Callaghan sniggered and held the prayer book to his chest. 'No, he's not like that. He has an honest face.'

He looked up at Foley again and his smile disappeared. 'I mean it.' He pursed his lips. 'He was very interested in what happened to me. I told him the nurses had pumped me full of medication for the pain, and it was making my mind duller than normal. That made him laugh. Anyway, I told him I remember you coming to the chapel looking for a statue. And for some strange reason I volunteered to drive you to collect your stuff from the pub you were staying in.' He paused and licked his lips. 'I remember having a few drinks in the pub and you having to drive me back here. I know we stopped somewhere but I can't remember why, then some eejit came out of nowhere and fired a shotgun at us. Everything was even more of a blur after that. Except for the pain where my hand got shredded. That was very real. And ferociously clear.'

The priest looked at the prayer book then held it to his lips. 'I remember being absolutely terrified that I was going to bleed to death. I wasn't ready to die. I'm not ready to die yet. I haven't made my peace with the man upstairs, you see.' His voice dropped to almost a whisper. 'I'm ashamed to admit I neglected to go to confession. I know I wouldn't confess all my sins, all my discretions. So I wouldn't be absolved. And the longer I avoided asking for absolution, the harder it became.' He glanced at Foley then looked at the prayer book. 'What I'm saying is, I'm the worst kind of hypocrite. I rage about sinners, and I'm embarrassed to admit that I'm one of the worst.'

Foley sat on the end of the bed. 'You're a human being,' he said. 'So you're as flawed as everyone else. There is no such thing as a perfect human being, Father. But you have a head start on the rest of us mere mortals. You already have your foot in the door.'

'If only that was true.' Fr Callaghan let his head sink back on the pillow. 'If only that was true.'

An awkward pause followed and for a moment Foley thought Fr Callaghan was about to cry. His eyes grew pink and tears filled them, but he pulled a handkerchief from somewhere under the blankets and wiped them away. Then he blew his nose and shoved the handkerchief away again.

'Anyway,' he said. 'Thank you for calling by. Look after yourself, Guard Foley.'

'Oh? Right.' Foley stood up. 'Before I go, can I ask …?'

'He wanted to know why you were looking for a statue.' Fr Callaghan closed his eyes. 'I said I had no idea. I said you turned up in the chapel asking about a statue of The Sacred Heart.'

Chapter Twenty-Six

The medication was wearing off now, and every move Foley made antagonised his aching body. He could feel the stitches in his legs weeping and his head throbbed. His arms felt like limp lettuce leaves. He needed to go back to the hospital and ask for assistance, but he had something far more important to do first. So he pulled his coat tighter around him and braced the bitter wind as he walked across the green to the chapel.

The door creaked as he pulled it open, and a waft of scented candles invited him into the warmth of the sanctuary. A shaft of evening sunlight coming in through the coloured window settled on the altar, and it made the silver cross shimmer as if it had a halo around it.

But Foley was too absorbed in his discomfort to appreciate the tranquillity. His pain was exasperated by the anxiety that squeezed his stomach. He groaned as he genuflected in front of the altar, and he had to grip the back of the nearest pew to help him stand up again. The holy water was cool when he blessed himself with it.

The big man with the mop of white hair standing in front of the altar was distracted by the noise coming from the back of the chapel. He turned slowly, keeping his hands joined in front of him. When he saw Foley he smiled. 'Are you alright there, Father?'

Foley walked down the middle aisle towards the inspector, and as he got closer he said, 'It's Guard, actually.'

Foley had forgotten how big Maranus was, not just in height but broad as well. In a certain light he could pass for a grizzly bear. He's also forgotten about the inspector's cold features that oozed menace.

'Guard?'

'Foley. Guard Eamon Foley.'

The cold grey eyes studied the visitor for a moment then he clicked his fingers. 'A Kerry accent? Of course. You are one half of that accident pair.' He gave a dry smile. 'Should you be out of bed? Your pal is in a bad way, so what are you doing wandering about?'

'Looking for you.'

Maranus gave a deep rumble of a groan. 'Looking for me? Why?'

'To tell you it's all over.'

Maranus gave the slightest shake of his head but he didn't speak. His eyes didn't blink either, adding another level of menace to his features. Foley felt compelled to fill the silence.

'The statue isn't here,' was how it came out. And it echoed around the chapel when he cleared his throat.

Maranus growled again then asked, 'What the feck are you talking about?' He turned to the altar and crossed himself. 'Sorry, Lord. Sorry for swearing.'

'You know what I'm talking about,' Foley answered. 'But you're too late. The statue isn't here.'

Maranus looked around at the walls of the chapel, his eyes squinting in annoyance. Then he sighed and focused on Foley again. 'I'm a very busy man, Guard Foley. I do not have the time or the patience to play your silly games. You have five seconds to explain yourself.'

The voice dripped danger and Foley felt his stomach tighten again. He unbuttoned his coat and let it hang loose, and as he clasped his hands together in front of him he judged how quickly he could reach the gun in his belt.

Maranus stood perfectly still and his posture was both relaxed and threatening. He didn't need to count down the seconds. Foley's heartbeat was doing that.

'I know you came here looking for the statue.' Foley's mouth was so dry he words came out slurred.

The inspector's eyebrows rose up almost to his hairline before dropping again and turning his eyes into angry slits. 'Again with the statue. What feckin statue, Foley?'

'Oh come on,' Foley yelped. 'Detective Sheffield told you about it. Father Callaghan told you about it. I'm not stupid, you know?'

The expression on the inspector's face was impossible to read and again Foley couldn't help filling the silence. 'That's why you're here in the chapel, isn't it? You're looking for the statue of The Sacred Heart.'

Maranus smirked and his shoulders gave a tiny shrug. 'Well, your pal *did* mention a statue. But he was very confused because of the stuff they gave him for the pain. So he was a bit vague about the details. However, there was another patient in the hospital who would probably know more about the statues in this place. The priest who served this parish. I saw you bringing him in and I felt it in my bones he was connected with you and your search for the D'Lacey deeds.'

The smirk turned into a darker sneer. 'But he was as vague as your detective friend. Even vaguer, if that's even a word. So I thought I would take a look, see if I could find out what was so interesting about this statue.'

'Only to find it isn't here,' Foley told him.

Maranus blew a puff of air down his nose and he held his arms by his side as stiff as a palace guard. And he gave Foley his most intimidating stare. 'So where is it?' The dead eyes advised Foley to explain.

'It's on its way back to D'Lacey.' Foley looked back at the clock above the chapel door. 'In fact it should have arrived there by now.'

The only thing that moved over the next few moments was the muscles of the inspector's jaw. They twitched, then he said, 'Let me get this straight, Foley. Are you telling me the D'Lacey deeds were hidden inside a statue?'

Foley nodded. 'Seamus Cassidy put them there on the morning your detectives killed his brother Tommy. And crippled his mother.'

The silence was louder than a rocket, filling every corner of the chapel as Maranus digested what Foley had just told him. 'So where was this statue all along?' he asked eventually.

'In Mrs Cassidy's kitchen. You saw the photograph. Sheffield showed it to you. The photo with the inscription *Safe in the Sacred Heart.*'

The look of surprise that made Maranus seem almost human didn't last more than a heartbeat. Then his features reset to their normal deadpan mask. He pulled his mouth into a thin colourless line.

'How did you know all this?'

'His mother told us.'

A hint of a frown skipped across the inspector's face. 'So you're telling me the D'Lacey deeds were in Mrs Cassidy's kitchen all this time? How did no one find them? The house was pulled apart. So how did we miss them?'

Maranus turned back to the altar and leant his head to one side as if he was struggling to grasp that information.

'So what happens to the reward money?' He said it in a tone of voice that sounded like he didn't really care.

Foley leant against the back of a pew to relieve his aching legs. 'I'm sorry to disappoint you, Inspector. It's going to Seamus Cassidy's mother.'

'Seamus Cassidy's mother? Why?'

'Because she deserves it. She certainly deserves it more than you do.' Foley noticed the sharpness of his voice caused Maranus to flinch, and his jaw muscles twitched once more.

'You're waffling now, Foley,' he said. 'I don't get what you're trying to imply.'

Foley swallowed to relieve his dry throat. 'I'm implying you were so desperate to get your hands on the reward money you didn't care who got hurt along the way.'

This caused Maranus to flinch again. 'Me? You think I was after that reward money?'

'Seriously,' Foley gave a mocking yelp. 'How can you say that with a straight face?'

This time the inspector's eyes flashed and he turned around and faced the altar. And Foley's heart skipped a beat as the inspector slipped his hand inside his coat. As he took it out again he swung around to face Foley. But when he saw the .38 Foley was pointing at his face he froze with his arm in mid-air as if he was posing for a portrait. Then very slowly he held out the packet of cigarettes to Foley, and to Foley's surprise he stepped forward so the gun was pressed against his neck.

'Drop your weapon, Inspector.' Foley kept his voice low to inject some authority into it, but Maranus just bent his head and stared at Foley.

'Your weapon. Take it out and drop it on the floor. Now.'

'Or what?' the inspector's eyes never blinked.

Foley stood up on his toes so their faces were inches apart and he gritted his teeth. He struggled to hold the hard unblinking stare the inspector was giving him. The dead grey eyes seemed to bore right into his very soul.

'Drop your weapon now, Inspector. I won't tell you again.'

'For feck sake, Foley.' Maranus gave a lopsided sneer. 'You're not going to shoot anyone.'

'Are you going to take that chance?' Foley's hand was beginning to tremble and he steadied it by grasping the gun with both hands.

'I am,' Maranus mocked. 'I don't think your conscience will let you shoot anyone.'

Foley couldn't stop the sarcastic splutter and he pointed to his own face. 'Like your conscience wouldn't let you do this.'

The inspector's eyes flicked over Foley's battered and bruised features. 'What the feck are you talking about *now*?'

'This,' Foley screamed. 'Your conscience didn't stop you trying to kill me. And Sheffield.'

There was just a hint of confusion on the inspector's face, a small dance of the eyebrows, but the eyes were still stone cold. He sighed as he turned and looked at the altar, then when he turned back again he pressed his neck harder against the gun.

'I still don't know what the hell you're talking about, Guard Foley.'

'You know exactly what I'm talking about, you murdering piece of cowshit.' Foley held the gun steady, noticing how the inspector's skin around the tip of the barrel had turned white. 'You shunted our car off the road. We're lucky to be alive. Then you tried to shoot us. But you mistook Fr Callaghan for Sheffield and shot him instead.'

'Fr Callaghan?'

'Yes. Fr Callaghan. You spoke to him earlier.'

'I know who Fr Callaghan is. And I also know *you* brought him to the hospital. And how do I know that? Because I saw you. I was in the hospital visiting Detective Sheffield when I saw you bring him in.'

'So you saw the damage you did to him.'

Maranus gave a deep throaty laugh. 'All right, clever dick. So explain to me how I managed to shoot your priest if I was already here when you brought him in.'

Foley was the first to blink and he moved back from the inspector. 'Well, you obviously didn't do it yourself. You got one of your cronies to do it for you.'

'My cronies?' Maranus moved forward by the same amount and put his neck against the gun again. 'Who do you think I am, Foley? A Mafia don? This is not Chicago.'

Then with the speed of an attacking rattlesnake Maranus swiped the gun out of Foley's hand and stepped back. He flipped open the barrel and checked the bullets, then flicked it shut again. Then he held it down by his side.

'Sit down, Guard Foley. Before you fall down.'

Foley felt a surge of defiance pin him to the spot, but that was quickly diluted by the embarrassment at being disarmed so easily. His whole body sagged and he shuffled to the pew and dropped down onto it. The stitches on his legs pinched even more where the dried blood had caked, and it was now being cracked apart by the pull of sitting down.

He forced himself to look up at the inspector, sitting up straight to show he wasn't defeated, but Maranus was looking around the chapel like a tourist.

'I haven't been in a church in ages,' the inspector said softly, almost as if he was thinking aloud. 'It's the strangest feeling, isn't it, being in a church? You can sense your soul being probed and all your sins exposed. The tranquillity focuses your mind, brings your subconscious to a higher level.' He let out a soft chuckle. 'It's almost impossible not to dash into the nearest confession box and pour your heart out.'

Foley snorted and immediately started to cough, and he had to stifle it with his handkerchief. He wiped his eyes and sat back up, and he shoved his handkerchief back in his pocket.

'You're a strange sausage, Foley. I can't figure you out.' Maranus leant against the altar rail in front of Foley and looked him up and down. 'Sitting there, you have the bearing of a priest. Not a policeman. You're too soft. And it shows. Maybe a change of career would benefit you. As I said, being a priest would suit you better.'

'Right,' Foley closed his eyes and bowed his head which was thumping in time with his throbbing legs. He felt a sarcastic quip working its way up his throat, and it came out as, 'And you would be happy to make your confession to me?'

Maranus raised the gun and studied it, then he lowered it again. 'I'm not sure I would even confess the time of day to you, you dopey cretin. Never mind tell you anything personal. Imagine that, hanging out my dirty laundry for some eejit like you to poke over. That would never happen, Foley. Not in a month of Sundays.'

'I'm not sure I could stomach poking over your dirty laundry anyway,' Foley laughed. 'Especially the things you would rather die than admit.'

Maranus gave Foley another intimidating stare. 'What the feck are you trying to say now, Foley? C'mon. Spit it out.'

'Naw. It doesn't matter. You will never admit it so what's the point?'

'Admit what?' The voice dropped a few octaves.

'That you shunted us off the road in an attempt to kill us.'

'For God's sake ...'

'And you followed me and Fr Callaghan today, and you shot at us, injuring Fr Callaghan.'

The inspector's eyes widened in fury and he waved the gun at Foley. 'I'm telling you for the last time, you bog trotting prick. I had nothing to do with what happened to you. So get that into your thick Kerry head. I had nothing to do with what happened to you.'

'Then how did your two cronies know we were shunted off the road?

'What cronies, for Pete's sake?'

'Guard Kavanagh and his sergeant. They joked about us being run off the road. So how would they know that if you didn't tell them?'

'I don't even know Guard Kavanagh,' Maranus gritted his teeth. 'Or his sergeant. Why would I tell them anything?'

'But how did they know, then?'

'The whole feckin world knew, you thick maggot. It was on the news.'

'Not about being shunted by a lorry, it wasn't. I didn't tell anyone about that. And Sheffield was unconscious so he didn't say anything.'

Maranus rolled his eyes. 'You were in shock. You were injured. In my experience of accident victims, they can't stop talking. They can't help it. They have a desperate need to go over the incident again and again, as if they're trying to justify their role in it. And that would be you, Foley. You look like a wimp who would gob off like a stuck record. By the time you were seen by the doctor the whole world would have known you were run off the road.'

Foley sighed in exasperation. 'No. I don't accept that. There's more to this than you're admitting.' Then he remembered something and he stood up, wobbled and sat back down. 'Sheffield saw you. When we were in the back of that tractor he suddenly woke up and he said he saw you. He was adamant it was you. He told us it was you. He saw you in that lorry.'

'Oh for God's sake,' Maranus snapped. 'How could he see me if I wasn't there? He was probably delirious.'

'No. He was sure. He saw you and you knew it. So you followed us today, but you mistook Fr Callaghan for Sheffield.'

'That's enough.' A cloud of spit came out with the words when Maranus snapped again. 'I already told you I was here with Sheffield when you say you were shot at.'

Foley rubbed his mouth with his sleeve and flinched at the stab of pain it caused to his swollen lips. 'And that's another thing. Why were you here in the first place? Don't tell me, you came to check how much Sheffield remembered about the crash. So what were you going to do if he remembered seeing you?'

Maranus rushed over and clipped Foley on the side of the head with the gun, then he went back and leant on the altar rail. Foley held his hand to his head.

'I live on the end of this street here.' Maranus waved the gun in the direction of his house. 'I pass this way every day on my way to work. I drive right by the front door.' He paused and waited for Foley to look up at him. 'I heard about the accident on the news, and I recognised the name Sheffield. I lived in Sheffield for a few years when I was younger.' He gave another sarcastic smirk. 'I'm afraid I didn't recall your name. I knew it was common, like Riley, or Murphy. But I did remember Sheffield. And due to the fact I had met him, I thought it was a compassionate thing to do, to drop in and check how he was doing.'

He stood up and walked across in front of the altar. 'And do you know something else? He did not mention seeing me in the lorry. Or any other time either. Don't you think that's odd? Considering you believe he definitely saw me.'

He stopped and stared at the tabernacle on the altar. He had an odd expression on his face that could have been mistaken for reverence. He bowed his head as if in prayer. Then he jerked up again and turned back to Foley. 'He was anxious to tell me about the statue, that you were coming to St Kevin's to find it. If he was so sure I tried to kill him because of it, why would he tell me anything?'

'Because he was terrified,' Foley argued. 'He opened his eyes and saw your ugly puss hovering over him. He was vulnerable, lying in his bed in desperate pain. And there you were like Satan himself. Of course he was going to tell you anything he thought you wanted to hear.'

Maranus looked at the ground for a moment then clicked his tongue. 'Actually, he was in no condition to tell me very much. His main concern was that you might be in danger and he wanted me to look out for you. He told me you were chasing after some statue here in St Kevin's, but he didn't have the strength to explain it in any detail.'

He waved the gun at Foley. 'And at that very moment you came along dragging a priest behind you and howling like a banshee with his bits caught in a door. Your pal was worn out by then and he drifted back to sleep.'

'So you went and frightened the crap out of Fr Callaghan.'

Maranus gave an angry growl and ran at Foley, and he pressed the gun against his temple. 'I have had enough of this shit, Guard Foley. I have told you. Whatever happened to you and Sheffield had nothing to do with me. I will not tell you again.'

Foley forced himself to sit up straight, and he mustered all the strength he could to hold himself together. At that moment he imagined how the official report of his death would play out. Injured guard found dead in the chapel?

Natural causes? No one realised how badly he was injured in the car crash, and when he went to pray in the Chapel he just quietly passed away? He could see his boy Mickey's face when the guards broke the news to him. He imagined his sister, Vicky, crumbling with the shock. He had no doubt Vicky would look after Mickey, but his heart almost broke at the thought of the hardship she would face trying to support her own five children as well as his boy.

He looked up at the furious face of the inspector and said, 'Just get on with it.'

Maranus pressed the gun harder, pushing Foley's head against the back of the pew, and he could feel his breath coming out in frantic puffs.

Then Maranus stepped back and dropped his arm to his side. 'If you're right and the deeds are finally back with D'Lacey, there is no reason for me to ever see your ugly Kerry face again.' He pursed his lips and snarled. 'But if I ever do, I might just forget to be nice.'

The front door of the chapel creaked open and Maranus straightened up, and he watched the elderly lady look around her before she crossed herself with holy water and genuflected in front of the altar.

In the silence of the chapel they could hear her rooting in her purse for her rosary beads. Then she shuffled over and stood before the first Station of the Cross. She glanced at Maranus then bowed her head and began her prayers.

Maranus looked at the gun in his hand. 'Where did you get this? You're not a detective.' Then before Foley could answer he said, 'You took it from Detective Sheffield, right?'

Foley nodded, and Maranus held it out butt first and shoved it at him. 'Then you better give it back to him before you cause any more trouble.'

Maranus didn't look at Foley as he took hold of the gun. Instead he watched the lady whose whispered prayers were loud enough to let you know she was there. Then he pulled up the collar of his overcoat with an exaggerated flourish and walked down the middle aisle.

There was another creak as the front door opened. And then there was a sharp thud as it was slammed shut again.

Chapter Twenty-Seven

Foley sat back in the large office chair and held the phone to his ear as he waited for the Tralee Garda switchboard to connect him with Sergeant John Guerin.

Foley's legs were freshly bandaged and the painkillers had dulled the pain from his many bruises. The hospital had found him a bed last night and got him cleaned up. But despite the warm milk and soothing medication, he could not switch off his mind and go to sleep. His eyes stung with the weariness. Every grunt and groan from the other patients during the night came at him like a wave of noise and punctured his thoughts, destroying any hope of concentrating on any of them. He tossed and turned, got out to the toilet, sat up in the bed, and sank back down again. But no matter how hard he tried to focus on the images that flooded his mind, he could not grasp them long enough to make sense of them.

The image of Inspector Maranus was everywhere. Foley could hear his voice, denying having anything to do with them being shunted off the road. But he would say that, wouldn't he? So why did he give Foley back the gun? Was it his way of saying he was innocent? Or was it a cynical ploy to miss-direct Foley? Did he realise it was all over now so he needed to put some distance between himself and what happened?

But the fact was, whoever was driving the lorry was following an agenda. It was not a random burst of road rage. And the attack with the shotgun that almost killed Fr Callaghan was certainly not a pissed off landlord annoyed at a couple of trespassers.

Foley needed to speak with Det Sheffield. He needed to establish what he actually saw before the lorry hit them. Who was *your man* in the rear view mirror? Could Sheffield positively identify him, or was it just someone that reminded him of the inspector and the nun?

So it was a long, long fretful night, and Foley was relieved to see the dawn and hear the hospital come awake again. And at the first opportunity he slipped out of bed and went looking for Sheffield, only to find an empty bed. Sheffield had been rushed to surgery because of complications during the night.

Back in his own ward Foley got dressed, wearing a clean shirt from his suitcase he'd retrieved from Fr Callaghan's car. He still had the key for the car. He decided to take it back, and he found the priest sitting up in bed holding a cup of tea. He looked dreadful. His skin was like off-white parchment paper, and his bloodshot eyes were reluctant to settle on anything. His hand trembled when he tried to raise the cup to his lips.

'Good grief.' Foley pulled a chair closer to the bed and sat down with a groan when his stitches pulled. 'Do you want me to call the nurse?'

Fr Callaghan sighed and raised his bandaged arm. 'She's been already. She thinks I have an infection in my ...' He cringed and forced a smile. 'I was going to say hand. But as you know, if I say *lend me a hand* now it will have a different connotation.'

He sipped the tea and pulled another face. 'No sugar? Are they still rationing the sugar? How can they still be rationing the sugar? Sick people need sugar to build up their strength.'

He put the cup down and looked at Foley as if he suddenly realised who it was. 'Where's my coat?'

Foley looked down at his uniform jacket and patted the front of it. 'I still have it. It's with my suitcase. Will I drop it off at the chapel before I go? I could collect my own at the same time.'

Fr Callaghan nodded absently and rested his head back on the pillow. His eyes drooped and he licked his lips. 'So you're off, are you?'

'I am, sure.'

'I hope you don't think you'll be missed.' Fr Callaghan tried to suppress the smile that twitched around the corner of his mouth. 'You know they're calling you Jonah?'

'Who's they?'

This time the priest did chuckle out loud. 'Well, just me. At the moment. But that could change when I'm well enough to get back to work.'

He gave a huge weary sigh and rubbed his eyes. Foley got the message. He stood up and held out his hand, but he withdrew it when Fr Callaghan jerked his head back and sniffed. 'Don't come any closer, Guard Foley. I want to keep what appendages I still have. So a quick wave from the door on the way out will be sufficient.'

'Right you are, Father.' Foley laughed out loud and chopped off a salute.

'Ah, there you are.' A nurse appeared at the door and smiled at Foley. 'You have a phone call.' Then she was gone. Foley looked back at Fr Callaghan who waved his bandaged hand and smiled, then closed his eyes.

Matron glanced up when Foley opened the door to her office and she clicked her tongue in annoyance. 'Where have you been? This is a hospital. We can't have the telephone tied up with a personal call like this.' She practically threw the receiver at Foley, stood up and indicated for him to use her chair. 'You look like death warmed up,' she grumbled. 'Sit down before you fall down. I can't afford to have you readmitted today.'

She went to the door and glanced back as she pulled it open. 'Get on with it,' she snapped. 'Say your piece and get out of my hospital.'

'Hello?' Sgt John Guerin sounded impatient, and when Foley answered he heard an agitated sigh.

'Where the feck have you been, Eamon? The Super is hopping up and down wanting to know what happened to you.'

'Good morning to you, John.'

'Don't be funny, Eamon. If we had a fan in the Super's office the shit would have hit everyone in the building. So what's going on?'

'I'm sorry, John. You're right. We had a bit of an incident here. Sheffield and I were in an accident ...'

'We know all that.' Guerin grunted before continuing. 'A guard called Kavanagh phoned here complaining that you drove your car off the road and almost killed Det Sheffield, and you refused to cooperate with the local guards who were investigating the crash.'

'That is not true,' Foley shouted, then he checked himself. 'Kavanagh is a right maggot. He would not listen to what I was trying to tell him. Actually, he's just a dog's body. It was his sergeant who was being pedantic. He wouldn't believe it wasn't an accident. I tried to tell him we were shunted off the road by a lorry, but he completely ignored me.'

Guerin gasped on the other end of the phone. 'You were shunted off the road by a lorry? Are you saying it was deliberate?'

'Yes.'

'Why, for God's sake?'

'Because we found out where those famous D'Lacey deeds were hidden. Someone was trying to stop us getting there before them.'

The phone crackled in the pause that followed and Foley looked at it. He could hear Guerin breathing and he said, 'John?'

'Sorry, Eamon. I'm just shocked that someone would try to kill you over some feckin deeds to a house. Kavanagh said Sheffield was badly injured, but what about you? How hurt are you? Is it bad?'

'No, John. I'm a bit battered and bruised, but otherwise I'm grand. So don't worry about me, alight?'

'Don't lie to me, Foley. If you're hurt ...'

'I'm fine, John. Honest to God. I've been discharged from the hospital and I'm heading home on the next train.'

'But what about the deeds? Are you still in danger because you know where they are? Should we call the local lads to help you?'

'Actually, there's no need to worry about the deeds anymore. They're back where they belong.'

'What? You actually found them? So where are they? Are you sure you don't need help?'

'I do not, because the deeds are back with D'Lacey himself. I gave them to a solicitor with instructions to take them back to their rightful owner. I was going over there to see him later to find out how it went.'

'Are you sure you can trust this solicitor?' Guerin lowered his voice as if he was worried someone would hear him. 'How did you know him in the first place?'

'Ah, sure, tis a long story. I'll tell you all about it when I get home. Hopefully that will be sometime this evening.'

'That's good. As I said, the Super is having a dicky fit here. He'll want to see you the moment you get back to Tralee. But before that, there's something he would like you to do for him.'

Foley held the phone away from his ear and studied it again, then he pressed it to his other ear. 'Oh?'

'Yeah. But first things first. How did you get on with Mr and Mrs Redigan? What was your impression of them?'

'Mr and Mrs Redigan?' The image of Mrs Redigan's perfect face made Foley sit up. 'Well, she was very … she was nice. Her old man was a bit odd. I couldn't put my finger on it, but he seemed very nervous. And a bit evasive. But apart from that … well, you can understand why. Losing your sister in those circumstances would upset anyone. But Mrs Redigan was …' he almost said beautiful but stopped himself. He didn't want to sound pathetically influenced by a pretty face. '… very nice, considering. But I will brief you on that too when I get home.'

There was an almighty crash and a string of curses, and the phone went quiet for a moment. Then Sgt Guerin came back on the line again. 'Eamon? Are you still there?'

'John? What the hell was that?'

'The bloody wind. There's a gale raging here. It nearly took the front door off its hinges. Isn't it the same up there in Dublin?'

'No. Well, I don't think so. But I haven't been outside yet.'

'Lucky you. Anyway, Eamon, there has been a bit of a development with the Appleyard case.' Sgt Guerin sounded as if he was flicking through notes. 'Remember Sean McGrath, the Birmingham Detective?'

'I do.'

'Well, he called in to see me yesterday. He'd been talking to the railway gatekeeper over in Clash. Roger Flaherty? He was out when we were interviewing all the neighbours.'

'Yeah, I remember him too.'

'Well, Sean met him in town. Roger said he'd been away visiting his sister in Cavan. And when Sean mentioned the Appleyards, it reminded Roger about something odd that had happened to him on New Year's Day.'

Foley could hear another page turning. 'Usually there wouldn't be any trains that day, Roger said, but there had been a dreadful mix up with a huge shipment of sheep, and the train had to get from Killarney to Tralee urgently. So Roger opened the railway gates as soon as he got the call. Anyway, he was standing by his cottage door when a big shiny car pulled up on the far side of the gates. He couldn't see who was in it, but the driver wound down the window and started shouting that he was in a desperate hurry and he wanted Roger to let him pass. Roger apologised and promised that the train wouldn't be long. But the train took longer than expected and the driver got out of the car and stormed over to the gate, roaring and flapping his arms like a demented penguin. He demanded Roger move the gate out of the way immediately, or he would do it himself. Roger told him that if he did he would have to call the guards and your man wouldn't be going anywhere in a hurry.'

Guerin chuckled at the thought of that. Then he said, 'So a woman got out of the car to calm the fella down, and she got him back into the car.'

Guerin paused for effect again and Foley rubbed his ear. 'So why are you telling me this, John?'

'Because Roger swears the woman was Bella Appleyard.'

Foley jigged the names around his memory. 'Bella Appleyard? But I thought the body in the house was Bella Appleyard.'

'Well, that's who we think it is. But that's not the point, Eamon. The point is, Liam Brazil could be telling the truth after all. If Bella Appleyard was in that car on New Year's Day it could mean she and her father were actually going away for a few weeks, like she told Liam Brazil. And that would put our estimation of the time of their death out by weeks.'

'I see.' Foley picked up a cup of tea from Matron's desk, noticed the lipstick around the rim and put it down again. 'So is Roger sure it was Bella Appleyard in the car? Didn't everyone say the two sisters looked alike? It could have been the other one. Lily?'

'No. He's positive. He recognised her by the way she walked.'

'Huh?'

'Yeah. Bella Appleyard walked with a pronounced limp. She had an accident when she was a child. I remember one of the neighbours telling us that.'

'God, I remember that too, sure.' As he spoke something rippled through Foley's memory and caused the hairs on his neck to twitch. But he couldn't quite grasp it and it evaporated as quickly as the mist when the sun came out. He cursed the numbing effect of the medication, the way it relaxed him to the point where he couldn't think clearly. But he was sure it was significant. He would remember it eventually.

'Eamon? Are you still there?'

'Yeah. Sorry.'

'Are you all right? You sound odd.'

'No, no. I'm grand, John. Honestly. I'm grand altogether.'

'So do you think you're up to calling on the Redigans again, just to clarify what happened on New Year's Day? See if you can find out if they did take Bella and her father away for a few weeks? Are you up to that?'

Foley leant his elbows on the desk as he considered the request. His train stopped at the town where the Redigans lived. And as much as he would love to see Mrs Redigan again, if he got off there to call to her house, he'd have to wait until the following morning to get the next train to Tralee. To be honest, he didn't relish having to stay at that pub again. His body was already protesting at the thought of sitting on a train for four hours. Now breaking the journey, getting a taxi to the Redigans house, then a taxi to the pub was a task too far.

If only he could borrow a car.

He put his hand in his pocket and took out Fr Callaghan's car key. That was why he went to see the priest just now, but somehow he got distracted. If he left straight away he could talk to the Redigans. And be back here in time to leave the car at the hospital and get over to the station.

Chapter Twenty-Eight

Foley pulled his collar up against the rain that was being whipped around him by the increasing wind, and when he rapped on the big front door the maid held on to it when she stepped back and looked him up and down. Then she said, 'you're that guard.'

Foley looked down at his uniform jacket. 'I am. I'm Guard Foley.'

It came out in a condescending growl and the maid bared her teeth. 'So what do you want?' she snapped.

Foley took a sharp breath. 'I want to speak to Mr and Mrs Redigan. If you don't mind.'

'Well Mr Redigan is not here,' she sneered and went to shut the door.

Foley stopped it with his foot. 'Then I want to talk to *Mrs* Redigan.'

The maid opened her mouth and looked as if she was about to start screeching, but instead she turned around and scurried down the hall before knocking on a door and going inside.

She was back out almost immediately and she beckoned Foley with a nod of her head. And the sullen stare followed him all the way to the door.

'Mrs Redigan will see you now.' She gave an exaggerated wave of her hand. Foley forced a smile and said, 'Thank you.'

Mrs Redigan was sitting in the same armchair as the last time Foley was here. There was a silver tray with a pot of coffee and several cups on the small table in front of her. She indicated for Foley to sit in the armchair opposite her, and she began pouring coffee into a cup.

'I'm afraid my maid has no idea how to make decent coffee,' she said as she pushed the cup towards Foley. 'So I made this myself. I hope it's still hot enough.'

She picked up her own cup. 'I like it not too bitter with a splash of milk. But I suppose you prefer it to be thick enough to stand a spoon up in it.'

Foley was aware he was staring at her so intensely he almost didn't hear what she was saying. He coughed into his fist as he sat down, and he leant forward and poured milk into his cup. He had to make a conscious effort to stop his hands trembling when he picked it up and sat back.

Mrs Redigan held her cup to her lips but Foley couldn't tell if she actually drank from it. She looked regal in the same black dress, sitting with her back straight and her head held high. Foley didn't think she looked as severe as the last time he was here. If anything, she seemed subdued. Her cheeks were slightly flushed and there appeared to be dark rings around her eyes.

Her unblinking eyes still unnerved Foley. He couldn't help staring at her, even though he knew he would never be able to concentrate while he was blinded to everything but her beautiful face.

He broke the spell by taking a long drink of his coffee. Then he put his cup on the arm of the chair and took out his notebook. As he fiddled with his pen Mrs Redigan gave an impatient sigh.

'What do you want, Guard?'

'Well,' Foley was taken aback by the sharp tone and he looked at his notebook as if he was referring to a transcript. 'I wanted to ask you about New Year's Day.'

Mrs Redigan gave a slight shake of her head but she didn't respond, and Foley looked down again. 'According to a local shopkeeper, Liam Brazil, Bella told him she and her father were going away for a couple of weeks.'

Again there was no reaction. Foley cleared his throat and continued. 'Later that day a witness told us he saw Bella getting into a car by the railway gates.'

As Foley paused for Mrs Redigan to make some sort of reply, the ticking of the clock on the mantelpiece was the only sound in the room.

Eventually Foley said, 'The reason we're asking is this, if Bella and her father *did* go away that day, it puts our estimation of the time of the ... *incident* ... out by weeks. So can I ask you if it was you who took them ...?'

'Stop.' Mrs Redigan held up her hand. Foley jerked up straight and almost knocked his cup off the arm of the chair. 'Please don't treat me like an idiot, Guard.'

'I'm sorry, what ...'

'I'm not stupid.' Mrs Redigan had assumed the regal pose again. Her face was emotionless. Only her mouth moved. 'And you are not a stupid man, Guard Foley.'

'What do ...?'

Mrs Redigan reached down and pulled up the hem of her dress, and she moved her foot to show the thick sole on one of her shoes. Then she let the hem drop again to cover it.

And at that moment a pulse of embarrassment surged through Foley as he realised what this meant. He wanted to shout at her that he *was* a stupid man. How in God's name had he missed such an obvious clue? He had seen the shoe the last time he was here. He had been told about the accident Bella had when she was a child. What was wrong with him? Of course he could put it down to the medication that was blurring his mind, but that was a feeble excuse. He picked up his cup of coffee and swallowed a mouthful to mask his shock, thankful that it wasn't too hot.

Mrs Redigan seemed surprised at his reaction and a frown rippled across her forehead. Then she said, 'I saw you looking, and I could tell what you were thinking. Why is she wearing a shoe with such a big sole? Has she got something wrong with her foot? And I just knew you were not going to let it go. So it was a matter of time before you put the pieces together and realised the truth.'

Foley sipped his coffee again as he juggled the words in his head, trying to decide on the right ones. 'So *you* are Bella Appleyard,' was how it came out.

'Bella,' Mrs Redigan whispered, and she looked down at her hands. Foley got an unexpected wave of sympathy for her, but he knew it wasn't right. If this really was Bella Appleyard, who was the unfortunate lady back in the house in Tralee?

'So what happened?' he asked and he pretended to write something in his notebook. 'Who is the lady we found in your kitchen?'

A tear sparkled in Bella's eye and she rubbed it away with her finger. 'It was never supposed to happen that way. It was a moment of uncontrolled madness. Something evil got hold of me and I couldn't control it. But no one else was supposed to get hurt. No one else was supposed to even be there.'

She held her hands together as if she was praying. 'But as usual *she* swanned in just at the wrong moment, and everything went to pot after that. But no one else was supposed to get hurt.'

The frown on her forehead deepened a little. 'I have struggled with the guilt every day since, Guard Foley. It torments me from the moment I wake up to the moment I go to sleep. Which is no longer possible without medical help.'

She picked up her cup but put it down again and pushed it away with her finger. Foley took a beat, aware that silence was his best weapon. Let the person fill the gap and they will eventually tell you everything you need to know.

He was right. 'There is no excuse for what I did, Guard Foley,' Bella said as she looked down at her hands again. 'No excuse. And carrying the guilt around with me these past months has been unbearable. I can't carry it anymore. It's become too heavy. I need to put it down.'

A grin touched the corner of her lips but in a heartbeat her mouth had resumed her Mona Lisa smile again. Then all that could be heard in the room was the ticking of the clock. Foley scribbled in his notebook but it was just gibberish. He didn't know where to start. When he glanced up Bella was staring at him again, her face back to her usual expressionless mask.

'Do you look forward to the New Year, Guard Foley? Or are you one of those who find it dreadfully depressing?'

'Well, I ...'

'I have always looked forward to the New Year.' She looked around the room as she spoke. 'To me it's like starting a new page, opening a completely new chapter in my life. Everything was going to be new and beautiful and I would feel alive.' She focused on Foley again. 'But as always it was just an elusive dream. As my father used to say when he was spreading the manure over the fields – *same shit, different day.*'

Foley chuckled at that but immediately straightened his face again when he saw the annoyance that flickered in Bella's eyes. He mouthed *sorry* and pretended to write in his notebook again.

'Please don't think I'm wallowing in self-pity, Guard Foley. Because I'm not. I don't want you to think I'm using my childhood woes as an excuse for what I did. I'm merely trying to explain what happened in the run up to the New Year.'

Foley gave a contrite nod. 'Yes, of course. I understand.'

'What do you know about my family?'

Foley shrugged. He decided not to lie. 'Nothing. Until recently I knew nothing about the Appleyards at all.'

'Then you're one of the few, Guard Foley.' Bella stared at him again, and Foley shifted in his chair as he tried to hold her gaze. 'Everyone in the south of Ireland knew the Appleyards. We were huge, rich, and pompous. We presented an image of grandeur and respectability. We had maids, housekeepers, butlers, and numerous farmhands. The house was always full of people. It was almost impossible to be alone in the house for more than a minute. So it's hard to imagine how a little girl could be so lonely in a house like that.'

Her voice faltered and she bowed her head as she wiped her eye with her finger.

'But I was.'

She picked up her cup of coffee and took a sip then licked her lips. As she put the cup back on the tray she said, 'The only friend I ever trusted was my Guardian Angel. You know about Guardian Angels, don't you? They watch over us and report directly to God himself.'

Foley nodded, and Bella absently made the Sign of the Cross and joined her hands together again. 'Of course people thought I was a bit soft in the head because I chose to do what I thought would please my Guardian Angel, and not do what they wished. And that made me more of an outcast than ever.'

'I'm sorry to hear that. It sounds really sad,' Foley said.

'Sad isn't the word for it.' Her answer was sharp and she glared at Foley again. 'I just didn't fit in. Everyone fawned over my bright and beautiful sister Lily. But I was invisible. She had the big birthdays and the big Christmas presents. I was just an afterthought, an irritation.'

Foley leant forward. 'I was told you and your sister were almost identical. Surely that would mean that you were as beautiful ... as pretty ... you know what I mean. You have no reason to put yourself down.'

For the briefest of moments her face lit up but she tightened her mouth again. 'Despite not wanting me around, they wouldn't accept that I wanted to be a nun. I knew I would make a wonderful nun. So as soon as I could, I joined a convent. And it was the most incredible time of my life. I was with people who thought as I did, who wanted to live their lives the way I did. I was so happy, so content. It was such a simple, uncomplicated life.'

Then she snapped her fingers. 'But it all changed in the blink of an eye. My mother died and my father turned into the Antichrist. It was bestowed upon me to do my duty and go home to care for him.'

This time the tear escaped and she let it creep down her cheek to her chin. 'Don't get me wrong, Guard Foley. I did what I always did. I asked myself, what would Jesus do?

He would do the right thing. *He* would put caring for his father before his own needs.' She licked her lips again. 'So I tried to take strength from that.'

She sighed and glanced at Foley again. 'Of course at the time I was younger and fitter, and if I'm truthful, I was thinking it would only be for a few years at the most. But the years rolled into each other, over and over and over again.'

She looked around the room again. 'But as the saying goes, I was thrown in at the deep end. I knew I was out of my depth right from the very start. I knew nothing about running a farm, and my father was absolutely no help. But I was bitter too, because I was put in this situation in the first place. Yes, I believed it was my duty. But I was struggling. I didn't want to be there, and it showed. The staff resented me and in a short time they all left. And I was all alone again. I prayed and I prayed and I begged my Guardian Angel to give me the strength and the patience to do my duty. I promised to accept my station. I promised to humble myself to the task. Sometimes it worked. Sometimes it didn't.'

She made a noise like a suppressed laugh but her face didn't show it. 'My father's health was compounded by dementia, and he spent his days in his room. The farm suffered. All the equipment and the animals were sold off. And somewhere along the way I lost contact with the real world. Everything in my life was turning to dust. All day, every day, I faced my father's abuse, the venomous name-calling, the bitterness that filled every corner of the house. There was no escape. Whether it was by design or just coincidence, I don't know. But the position of his room at the front of the building meant he could be heard all over the house. There was no hiding place. Day or night.'

She closed her eyes for a second then sat up straight again. 'Then suddenly it was New Year's Eve again. And I hoped again. I was looking forward to the new chapter, to opening a new page. So I stayed up until midnight to see in the New Year. I looked out over the town, listening to the celebrations and the cheering echoing all over the valley.'

She let a shiver ripple through her body. 'Then his roaring started, and the spell was broken.' When she looked up at Foley her eyes were pink and glistening with tears. 'It didn't matter that it was past midnight. He wanted me to write a letter to each of our tenants telling them I was increasing their rent, effective from 1st January. Not *him*. *Me*. I was to play the miserly landlord. I was the one they would despise. Again. So I suggested maybe I should sell off some land to raise the money. He looked at me like I had suddenly grown two heads. That would be up to Lily, he said. Then he realised I didn't know, and he gave one of his cruel sarcastic laughs. He's already signed everything over to Lily. Well, why wouldn't he? I was a nun. Why would I want it?'

She licked her lips again. 'I *didn't* want it. But that wasn't the point. It was the fact that I wasn't even consulted. And for some reason that cut deeper than all the other insults he's ever thrown at me. So that was what they really thought of me. After all those years of sacrifice, of abuse and disrespect, of struggling to put food on the table, of going out in the bitter cold mornings to collect wood for the fire. Darning clothes to make them last a little longer, repairing shoes to keep the wet out for just a few weeks more. And they didn't have the decency to include me in such an important decision. That was what I always believed, of course. But now it was actually spelt out to me – I was *nothing* in their eyes.'

She paused and studied her hands in her lap. 'As I sat in the kitchen later that night – or was it that morning - writing the letters, the pain festered in my heart until it grew so big it cancelled out every thought I had of living a pure and simple life. I turned my face away from my Guardian Angel. I let the anger and resentment consume me. By the time the sun came up it had totally overwhelmed me. I could no longer go on like this. I made a plan. It was simple. And final.'

Foley reached his hand out to her. 'Can I stop you there? I'm not sure where you're going with this, but I think you might want to seek legal advice before you tell me anything else.'

Bella's face changed shape and her eyes blazed, and she almost jumped out of her chair. 'I do not need legal advice,' she screamed. Then she sucked in a huge breath. 'What I want is for you to listen to me. Don't you understand? I need to purge my sin. I need to confess that I have committed the biggest sin of all. If I do not repent I will go straight to Hell. I want to confess, Guard Foley. I want to repent.' She sagged back in her seat and sighed. 'I am deeply sorry for what I did. But I'd had enough. They had pushed me too hard. I remember trembling with the fear of it. But I also remember the unbelievable thrill of it too.'

She made the Sign of the Cross again and kissed her hands. 'I remember lifting my foot off the floor to ease the pain in my leg as I made his breakfast. An arctic wind was tormenting the west coast of Ireland, and an old house like ours had so many gaps it reached into every corner. I dreaded the cold. It caused the pain in my leg to become unbearable, which is why I depend so heavily on powerful painkillers.' She absently rubbed her leg. 'I remember taking some that morning, and I remember flicking one of the cats away from the breakfast tray. Nelson. Or was it Drake?' A smile touched her mouth for a moment. 'I loved my cats. But there were so many of them now I was losing track of which was which. Miss Kitty had another litter, and so did Lucy Lastic. So now there must have been at least twenty scattered around the place.' Another pause, but the smile had vanished leaving her mouth a tight thin line again. 'Anyway, I scooped his porridge into a bowl and put it on the tray next to the toast and the mug of tea. Then I stirred in a lethal dose of my crushed painkillers and scattered sugar over it to kill the taste. And when I picked up the tray and crossed the kitchen floor I was seeing everything with a clarity I had never experienced before. It was as if I had actually woken up for the first time in my life. I could see the real world, the world I had always averted my eyes from. The clean and sanitised path I had religiously followed all my life was crumbling before my eyes and it scared me. But it also brought a cold sharpness to my mind.'

There was a loud rap on the door and the maid bounced in. She glared at Foley then gave a half curtsy to Mrs Redigan. 'I'm off now, missus. Tis my half day. So I'll see you in the morning.'

Before Bella could respond, the maid had pulled the door shut behind her. Bella stood up and picked up the tray. 'Would you like more coffee, Guard Foley? Or perhaps something stronger?'

Foley stood up too, surprised at the sudden change in the conversation. He went to speak but she waved him to sit back down. 'Coffee would be fine,' was all he could think of saying.

As Bella closed the door behind her, Foley was suddenly aware of a vehicle approaching. It went around the side of the house and stopped, then a dog started barking and was met with a cheery greeting. They faded quickly around the back of the house and were lost in the rattle of the rain being blown against the window.

Foley turned when the door handle clicked and the door swung open, but instead of Bella bringing in a tray of coffee, it was Sean Redigan who breezed in. He was saying something about the rain and the flooded road, and when he realised the only person in the room was a garda officer his smile disappeared.

'For feck sake! What are you doing back here? God almighty, this is ... what do you ... why are you here again?'

Before Foley could reply Redigan spun around and ran out of the room, pulling the door shut behind him.

Foley waited, expecting Bella to reappear, but when no one came he stood up and went across to the window. And he cursed out loud when he saw Sean Redigan opening the cab door of a Bedford lorry with the distinctive bull nose grill.

And reach in and pull out a shotgun.

Chapter Twenty-Nine

Foley pulled the .38 from his pocket and looked around the room for suitable cover, but no matter where he went he would be too exposed. He stood back behind the door, taking deep breaths to control the thumping of his heart that was making his ears ring. He pressed his head back against the wall and forced himself to think. Where was Bella? Is she aware that Sean is coming back with a shotgun? How will she react when Sean points it at Foley? He decided he wasn't going to hang around to find out.

A gust of wind came down the chimney and blew out a cloud of smoke, and the rain did a drum roll on the window again as Foley whipped the door open and sprinted down the hall to where he thought the kitchen might be.

Bella yelped in surprise when Foley charged in waving a handgun, and she slammed down the pot of coffee on the top of the range. 'What the ...'

'Get over here.' Foley grabbed her arm and pulled her over to the far side of the room behind the large table, and he pushed her down on a chair.

'For God's sake, Guard Foley. What's going on? Have you gone completely mad? Why are you pointing a gun at me?'

'Sush.' Foley crouched down with his elbows on the table. Footsteps clattered along the hall and a door crashed open. And Sean Redigan gave a ferocious roar of anger. Then his footsteps headed towards the kitchen.

'Bella, where are you? Where the feck is that guard I just saw?'

Sean ran into the kitchen so fast he was in the middle of the floor before he saw the two figures crouching behind the table. He raised the shotgun to his shoulder and held his eye against the sight.

'Bella, move,' he yelled.

Foley pointed the .38 at Sean's head. 'Put the weapon down, Sean. Put it down or I will shoot you.'

Sean gave an angry roar that turned into a mocking laugh. 'You might hit me with that peashooter, you maggot. But I will blow you to smithereens. They'll be picking bits of you off the walls for weeks. So *you* put that thing down and stand up.'

'For God's sake, Sean,' Bella yelled. 'What are you doing? What in God's name is going on?'

'I said move.' Sean shook the wet hair from his eyes. 'Get out of the way.'

'No,' Bella screamed. 'You are not going to fire that thing. Do you hear me? You are not going to shoot anyone. Especially a guard. So just put the gun down. Please, Sean.'

'Bella, he knows everything.' Sean's voice had desperation in it. 'I saw it in his eyes when he was here. He knows what happened.'

'Is that why you ran us off the road, Sean? Because you thought we knew what you did in Tralee?'

Bella looked from Foley to Sean and her face drained. 'What does he mean you ran him off the road? Sean, what does he mean?'

'It wasn't planned.' Again Sean's voice was high and pleading. 'I was coming back from Reilly's place when these two eejits almost hit me at the crossroads. I recognised them immediately. I was already worrying about what they were going to do about us. Were they going to be coming back to arrest us? Were they going to put us in jail? I couldn't stand it. I was frantic. Then suddenly there they were, and I was presented with a solution. A country road. A wet and miserable day. It was a chance I had to take.'

'Oh my good God, Sean.' Bella threw her hands in the air. 'They knew nothing. Guard Foley didn't know a thing until I told him about it just now.'

Sean's face twisted in confusion. 'You told him what happened in Tralee? For feck sake, Bella. Why would you do that?'

'Because I'm tired, Sean.' Bella flapped her arms in frustration. 'I'm tired of living like this. I can't go on living a lie. I have to confess my sin. I need to repent. It's eating me up inside. It's time for it to stop.'

'And now he'll get the two of us hanged. Have you thought of that?'

Bella bowed her head and pressed her forehead on the table. 'Of course I thought of that, Sean. But I am a thousand times more frightened of going to Hell than I am of being hanged. I need to confess. I need to repent and beg God to forgive me.'

'Move out of the way, Bella,' Sean barked at her again and she jumped back in her chair. 'You told the guard what we did so it's your fault we have to do this.'

'My fault?' Bella pushed her chair back and jumped to her feet. 'How dare you. None of this would have happened if you and herself hadn't turned up out of the blue on New Year's Day. You were not supposed to be there. No one was supposed to be there.'

'No, no.' Sean lowered the shotgun from his shoulder but kept it pointing at Foley. 'We always called on New Year's Day, Bella. It was tradition.'

'No, it was not.' Bella ran her hand over her face. 'When on God's earth did you ever call to see us on New Year's Day? When, Sean? It never happened.'

'We did, Bella.' Sean bared his teeth in defiance. 'We always did.'

Foley grabbed Bella's arm and pulled her back down onto the chair. 'Sean, put the gun down and we can discuss this. Please. Just put it down and we can clear things up now. C'mon, Sean. Just ...'

'Shut up.' Sean whipped the gun back up to his shoulder. 'Shut the feck up and put *your* gun down. Put it down now.'

'You know I can't do that, Sean'

Sean made a screeching noise and the shotgun trembled in his hands. Spittle glistened on his chin as he shouted, 'You can. Put it down. I will not tell you again.'

'Sean, if you fire that thing you will not just hit me. You will hit the both of us. So please, stop this crazy nonsense and just put the gun down. Then you can tell me what really happened back there in Tralee.'

The whimper Sean gave made Bella groan and she slapped her hand on the table. 'Sean, just do it. Please.'

'I can't, Bella. I can't let him arrest us. I can't go to jail. I … you know how I feel about you. I … there's no way I'm letting you be put in jail either. I won't let it happen.'

'Sean.' Bella lowered her voice to almost a whisper. 'Apart from Guard Foley, the guards haven't got a clue about what happened in Tralee. I'm promising you. Guard Foley knew absolutely nothing when he came here today.'

'Then why did he come back? Ask yourself that, Bella. Why did he come back if he didn't know anything?'

Bella joined her hands together under her chin. 'Sean, please. Stop this now. It's gone far enough. Put the gun down. The guards do not know what happened. All they have are assumptions and guesses. But they have no evidence to link us to any of it. So they have no reason to come here to arrest us.'

The shotgun was becoming dangerously heavy and Sean pulled it tighter against his shoulder to stop it trembling even more. 'Bella, please …'

Bella pushed her chair back again, only this time more slowly. She put her hands up as she got to her feet and calmly moved around the table towards Sean. Sean looked startled, uncertainty making his eyes open wide.

Holding her hands out as if she was going to give him a hug, Bella kept eye contact with Sean as she got nearer. Foley got up too and held his hands out, and he cautiously edged his way around the other side of the table until she was right behind Bella.

'Sean?' Very gently and carefully, Bella reached out for the shotgun, and Sean had tears in his eyes. He looked as he was about to let her take it.

At that very moment a gust of wind threw the rain against the window with a crash that sounded as if it was being battered by a shower of rocks. Sean jumped and let out a yell, and he swung the shotgun at Foley and pulled the trigger. But Bella threw herself forward at the same time and slapped the gun out of his hands. It discharged into the concrete floor with a deafening roar. And a scythe of pellets swiped the legs from under all three of them.

Foley bounced off the table and landed on a chair, and every part of his already bruised body screamed in pain. The ringing in his ears disorientated him, and for a moment he couldn't figure out what part of him had been hit. It didn't take long to realise his ankle was raging in a deeper pain, and he reached down and grabbed it.

Several pellets fell on the floor when he pulled up his trousers leg and pushed down his sock. There were angry marks but luckily none of the shot had broken the skin, though the throbbing was severe enough to make Foley think there could be broken bones beneath the bruises.

As he rubbed the pain away he looked around at the others. Bella was under the table holding her leg. Her face was pinched in agony and tears filled her eyes. Foley eased himself down onto his knees and reached out to her. 'How bad are you hit?'

'I don't know.' Her laced up shoe reached above her ankle and she was rubbing it. 'This is my bad leg. It's always painful, but now I think it might be broken.'

As Foley shifted closer he could see several pellets embedded in the side of the shoe and he instinctively went to brush them off, but Bella pulled away. She had noticed Sean and she was staring at him with an expression of horror on her face.

Foley spun around. Sean was sitting with his back to the wall and blood was spurting out of the ragged stump where his food had been. His shoe was hanging to the wound by a strip of skin, and the bone looked unnaturally white as it poked out like an accusing finger.

Foley tried to crawl over to him, but the fury from his own pain made him stop. He cursed out loud and tried to get back up onto his feet. He heard Bella calling at Sean to stay awake. She had to shove Foley out of the way so she could grab the table and haul herself to her feet. Then using what furniture she could reach, she hobbled across the kitchen to the cupboard near the range.

She pulled the cupboard door open and grabbed a heap of kitchen towels, and she threw them to Foley. 'Can you reach him? Use these to stop the bleeding.'

She found a broom and she was using it as a crutch as she hobbled towards the kitchen door. 'I'm going to phone for help. Try to stop him from bleeding to death.'

When she reached the door she looked back. 'I have some strong painkillers in my purse. I should have enough for all of us.'

Foley could hear her tapping down the hall, and he dragged the towels across the floor towards Sean. Sean's red watery eyes were looking at Foley but it was hard to tell if he was seeing anything. He had clamped his hands over the wound, but he couldn't stop the blood from escaping in pulsating streams from between his fingers. Foley had to use brute force to unclamp the hands, and he pressed a towel against the damaged leg. Sean screamed and wriggled back against the wall, and when he shook his hands in agony he sprayed Foley with a shower of bloody droplets.

'Sorry,' Foley called to him. 'Brace yourself. There's more.' He used another towel to fix the first one in place, then he tied a third one around it to hold them all in place.

Sean wasn't wearing a belt so Foley looked around for something else to use as a tourniquet. He settled for the laces from Sean's shoes. Luckily Sean's leg was thin enough for the laces to fit around, and be pulled tightly to staunch the flow of blood.

Sean's head dropped onto his chest and Foley realised he'd passed out, so he used the moment to ease him onto his back. Then he pulled a chair closer and raised the injured leg onto it.

Another burst of wind rolled over the house like an express train and Foley shuffled back against the wall. His ears hadn't cleared from the shotgun blast but he could still hear Bella's voice bellowing from somewhere in the house. Seconds later he could make out the clatter of her broom as she came back down the hall. She waddled into the kitchen and headed for the sink, grabbed a cup and filled it with water. She twisted the cap off a bottle of pills and shoved some into her mouth, washing them down with a long drink. She rested against the sink with her head bowed for a minute, then she put the broom under her arm and hobbled over to where Foley was sitting against the wall.

'I got through to the guards. They were surprised I still had a phone line. The storm is wreaking havoc all over the country. Phone lines are down, trees are falling, there's floods everywhere.'

She gasped when she noticed the pool of blood that Sean was sitting in. The towels were sodden and glistening in the kitchen light. 'Holy Mother of God. How much blood is there in a body? Surely there can't be much left in him.'

'Now he knows what Father Callaghan felt when he shot him,' Foley said.

'What? Who is Father Callaghan, for heaven's sake?'

Foley could feel the effort of talking draining him. 'Sean followed us. He thought the priest was Det Sheffield and he fired his shotgun at us.'

'Oh, dear God. Sean shot a priest. Oh, my dear God. How many more people will he kill?'

'No.' Foley put out his hand to her and she eased herself down onto the floor beside him. 'Lucky for Fr Callaghan, Sean was a poor shot. He was hit in the hand. Or not lucky, actually. He lost his hand.'

Bella shook her head as she passed the bottle of pills to Foley. He shook two into his hand and swallowed them.

'They're very strong,' Bella said. 'But I think you will probably need more than two.'

Foley handed the bottle back. 'I'm already dosed up with whatever the hospital fed me this morning. Any more and I'd probably keel over.'

Bella looked at the bottle in her hand, studying the instructions on the label. 'Yes, they are very strong,' she repeated. 'I've been taking them since I was a little girl. I've had to increase the dose recently to get any relief. I must be getting immune to them.'

She looked over at Sean and cringed. 'We can't leave him like that.'

'You're right,' Foley agreed. 'What did the guards say? How long will they be?'

Bella pulled a face. 'Well they won't be here anytime soon. There's no one available right now. They're all out dealing with emergencies. Apart from that, they've got trees down across the road by Cashman's farm, so if there was anyone available they couldn't get here anyway. The only other way is by Lynch's Dip on the lower road and that's under four feet of water.'

'Bella.' Sean raised his head and looked around, and when he focused on Bella he gave a relieved smile. He reached out for her then let out a dreadful howl when his leg slipped off the chair and hit the stone floor. Foley and Bella crawled over to him and made soothing noises as they tried to comfort him.

Bella took the cap off the bottle of pills and shook some into Sean's mouth, but he instantly started to gag and spat then out again.

'Sean,' Bella shouted at him. 'You have to take these. They'll help you. You need them for the pain. They'll help you with the pain.'

Sean pushed her away and his whole body started trembling.

'This is not good,' Foley said. 'We have to get him to a doctor.'

'How?' Bella asked. 'I told you already. Both the roads out this way are blocked by fallen trees. Or flooded.'

'What about the lorry? We could use that. We could drive through the flood with that.'

'No, we could not.'

'But it has to be worth a try,' Foley insisted. 'We can't just sit here and watch him bleed to death. We have to do something. We can carry him to the lorry between us.'

Bella cursed, using words that were unbecoming of a nun. Then she pulled the chair closer and used it to get to her feet, and she nodded for Foley to do the same. He had to brace himself for a moment, then he scrambled to his feet as well.

'Right,' Bella said, and she shuffled over to the cupboard where she got the towels from. She pulled out a large tablecloth and threw it at Foley. 'Get that under him. We should be able to drag him along on it.'

Foley wasn't convinced, but he spread the tablecloth out anyway, and when Bella got back they grabbed an arm each and tried to lift Sean onto it. But the pain was too much for Sean and he kicked out in agony. He let himself flop into a dead weight forcing Foley and Bella to drop him again. And they both fell back against the wall. The roar of the wind outside dulled the whimpering that was coming from all three of them.

After a while Foley forced himself to sit back up. 'We can't just lie here all night,' he said. 'Sean needs help now. He won't last the night like this. There must be something we can do.'

'Can you get some water?' Bella rattled the bottle of pills she pulled from the pocket of her dress. 'If we can get him to take these they might give him enough relief for us to drag him out to the lorry.'

Sean's face was colourless, and his eyes were staring at his hands which were clamped around the towels on his leg again. His blood was everywhere, spread across the floor where Foley and Bella had knelt in it while trying to help him. Their clothes were smeared in it, and their hands were like red sticky gloves. Bella even had some on her face and neck.

As Foley got back onto his feet Bella crawled over to Sean, but he pushed her away.

'Guard,' he coughed. 'Listen to me, Guard.'

Foley looked at Bella and she shrugged.

'Guard, I want you to know that it was me.' He coughed again and squeezed the towels. 'You have to know ... Bella had nothing to do with any of this. It was me that killed Lily.' His eyes opened wide and he reached out to Foley. 'I'm making a deathbed confession. You have no choice. You have to believe me. That's the law.'

'For God's sake, Sean,' Bella shouted. 'Stop it. Guard Foley knows what happened. I told him already. So don't pretend you're responsible ...'

'Bella.' Sean's words came out in a rasping whisper and he coughed to clear his throat. 'Do not say another word. The guard has no choice but to take my word as gospel. Tis the confession of a dying man.'

'Stop it,' Bella screamed at him. 'You're not dying, you big eejit. So just swallow some of these pills and they will help you with the pain. Then we will try and get you out of here and to a hospital.'

She poured some pills into Sean's hand and he studied them. 'Are these the ones you gave to your father?'

Foley came back with a cup of water and handed it to Sean. Sean took his time deciding whether to take the pills or not, but eventually he swallowed them and washed them down with a long drink. As he sagged back down onto the floor he said, 'Guard, I still want you ...'

'Sean!'

Sean closed his eyes and sighed, and lightning flashed outside the window and was followed by a crash of thunder that shook the house. When they sat back down on the floor Bella moved closer to Foley and covered her ears.

'Holy Mary, Mother of God, Blessed are you …'

Two more explosions of thunder had her praying even more, and when it eventually passed she opened her eyes again and looked at Foley. He was still fascinated by her perfect face, but somehow his initial attraction was dulled by the fact she had poisoned her father with a dose of very strong medication. And she was involved in the death of her sister too. Yet when her eyes met his and held his stare, he could understand how any man would be intoxicated by her.

'Are you alright?' she asked. Foley wanted to wipe the blood from her face but he wasn't sure if she would appreciate it.

'I wouldn't say I was all right.' Foley tried a smile and Bella parted her lips but didn't smile back.

'Don't listen to Sean,' she said. 'He didn't do anything. His only crime was to panic and try to cover it up.'

'No,' Foley contradicted her. 'His crime is trying to kill two guards, and shooting a priest.'

Bella cringed but she didn't look away. 'Tis a strange world, Guard Foley. A very strange world when someone tries to save someone by trying to destroy someone else. It never ends well, does it?'

Foley waited for more but she just stared back at him. Even with Sean's blood smeared in her hair and streaked on her face she was intimidatingly attractive. In another time and place Foley wouldn't have been able to resist the temptation to wrap her in his arms and kiss her on her beautiful mouth. But now all he did was say, 'So what was Sean trying to cover up?'

Bella pointed to the cup on the floor by Sean's legs. 'Is there any water in that?'

Foley picked it up. 'Maybe a mouthful.'

He passed it to her and she looked at the thick bloody fingerprints all over it, and she decided she didn't want it after all. She put it down and joined her hands together in her lap.

'So?' Foley shifted his legs to ease the cramp that was annoying him.

Bella gave him a look that said she was thinking how best to describe the events of that fateful day in Tralee. She wiped her mouth leaving more streaks from her bloody hand.

'Do you know what Murphy's Law is?'

'Murphy's Law,' Foley repeated. 'Isn't that *if something can go wrong, it will*?'

'And it did.' Bella looked into the distance as she scooped up the memory of that day. 'What was such a simple plan turned into my worst nightmare.' She fixed her eyes on Foley again. 'I was so angry that morning. Rage was sitting in my stomach like a tumour, bloated and painful. I couldn't bear it any longer. So I crunched enough pills into his breakfast to fell a buffalo. I honestly thought he would just lie down and go to sleep. Then I would make it look like he took an overdose. I was going to wash his breakfast dishes and scatter some pills around his bed. I intended to leave it a while before I called the guards, then I would play the distressed daughter who was devastated by the loss of her beloved father,'

She rubbed her hands together. 'But for some strange reason I didn't hear the car arrive. And I nearly fainted with the shock when Lily appeared in the kitchen dressed up like Lady Muck and dragging poor auld Sean behind her like a faithful little puppy. And the minute she saw me she started ranting about the state of the kitchen with all the cats and the dirt and the smell. She kicked at the cats with her expensive shoes and she howled at Sean to throw them all out of the house. She said this was the last straw. She was going to sell the place and buy a smaller house near where she lived so she could keep an eye on her father and make sure I was looking after him properly.'

She stared at Sean for a moment. 'Then in the middle of it all there was this almighty howl. It sounded like a pig being slaughtered, and it was coming from my father's room. I told you his room was like an echo chamber. The noise carried all over the house. We were frozen to the spot. Then Lily was screaming at Sean to call the guards, and she was screaming at me demanding to know what I'd done to her father. Then everything became confused. I remember trying to stop her from going upstairs but she was like a mad woman. She was lashing out and slapping me, and I wasn't strong enough to hold her back. So the both of us were locked together as we wrestled up the stairs.'

She rolled her eyes in disgust. 'Those ridiculous shoes. How anyone can wear such stupid shoes is beyond me. They had long heels that were as thin as knitting needles. She had a fistful of my hair and she tried to turn me around, and the next thing one shoe spun up into the air and Lily did a backward flip and rolled down the stairs. She hit the floor like a sack of spuds, and Sean and I just stood there staring at her. Then, unbelievably, I saw Liam Brazil's van coming up the drive. It was as if my Guardian Angel was determined to punish me by exposing what I'd done to the whole world. He was not going to let me just walk away from my sin.'

She frowned at that. 'Anyway, I knew I had to stop Liam from going around to the back door. He usually walked straight into the kitchen and I couldn't have that. So I rushed out the front door and waved him down. I needed time to think. I needed to find a way to keep everyone away from the house until I could sort things out. So I told Liam we were going away for a few weeks. Three, maybe four. He looked disappointed but that was probably because they relied on our business, for what it was worth. Then I remembered the letters for our tenants in my pocket and I asked him to deliver them for me.'

There was a pause as she shifted position on the floor. 'When I got back to the house Liam had carried Lily into the kitchen and sat her in an armchair by the range. And again the two of us just stood there like a couple of frozen dummies unable to speak. Or think straight. Sean looked like he was on the edge of hysteria. His whole body was trembling. Then he asked me what I did to my father. But before I could answer he said I gave him something, didn't I? Poison? What did I give him? I couldn't speak. My mind had turned to cabbage. I thought it was all over. It was time to call the guards.'

Bella rubbed her hands together again. 'Then to my surprise Sean picked up Lily's purse. She'd thrown her very expensive jacket over the back of a chair, and he picked that up as well. And he told me to put it on. I asked him why and he said just do it, we had to go. He shut the door to the hall and looked around the kitchen, picking things up and putting them down again. He said to take everything that belonged to Lily. We couldn't leave anything of hers behind. I was even more confused now, and I asked him what he was talking about. He said he was talking about how me and Lily looked so much alike, and if I was wearing her jacket no one would know the difference. I told him he was mad, but he said all we had to do was drive away. He said I'd told them often enough how no one ever comes to the house these days, so we should leave everything as it is and go home.'

Bella made the Sign of the Cross and clamped her hands in her lap again. 'And to my eternal shame, that's what I did.'

Lightning flashed outside and a minute later the thunder hit, but it was noticeably weaker now. The rain was still vicious and it rattled the windows with each gust of wind. Bella shivered, then she said, 'I have regretted it every day since. Living a lie is not easy. Pretending I was my sister was impossible. She was loud and screechy. She ran a business with hundreds of employees. She met sales people. She had meetings with businessmen. She went to events and social gatherings. It was a life I was not familiar with. It was a life I did not fit into.'

She looked at Foley to see if he understood. He nodded. 'So we sold our house and moved out here where no one knew us,' she continued. 'Sean took over the running of the business. But as I said, it was not a comfortable situation. The longer it went on the more paranoid Sean became. And the more depressed I became.'

She gave a coy smile. 'I think Sean was hoping I would replace Lily in every sense. But that was just nor possible. Apart from being a nun and being married to God, there was absolutely no attraction there. Anyway, physical involvement with any man would be repulsive to me. But with Sean it would be even worse. He was my brother-in-law, after all.'

She stared at Foley again, and for a moment he thought he saw a twinkle in her eyes and the impression of a smile on the corner of her mouth. He distracted himself by glancing at Sean.

'When we found your sister's body in the kitchen there was a large rosary beads around her neck,' he said.

Bella frowned, unsure of how to answer that. Then she said, 'Yes. That was mine. My father wouldn't let me wear it in the house so I kept it in the kitchen. Sean obviously thought it would make the guards think it was me sitting there, and not Lily.' Again there was a short pause. 'Strangely though, I didn't even notice it until I looked back when we were leaving. And it looked really odd, hanging like it did. I remember feeling uneasy about it. Suspicious, I suppose. But I tried not to think about it. Sean had suffered the same kind of abuse from Lily that I had suffered from my father. So I didn't ask. And Sean didn't say.'

Sean started mumbling and twitching, and Foley got up onto his knees again. The tablecloth was still spread out beside him. Foley slid over and put his hand on Sean's forehead.

'Sean, we have to get you to a doctor. If we can get you on this tablecloth we can haul you out to the lorry and drive you to the hospital.'

Sean's eyes were unfocused and whatever he was saying was incoherent, so Foley lifted Sean's legs just high enough to slide the tablecloth under them. Bella appeared beside him and she put her hand on Sean's face.

'C'mon, soldier. Help us. Lift your arse so we can pull this under you.'

Little by little they got the tablecloth under the patient, and when it was up to his shoulders Bella took one corner and Foley took the other. And together they pulled it across the kitchen floor. Sean made little whining noises but the pills appeared to have taken effect and dulled his senses. But they also drained the strength out of Bella and Foley. When they got through the door into the hall they both had to flop down and take a breath.

The wind had died down and the rain was not as sharp against the windows. After a few minutes Foley got back onto his feet and took both corners of the tablecloth. Bella scowled and scrambled to her fee as well.

'No,' Foley told her. 'You stay there and rest. If I can get him to the door, you can help me get him across the yard. Then I'll need you to help me get him into the cab.'

'Oh, don't be so stupid,' Bella snapped. 'We'll do this together.'

When they reached the door to the lounge Bella stopped. 'It's still raining heavily. We should get some coats. There should be some in here.'

She opened the door to a boot room on the other side of the hall and stepped inside, and she immediately let out a startled cry. Foley rushed over, putting his hand on the gun in his pocket.

'The window,' Bella whispered. 'There was someone at the window.' She pointed to the glass panel down the middle of the door that led out the garden.

Foley rushed over to it but all he could see was his own reflection. 'Who was it? A neighbour. Did you recognise him?'

'No. It was too quick. I just caught a glimpse of a face and then it was gone. But I saw someone. I'm not making it up. I definitely saw someone. I saw a face.'

'All right.' Foley took her arm and led her back out to the hall. 'It could be someone coming to check if you're alright. A neighbour looking to see if everything is alright.'

Bella shook her head. 'No. We don't know our neighbours.'

'Still, I better check.' Foley started heading for the front door and Bella grabbed the back of his jacket.

'Be careful. It could be anyone. It could be someone trying to rob us.'

Before Foley could reply there was an almighty hammering on the front door. Bella yelped and held on tighter to his jacket, and he put his arm around her.

The hammering shook the door again, and a voice rang out. 'Gardaí. Open up.'

'It's the guards,' Bella cried. 'The guards have arrived.'

Foley hesitated before cautiously pulling the door open, and two soldiers pointed their rifles at him. One of them shouted, 'Put your hands up. Put your hands up.'

'I'm a guard,' Foley shouted back. 'I'm Guard Foley. I'm a guard.'

Bella and Foley were pushed back into the hall. 'Show me your hands,' the soldier shouted, and when Foley hit the wall the soldier patted him down. He found the .38 immediately and shoved it in his belt, then he spun Foley around and patted him down again.

The second soldier rushed at Bella and she stopped him with a ferocious bellow. 'Don't you dare. I am Sister Mary Claire. You do not touch me.'

The soldier jumped back as if he had an electric shock, and the one searching Foley stepped back too.

'Who else is in the house?' His voice was still harsh but he lowered his rifle.

'Only him.' Foley pointed to Sean, and as the soldiers got closer they both hesitated when they saw the blood on the tablecloth and the trail coming out from the kitchen.

'Holy Mother of God,' one of them muttered. 'What happened to him?'

Two garda officers appeared at the front door, and the one with the stripes on his sleeve looked at Foley's uniform as they entered the hall.

'Where's the gunman?' he asked, looking past Foley at the soldiers who were cautiously following the trail of blood into the kitchen.

'That's him.' Foley said, and the sergeant and the other guard approached Sean. They stood looking down at him for a minute before the sergeant stooped down and felt for a pulse.

When he stood up he said, 'I'm Sergeant Galvan and this is Guard Maher. We were told people were shot. One of them was a guard. Are you injured?'

Foley raised his foot. 'Not too badly, thank God. He misfired and the shot hit the floor. He took most of the blast. His leg is in a bad way. And as you can see he lost a lot of blood, which is why we were trying to drag him out to that lorry out in the yard. We were told the lower road was flooded, but we thought the lorry would be high enough to get through.'

The sergeant took off his cap and shook the water from it. 'The roads are flooded all right.'

He saw the question in Foley's eyes and he grinned. 'We wouldn't have made it without the help of the Civil Defence lads. Fair dues to them, when the call went out that there was a guard being attacked, they sprang into action. You should see the size of the truck they brought us here in. It could cross the Shannon River itself. A bloody brute of a thing.' He looked around and smiled. 'But you seem to have it under control, Guard …'

'Foley. Eamon Foley.'

He looked at Foley's shoulder tags. 'And a Kerry accent, too. So what are you doing way up here on the other side of the country?'

He suddenly noticed Bella standing back against the wall, and even with the blood in her hair and on her face he was obviously impressed by her delicate features. 'And you are?'

'Sister Mary Claire.' She held out her hand and there was a look of disappointment on the sergeant's face as he gave it a quick shake.

'Sister Mary Claire,' he repeated. Then he turned back to Foley. 'You were saying? What are you doing in Dublin?'

'There was an incident in Tralee. Two bodies were found in unexplained circumstances. I was asked to come up here to give my condolences to the victim's relative, Sean Redigan and his wife Lily.' He glanced at Bella but she was looking at the floor. 'Unfortunately I then discovered that they were actually implicated in the deaths in Tralee. Sean took exception to that. He thought he could erase the evidence. Thankfully Sister Claire reacted bravely and saved my life.'

Sgt Galvan digested that for a moment, then he asked, 'So where is Mrs Redigan now?'

The soldiers were back. 'The house is clear, Sergeant,' the loud one called. 'What do you want us to do now?'

'We have to get Sean to a hospital,' Foley stooped down beside him. 'He's lost a lot of blood. We have to hurry if we want to save him.'

Sgt Galvin and Guard Maher went to one end of the tablecloth and the soldiers took the other corners, and the sergeant grinned at Foley. 'He's not likely to run away so we won't be putting the handcuffs on him.'

Bella was helped into the cab of the Civil Defence vehicle next to the driver. Sean was loaded into the back, then the sergeant helped Foley climb up beside him. When the soldiers and both of the guards were settled in, the wagon shuddered into life and rumbled down the drive.

The sergeant took out a small bottle of whisky and passed it to Foley. 'Take a good swig of this, Guard Foley. Then tell me what the feck is going on.'

Chapter Thirty

'I don't understand.' Vicky was unpicking an old knitted cardigan and rolling the wool into a ball. 'I thought I would feel something. You know? I thought I would feel relief, or some sense of an ending to it all.'

She gave an aggressive tug at a stubborn piece of wool and swore when it snapped. She threw it down on the small table beside her chair, stretched her arms and sat back. 'But I feel nothing. Absolutely nothing. Even after everything that happened. That pompous maggot D'Lacey was so desperate to save his family's reputation he caused a pile of other families to suffer. People died because of him. People actually died.'

She glanced up at a photograph of Inspector Liam Edge on the mantelpiece and she blessed herself. 'God rest their poor souls.'

Vicky's husband Stefan was sitting in the armchair at the other side of the range, and he watched her intently. There was a look of both admiration and concern on his face, and several times he looked as if he was going to say something. But each time he closed his mouth again and just nodded.

'Can that be right, Eamon?' Vicky looked over at her brother sitting at the table reading a newspaper. 'Am I being weird? Can it be normal to feel nothing at all? To not feel bitter about what happened? To not feel hate for that moron D'Lacey and his dope of a son? To just feel ... *nothing*?'

Eamon Foley put down the newspaper and sat back in his chair. Two weeks of sitting around the house with his foot in a cast had frayed the edges of his patience, and he wasn't in the mood to debate the psychology of his sister's feelings. What he really wanted to do was go back to work. But Superintendent Flynn made it plain he wasn't to even think of it until he got the all clear from the force's doctor.

Most of Foley's bruises had faded now, and his stitches had been removed by the nurse who called on him. His foot was still sensitive so the doc wanted the cast to stay on for a few more days, just to be sure. But his confinement was like an itch that Foley couldn't scratch. There is only so much reading a person can do before the words merge into a meaningless blob. There is only so much radio a person can listen to before the opinionated voices grate on their nerves and they actually start to argue with them. Foley needed to get out of the house. He needed to get back to work.

'Eamon?' Vicky was staring at him with a look that demanded a response.

'I don't know, Vicky.' Foley picked up a packet of cigarettes, shook one out and put the packet down again. He flicked his lighter as he put the cigarette in his mouth, and he took his time lighting it. 'Maybe it's because it happened so long ago. Maybe the memory is not as raw anymore.'

'How can you say that?' Vicky's face was pinched with the thought that such a major event in their lives was being allowed to fade into the mist of time. 'We will *never* forget what happened to us, Eamon Foley. We cannot let it be forgotten. Ma would be furious if she heard you say such a thing.'

Foley blew out a cloud of cigarette smoke and wiped a bit of tobacco off his lip. 'That's not what I'm saying, Vicky. You know it isn't. I'm saying that pain eases with time. It's a fact. It never goes away, but it does ease.'

'Well she'll be here tomorrow.' Vicky glanced up at the clock. 'You can tell her that when she gets here. She's already mad at you for not telling her you were hurt.'

'Well she wouldn't be if you hadn't told her in the first place.' Foley blew out another puff of smoke.

'What did you expect, Eamon? Of course I bloody told her.' Vicky sat up in her chair with an angry scowl. 'The cut of you when you came home. You went away for a couple of days and you came back looking like you'd been attacked by a herd of Reilly's bulls. I nearly had a heart attack when I saw the state you were in. Then your Super casually tells me how lucky you were to walk away from a car crash that left Det Sheffield in a coma.'

She flapped her hands in horror. 'Then he adds that you were shot as well. My good God, Eamon. You looked like a dead man walking. I couldn't keep that to myself. I had to tell Ma. I needed her support. So I wrote her a letter straight away.'

Foley put his hands up. 'You're right. I'm sorry, Vic. It wasn't fair of me turning up like that. Someone should have warned you. I am sorry.' He flashed her a smile. 'I'll try not to let it happen again.'

'Ha, bloody ha.' Vicky rolled her eyes, picked up her cardigan and continued picking at it. 'Next time I won't be so sympathetic.'

Of course Foley knew Vicky was right. He should have stayed in the Dublin hospital until he had recovered. But he was too anxious to get away from there and back to his friends and family. Superintendent Flynn and Sergeant Guerin met him at the station and escorted him through the mob of reporters who were hoping for an update on what they called 'The Appleyard Murders.'

Superintendent Flynn looked like he was leading a champion racehorse around the royal enclosure. The pride on his face highlighted his dimples. When they got to Foley's house in Rock Street he turned around and addressed the reporters, telling them that Bella Appleyard and Sean Redigan were being detained in Dublin for the moment. And Guard Eamon Foley was being recommended for a commendation for his outstanding contribution in bringing them to justice.

Vicky had pulled the door open to see what all the commotion was about, and she clamped her hand over her mouth in shock when she saw her brother.

'Now don't be worrying there, Vicky,' the Super told her in his most assuring voice as he and John Guerin practically carried Foley into the kitchen and sat him in the armchair. 'Your brother's injuries are mostly superficial. They look a lot worse than they are. A few days rest and he'll be back to his old self.'

Vicky's automatic response was to put the kettle on.

The Super told them he couldn't stay long because he had a court case to attend. But before he left he told them he'd been instructed from above to clarify the Garda Síochána's position regarding the D'Lacey episode. Of course there was tremendous relief that the incident was now closed. But there was also a deep sense of embarrassment that the Gardaí had been so brutally manipulated without the slightest resistance on their part. Guard Foley and Det Sheffield were recognised for their skilful recovery of the items in question, and they were going to be rewarded. But they are strongly advised that the incident is now relegated to the archives, never to be discussed again in their lifetimes.

The advice also applied to Vicky, the Super said. But Vicky didn't seem to be listening. She was too concerned about her brother slumped in the armchair holding a cup of tea to his bruised lips. Foley and Guerin gave their verbal agreements, which were going to be put in writing and signed at a later date.

As the weeks went by the initial flurry of activity by the reporters gradually died down, and the requests for an interview were less frequent. In fact, this week's Kerryman made no mention of the Appleyards at all.

Then a letter arrived from Foley's mother saying she was coming down from Limerick for a few days to see for herself how badly hurt her son was. And it stirred up some uncomfortable feelings for Vicky. It was as if the Super's instructions about never discussing the D'Lacey incident had not registered with her until that very moment. And she spent the rest of the morning analysing it, dissecting her feelings, trying to remember the emotion she'd felt when Det Sheffield first told them the famous envelope everyone was looking for was nothing more than the deeds to some posh knob's house.

But no matter how she tried to juggle the words, Vicky couldn't generate a coherent response. Which made her feel even guiltier. She really believed she should be feeling *something*.

Stefan looked at the clock and shuffled to his feet.

'Is it that time already?' He picked his cap off the back of his chair. 'I must go back to work.'

Vicky stood up too and walked him to the door, reminding him that they were going to visit her friend Daisy McGrath that evening. They reached the door just as someone rapped on it. When she pulled it open she gave a cheery greeting.

'Good afternoon, Sergeant Guerin,' she chirped. 'And how are you this fine day?'

John Guerin stepped back to let Stefan out, and the big Polish seaman straightened his cap as he kissed Vicky on the cheek. Then he nodded to Guerin.

'Good day, Sergeant.'

'Good day to you, Mr Zedenski.'

Eamon Foley was relieved to see his friend, and he pushed the kettle onto the hot plate on the range. 'You're a bit late for lunch,' he told the sergeant. 'But I'm sure Vicky can rustle you up a sandwich.'

'No bother at all.' Vicky went to the breadbin and took out a loaf. 'I have cheese.'

'No, no.' Guerin brushed the idea away. 'You're grand, Vicky. Sure didn't I have lunch in the canteen? It's probably supper as well because it was so heavy it's stuck to my insides and isn't likely to digest any time soon.'

All three of them laughed at that. Foley nodded for Guerin to sit in the armchair by the range but Guerin pulled out a chair by the table and put his cap on the back of it as he sat down.

'So what's new, John?' Foley relished Guerin's visits like a gust of fresh air because he brought updates of what was happening in the outside world.

'Well,' Guerin sat back in his chair. 'Your friend Mrs Brazil, who has that shop over in Racecourse Road, turned up this morning asking to speak to you.'

'Me?'

'She asked for you by name. Guard Eamon Foley.'

'Did she now?' Foley grinned at the way Vicky pulled a face. 'So what did she want?'

Guerin tried to ignore Vicky but still couldn't resist grinning as well. 'Remember Tom O'Gara telling us he was almost hit by a van similar to Liam Brazil's speeding out of the Appleyard's gate? He said it was the day the big snow began, around the 23rd of January.'

Foley cast his mind back to the interview. 'Yeah, I remember that,' he said. 'But Mrs Brazil swore blind it couldn't have been her son Liam because he was in hospital in Killarney.'

'He was, sure,' Guerin pointed at Foley with his finger. 'But did we ask if anyone else had access to that van?' He paused for effect and smiled even more when the answer dawned on Foley.

'Don't tell me. It was Mrs Brazil herself.'

'Correct.' Guerin clicked his fingers. 'She used the van for deliveries as much as Liam did.'

'Well, that's interesting.' Vicky put a cup and saucer on the table in front of Guerin then went back to the range and scooped a spoonful of tea into the teapot. Then she dropped back into the armchair. 'And it didn't dawn on you to ask her,' she mocked, still grinning at her brother.

Foley flinched. 'No, it didn't. Perhaps I'm old fashioned, Vicky, but I still think it's rare to see a woman driving a grocery van. What's the world coming to, I ask myself.'

Vicky pretended to throw a ball of wool at him. 'Go on with yourself,' she chuckled. 'If you had your way women would still be chained to the kitchen sink.'

'Well, yeah.' Foley tried to pull a serious face. 'Sure isn't that why women have such small feet, so they can stand closer to the kitchen sink?'

The kettle started to boil and threw out a cloud of steam, and Vicky laughed as she jumped up and poured the boiling water into the teapot.

Foley turned back to Sergeant Guerin. 'So what did she want to see me about, John?'

'Well, according to Mrs Brazil, the day the van was seen coming out of the Appleyard's gate, business had been very slow in the shop and she was getting anxious. She had bills to pay, stock to order, and out of desperation she decided to check if Bella Appleyard and her father had come home yet. It was over three weeks since Bella told Liam they were going away, and Mrs Brazil was hoping that if they had come home they would be wanting some groceries from her.'

Guerin moved the cup and saucer closer. 'As usual she drove around to the back door and knocked. When she didn't get an answer she tried the handle, and because the door was unlocked she went straight into the kitchen. And into her worst nightmare. The smell was what hit her first. Then the sight of all the cats crawling over everything. Finally she realised someone was sitting in the armchair by the range. She knew she shouldn't have looked, but curiosity got the better of her. And the image is still with her to this day, according to her.'

'Oh holy Mother of God.' Vicky blessed herself. 'The poor woman. How would you ever sleep again after seeing something like that?'

Foley nodded in agreement, then he asked, 'So why didn't she call us straight away? We would have saved a lot of time if she'd called us immediately.'

'She didn't call us because the first thing that entered her head was that her son Liam might have been involved,' Guerin said. 'Imagine how she felt at that moment. The poor woman was sick to her stomach. Actually she was sick all over the floor as well. She was frantic, and all she can remember after that was trying to get away from there as fast as she could.'

'The poor woman,' Vicky said again. 'What did her son say when she told him?'

'Actually, according to her, she didn't say anything to Liam. She just watched and waited to see if he let anything slip. He didn't. In fact, the shock on his face when you turned up the day you found the bodies convinced her that Liam had nothing to do with any of it.'

There was a pause as Vicky poured the tea into Foley's cup then put the teapot on the table by Guerin.

'So why didn't she tell us then?' Foley picked up his cup.

'She couldn't risk it.' Guerin told him. 'She thought she'd be in trouble. She thought she'd be arrested and put in jail. Liam was already disturbed by Bella Appleyard being dead, and she didn't want to leave him on his own. She didn't know how he would cope.'

'I don't know,' Foley took a swig of his tea. 'She put on a good act the day I called to her shop. She was ... well, is *composed* the word I'm looking for?'

Guerin thought about that for a moment, then he remembered that Guard Hurley had called there before Foley did to use the phone. That would have put her on her guard, he said. She would have prepared herself in case she had another visit from the guards.

'The poor woman,' Vicky said again. 'She must have been sick with worry all that time. She must have been driven half mad. So how is Liam now? Is he still in Killarney?'

Guerin looked sheepish. 'You know, I didn't ask her. Sorry. That was careless of me.'

'So why did she come forward now? What changed her mind?'

Guerin pointed to the Kerryman on the table. 'She saw the newspaper. It was like a weight had been lifted off her shoulders when she read that Bella Appleyard and Sean Redigan were arrested over the death of Lily Appleyard and her father. She was hoping they would hang for what they put her through.' Guerin gave a deep sigh. 'The poor woman, she's going to be terribly ...'

When he didn't finish the sentence both Foley and his sister questioned him with their eyes, and he made a big show of pouring tea into his cup, adding milk and then a spoonful of sugar.

'She's going to be terribly *what*?' Vicky couldn't wait any longer.

Guerin looked at the floor as he searched for the right words. Then he said, 'According to the Dublin lads, Sean Redigan died two days ago. His wound had become infected and they couldn't control it. Anyway, before he died he got a solicitor to come and witness his confession. He swore that he alone was responsible for the death of Toby Appleyard and his own wife Lily Redigan. He said Bella Appleyard wasn't even there at the time. He said he and his wife Lily had taken her to their house in Dublin for a holiday. Their father Toby Appleyard was being obstreperous and had refused to come with them. But they went back the next day to try and persuade him again that a holiday would do him good. A row developed resulting in Sean killing Lily in the kitchen. Then he poisoned Toby. After that he went home, and he held Bella hostage in his house. He professed he had feelings for her and was trying to establish a relationship with her.'

Foley and Vicky stared at him in disbelief. Eventually Vicky scratched her head and said, 'So what does that mean? What's going to happen to Bella Appleyard? Surely they're not going to just let her go.'

Guerin gave a wry smile. 'Sorry, Vicky, but that's exactly what they're going to do. In fact, according to the Super this morning, Bella - or Sister Mary Claire as she's known in the church - was actually returned to her convent the very day you arrested her, Eamon.'

'But surely ...'

'The thing is, Sean was telling everyone who would listen that Bella was not involved in any of it. And Bella was a nun. No guard wanted to lock a nun up in their cell.'

A shiver made Foley stand up, and he walked to the window and stared out at the real world going about its normal business.

'Well, well, well,' was all he could say.

The End